UNIVERSAL ORDER:
RETURN OF THE CLAVE WARRIORS

To Bob & Sharon Ahlgren,

Thanks for your support! Enjoy!

UNIVERSAL ORDER:
RETURN OF THE CLAVE WARRIORS

TONYA TETTEH

Tonya Tetteh

Published in the United States by
Tonya Tetteh
tct@tonyatetteh.com

www.tonyatetteh.com

Library of Congress Control Number: TXu 2-031-009

ISBN 0-692-94581-4

Printed in the USA

Cover design by Nathan Fisher

Text design by Sandra Williams

Dedicated to the memory of Gregory Allen Smith, Sr.,
My brother, my best friend, my inspiration.
Your encouragement made this project a reality!
Rest in Peace, my hero!

Table of Contents

PART III:

PART IV

Acknowledgements

I thank my mother Adelia Smith for reading my book and giving me feedback on how I could improve the content. Mom, I want to also thank you for spending endless hours re-reading and editing to clean up my many punctuation, spelling and grammar errors.

Thanks to my aunts Jacquelyn Cammon and Georgia Sims for helping with the editing process, which allowed me to finish my book more quickly.

Thanks to my Aunt Sandra Williams who took on the task of doing the layout for my book and taking care of all the tasks required to get the book to publication.

Thanks to my cover designer Nathan Fisher for creating a cover for my book and for valuable advice on how to prepare my book for publication.

Thanks to God for giving me the gift of imagination which allows me to create dynamic characters and vivid settings that keep readers engaged from beginning to end, and leaves them wanting to know more. I am also eternally grateful for technology advancements that allow me to write even though I am legally blind. I am truly blessed.

Prologue

The Keepers of the Gates, also known as the Clave Warriors or Clavemen, had life-long duties: to keep the keys to the gateways throughout the galaxies hidden and secure and to maintain peace and order among the different world governments behind each gateway. During times of peace in the old days, there was no reason to keep the gateway keys hidden because everyone knew that the Clave Warriors had them on the planet of Shangri-La, the planet which was the stronghold of the Clave. Additionally, no one dared to cause problems by attempting to take the gateway keys because Clave Warriors enforced the rules of the Universal Order. During times of peace, all planets cooperated, had fair trade, and smooth relationships. However, this peaceful interaction that had existed several decades ago, does not exist in the present where an evil dictator usurped power and disrupted what had been an ideal form of existence. The Clave Warriors are nothing but an old legend told by old men to the young with hints of truth. The Clave was rumored to have died out long ago, and the keys to the galaxies were but scattered treasure to be sought after for a sizable price.

Now a new Order would take over the ways of life in the galaxies. This new order would have to demand change in all the galaxies by forcing the present government that ruled the universe to be seized and brought to justice, tried for their crimes, and sent to universal prison, a place where one was simply forgotten.

What many did not know was that the Clave Warriors did exist, and they had not died out as rumors had spread. They were only hidden in secluded and out of the way places of the universe. And the Clave Warriors had reasons to hide. Now they had reasons to return. However, timing was most important. It had to be the proper time for the Clave Warriors to return and with the support of the right people.

If one were to believe that we are not alone in the universe, and that other worlds hold different life beings like ourselves, then the story you are about to read will not seem too far from reality. The Universal Order, a government run by Senators from each world, also called the UO, kept order and peace in the galaxies. To do this, they needed the Clave Warriors to enforce the laws enacted by the UO.

At one time, an evil warlord, Zymon Keltor, fought against the UO and the Clave and took over control of one of the galaxies. As he did this, he also dismantled the Clave. Having killed the leader of the UO, Keltor sought to take control of Shangri-La, which was the Clave stronghold.

PART I

Chapter One

Aliens, Secrets, and Escape

One such Clave Warrior, Odan Amir, clad in his Earthly clothes, khaki trousers, white shirt and a wide-brimmed straw hat, kneeling down in the front yard of a rather large house, pulling up weeds out of the flower bed. Three men dressed in what looked to be monks' robes walked toward him. Before they reached him, Odan's head turned slightly, and a huge smile spread across his face. He jumped up, discarded his straw hat, and wiped away the salty water pouring from his brow. Pushing the strands of hair that had fallen around his temples, making them blend in with rest of his salt and pepper hair that hung in a ponytail down the middle of his back, Odan raced toward the visitors and shouted in delight.

"Markel, Justin and Gorn!" he exclaimed while spreading his arms wide to embrace the three dear friends that he had not seen in over a decade, when the Universe was different. The four of them embraced, laughed and exchanged handshakes for several minutes before releasing each other. For it was true that they had not seen one another in a good ten years or more.

Markel took the hood off his face, revealing his shaved, bald head and his tan, brown skin.

"Footsteps can be misleading, brother," Markel remarked as he slanted his eyes toward Odan Amir, making his point clear that the three of them could have been anyone mimicking their footsteps to trick him.

"With feet like yours, I fail to see how," Odan replied, as he, Justin, Markel, and Gorn embraced and joined in a loud belly-wrenching, thunderous laugh befitting of four friends reuniting after ten years apart.

"I think he has spent too much time with the Earth people," Justin commented as he removed the hood to reveal his light, pale skin and his long, dark brown hair, which he had braided in a single braid down his back.

Gorn, also bald, smiled and nodded. "Our coming is not to be taken lightly Odan. Where are the younglings?"

"Off doing what younglings do on Earth. They get into trouble and cause all sorts of mischief! Come on inside. They should be home shortly. What in the blazes brings you three to Earth? I mean, I thought we were on a no contact status."

"We came to warn you, Odan, and to help if we can. It is no longer safe to stay here with Premier Zeger's children."

Odan ushered his guests into the sitting area of the kitchen as the door automatically shut behind them. When the three had settled themselves comfortably around the oblong wooden table, Odan began brewing tea. The kitchen table sat in front of a large bay window that over-looked the small lake behind the Tudor-styled house. The medium-sized table could easily accommodate six adults. To the right, separated by top and bottom oak cabinets, was the kitchen area which housed all the appliances, and where Odan Amir now danced around whipping up tea and refreshments for his friends. His dancing around was limited to the area near the sink and the cabinets near the doorway leading to the dining area, which was to the far right. With the use of his supernatural powers, he moved the tea kettle through midair without touching it and positioned it under the stream of water from the faucet until it overflowed. With those same powers, he shut off the faucet and moved the tea kettle kinetically to the stove to heat the water. He did all this while standing at the cabinet and looking for a certain flavor of tea for his friends.

"Why? For some decades nothing has happened. Why is it not safe now?"

"There is a leak within our …within our own numbers."

Odan stopped what he was doing and nearly dropped the tea pot of hot water on himself. "What? But who would do such a thing as…"

Odan turned his head in disgust and bewilderment.

"That is why I have come to help you," Markel stated.

"Help me do what exactly? These children are nowhere near ready for this."

"Haven't you been preparing them?"

"Yes, yes, of course. I've trained them in what they should know. Hand-to-hand and sword fighting and mind control…all of that, but they are nowhere near ready to lead the people to over-throw the current regime. Seth is just 17 years old, and Cassandra is—"

"No matter. They will have to learn faster is all," Gorn interrupted.

"They don't even know WHO they are yet. I was waiting until they could better understand."

The front door opened and the pair of twins burst into the home. Cassandra entered first, her long dark-brown locks of curls swaying as she walked. The younger of the twins behind her.

"Grandpa Odan! I need to go to the store please!" she cried out as if she knew he was somewhere in the house.

Markel looked to Odan. "Tell them now. We have no time to lose. We can't be sure whether we have been followed or not."

"Cassy, Seth, come here, now!"

Cassandra bounced into the kitchen area, stopping in surprise when she saw the three men dressed like monks sitting at the table. Her jaw dropped in amazement. Catching herself, she smiled and nodded to them.

"Hi!" Cassy greeted them cheerfully.

"Cassandra, these are good friends of mine. This is Markel, Justin and Gorn."

"Hello," Justin and Gorn replied in unison.

Markel nodded as he looked at Cassy and then back at Odan and grinned.

"She looks just like her mother, Odan. Pleased to meet you."

Seth walked into the kitchen from the foyer and noticed the three monk-looking men, too.

"Whoa, Grandpa Odan, you joining some cult we don't know about?"

Laughing at Seth's joke, Odan glanced at his friends. "Don't mind him, he's just trying to be humorous. Seth, these are my good friends Markel, Justin and Gorn. They have come a long way to talk to us about a serious matter."

Taking a seat, Seth looked at Odan. "Us?"

"Yes, but before we get into that, there are some things that I must tell you. I hope that you will understand the 'whys and whatnots' after I tell you what I can no longer hide from you."

"Hide? Why are you hiding something from us?"

"To protect you. You have to understand that the less you knew, the better off you were. After all, it was my duty to keep you safe and hidden."

Seth and his sister gazed at each other confused before turning their attention back to who they thought was their grandfather.

"Duty?" Seth directed the question to Odan.

"Yes. I am not your Grandfather by blood, but I have loved and cared for you as if you were my grandchildren. I am a Clave Warrior, a group established by the Universal Order to enforce the laws in the universe. Markel, Justin, and Gorn are also Clavemen. We now have the responsibility to keep the keys to the gateways throughout the galaxies hidden from the rebels and out of the hands of those who would use them for evil and destructive purposes." Odan paused to see if the twins were listening and understanding what he was trying his best to explain.

Seth spoke for the two of them. "Go on, Grandpa, we are following what you are saying so far, but we are waiting for you to explain how we fit into this puzzle."

"Let me explain. During times of peace in the old days, there was no reason to keep the gateway keys hidden because everyone knew that the Clave Warriors had them on the planet of Shangri-La, the planet which was the stronghold of the Clave. Additionally, no one was after the gateway keys to cause problems because Clave Warriors enforced the rules of the Universal Order. During times of peace, all planets cooperated, had fair trade, and smooth relationships.

However, the peaceful interaction that existed several decades ago, no longer exists. A rebel, Zymon Keltor, overthrew your parents in a surprise attack, killing them, as well as other Clave Warriors in the process. His mission was to destroy the Clave. Before your father took his last breath, he ordered me to take you two into hiding so that when the time was right, you could return, revive the Clave, and continue what they had devoted their lives to building, a peaceful universe.

Cassy interrupted him. "Grandpa, how many of our siblings did this monster kill?"

Odan paused before he could answer. "You had two older sisters and two brothers. They were just learning how to be Clave Warriors at the time."

As Seth listened to the story about the fate of his family, he turned red with anger, clenched his fist, and exploded into a verbal tirade. "How could they do such an awful thing? The ones who orchestrated this crime must be punished. I will see to it!"

Odan continued his story. "After the coup, Zymon Keltor, the leader of the Rebels, set himself up as the leader of the new order and demanded to be called the emperor. He proceeded to rule like a dictator, caring nothing for peace and equality. All he wanted was power, which he abused. Under his leadership, many Universal Order government officials were seized, unjustly tried and sentenced to universal prison, a place where they were simply forgotten."

"What many did not know was that most of the Clave Warriors had gone into hiding. They hid in secluded and out of the way places of the universe. And the Clave Warriors had reason to hide because of the events that I just described. I had to select the best place for your safety. So I hurried back to Shangri-La, collected you two, and headed to planet Earth, the only place I was sure Keltor did not know about."

"Why did you choose Earth," asked Cassy?

"Your parents here on this Earth were old friends of mine. I was an orphan and they adopted me, raised me and taught me things that helped me survive. It was later that I found out that I was actually left on this planet by my real parents, who were also Clave Warriors. I was left here on their doorstep. They said, if I ever needed help, that they would help me. When I came with the two of you, I am sure they didn't expect two young babies. But they opened their doors and arms to you two like you two were their own. I pretended to be Grandpa, just to stay close in case something happened such as what is happening now. When your parents on this Earth left us, I thought it might have been Zymon's men, but I couldn't be certain. Now I am sure. I know it must have been them. The time has come to go back and revitalize the Universal Order and the Clave with both of you taking on leading roles."

"What is happening? What the heck are you talking about, Grandpa Odan?" Cassy asked.

"My friends have come to tell me that there has been a leak of your whereabouts. We must leave this good Earth and go elsewhere."

Seth began laughing as he looked at his sister. "Just like that?" Seth asked. You know what I think? I think you have lost your marbles! Everyone knows that aliens do not exist!! Aliens didn't kill our parents! You are just old and are probably experiencing Antimeres, or you've been watching too much Star Trek."

Cassandra laughed. "Like, yeah our spaceship is in the back yard and we can zip off to the next galaxy in a few minutes."

"Deeetaadaaa!" Suddenly the entire group levitated off the floor about four feet and hovered in midair. "I know this is a lot of information to swallow, but the situation is urgent and I have no time for games."

As they floated in midair, they struggled to grab hold of something, desperately trying to get a foothold, but they were not so lucky.

"What the heck is going on here? Let us doooown!" Seth cried.

"You ready to listen to me now?" Odan asked.

"All right! I believe you," Seth cried out.

"Me too," Cassy replied as well.

Odan lowered them from mid-air to their seats and exhaled in a deep sigh of relief.

"I didn't want to treat you so harshly, but we have no time for childish things now. These people are out to kill you and the rest of us with you. And we have no time to waste."

"You seem afraid now, Seth," Markel stated.

"You bet your Twinkies I am," Seth replied. "It's not every day that you learn you're an alien!"

"Or that the parents you thought were your parents are not your blood parents!'

"Please, you must try to understand. Odan is not lying to you. Surely you have seen some signs of your abilities, by now," Markel butted in.

"What do you mean?" Seth asked.

"Like running, for example. Are you not faster than the average young man?"

"Somewhat."

A few moments passed.

"Okay, so yeah I run faster."

"You see far better than average."

"Yeah."

"You get all A's in your classes because you know the material better?"

"Honor roll student."

"Then you know you are different," Markel interjected.

"Cassy and I have this connection with our minds. We can speak to one another without talking out loud. I always thought it was something we had because we are twins," Seth replied.

"No. Nonverbal communication is an ability among many alien species in the known galaxies. It's not a special sibling thing," Markel stated.

"Well, I happen to like where I am right now. I had no plans on leaving! Why can't we fight them and stay here?"

"Would you want to be responsible for bringing Earth into the Galaxy wars?" Gorn asked.

"Well…No. I don't think people would appreciate it very much."

"If we stay here, the Rebels will come with full force and attack. They will come only because they know you both are here. But if you are not here, perhaps they won't come. Then we could leave Earth in its peaceful state. WE MUST go before they get pulled into this thing."

"When do we go?" Seth asked, looking at Markel and Odan.

"Tonight." Markel replied.

"We don't get to say goodbye to anyone?"

"It would work out best if no one knows that you are leaving. No letters …no leads.

Seth's hand covered his face and Cassy reached her hand out to his other hand. There were no words spoken. But Markel caught on to something else. Their minds were in conversation, but he only detected a part of it.

"Don't worry, Seth. Jordan may wait."

"I can't even ask her to, Cassy. You heard them. No goodbyes."

"Text her now," Cassy suggested. *"After this little talk just text her and tell her that no matter what happens, she is to wait for you."*

Seth grabbed his sister's hands, and a broad smile spread across his face. He winked at her to communicate, *"Thanks, Sis! That is a great idea!"*

"You obviously had a problem with the 'not saying goodbye to people you know here, Seth. Anyone special?" Markel asked.

"I have a girlfriend. Her name is Jordan."

Markel smiled. "There will be plenty more, I assure you."

"Not like her."

"It would be better for you to forget her. Once we leave this world, there will be no coming back. Earth is not a realm that is within the Universal Order yet. They are a primitive people that still wage war against their own kind. You see it on your news day in and day out. It is a miracle that they have survived this long," Markel added.

Seth looked to Odan with pleading eyes. "He's not telling the truth, is he?

"He is. Once we go, we will go for good. You have a destiny that does not include Earth. You both are the offspring of very important people, who were the leaders of nations, which both of you will be also. Don't become too attached to this place or any other for that matter. From here on out, we will spend a very short time in places we go. It is best not to get too attached. It would ruin your objectivity."

"You didn't tell us this Odan!" Seth's hand hit the table hard as he shot up from the table, enraged. "What the heck! You're not our grandfather! You're some strange man that—"

Odan rose up from the table and stretched his arm out to Seth's shoulder.

"I know, Seth. It will be all right."

"No! It's not!" Seth shouted.

"Just take it all in and accept it. Remember what I taught you about controlling your emotions?"

Seth exploded in response. "You're telling me our parents aren't our parents! That some other man and woman are our parents! That our destiny is to lead ....lead what? That we don't belong here on this planet, but elsewhere?"

"I know this is confusing to you now, but you will soon understand it. Right now, you must trust that I would not lead you astray."

Seth stared at everyone looking at him. He plopped down and held his head in his hands trying to digest all the information that had been dumped on him at once. Cassandra's heart raced, and she squeezed her hands together underneath the table in an effort to be strong for her brother. Though equally upset, she was better at hiding her emotions until she was alone. However, the unspoken communication between them alerted Seth that she held back a river of tears and sorrow at this news also. That made him even angrier.

"You are going to have to prove that we are who you say we are and that you are who you say you are. Aliens? People don't even believe in Aliens on this planet, Odan! You expect us to just trust you and believe all this crap!?"

Odan raised his eyebrows when Seth challenged him. Then he shrugged his shoulders and nodded.

"You still don't believe me after all these years? Alright. Stay here I'll be right back. You want proof, I'll give it to you."

Odan moved swiftly and exited the kitchen area into the corridor of the house that led to his bedroom. He reached into the closet and rumbled through a back pack, pulling out a device, which was circular and black on one side and silver on the other. He walked down the corridor and re-entered the kitchen.

Setting the device on the table, Odan placed it in the center of the table and tapped the silver side.

In a bluish haze of florescent light, images of a man that looked like Seth and a woman that resembled Cassy appeared with four other children. The couple held two babies, and it was obvious that the image was that of a family.

"You want proof? Well, here are your parents and your mother and father holding the two of you. The others are your siblings."

"Other siblings?" Cassy questioned.

"Yes, of course. There's Theo, Hector, Andromeda and Sicilia."

"Don't tell me they are dead, too?"

"We aren't sure about them," Markel replied. "But we believe they are. They did not go into hiding like you did."

"Why not go get packed up?" Markel asked.

Seth looked at the strange image of the people, and he could see some resemblance in the features of their faces. He could see that the babies were actually he and his sister, Cassy. He glanced at Cassandra and raised his eyebrows. She spoke using her mind.

"It's us!" exclaimed Cassy.

"Yes. It is," Seth replied.

"You don't waste any time, do you? Our lives are being turned upside down, and all you can think of is getting us out of here as fast as possible. We have made roots here! We have made friends here! You don't just up and disappear!" Seth yelled. "With strangers!"

"Seth, you will check your voice when you are speaking with your elders! Now, get up and get some clothes into a duffle bag, towels, whatever you need and get back down here so we can leave. As Markel stated before, we might not have enough time. Zymon's people could have followed them," Odan reminded him.

Seth stood up and gave a glance to Odan and knew by his tone that he should not say anything more. He cursed under his breath as he bolted out of the kitchen. Cassy rose taking her things with her. Odan followed her then turned back to his guests.

"We won't be long," he assured them.

"Good," Markel replied. "We are already pushed for time."

Seth raced into his room, slammed the door, and grabbed his duffle bag. Pausing for a moment, he thought about his situation. Then, as if he were running away from something sinister, he opened the window to his room, took out the screen, and jumped to the ground just a few feet below. He hit the ground running.

Darkness had fallen on the Florida suburb, and the only lighting was the tall road lights. Seth took the lighted path to Jordan's house, which was only 10 blocks away. If he ran, it would only take some ten minutes. He knew time was against him. Odan would soon come to his room and find him gone.

Not long after helping Cassy with her things, Odan rushed to Seth's room and found it empty. He noticed the open window and that the screen had been removed. Sighing with disgust, he rushed down the corridor and into the kitchen to inform his friends that Seth had run off. Cassy walked into the kitchen with her bag.

"I know where he went," Cassy stated.

"Jordan's?" Odan asked.

Cassy nodded.

"Cassy, I want you to go with Markel, Justin and Gorn." Turning to his old friends, Odan confirmed that they knew their destination. "You know how to get there, right?" Odan asked.

"Yes, I do," the three answered in unison.

"We will be taking the boat out to where we need to go."

"What about you and Seth?"

"I will find him and meet you at the dock," Odan reassured her.

Markel rose, taking the device from the table that held the picture of the Zeger family. Handing it to Odan, he reminded everyone of the importance of the secrecy of their mission. "We should not leave clues," he remarked.

Odan took the device. "True."

Taking one of two cars that belonged to the earthly family, the three friends of Odan rose and exited the place. After loading his things into the bed of the old pickup, Odan sped off to find Seth.

Meanwhile, Seth had arrived at Jordan's home. Instead of ringing the doorbell, he went to the back of her house and threw pebbles at her window to get her attention. After two tries, Jordan's face appeared at the window, and she opened it when she saw Seth.

"Seth? What are you doing?"

"I was in the neighborhood."

Jordan smiled. "And you thought to come and see me?"

"Certainly."

Jordan smiled. "You're so sweet."

"Truth is that I'm going away, and I wanted to tell you goodbye."

Her smile disappeared, and her brow furrowed. "You're leaving me?"

"Yeah. I doubt I'll be back soon."

Seth found this hard to say to her. But she deserved to be told rather than left wondering about him. At that moment, Odan's truck pulled into the yard. Seth could feel it.

"I don't have much time left, Jordan. But I wanted you to know that I love you. I would rather stay here, but I can't. So I had to come and tell you goodbye because I respect you and don't want you wondering about me when I'm not around."

"Where are you going? Take me with you."

"I don't know if you'd want to go, and I don't know if you can. It's better if you stay here and go on with your life," Seth continued.

Then, the back door to Jordan's house opened, and Jordan's father came out with Odan following.

"I thought I'd find you here, Seth."

"You were right, Mister Odan. He is here wooing my daughter. Seth, if you want to talk to Jordan, you could have rung the doorbell."

Seth's face turned red, and he glanced at Jordan who was smiling at her father. It did make sense. Seth turned to Jordan's father and nodded. "Yes, Sir, I was a little pressed for time."

"Come on Seth. We need to go," Odan urged.

"Next time I'll take your advice and use the front doorbell, sir."

Seth shook hands with Jordan's father and followed them back through the house and out the front door. Seth turned back to see Jordan on the steps, as she waved goodbye to him. He was not sure, but he thought he saw tears in her eyes.

Seth walked up to the truck and got inside, sitting on the passenger side, while Odan took the driver's seat. Silence was deafening as Odan backed the truck out and headed for the yacht. He struggled to contain his anger at Seth for disobeying his request for secrecy. He drove several miles before speaking.

"We said no goodbyes for a specific reason, Seth. We didn't want anyone to know we had been here at all. Now, Jordan knows we are leaving, which leaves proof that we were here."

"I....I'm sorry, Grandpa..... Odan. I had to tell her I was leaving so she wouldn't be left wondering about me."

"What would it have mattered? She would grow up and forget about you and marry some other man, Seth."

"I know that. I just wanted her to know that I love her enough to tell her the truth instead of just leaving her hanging."

"I'm sure she appreciates that, Seth, but you have to look at the big picture here. By letting her know you are leaving, you have left proof that you were here. It links this good Earth to you and, thus, involves Earth in universal affairs. I hope, for your sake that it doesn't—"

Suddenly, there was a bright flash of white light, and Odan cried out. "Get down!"

Then Odan spoke his native Clave tongue, "Entukas-Ven!"

Odan let go of the steering wheel and ducked down like Seth. Seth's mouth dropped, and he looked at Odan in awe. Odan was using his supernatural powers to drive the truck while he ducked down out of harm's way.

"What are you doing? You have to drive the truck!"

Odan nodded. "Don't worry, I am. I just don't want to get killed in the process. I think we are being followed and shot at by Zymon's men."

As if it were being driven by someone, the truck rolled in and out of the traffic and zipped through yellow lights, speeding forward, while Odan and Seth ducked and kept their heads out of the line of laser fire.

Glass shattered as the laser shots hit the rear window of the truck.

"What do we do? We will lead them to the others!" Seth cried.

"Our only hope is to get to the boat and get to the gate. They won't be able to follow us without a boat."

"I hope you're right."

Arriving at the marina, Seth and Odan got out of the truck, and Odan used his powers to send the truck down the pier into the water. Then, they ran to the docks where the yacht that belonged to their earthly parents rested. Odan then turned into the Captain of the boat and followed what he had learned from his earthly friends. Before long, they were heading out of the pier at a no-wake pace. When they cleared the no-wake zone, Odan revved the engine and the boat bounced over the 3-foot waves as its passengers held on for dear life, rocking this way and that way. Seth looked to Cassy as they sat on the back of the boat with their backs to the engines, and they began to communicate without talking.

"What do you think, Cassy?"

"I'm pinching myself to see if I'm imagining this but...it's real, and I still can't believe it."

"I know. I think we were just chased by some aliens. It's like something out of a comic book or something. But if it is true, and our

parents are some political leaders of some far off world government, don't we owe it to them to return and change things back to the way they were?"

"No one is forcing us. I'm sure if we told Odan we don't want to be part of this, he'd listen to us."

"But that would disappoint a lot of people."

"People we don't even know."

"People that care for us and people that have counted on us to be the force that would change the tides."

"I think you like the idea of helping Odan overthrow these enemies of our parents, whoever they are."

"It doesn't matter who they are. They saved our lives by hiding us from him."

"True."

"Now we should pay back."

"I suppose so." She nodded and smiled at her brother.

Odan surrendered the steering wheel to Markel so that he could speak to Cassy and Seth.

"I know all this is rather sudden and pretty unbelievable. But no one is making you do something you don't want to do here. Thing is, I must consider your safety and the peaceful state of this galaxy. Earth has been and always will be a relatively peaceful realm. It is the reason I brought you two here in the first place. I knew Zymon would not look for you here. But once we pass over to another galaxy, you can be sure that your safety will be in jeopardy. Thus, it is imperative that you remain with us because you do not know your way in the other realms yet."

Seth's eyes narrowed, "We didn't sign up for this, Grand…Odan." Suddenly, he did not know how to address the man he had always known to be Grandpa. He continued with his statement after an awkward pause. "We have no choice but to come with you anyway!"

"Grandpa Odan, we were talking about this together, and we decided that we will go along with it. But we don't like how this has come about.

All these secrets make it very hard to trust you. I know you were only doing what you thought was best, but, by not telling us, you left us totally in the dark. We have lived this long thinking Michel and Annie were our parents, but they were not. And now we don't have a clue as to who our parents were or who we are, except what you've told us, which isn't much. We know they were leaders of nations and that they were betrayed and slain by this Zymon guy, who is out to kill us."

"I know. I-"

"Don't repeat yourself, Odan. I know you were trying to protect us."

Odan nodded and then sighed. He could only hope that this breach in their previous bond of trust would be mended somehow.

Then Gorn and Justin moved slowly to the back of the boat, holding on to anything they could to keep from falling overboard.

"We are nearing the coordinates. By my calculations, the portal will be open in ten minutes. We must be prepared to open the gates.

Odan nodded and rose to his feet. He reached into his shirt and pulled out a medallion he wore around his neck, as did the other three monk-looking Clave Warriors. After a few moments, Markel stopped the engines, and the boat just drifted.

"Seth, Cassy! Come join hands with us."

The twins joined hands with Odan and his friends and watched in amazement as Markel, Justin and Gorn produced similar medallions from their shirts. The four friends began to speak aloud in a language the teens did not recognize. Suddenly, the sea around them whirled and churned like a category 5 hurricane sea, sending the boat into a clockwise spin faster and faster in sync with the whirling water. A bright light beamed on the party below, and they were caught up into the air slowly, then faster and faster. Had it not been for the supernatural powers of the four aliens, Seth and Cassie would have lost consciousness.

One thought was crystal clear in Seth's mind as he was passing through the gate. "Goodbye, Jordan."

Chapter Two

The Return Home

Andromeda Galaxy: Planet Romes IV

F ar, far from Earth, deep within the Andromeda Galaxy on a jade-colored planet, something that was once dead came alive. In an abandoned, old building, deep in the city of Romeria, in what used to be called the grand hall where the Clave Warriors met to discuss matters of the universe, something came alive that had been dead for many years. In the center of the room, the ground began to move in a circular motion. Orbs of light that had not burned for some decades erupted into flames, and a fierce wind blew in opposite directions.

The party from Earth appeared as they had departed from the Bermuda Triangle, still holding hands in a circle. After breaking from the circle, Odan, Markel, Justin and Gorn raised their hands and spoke in unison. Immediately, the winds died down, and the floor stopped its circular motion slowly. When it was fully motionless, Odan looked to Seth and Cassy.

"Do you feel okay?" Odan asked. "Sometimes the jump from one place to another affects people differently."

Cassy shrugged her shoulders. "I feel fine, actually. I feel a bit better than I did before."

Seth nodded. "So do I."

"You should. You were born here on Romes IV. This is your real home, your native land."

"Enough of the history lesson, Odan. We need to get out of here unnoticed, and these kids need to get out of those clothes or cover them up so that they won't draw attention to themselves," Markel interjected.

Odan consented and walked over to a stack of robes hanging on a rack. Grabbing two of them, he handed one to each of the twins to put on over their clothes. As they did this, the others searched for a safe exit from the building.

Gorn motioned for them all to follow him, for he had gone down one corridor leading from the hall.

"If my memory serves me best, I think this leads to a side exit."

The party followed him down the corridor, taking the orbs of light from the great hall with them to light their way in the dark and dusty corridors. They took a winding pathway that soon led them to a side door. The door had been locked from the outside, but such a lock would not stop a Clave Warrior. Markel grasped the door knob, bent down as if to whisper a few words in a strange language so that only the knob could hear. A loud series of clicks echoed through the hallway, and a chain fell to the ground outside. The door then opened slowly, and fresh air and the night sky of Romes IV greeted them.

Slipping out into the alley, the party quickly headed down the path and onto a somewhat populated street.

Odan whispered to the children. "Don't stop to talk to anyone. We are here to gain transport."

They moved on through the city streets without incident and soon came to a loud, and over-populated tavern. Moving as a group inside, they found a table, and Markel motioned for them to sit.

"Remain here, I'll get us transport."

Markel moved deeper into the establishment until the smoke and moving bodies made it difficult for the others to see him.

A strange looking female waitress with green skin and four arms came to their table. "What'll you have, travelers?"

Odan unhooded himself and nodded to the lady saying, "Blue Rivers all around, please."

Cassy looked to Seth and smirked as she turned back to Odan and wondered what blue rivers was. She waited until the waitress left and asked him, "What is Blue Rivers?"

Odan smiled. "Purest Water they have."

"I thought you were getting us alcoholic beverages."

"That would kill you. No, my dear, you can't handle their alcoholic beverages. They are too strong."

Meanwhile, Markel sat down with a rough looking humanoid male, who seemed somewhat trustworthy.

"You looking for transport, you say?" the humanoid stated. "What's the cargo?"

"Passengers. Six of us altogether."

"Where we going?" The humanoid took a gulp of his drink.

Markel leaned closer to the man and spoke in hushed whispers so that only he could hear him. "Shangri-La."

When the man heard this, he spewed out his drink, coughing as he almost choked on it. He coughed again and cleared his throat. "Heeek-errmmmm-Shangrala? That is a dead planet. No one goes there unless they want to get thrown under the ne*ares*t prison planet. Any ship that tries to go there is either shot down or boarded or both!"

"Even still, that is our destination. If you can't take us there, then I will find another pilot who can."

"Woe, hold on there. I never said I can't do it. I am just saying that it won't be an easy thing. You must be—"

"The deal is six passengers and no questions. You get us there without any Rebel interactions, and I will give you 5 million gold terrons."

The man's mouth dropped open wide, and then he smiled and chuckled as he took a sip of his drink, finishing it in one final noisy gulp.

"You got yourself transport. This won't be easy, but I love to play hide and seek with those Rebel scum. I just never liked the way they took over things. They were bad for business; making my line of work so much harder. I'll get my crew, supplies and whatever else we need. Meet us in hanger 45E in 30 minutes."

Markel stood. "30 minutes. We'll be there."

Markel gave the man a nod and walked back to the table where Odan and the others were sipping their pure water. Odan gave Markel one, which he accepted and took a seat with the others.

"I've arranged transport for us. We meet them in hanger 45E in 30 minutes. We should get supplies we might need now. Cassy and Seth will need more clothes that don't look odd."

"I'll see to it," Odan agreed.

"I hope those that followed us to Earth have not followed us through the gates," Justin stated. "Maybe we will be gone from here before they can follow us."

"At any rate, we have involved Earth. I hope the Rebs don't bring Earth into this on a larger scale."

"If they do, we might be going back, won't we?" Seth asked.

"Perhaps," Odan replied. "Perhaps so."

"Well, let's not waste time," Markel added, rising from his chair.

The party rose and moved out of the establishment toward the many shops. They purchased robes and other garments and bags to put things in. They also bought Blue River bottles in abundance.

Odan helped Cassandra buy some ladies' attire. She chose jumpsuits and dresses with matching robes and two pairs of durable, leather boots to match her outfits. Altogether, she purchased about ten interchangeable outfits. The clerk smiled, thrilled for the business, as she packed the purchased items into a tote for Cassy. Markel volunteered to carry the load to the ship. They also bought weapons along the way, some suitable for a lady to wield. Justin assisted Seth in buying some manly items, such as trousers, boots and tunics. They also bought weapons for him.

After their shopping spree, the party made their way to hanger 45E. It didn't take them long to find the hanger where the ship was docked. When they entered, they were greeted by the Captain of the ship.

"Greetings. Welcome. We are just about to make final, preflight checks. You all are just in time to put your things in cargo hold. My name is Maximillion Rex, but people call me Rex. The ship will accommodate you all quite well. I'll show you to the common cabin area and then your quarters."

"We will be needing separate quarters for the lady."

Rex turned about and looked confused. "Lady?" looking at all the hooded figures with them. "Which one of you is a lady?"

Cassandra took the hood off her head, revealing her long, curly, brown hair and her striking, blue eyes. "I am."

Taken in by her beauty, Rex was struck into silence for a few seconds. He stared at her, and then snapping out of it, he looked away and cleared his throat. "Right. You can have my quarters. They are private and secure. I'll bunk up with the crew."

Cassy gave a slight smile at this reaction and nodded. "I thank you for your hospitality, Captain Rex."

"It is quite gentlemanly of you," Odan stated.

The party moved into the corridors of the ship, which was a medium-sized vessel, capable of high speeds. After giving them the grand tour of the vessel, Captain Rex parted his passengers' company in the common cabin area where three of his crew stood ready. He introduced them to the passengers before he left.

"This is Dexter, an engineer who knows the operations of the vessel. The red-headed gal is Langstrom, the Doc and science officer. We call her Doc. The black dwarf is Raymond, the tactical and security officer. I handle the helm and communications. If you need anything, let one of us know. Okay?"

Everyone seemed to understand what was expected, and Rex, satisfied with the passengers and crew, decided to get the ship moving. "All right. Let's get the show on the road then! Crew, to your stations."

The three crew members and Rex went to the front of the ship and got themselves ready. Odan's party took their seats in the cabin area and waited. Minutes later, Rex's voice sounded over the intercom. "We asked for departure clearance, and we've been told to hold our position.

Odan turned to look at Markel. "Could they have followed us?"

"Perhaps. But let's hope not."

Rex's voice came through again. "We've been told to shut down our engines. Damn it! This has never happened before!"

Rex came out of the cockpit and looked to Markel. "What's going on? We're being boarded!"

As Captain Rex spoke, several Rebel patrols entered hanger 45E armed to the teeth and carrying scanning devices. A sea of blue uniforms flooded the hanger. Rebels surrounded the octagon ship.

Markel, using his powers, could feel the Rebels crowding into the hanger.

He looked to Rex, "Is there some place you can hide us?"

"Follow me!" Rex cried.

With all swiftness, the parties moved to the cargo hold and were put under the bulkheads between the frameworks of the ship. Just as he finished hiding Seth, the Rebel guards boarded the ship to search it.

Rebel Warrior stepped up to address the Captain as several Rebel patrols moved through the ship using their scanning devices. "What is your destination?"

"Appolis IV."

"That is far. Why do you go there?"

"Business."

"We are looking for Clavemen. They are known to look like monks dressed in robes. Have you given them your ship, perhaps?"

"No. I go to Appolis IV for trading business, a trip I always take."

"I would be careful then. There are a few battles going on along the way."

"So noted."

The Rebels, who had boarded to search the ship returned to the one Rebel standing next to Captain Rex.

"Ship is clean, Sir."

"Nothing but the crew in the cockpit, Sir," added another.

"Very well. Be on your way," the Rebel officer replied, giving the ship permission to continue its voyage.

After the last Rebel Warrior had deboarded and cleared the landing bay, Rex blasted his ship off the planet and headed on course for Appolis IV, the destination he had told the Romerian Command he was headed. When he felt enough time and distance had passed, he freed his passengers from the secret workings of this vessel.

When all had returned to the cabin, Rex sighed. "That was close."

"Thank you for your clever answers to his questions," Markel complimented the captain for his quick thinking and responses to the interrogation of the Rebels.

"No problem," Rex smiled. "I liked lying to them. I only told the truth partially. We are headed to Appolis IV. We will stop there to refuel before going on to Shangri-La."

Markel nodded. "How long will we be residing there on Appolis IV?"

"That would depend on the number of ships in line for refueling. Appolis IV is the only refueling station in the Outer Rim. Plus we are trying to avoid Rebel ships. It might prove difficult to get the fuel without being boarded again."

"Well, at least for the moment we don't have to worry. We have managed to outsmart them thus far, and I believe we shall outsmart them again," Odan's confidence resounded and reaffirmed hope in the others that their mission would be successful.

"They know we made it through the gate, Odan. They will be looking for us harder than they ever have before. They know if we start making contact with the others, we pose a threat to them," Markel interjected, still unsure of the mission's ability to elude the rebels forever.

"You are Clavemen, aren't you?"

Silence fell on the group in the cabin as they all stared at Captain Rex. Then after a few odd seconds of silence, Markel rose to his feet.

"Who we are is of no concern to you, Captain Rex."

"I beg to differ," Rex replied. "I'm risking my life and the lives of my crew to aid you and your friends. I think I deserve to know why I do this. If it is something that I believe in, then I have no problem taking you to Shangri-La. But do not keep me in the dark. I'd like to know why I might be dying, and I know I speak for my crew when I say this."

"Very well, Captain Rex," Markel agreed. "We are Clavemen on a mission to revitalize the old brotherhood. We have what is necessary to take back control from the dictator, Zymon Keltor and his rebels. The Zeger family heirs who are aboard this ship will serve as Senators of the Universal Order."

"The Zegers' Offspring were all slain."

"All but two," Odan corrected.

Rex looked at the lady of the group. "Her?" he asked in surprise.

"And her brother."

Rex nodded and understood. "I understand why you are trying to avoid the Rebels. They would seek to kill those two."

Markel turned to Rex." Can we count on your silence?'

"I will do all I can to assist you and the royals."

"You will be handsomely rewarded."

"Forget the money. I just want to see the Rebels put in their places for once."

"A deal is a deal, Captain Rex," Markel responded, happy to know that the captain was on their side. Without his support, they would never make it to their destination in time.

"If you insist," Rex smirked. "I would suggest you get some rest while we are not being pestered by the Rebels," he added as he walked toward the cockpit. "I plan on hitting hyperspace which would get us there within a few days."

When Rex disappeared into the cockpit, Odan looked to Seth and Cassandra. "You two should get some sleep."

"It's been a long and trying day," Cassandra agreed. "Rest sounds good right about now."

"A lot has happened," Odan replied. "Some rest will do you well."

"I'd like to sleep," Seth yawned while stretching his arms in an effort to release the stress of the past few hours. Odan rose to his feet and escorted Cassy thru the ship to the Captain's quarters where he checked the room to make sure she was safe. Then he hugged her and left her alone there in Captain Rex's quarters.

The captain's quarters were dimly lit, but Cassy could see that clutter spread throughout the room. Clothes hung on several different chairs and the bed, as well. The walls, however, were adorned with several different kinds of weapons: blades, swords, bows and arrows, and laser pistols. All of them were organized neatly on the four walls, in contrast to everything else in the room. This led Cassy to believe that he knew how to use all those weapons very well. She walked over and admired some of the swords, her hands clasped behind her back, remembering what Odan had told her when they had arrived at Romes IV, not to touch anything that didn't belong to her. Then after a few moments of studying the captain's arsenal, she crawled on top of the clothes on the bed and exhaled, releasing all the pent up anxiety of the recent happenings.

Sleep came almost instantly. Before she could rehash the experiences of the past few days, she fell into a deep and dreamless sleep, one in which she acquired the most rest, which her body needed. Without her noticing, Seth slipped into the Captain's Quarters to watch over his sister. He quietly took a seat on one of the chairs, taking care not to rouse her, and fell asleep with his boots propped up on another chair. He was taking no chances that someone on the ship might try to take advantage of her.

Chapter Three

Transport to Shangri-La

As he sat in the pilot's throne of the cockpit, Captain Rex could not get the vision of the lady among their passengers out of his mind. She was beautiful, young, and he found himself thinking about her more than he was thinking about his work. The voice of one of his crew snapped him back into the present.

"So what's the story of these people, Rex?" Dexter questioned.

"There's no story. We are just giving them a ride somewhere is all."

"Where exactly would that be?" Dexter asked. "And why did those Rebels force us to power down the ship! Why did they board us?"

"They were looking for..."

"Them? Weren't they?" Dexter blurted out.

"Now, hold on a minute. Yes, they were looking for them, but we don't need to worry about that now." Rex stated. "They didn't find them."

"Rebel patrols sweep every inch of the Andromeda, Rex. They will board our ship and search it if they have an idea the wrong sort is among us."

"They found no one on our ship before we left Romes IV, so they have no reason to board us. Just relax."

"Who are they?"

Raymond chimed in then. "Clavemen. They are the only sort that hide themselves in crowds."

"Look, we are being paid handsomely for this run. This could be the run that will retire us early. Five million terrons!"

"I never knew you could be bought until now," Dexter replied.

"It's a handsome price, and I know they are good for it. Clavemen have never been known to tell lies."

"You just sold our hides to the first Rebel patrol that will seek these misfits."

"Not if we avoid those patrols," Rex retorted.

"You know what I think?" interjected Dexter.

"No, what?" Rex asked.

"I think you like the young lady."

"What is not to like about her? She is beautiful; very easy on the eye. You got me all wrong, Dex. I'm not doing this for love. I don't even know the lady."

"With all the teasing aside, you have put our lives on the line on this one, Rex, without asking us whether we wanted in on it or not."

"I'm the captain of this ship, and you are the crew. You all go where the ship goes if you wish to be paid your wages. I didn't have to tell you about our job, but I felt you deserved to know. If you want out, you know where the life pods are. You can take off and hope for transport because I'm not turning around."

"Jumping stars! There's a battle in our pathway! I'm picking up radiation emissions in great numbers. If we continue at hyperspace, we may run into a ship or something worse!"

"Frock!" Rex stated. "Can we go around it?"

"It will take us by Soma II, a Rebel outpost."

"We'll stay on course and hope we squeak by," Rex decided. "We cannot risk going near Sona II. Not with this group we have here."

"We will gather too much attention, Rex. They will check us out, coming in hot like this."

"We don't have a choice." Rex stated. "Keep an eye on the battle up ahead. Let me know if anything changes." After a few seconds he asked Dex another question. "Who is in the battle?"

"Looks to be Rebels firing on ...a small fleet of ships."

"Can you identify those ships at this range?"

"Not this far out. I know the others are Rebels because the lasers are signature laser beams, high voltage bursts or radiation…definitely Rebel in design," Dex replied.

"How many Rebel ships are there against the others?"

"The other unknown ships are outnumbered by 3 to their 1 ship. They are being clobbered."

"When we reach there, drop us out of hyperspace and let us engage the Rebels."

"What? Did you say what I thought you said?" Dex asked.

"Yes. I did not stutter. We will engage them and catch the Rebels by surprise and make friends with the others on that ship."

"You are out of your mind! We'll be on the hit list!'

"Dex, anytime you want out, just hit the pods and go. Alright."

"You keep saying that and I'm likely to do it!"

"Fine."

"Fine then."

"Pipe down, ladies," Raymond teased. "No one is going anywhere. But I have to ask you Rex, why do you want to do this?"

"It's time for the Rebels to get a taste of their own medicine."

"Don't you think that with these passengers that would be unwise?" Raymond asked.

"No, I don't. Those aboard the ship being destroyed need help. We can help them. Why not let it be us?"

"I believe that helping that ship will drastically endanger our mission, whatever the hell that is! If we have people that don't want Rebels boarding our ship, then we should pass them by and try not to draw attention to us."

Raymond always knew what to say at the right moment. He always was the voice of reason and plain common sense. There was no drive of heroism in him, despite his line of expertise. He simply told it like it was.

"We will try to pass through the battle and make it to Appolis IV. We might have to do some fancy talking."

"As I do recall, that's your department, Rex," Dex stated. "And thanks Raymond for speaking wisdom into his brain."

Raymond's deep baritone voice chuckled through the head gear. "We'll see how long that lasts."

Rex's face cracked into a grin as he checked the instruments of the helm. "Don't you worry about me none; I just felt like being the hero for a spell."

"You know darn well anyone who plays the hero winds up getting killed these days," Raymond offered.

"Yeah. I know." Rex shook his head. "I must have been talking too much with our passengers. They've inspired me to a degree."

"What have they been saying?" Langstrom asked.

"They are trying to bring life back into the Clave and to revitalize the Universal Order as it was long ago before the Rebels took over."

"You're kidding me?" Dex stated.

"That would be hard to do. The Clave are scattered all over the universe by now."

"In order to bring back the Universal Order and the Clave Warriors, they would have to have a Senate Leader."

"We have two Senate Leaders aboard."

"What!"

"Yeah, and keep your mouths shut about it."

"Now, I understand why you wanted to take on the world," Dex exclaimed, as if he just had a sudden revelation. "If I saw that, I would be inspired, too."

"Do any of you realize that we are making history because of what we are doing right this minute?"

"Isn't it a rush?" Rex exclaimed.

"Truth be told, it won't be easy to get them to where they are going, and I don't even know where that is yet," Dex replied.

"They are going to Shangri-La," Rex revealed their destination to his crew, somewhat assured that they were all in agreement that this was the right thing to do.

"Okay, that might be impossible. That planet is heavily guarded and scanned by Rebel patrols, specifically to keep the Clave from regrouping there."

"I believe that with the passengers' aide, we can sneak by the patrols and land on Shangri-La without the rebels picking up our ship," Rex stated. "The Clave were known for their mastery of stealth and their ability to camouflage themselves, despite their present state of being."

"So you think they could use their powers to assist our efforts to get them to Shangri-La?"

"I do," Rex readily replied.

Suddenly, the ship dropped out of hyperspace speeds and slowed down to just under light speed. Rex grabbed the controls and turned the ship to avoid entering the gravitational well of the nearby planet. The ship shuddered slightly, as Rex swore under his breath in his native Angolian tongue. Dexter also cursed as she placed her feet on the sides of the metal ladder and zipped down. She opened the bulkhead under the ladder and continued down another ladder to the corridors underneath the ship, leading to the ship's interworking that controlled the ship's engines.

Ahead, about a few clicks, a battle being played out, and as they continued at light speed and dropping-in speed, Rex wondered if they could avoid being boarded.

"Dex, get that hyperspace back up, please."

"As if I didn't know that already! Cap. I'm working on it!"

"Make it fast! We are approaching the edge of the battle!"

"I heard ya! I know what's at stake. I'll get it up and running! Give me a few, will ya?"

"That's all we have is 'a few,' Dex," Rex stated. "You know I trust you, babe."

"Oh, so when you need me, you trust me? What about those other times?"

While she talked to Rex, her hands had a mind of their own, as they moved and checked and reconnected the wires. She worked with what looked like hands full of snakes and wads of mating clusters of those snakes. She didn't mind the idea of playing mother hen to those wires and clusters. As long as she got those wires and clusters to cooperate and give her green lights, she was happy. Finally, she used a system-checking device to make sure her work was finished. She checked the hyperspace drive and found a green light and whispered a silent prayer to her God for his blessings.

After double checking her work, she nodded when she got green lights and gave herself a big cheer before contacting Captain Rex.

"All clear! We can make the jump to hyperspace now!"

"You're beautiful, Dex. Nice job!" Rex replied. "Everyone hang on!"

For the second time, since they started their voyage to the planet known as the mysterious Clave stronghold, Shangri-La, the medium-sized ship lurched into hyperspace speeds, taking them well above light speeds. Before it, an intense battle played out; ships fired on ships, creating what looked to be a great fireworks display. But there was no celebration associated with this bombardment. As the medium-sized ship etched closer to the battle field, it became more noticeable. Presently, they were contacted on normal communication frequencies.

"Approaching vessel, this is the Rebel Flag Ship *Lunar II*, Please state your name for our records and the name of your ship and your business, or we will open fire on your vessel and consider you part of the riffraff that is among us now."

"We are just a cargo and freight ship, heading to Appolis IV for a bit of trading business," Rex replied. "Ah… we also need to refuel."

"From what planet did you originate?"

"Romes IV."

"Did a patrol check your ship before departure?"

"Aye, Sir. They searched it and found nothing amiss."

"Hold on here until we communicate with Romes IV Security to verify your story." He then switched channels and directed orders to his fighter cruisers. "Hold this ship until I check out their claim. If the ship makes any attempt to flee, fire full power to destroy it, understood?" Upon this, he turned to the command center communication technician. "Get Romes IV Security for me, now!"

Rex did as he was told, praying that the *Lunar II* patrol would not demand a new search. His crew would not have time to hide the cargo. He tried to maintain his cool demeanor, though his heartbeat accelerated and sweat poured from his brow. The Rebel leader only took a few minutes, but to the *Raptor's Claw* crew, it seemed like hours. Finally he reappeared and announced his decision.

"Romes IV confirms your story. You understand that we had to check it out. The Emperor will have our heads if we let the Senators and Clave members slip through without searching every suspect vessel. I see no reason to check what has already been checked out. I will inform the other Rebel ship in this engagement to give you passage to Appolis IV."

"I do thank you, Sir. Captain Rex, out."

Rex smiled and uttered a sigh of relief. He propped his knee-high, leather boots upon the control panel, careful not to touch any of the controls, clinched his hands behind his head, took out a cigar, lit it, and took a long puff, exhaling the smoke through his nostrils. He then addressed his passengers and crew.

"I guess you can say we got lucky this time. We have been given clearance. Continue to destination."

Dex entered the cockpit. Seeing him, she put her hands on her hips, and shook her head.

"We are damn lucky not to get boarded."

Rex took the cigar out of his mouth, leaving smoke spiraling out as he tapped into a metallic can on the side of the pilot's throne. "Darling, I must teach you the art of smuggling one of these days. First lesson is to hide what you have, and the second lesson is to make up a lie to tell them so you don't have to lose your stake."

"How do you plan to keep them from searching us when we get down there? "We are a few days journey to Appolis IV. I think we can come up with a workable plan that will trick the Rebels again."

Raymond scrambled up the ladder from his station and entered the cockpit. "Hey, no sloughing off on the job! You loafers get back to work." Raymond grinned as his short frame barely reached the top of the back of Rex's pilot's seat.

"We were just talking about when we get to Appolis IV. You know darn well they will search this ship when we arrive. It is procedure," Dex reminded them.

"She's right. They do that in every station nowadays."

"We will have to come up with some sort of trick to make them think we don't have passengers," Rex answered, taking a puff of his cigar.

Langstrom strode into the small cockpit, taking her place at the entrance. "There's a way, but we will have to put it into effect soon if we are to do it."

"Doc? We don't often hear any hair brain ideas from you! What's on your noodle?"

"We can give our passengers a sedative and medicine combination that will slow their heart rates down to a low level to make them appear to be dead. We can put them in the ice chamber until the Rebels have searched the ship. We can tell them that we are delivering the bodies to a science lab near Detonia VI. I can apply makeup on some of them to change their appearances from what the rebels are looking for."

Langstrom folded her arms and sighed.

"It would work but the passengers would have to agree to do it."

"They would have little choice. It's either that or hide in the inner workings of the ship, and that's not going to work for long," Langstrom replied. "It might have stumped those idiots back there, but they were supposed to search those areas, too. I was surprised they did not look there in the first place."

"She's right, Rex," Dex concurred. "We will not be so lucky next time around."

"Alright then. Let's go present this idea to our passengers and see what they say," Rex agreed. He turned to his console and programmed the auto pilot and set the ship's alarm system so that it would warn him when they neared Appolis IV. He then accompanied Dex and Langstrom to the main cabin to discuss the new plan with the passengers. When all were seated, Rex cleared his throat to gain their attention.

"Excuse us, but we need to talk about something concerning this trip."

Markel nodded. "Speak on."

"Are the two Senators sleeping?"

"They are resting," Odan confirmed. "Do they need to be awakened?"

"I would prefer we talk to everyone."

Odan left the cabin and returned with the twins minutes later. Both Cassandra and Seth rubbed their eyes and yawned as if they were still in a sleep mode. They sat and looked at Captain Rex.

"I thank the gods that we have made it this far. However, luck was on our side. When we reach Appolis IV, the Rebels will do a thorough search of our ship. The places where I hid you on Romes IV will be searched. Therefore, Doc Langstrom has come up with a way to fool the Rebels. I will let her explain it."

Langstrom rose and flipped her red hair back to her shoulders. "What I can do is put you in cryostats, which is almost a dead state while administering to you a sedative that slows down your vitals, followed by a medication that will slow down your heart rate. Then I put you on ice. Your body will go into hypothermia, a state which the body can tolerate for a short while. After the ship is searched, we can slowly bring you out of the coma and back to your original selves. Of course, it will require that I monitor you constantly."

Markel looked to Odan, Justin, and Gorn. Odan nodded slightly at the thought of it. Markel was shaking his head, no. Then Seth spoke up.

"The question is do we trust you all to safeguard us while we are out of it, and do we trust you to bring us back? I say we do it. We have trusted you this far, and besides that, we have no choice. You are the Captain, and having dealt with them many times before, you know what they will do."

Cassandra nodded, "I agree. I never played dead before. Should prove interesting."

Markel nodded in agreement. "If the two of you agree, I will go along with it. I don't see any other way to avoid the search."

"How long do you need to get them ready, Doc?" Rex asked.

"At least twenty-four hours."

"You should start now then," Rex replied.

"Take the two Senators first," Markel suggested.

"All of you come with me to the medical area, and we will get started," Langstrom directed with a smile.

"Very well, let us get going then," Odan stated.

The two Senators, Odan, Markel, Justin and Gorn followed Doc Langstrom to the medical area of the ship, which was one level down and almost in the center of the vessel. Getting to the medical wing was like finding one's way through a corn maze on earth. After stepping through many hatches along the way, they finally arrived at their destination.

"Doc, are you absolutely certain you can bring us out of this comatose state once the ship has been searched?" Odan asked, still not convinced that this was the best solution to the problem.

"I've done this several times before," she replied while scanning Cassandra.

"Our mission is very important to the future of many nations, and if anything happened to us..."

"You don't need to sell me on your mission. I'm already on your side. I know you all are Clave men, and the two here, the young man and lady are Senators of the old Universal Order. You're planning to rebuild, right?" The doctor interrupted reassuring him that she would take care of them.

Markel nodded. "Captain Rex told you?"

"As I said before, he didn't need to tell me. I can look at you and tell you are Clave men. The two here are young. I figured they are apprentices or something. I didn't figure them to be Senators. But you should not worry about us bringing you back out of the comatose state. There is the little matter of the monetary payment that is still due us after we deliver you to your destination; that should ease your mind. If that doesn't comfort you, then I don't know what will."

Seth chuckled. "Point made."

"Believe me, no harm will come to you. It's not just the money either. Everyone on this ship hates the Rebels. They've made earning a living so much harder for common folk. It's to the point where people are becoming desperate, doing desperate things, such as stealing, killing and pirating, all for money and favor of the Emperor Zymon.

Doc Langstrom scanned each passenger to get a baseline of the normal vital readings. Then she administered the sedative and helped them into the status units built into one of the wall panels. As they drifted off to sleep, she began the alterations on their faces. This was mainly to deceive anyone who looked through the glass. After that, she administered the medicine which would slow the heart rate, and at the same time, she began the deep chill. Slowly, but surely, their heart rates decreased, as their bodies began to drop into hypothermia. She worked well into the wee morning hours, monitoring their drop into cryosleep mode. Just as she had done to several other people before. She stopped the deep freeze at a level that she knew to be the jagged edge of death.

"Doc to Rex."

"Rex here, Doc. How's it going with them?'

"They seemed a bit edgy going through with this, but I have reassured them that everything will be fine."

"Good. So they are in…"

"They are in cryostats as we speak."

"Good, now, this is an order from your Captain. Get some sleep, why don't you. It's late."

"No, no. I have to watch them," Langstrom replied with a sigh. "Their vitals might drop or something, and if I'm not here to make adjustments, they might die."

"I don't envy you, Doc." Rex stated. "I'm out."

Chapter Four

The Wrath of Zymon Keltor

Regil Centuri: Caprica

On the other side of the Andromeda Galaxy, on a planet known as Regil Centuri, Zymon Keltor sat before a communications console with bluish images floating in the midst of the holographic light. The images of the faces of his men moved as they reported their findings.

"We found evidence of two of Zeger's offspring on a remote planet known as Earth in the Milky Way Galaxy. However, knowledge of our search for them was leaked to the Clave and they have four Clave Warriors protecting them now. It will be difficult to make a hit on them now.

"I don't care how difficult it is! If they come back through the gates, they will gain the aide of the remaining Clave Warriors and the remaining Senate Leaders who still believe in the old ways. If they make it through the gates, it will be more difficult to catch them. Understood? We will make an attempt, but as I said before, they do have assistance now."

"Don't make me repeat myself! Get them before they come through any of the gates! Zymon out!"

Zymon rose to his feet in his throne room chambers and walked to the lookout view port. He placed his hands behind his back as he admired the lights of the city Caprica. In the night on Caprica, the red moon shone brightly, giving off an orange hue in the darkness. Zymon's long white hair hung down his back in one long braid bound by a leather tie. His robe made of the finest cloth kept him warm, but, as he stood there, he felt a slight chill.

He thought that he had killed all of Zeger's children, and he was certain that the Clave had been put to rest, but this news that he heard from the lady crushed his joy. He was no longer certain that he would continue to rule the nations of the universe. Despite the efforts of the nations that opposed his leadership, he had managed to force his way into power. However, now, a legitimate threat was possibly coming his way. If the Clave Warriors and the Senators succeeded in regaining any foothold against them, they could become a formidable force and overthrow his régime. It was enough to make him slightly paranoid and overly anxious.

Not long after the first communiqué, another communication came through from the same person. "Sire."

"Speak."

"I am afraid that the Senators and the Clave Warriors that were on Earth have made it through the gate to Romes IV. We are searching for them now but have not located them.'

"They will be looking for transport. Search departing vessels!"

"Aye, Sire."

Zymon's fist hit the table beside him and all the vessels on the table came crashing down, shattering into pieces. As servants rushed to clean up the mess, Zymon stormed into an adjoining room where a man dressed in a uniform rose and saluted him.

"Sire."

"I want all Rebel outposts and ships to search for the offspring of Zeger and the four Clave Warriors they are traveling with. They should not be hard to find. It is possible they have acquired transport from Romes IV. Have Rebel patrols search all ships from Romes IV thoroughly."

"I will send the message over a secure frequency and encrypt it, Sire."

"Good. As soon as they are found, detain them. I want them alive and brought here to Caprica."

"Understood."

Zymon retreated to his chamber where he ordered six of his concubines to entertain him for the night.

/////

Appolis IV: Starbase Omega One

Meanwhile, the lone ship from Romes IV dropped out of hyperspace and approached Appolis IV's gravitational well. However, before they could get closer, they were hailed on the communications. Rex perked up when he heard the coms.

"Approaching vessel, this is Appolis IV Omega One Command. State your departure point and business in Appolis IV."

"This is *Raptor's Claw* One, departed from Romes IV. Our business is trading and refueling. Our estimated time of stay is 24 hours more or less, depending on the line to refuel, over."

"Do you mind a boarding and search of your vessel? It is ordered by the Emperor himself. We must search all vessels. They are looking for someone."

"Not at all. I just have to be present during the search."

"Proceed to docking bay 44A. There are searches going on at the moment, and our patrols are currently booked. I can get with you in the morning around 8 a.m. Is that doable?"

"Seems fine. I will get my business done and refuel and we will wait for the search tomorrow then."

"Sounds like a plan."

Rex flicked off the communications and sighed. Then he turned on the interior coms.

Rex to Doc."

"Doc here."

"The search will be tomorrow morning, Doc. Are we good?"

He was asking without really saying what he was referring to. He hoped she understood. But Doc was swift, and he knew she would catch what he meant.

"We're good," was all she replied.

"Rex out."

"Doc out."

Deep within the Andromeda galaxy the *Raptor's Claw*, a medium sized freighter and cargo ship docked with Omega One, the most popular starbase in the galaxy. Following the directions of the command center of the starbase, Captain Rex docked at docking port 44A. He shut down the engines and flicked off all switches. Then he checked in with his crew.

"Rex to Crew."

"Here, Cappy,' Dex replied.

"I got my ears on, Captain." Raymond chimed in.

"Doc here," Langstrom added.

"This will be a short overnight stay, folks. I have to go off ship to make some contacts, but I would recommend that all of you stay aboard the ship. By the way, the Rebs should be coming through to search the ship in the morning. I want my crew to look lively and cooperate with them. They are pretty swamped with checking other ships at the moment."

"I was looking forward to some R&R, Captain. If only for a few hours."

I would prefer that you remain aboard the ship. I don't want any of you to get involved in some tavern brawl"

"Meaning you don't trust us to stay out of trouble," Dex stated.

"That's not the only reason. The Rebels have Readers all over the stations now, mind readers that can read you like a good book. They can sniff out information. What I don't want is any of you to be read by the mind readers on the station."

"What about you? They can read you just as well."

"I'm Angolian, I can block a mind reader." Rex stated "I'll take the cargo we have to its destination and complete that deal. I'll bring back the money and split it with you as promised. We'll refuel tonight, get some rest, get the search out of the way in the morning, and continue on to our destination."

"What about…-

"We won't mention that while we are docked here." Rex said shaking his head to Dex. "Out of sight, out of mind.'

"All right, Capp," Raymond stated. "Can I ask you to get me something?"

"Depends on what it is," Rex replied

Raymond moved over to Rex and stood on his tippy toes to whisper in his captain's ear. Rex grinned and shrugged, "No problem, I'll get it." He looked to the ladies. "Anything you two want."

"Sassaphire Rum," Dex stated."

"Make that a double."

"You two are going to die of an overdose of that stuff," Rex teased.

"We'd get it ourselves, but YOU won't let us go from the ship, Master Cappy dude."

"Very well, then I'll get it for you with no complaints."

He spoke as he walked through the corridors of his ship, his mind on his passengers and the reason he was making this risky voyage. It was a routine job, one that he had been running for years, since before Zymon came into power over the realms. Zymon's patrols made it more difficult to run this route, but everything seemed to run smoothly when he made this particular run. He was beginning to think humans were Rymelions. Ever since he started making this run, not once did he have any Rebel encounters. No Rebel patrols boarded his ship with this Rymelion's cargo aboard. Was it luck? Or was it coincidence?

Rex put on a long, sleek, black, leather duster that matched his present outfit. He moved through the ship to his chambers and pulled several knives off his wall, slipping them on and making sure they were easily accessible. He also selected one laser pistol and put it in his hip holster. He placed another pistol in his back waist, and yet another in a holster on his left leg.

When it came to being prepared, Rex was always ready for a fight. He never underestimated anything. The worst case scenario was always on his mind. At the moment, he was concerned that the Rebels would see through their trick and find the passengers on this ship. He knew if they got caught, they would be prisoners of the Rebels, but he also knew that they would be even more special enemies of the Emperor because they were smuggling Senators on their ship across Rebel space. So far they had managed to trick them, but he knew they would not be able to trick them for much longer. Only a number of ships had left Romes IV since the Clavemen arrived there. They would soon pin point that it was their ship that had taken them. So far, they had not figured it out yet, which was good for them. The less they knew, the better off they were, and the more time they had to reach Shangri-La.

Suited up and armed to the teeth with his knives and his laser pistols, he moved through the ship to the airlocks, where he passed through and met security guards who aimed their weapons at him.

"Name and ID!" the security guard bellowed.

"Captain Rex Faraday, Captain of the *Raptor's Claw*. This is my ship right here, and I'm going on the base to take care of some business."

"What type of business?" "A bit of trading." Rex answered while handing him his permit and ID.

"Be on your way."

Captain Rex nodded to them and moved down the corridor to the elevator, slipped inside and continued downwards into the thick of *Omega One's* Common area. He stepped out of the lift into a smorgasbord of the galaxy's species and creatures. Instead of feeling uncomfortable or out of place, he blended in and felt right at home, as he notice the diversity of faces that passed. And he was careful to avoid some faces he didn't wish to encounter. In all the years he had been Captain of the *Raptor's Claw*, he had acquired some enemies. Being on the number one most popular places in the galaxy made his chances of encountering an enemy really high. So he was trying to remain quite invisible.

Chapter Five

Connections

Half way around Regil Centuri, on the dark side of the planet, in the mountain side castle known as Dezmun, Lady Shatra and her followers dwelled in luxury. Having once been a Clave Warrior and having sat on the Clave's inner council, she knew all there was to know about the Clave. She knew that there was one Clave Warrior who knew where Zeger's children were.

That was Master Odan Amir.

As she sat on the terrace of her chambers in the warmth of the night on Regil Cenguri, she closed her eyes and thought of the past. She thought of Odan Amir and how she had once known him well. Her mind reflected to a time long ago when they were young and just coming up in the Clave as apprentices. They had been paired off in a duel that would determine where they would be placed in the Universal Order. The one left with their weapon was the winner. Shatra remembered she had been overly confident because she knew of Odan's attraction to her.

"You like what you see?" Shatra had asked.

"I don't only look with my eyes," Odan replied.

"You had better look deep."

Their swords had clanked together before them and in a blurry haze of whipping blades, they had engaged in combat. The other up and comings had surrounded them cheering while the council members also looked on from their seats in the balcony. They had the best view. Odan and Shatra had tried every trick on each other and then Odan modified his approach on her by altering what they had learned and interchanging different combinations to trick her. The change had caught her off guard, and she lost her balance and her sword. Odan flicked it right out of her hand and caught it. Backing away from her, he decided to help her up. He held out his hand to her, but she refused the help and got up on her own.

The Master of the Clave stated the obvious winner of the duel. As a result of that duel, Odan became an apprentice in training to become a Master.

Odan only spoke of his love of Shatra once and said nothing of it ever again. When he had become a Master in arms, a true Claveman, he had spoken to Shatra alone. They had been on an assignment to escort a Senator to an outer rim planet. It had required a journey through different terrain, but it gave them many chances to talk. When they were hiking through the Rain Forest, Odan had spoken to her in the darkness of the night.

Even in the darkness of the night, her beauty radiated like a brilliant star. He would even go as far as to compare her to the brightest in the cosmos.

"You are a very beautiful lady, Shatra. I wish you were not a Clave Warrior."

"What? If your wish had been granted, we never would have met."

"Yes. I know. If only things could be different. I would take your hand in mine." He took her hand and squeezed it. "And I would take you as mine."

"We can't.'

"Believe me, I know we can't. I'm going away after this mission. I probably won't see you in many years. But I wanted you to know how I felt."

"You shouldn't have told me."

'Why not?"

"It will hurt to know that I can't have what I want."

"It's all for the best. We gave our lives to serve the greater good of all nations…everywhere."

"It's so easy to say that and yet so hard to walk that path, is it not?"

"I will walk that path, my love. I know you to be strong and can overcome anything. Just like you will forget about me, after a time. My hope is that you stay the course and not stray to the other sides of this battle."

"Why are you worried about that?"

"I've seen the way Keltor looks at you. It would be best if you stay clear of him. He will ruin your life, Shatra."

"Listen, as I do remember, I am calling the shots with my life. I think I know what is right and what is wrong for me."

"Very well, I have warned you about him. He's an ambitious man and only seeks power and fame and fortune. He *cares* nothing of the people and what they want or need."

"And you do?"

"I would like to say that I do care for the people of the state of the universe, Yes, Yes, I do care. I'm just suggesting you be careful who you make friends with."

"So noted, what shall I call you, Master Odan?"

"I'm not a master yet. The way you say that makes me wonder if you are thinking I don't deserve to be a master."

"No, you deserve it. The duel was fair," Shatra admitted.

Suddenly the forest became a target of a cloudburst, as raindrops pelted them. As they turned to head back to their headquarters, Odan offered a word of confidence he had in his friend's future in the Clave.

"You will become a Master soon enough. I am being sent through the gates to Romes IV. I will be the Clave Warrior there and report to the Council."

Nodding, Shatra smiled at Odan." You finally get your assignment and a gate key."

"Yes. But it is a busy one. The Andromeda Galaxy is riddled with many disturbances to unravel. I will be very busy there. I am thinking that they are on the verge of war."

"You will do well."

"I am wondering if it's too late," Odan replied. "Zymon's home worlds and lands are there, as well as Senate Leader Zeger's wife. There is unrest and confusion."

"Perhaps you can bring understanding and patience."

"Hopefully."

"At any rate, good luck."

"I do thank you for that. I will need luck and prayers."

They walked hand in hand in the darkness back to their camp for the night, not noticing that they were hand in hand.....

Before they made it back to the campsite, Odan stopped, pulled her close to him, and kissed her. Shatra, returned the display of affection with her own kiss. When they parted, they looked into each other's eyes, wishing that they were miles away from where they were, wishing they were someone else and not what they had become.

It was Odan who broke the silence as his mind flashed back to his own parents who were Clave Warriors who had been caught up in love and had left him on someone's door step to avoid the repercussions of their love. They had hid him from the council and from the world just to live the rest of their lives without shame. Their big secret never came to the light of day until they were old and grey. By that time it didn't matter to them what came out of the closet.

"By the stars, I... I won't ever forget that, Shatra, but, I can't...I... if only things could be."

Shatra put her finger over his lips then. "They aren't different, Odan. Things are as they are, and we must live out our lives....alone... unattached to...to anything or anyone. It would hinder us from giving 100 percent to the Clave."

When she opened her eyes from her memories of Odan and the Clave, a tear slid down her face. She wiped it away and stood up. Wrapping in her shawl, she moved to a communication's panel. "Shatra to Zymon!"

After a few seconds, Zymon's face filled the blue and white lights on the viewport. "What is it?"

"'He is back. I can feel him."

"Who is back?"

"Odan Amir is one of the Masters of the Clave. "

"I know he is a Master of the Clave, but how do you know he is back?"

"Trust me, I know. He will be going to Shangri-La, if he is not already there."

"He got past my men on Earth and on Romes IV. I don't believe he's made it to Shangri-La just yet."

"Your men are useless, pathetic idiots! Once he gets to Shangri-La, he will have power to recall the entire Clave! Then you can start biting your nails and having ulcers, if you haven't already! Once he has organized them, they will be unstoppable! They will have followers of Zeger behind them, which will shift the nations that are still resisting your leadership to them. They will start to outnumber our numbers. We will no longer have the majority against them."

"How do we stop them?" Zymon asked her.

"We should hunt down their ship. I don't know the rest of them. But I do feel Odan's presence. This should aide me in the search. You should up your efforts to search ships for him."

"I've done that already."

"You should have sent me to find them. I think like a Clave Warrior. I would be able to find them for you a lot sooner than those lame brains! I have a connection to Odan Amir that many don't know of. He and I were once close, close enough that I can use this connection to our advantage."

"You know what? Why not? Go and find them for me. If you fail me, I will treat you as I do my men. I will not spare my sword because you are a lady and a friend, Shatra. This is serious business. If these people succeed in getting to their destination, the blame will be on your head, not my men. I hope we understand one another."

Shatra smiled. "As you wish."

"From what I know, they must have gained transport on Romes IV."

"I'll start there. Shatra out."

/////

Appolis IV

Back on Starbase Omega One, on Community Deck 33, in a popular tavern known as Cymon's Cove, Captain Rex sat with old friends talking business. After all it was part of the reason he had come to Appolis IV.

In the dimly lit and smoke filled bar, Rex conversed with a Rymelion, which was a being that could transform from a human into a lizard-faced being. At the moment the Rymelion was looking more humanoid for Rex's sake. Usually when Rymelions were angry, they resorted to what was more natural for them, which was their lizard looking forms.

I have the shipments in my freighter. It's docked here on the station. Have your men to come to hanger 44A and retrieve it."

"You have all the crates?"

"All 56." Rex replied. "And you had better be glad for that. We were boarded on Romes IV. But the Rebel's didn't even look into those crates. I'd say we were lucky"

"Luck seems to follow you around, Captain. If it had been any other way, I would seek doing business with other pilots who have far better ships."

Grinning and showing his teeth, he continued, "They might have a better ship, but they don't have the golden touch. I've never failed you or any of my customers."

"Which is why we continue to use your services. I have another run for you to make."

Rex held his hands up. "I'm already hired out."

"You have a run already? To where?"

"I can't disclose that information. You know that. Where does it have to go?

"Teranosis."

"I suppose that's on the way to where we are headed."

"If you drop it for me, I will pay you in advance. I trust you to get it there."

Rex hesitated a moment, then reached out and took the small box that was in his friends hand.

"You know the rules. Don't open it, just deliver."

"Right. Who do I give it to?"

"A Rymelion female named Cameliea. Now. No more of your nosy questions. Deliver and then be on your way to complete your other run."

"Right. I'll do it. No more questions."

Here's five thousand terrons for delivery. I guess I'll be seeing you another time.'

Captain Rex slipped the terrons into his jacket pocket and put his hand there. He got up, finished his drink in one gulp, and walked off, not looking back. He moved through the crowd in the tavern and out through the exit. He then did a little shopping and returned to the ship to retire and check up on his crew. First he went to Dex's chambers. He buzzed her door by placing his hand on the red crystal light beside it which blinked "occupied".

'Come in, Rex.'

The door slid open and revealed Dex in her onesuit with her hands on her hips. He passed a bottle of what she ordered. Smiling, she took it, opened it, and offered him a sip. Rex shook his head. He didn't like that drink, and besides, he had just had a whole bottle of his favorite spirit.

"I've had my fill already. Rex declined, waving his hand as if to shield himself from the offer. "No thanks! I'm good."

"I've run diagnostic checks on the engines. I dare to say that we won't have another problem like we had coming here again."

Nodding, Rex brushed his head back and sighed. "I hope we don't. That situation could have killed us all."

"I get that. That's why I rechecked everything."

"I'm glad you took the initiative to do that, Dex. That means you're thinking ahead of me and that is good. I like that about you. Sometimes I don't have to tell you everything."

Dex smiled. "I guess that's a compliment?'

"That's about all you'll get from me.'

Dex laughed as did Rex.

"I should have known."

"You should know by now, I don't pat you on the back when you do something good, Dex. I say something when it happens, and then I leave it where it is. I don't go out of my way to give anyone extra credit for anything. If you're waiting for that, I should tell you one thing…I'm not your frigging mother! Got me?'

"Yeah, I got ya. Well, sometimes people like to hear that they've done something well, Rex. And I think we've been around one another long enough to know when it is expected."

"Girly, you had better get used to me. You'll be waiting a long time to hear something from me.'

"Why can't you just say, 'Good job, Dex.'"

"I've said that at the time it happened. One time is enough, isn't it?"

"I suppose it is."

"Look, I don't think I need to tell you that. You should know when you've done a good job. If you don't know that, then I'm sorry."

"I just like to hear it from you."

'We're talking in circles here, Dex. Now, I've explained myself and you've told me what you want from me. I'll think about it and try to remember it, but I won't make any promises. Okay?"

"That sounds good to me."

"Now I've got to go check on Raymond and the Doc."

"Thanks, Cappy."

"No, problem," Rex stated as he walked out of the door of her quarters.

After leaving Dex, he made his way inside the medical area. The poignant smell of antiseptics hit his nostrils immediately. Langstrom kept clean quarters and a pristine work area. Her job demanded it from her, and it became part of her everyday life.

She was sitting at the computer, coffee cup in hand, monitoring the vitals of their passengers.

'How goes it, Doc?' Rex asked.

"All goes well, Captain. They are holding up well.'

'Good. I like to hear that. It's good news. I bought your drink while I was out.'

At those words, Langtrom rose and walked towards him. She held out her hand to take the bottle. When she offered him a drink, he declined the offer.

'I had too much of my own on the station already.' Rex explained.

"Ah. Another time. We can have a toast after the completion of our mission, maybe.' Doc stated.

"Rain check. That's a deal."

"I have to check on Raymond. We'll be unloading our cargo tonight. It's mandatory that you be there. We're the only somethings on the ship right now so we don't want them thinking we're holding out on them, do we?"

"I'll be there."

Raymond sat in the security office cleaning the guns, swords, and all the other artillery in the confines of the armory. He might be a bit short, but he knew the ins and outs of lasers, swords, knives, bows and arrows, and the like. When he heard the footsteps of his Captain, he quickly took up a sword and got on top of the desk to greet his boss properly.

The door slipped ajar, and Rex entered. Raymond flew from the desk to attack his boss.   Rex took his sword from its holster and their blades clanked together.

"RAY!" Rex cried out, "Hold on a blazing minute!"

'What's this, an Algonian caught off his guard?"

Rex laughed. "You got me this time, you little –

"Did I hear the word little?"

"Oh! Well, I … ah—?"

"Did you get it?"

Rex handed him the item he had purchased for him on the station, and the dwarf put his sword away. He was all smiles. "Thanks Boss!"

"We have a shipment to unload. Meet me in the cargo hold in one hour."

"I'll be there, Cap'n."

Chapter Six

Detours, Old Relationships, Rebel Trickery

General Zolotan, head of the Rebel Forces in the Andromeda Galaxy, resided on Romes IV. He learned about the party of Clave Warriors and Senators only after the five ships had departed from Romes IV. As he walked briskly down the corridor of the command towers to the lift, he wondered if he had known about this situation sooner, would he have caught them. Entering the command center, he quickly prepared information on the five ships that had departed Romes IV and their destinations. At least they had the destination each captain had provided the tower command before permission was granted for landing. Usually, most Captains provided truthful information about their destination points. However, if they were smuggling people, they might lie about that. Zolotan surmised that they could be lying. Then again each ship had locked in courses heading toward their destination points. So they did not lie. Yet one thing was clear. One of those ships had the party they were looking for aboard.

Zolotan raced into the conference room and tapped a button on the console on the table before him.

"Now hear this Alpha, Delta, Beta, Omega and Gamma Patrols! Report to the conference room of the command center on the double! General Zolotan out!" Zolotan thought over his words as the members of each patrol gradually filtered into the conference room and filled up the seats. When those seats were full, they took up positions around the table. Zolotan checked and cleared his wrist piece.

"A few days ago, a group of Clave Warriors and two Senators came through here and acquired transport from one of the many freighter pilots who hang out in the taverns looking for such business for the highest price. The Clave pays in gold, and they would pay much for such a service. They were probably paid not only for the transport, but also paid to keep their transaction hidden from our Rebel forces. Thus, when we boarded their ship and searched for them initially, we didn't find them because they hid from us!"

Zolotan looked around the table and sighed. "And we did a half-ass job at our search because they probably got away by hiding behind the bulkheads. That is the only place they could have been! When you were all trained, did we not tell you to look behind the empty spaces?"

"Yes, Sir!" They all yelled in unison.

"Now since you did a half-ass job, you will all go out and complete the job you were supposed to finish in the first place. Each patrol will be assigned a ship to hunt down and re-search it. If they have delivered their party already, you must find them, capture them, and bring them back here! Emperor Zymon wants them alive."

Zolotan handed out the assignments and rose to his feet. "Good luck and don't come back here empty-handed. Send in to me twenty-four hourly reports, encrypted to this command center. Get what you need and launch when ready."

General Zolotan walked to the command center, not looking back.

/////

Starbase Omega One: Raptor's Claw Cargo Bay

Smoke rose from the cigar in Maximillion Rex's mouth as he puffed at it and looked at the time piece on his wrist. It was not like he was in a rush. The reason he was pacing and taking long drags from his cigar was that his contact was late. Tardiness in this business was never a good sign. It either meant something bad was happening on his part, or something was wrong on their part. In any event, something had gone wrong. At least, that is what Rex usually thought when people or aliens were late, in particular, aliens, because they usually got into more trouble than people.

Raymond looked at Rex in that way he usually did when Rex got nervous. "It doesn't help you wearing a hole into the floor. They'll be here. Give them a few minutes."

Rex stopped pacing and looked at Raymond. "How can you be calm?"'

"Because we've been dealing with these guys for nearly ten years and that is why we trust him to be here soon," Raymond replied.

Finally a noise of footsteps sounded of men entering the bay. Rex sighed, and Dex rose from her position on the floor, slipped on the gloves, and put her hands on her hips. "It's about time!'

The Rymelions, nearly ten of them, entered the docking bay and began to check the crates as Captain Rex and the Rymelion dressed in fine garments talked.

"Do excuse my tardiness, Captain, I had something come up that I could not avoid looking into."

"Not a problem. It was only a few moments," Rex stated, as he watched the cargo being hauled off.

"Here are the terrons for the 56 crates. Now that I see them all, I believe our business is done for the time being."

"One more thing," Rex started. "Tell me one more time the name of the Rymelion female you want me to give that parcel to and where can I find her.

"Her name is Camelia. She is very beautiful. She works at a bar called the Starlight Lounge. You'll find her working there. Remember, no questions, and don't open the box. It is only for her and her alone.

When you give it to her, be sure to leave her company. I want you nowhere near her after you give it to her

Rex wondered then what it was. However, he was a professional and his job insisted he not involve himself in his work too deeply, meaning he could never know too much or too little. Now his current job with the Clave Warriors required him knowing a lot more than a little because he had to stay clear of the Rebs.

This job with the Rymelion required he know very little because he smelled something sinister in the works. The whole idea of his getting clear of the lady after he delivered it usually meant that it was either a bomb or something equally as deadly. It made him think twice on delivering it at all, but he had agreed and had set his hands to it and had even taken the money. He was stuck with it.

As he stood there smoking his cigar, talking to the Rymelion, he thought on the possibility that he might never see him again. The job was dangerous. At least he had suspected it was. It could be that the box contained nothing dangerous as he suspected and was just a harmless gift that the rough and gruff Rymelion didn't want anyone else to see. Rex inwardly chuckled at that. His mind had gone off on its own little tangent and invented some terrible story. Boy, did he need to sleep.

Who was he kidding? Sleep was something people who didn't have their own ships enjoyed. He was lucky to get in about three to four hours of sleep and be happy with that. No, there was too much to do on and off his ship to worry about getting ample rest. Once in a while, every blue moon would come around and grace him with eight hours of rest. This of course, would throw him way off track. Everything would be out of synchronization because his body would be so weak from having so much time for resting. Even when he had time to sleep, he usually stayed awake doing something, and if there was nothing to do, he'd just find something to do to occupy his brain until it became sleepy, which left him only three or four hours of sleep time. Dex had called him an insomniac, and Langstrom had prescribed pills for him to take to make him sleep better.

The initial bottle was still in his room somewhere. He had no idea where. Somewhere beneath the clutter.

Everything was going like clockwork. Soon the last crate was lifted from the *Raptor's Claw*'s cargo hold, and the crew of the *Raptor's Claw* said good bye to the Rymelions. The Rymelion who was talking to Captain Rex bowed his head and lifted up his head to show his reddish eyes. As Rex looked at his face, one of those eyes closed and reopened. Then the Rymelion gave Rex a full, toothed smile.

"I have liked doing business with you, Captain Rex. For a man in this business, you have a certain integrity that is quite non-existent in other business captains. I wish to continue doing business with you. However, to do this, you will need to know me a bit better than you do."

"I would definitely like that. I would find that a win-win situation. What do you have in mind so far?"

"We've been getting along well without your knowing my name, but now I think it is time that you have earned my trust. My name is Zydak."

Rex's face cracked into a slight smile. He was caught by surprise with this. He was not expecting this Rymelion to give him such an honor as to know his name which was, usually, something intriguing. Not many humans gained the respect of the Rymelions because the Rymelions thought they were far superior in many ways. Usually, Rymelions ignored humans unless they had to deal with them. It wasn't often their paths crossed. Zydak and Rex were an exception. Zydak bowed his head, keeping his eyes on Rex the entire moment. As he rose from the bow, he spoke, saying, "Be well, Captain Rex."

Rex nodded, took a puff of his cigar, smoke circling around. As he exhaled, the horrible smelling thing burned. "You be well, too."

Rex, Raymond and Dex did the last job for the night, which was to connect the refueling tubes so that the trilithium plasma would be loaded into the plasma holding tanks aboard the *Raptor's Claw*.

"Ray, go into the cockpit and contact the command center and get us in line for refueling."

Ray nodded. "Aye, Captain."

"Dex, make sure there are no leaks anywhere."

"Already on it, Captain."

Through his ear piece, Rex heard Ramond's voice come through.

"We're next, Captain."

"Good. After this we can get some well needed rest."

"I'm for that." Dex replied, butting in.

"I think we all could use a little shut eye." Rex stated. "In fact, I strongly recommend we do that. This might be the only time we have for it."

Raymond grunted. "Sleep is for sissies. I'm a lean, mean, fighting machine, and I don't need any doggone sleep!"

Rex chuckled. "Who wound you up like a chicken?"

"It's that stuff you bought him on the station," Dex replied, half laughing. "He's a walking time bomb."

Rex smiled at her description of Raymond. "He is small enough to be a time bomb, isn't he?'

"Enough of the short jokes! It's not what he brought back. I have yet to indulge in that treat. Dwarfs of Indegos II need very little sleep remember.

"I insist that you at least close your eyes and see what happens if it is only for a short while."

"Very well, Raymond sighed. "I will try."

After what seemed a short period of time, the refueling was completed. Nothing left but to clean up the docking bay, which Dex appeared to be doing when Rex caught a glimpse of her, peeling out of her protective suit as she climbed the ramp leading into the ship. She entered the ship and went back to work, checking on the ship's systems and making sure everything was running at specified levels. This process took about two hours to complete, but it was worth it to prevent being caught by the rebels. As she worked, she thought of what might happen to them if they got caught smuggling their cargo. Then, she recalled what Rex had told her. His voice had been so confident. "Out of sight, out of mind." She shouldn't be thinking about them. She tried to think about something else, like finishing her work here and getting some rest time, if not all of it, some would do.

Langstrom poured her tenth cup of energy supplement, tipped it the container to her mouth and gulped it down. She sighed and wiped her mouth with the sleeve of her light blue jacket which had all sorts of things hanging out of the pockets. Most were just medical gadgets she used often. She had learned to make good use of her med jacket in this manner, which was to have her instruments handy when needed. Having it any other way could mean the life or death of someone. She prepared herself to handle any situation that might arise. Walking to the far wall where the status units were located, she checked readings. Everything registered stable, and her six patients rested as she expected.

With a nod, she double checked all the read outs. She would settle for nothing less than her best. Of course, she needed rest, but she knew she could not bat an eye for fear of not being alert if something should go wrong. She knew Rex would protest, but she had to do her job. And in this case, sleep came last on her priority list. She wondered when he would confront her about it. She knew she had to stand her ground, but perhaps she could meet him half way and try and get some Z's on one of the operating tables. They were not the most comfortable, but they would serve the purpose while keeping her close enough to the cyro status units. She filed that idea away as a last compromise. Perhaps she would never have to use it.

Rex moved through the corridors to check on Langstrom and see how she was holding up. To go without rest for hours on end was not good for the ship's physician. He needed Doc to be wide-eyed and perky. As he placed his hand on the crystal panel beside the door, his palm print gave him access to the medical wing.

"Doc? You still awake in here?" Rex called out.

Langstrom heard the Captain's voice and moved from around the corner where the cyro-status units were located. "Over here.'

Rex walked to where she stood and looked into her eyes. He frowned slightly. She looked tired and worn out. He hated to pull rank on her, but this was going way beyond the call of duty. "Doc, you've been on this duty since the day before yesterday. I can't ask you to go another night without some sleep."

"You know what I'm going to say to that. It is my job to watch over the units."

"Okay, so sleep in here then. Just get some sleep somehow. It is starting to show, and if the Rebels come aboard and see you without sleep, they might get suspicious about what is keeping you up." Rex folded his arms and spoke with authority. "I won't take 'no' for an answer. Find a comfy spot in here and shut those pretty eyes of yours for a few hours at the least tonight. Do I have to make that an order?'

"It just so happens I was going to suggest the same thing," Langstrom teased. "You don't have to pull rank on me though."

"I just don't want you to wear yourself out. Plus, we don't know what's in store for us on this trip. The skills of a doctor will be needed wherever we go. I'm no doctor, and I know Dex and Ray aren't either. Call it what you will. I'm protective of you," Rex chuckled. "Seriously, it concerns me if you don't take the time to rest. It means that your performance might not be up to par. Not that it will be that, but it's likely to be the case. To avoid all that, I'm willing to compromise and meet you half way. I know you are a stickler for doing what's right, but so am I. It is wrong for me to allow you to go without sleep. So I will allow you to sleep on the job. This is not something that I would ever do, mind you. It's just that the situation demands it. We don't have the man power, so all of us have a lot on our shoulders.

"Captain, you are rambling,' Langstrom blurted out. "I get it. Not to worry, I won't ever think you would allow the crew to sleep on the job. This is an exception to that rule. Now shoo, so I can get the most of my rest time."

"Sometimes, Doc, I think of you as a mind reader."

"Why? Is it because I complete your sentences?"

Rex smiled. "Yeah."

"Not to worry, Captain. I'm no Reader. I've been able to complete people's sentences since I was a kid."

"Now that is extraordinary," Rex stated. "With perfect strangers or people you know for a while?"

Langstrom smiles. "People I know for a while, of course. Strangers are hard because I can't tell what they are going to say; the possibilities are endless. But with you, for instance, I've know you to say certain things at certain times, and after certain events in time, you say them. It is something you learn to do."

"You must do it just to 'Wow' someone, right"

"Maybe to get their attention or to refocus their attention on me. But I do it for medical reasons. I have something important to say, I could utilize that tactic to get people's attention by blurting out what they are saying taking over the conversation. It is seen as rude and aggressive, but it works in crowds."

"When I go to bidding auctions for ships, remind me to take you."

"Now get moving, I know the Captain has more to do than talk to the sleepless lady in medical."

As she said her last words to him, she gently pushed on his chest.

Rex chuckled as he exited medical and headed off to his quarters.

As soon as Maximillion Rex's head hit his pillows, he was already snoring peacefully. Prior to crashing on the unmade bed in his quarters, he put away all his weapons, took off his smelly boots, and hung his leather duster on a rack on the wall. He didn't bother to change clothes before diving into the unmade bed. He could instantly smell the female Senator's perfume, where she had rested the night before.

But even that was far from his mind. His last words before he shut his eyes were to the computer console on the wall with his weapons.

"Voice recognition, Captain Rex."

"Voice recognized as Captain Maximillion Rex Faraday. How may I help you, Captain Rex?"

"Set alarm clock for three hours from now."

"Acknowledged. Alarm will sound in T-minus 2.59 minutes and counting. Sleep well, Captain."

He could feel the thumping of his heart, and it truly felt as if it would jump right out of his chest. Someone was tugging at his hand, pulling him onward as they ran. Then he began to notice who was with him. It was the passengers of his current ship run to Shangri-La. Then he began to notice his immediate surroundings. They were no longer on his ship. He wanted to go back for it, but something was urging him onward with the others. What was making him and his crew and the passengers of his ship run so fast?

"We will be safe once we get into the fortress of Shangri-La," Odan stated "We need to keep moving. They are not going to stop, and we must not either."

"Are you sure that we'll be safe? Rex found himself asking, "What about my ship!"

"I'll get you a better ship, Rex. Bigger and better," Markel assured him.

Rex smiled and then there was a great flash of light, an explosion. Something had gone wrong...

Sweating and panting, Rex bolted upright. He immediately checked his body to make sure he was still in one piece. He knew it was a bad dream, but it had felt so real, as if it had been really happening. Some people would call it a vision or a fore-telling moment, but Rex simply didn't believe in all that hogwash. It was just a strange, weird dream that ended badly. Perhaps he had been thinking about the smuggling that he had taken up with the Clave Warriors and the two Senators. It could very well end badly as the dream had, but it was just his mind playing tricks on him. What were the chances of things turning out just like that? About a million to one, not even? He pushed the dream aside and looked at the time piece on his wrist. He still had an hour left to doze. This time he slept well enough to take the edge off. When the alarm sounded, he got up, took a shower and changed his attire. He had about an hour before the Rebels came aboard for their inspection. He prayed they wouldn't bring any Readers aboard his vessel. But he couldn't exactly stop them either.

Still pondering about the dream, he changed into another set of black trousers and a black, long sleeve shirt. He pulled at the fabric to adjust it and sat on the bed to put on his insulation socks and boots. Stomping on the metallic floor with each foot until his feet were happy, Rex left his quarters and hurried to the cockpit.

His mind flashed back to the day Markel approached him in the bar and the mission he hired him to do. *"Why did he choose me to get the group to Shangri-La? Is my ship capable of getting them to their destination? What those passengers need is a battle ship, not some freighter."*

He actually gave this a lot of thought. His ship had weapons, but they could not compete with that of the Rebels arsenal. Just one of their shuttles could tear the *Raptors Claw* to pieces. What made the Clave Warrior so confident that they could make it to Shangri-La? This puzzled him. Markel had said that if he didn't agree to take them, he'd find some other pilot who would, which meant that he thought it was possible, unless Markel knew something that he didn't know about the place. Whatever it was, the Clave Warrior Markel was willing to put down 5 million terrons or more. Rex had trusted him after that, and despite all the difficulty in seeing this through, he still believed they could make it there. Dex had been right, he had bet their lives on it.

Rex ran some diagnostics on the ship's systems and noted that Dex had been busy tweaking the systems all night. He was lucky to have such a dedicated engineer. The only thing about her was that she always wanted his approval. A few years before, they had had a relationship, but it didn't last because it got in the way of being Captain and leading the ship. He also found himself worrying about her when he should have been paying attention to his job. She was a distraction that he didn't need. They had parted on good terms though and agreed to be friends, which was why she was still around. However, she still wanted him to show some affection in a way that he couldn't afford. He thought about confronting her about this, but decided it wouldn't make any difference. It would start an argument, and he wasn't looking for that.

Rex turned on the interior communications. "Rex to Raymond. You awake, bud?"

"Wide eyed and perky, Captain. I'm heading to the air locks to greet the search party. They said they would be arriving at 8 a.m. sharp."

"It's about that time. I'll be right down to join ya."

"Works for me, Capt."

As soon as Rex stood up, the officers began barking to them over the transmission system. "Command communications to *Raptor's Claw*, do you copy?"

"Loud and clear, command. We're here and ready for inspections. Give us five minutes to reach the locks and we'll open up."

"Acknowledged. Search party will stand by."

Rex moved as swiftly as he could in the confined space of the cockpit. He slid down the ladder as he had been doing for decades until his heavy boots landed on the metal floor where the locks were located. He then speed-walked through the corridors and portals until he arrived at the air locks where Ray was waiting for him.

"Sleep well?" Ray asked, looking up at his Captain and tugging at his artillery draped over his chest.

"What's this stuff, Ray?" Rex asked.

"Got to look the part, Cappy. I'm the ship's security, so I must have things on to display a security atmosphere."

"Am I the only one who knows how to be diplomatic?"

"No. You're the only one who *cares* to be with these Rebel scum," Raymond chuckled.

"You may open the hatch now."

"Nah. I want to make them wait some more." He laughed and began depressurizing the lock so that the outside and interior were the same pressure. Ray monitored the gage, and when it beeped, he turned the lock up and tugged at it. The familiar hissing sound ensued, but lasted only a second. Rex stepped out and held out his hand to welcome the one who looked to be in charge.

A man wearing two stripes on his shoulder jacket stepped forward and shook Rex's hand. "Greetings! I am Sargent Miller. We are here to conduct a thorough search of your vessel. I hope you don't mind. We are in search of some people who are wanted by the Emperor himself."

"Really? Sorry for them. What crimes did they commit?"

"I am sorry, but that information is classified."

"I see. Well, proceed with your search. I'm sure you won't find anything out of the ordinary. I'm a freighter, running my routine voyages across the galaxy."

Dex and Langstrom had been right about them searching behind the bulk heads this time around. They did look in all the cubby holes and nooks and crannies of the ship. And this time around they had found nothing, thanks to Langstrom. Rex was about to sigh with relief until he saw the bald-headed Reader enter the hanger. Immediately, he thought of happy thoughts. As the female Reader came toward him, she smiled at him.

"This one is Anglian. I won't be able to read him." She looked at Ray who stood beside Rex. "Dwarfs are difficult, as well. Where's the rest of your crew, Captain Rex?"

"Aboard."

"Come on then. Introduce me."

Rex looked down and then sighed as he nodded and led the way down the corridor, taking her hand as they stepped through the threshold of the air locks and into the ship. As they walked the corridor in silence, Rex could think of nothing to fill the dead air between them. Yet he should think of something to say, he just didn't know what. He hadn't prepared for this.

It was the Reader that ended the silence instead."

"Why are you afraid of me?"

He glanced at her and then laughed as she glanced away coughing to cover it up. "I'm familiar with command stations sweeping ships with search patrols, but not with Readers. Whoever these people are, you must be really after them to have such a search as this. You would think the sweep would be enough."

"One would think that. But we are not dealing with ordinary people, Captain. Are we? "

"I have no idea"

They came to the medical area and Langstrom was at her computer, typing away. She turned and saw the bald headed lady and her eyebrows rose as she glanced at Rex. She immediately knew she was a Reader

Langstrom came towards them and shook the Reader's hand. 'Greetings. I'm Doctor Langstrom. I'm also the science officer."

"I see you run a neat and clean area here, Doctor."

"I do try," Langstrom replied.

"So you patch people up?"

"Haven't had to do that in a while though. Rex gets more use out of me in science."

"Any science projects?'

"Not of late.'

Langstrom could feel the mind intrusion, but Doc successfully blocked the female's digging deeper into her mind. It felt like a dull headache was coming on.

"What's in your status units? I notice that they are active."

Langstrom looked at Rex who quickly spoke up. "We have six corpses that we are taking to a medical facility on Dengrom Star Command."

"I see," said the Reader, looking into one of the ice chambers. "Take me to the other woman on this ship."

"Right this way," Rex stated.

Finding Dex proved to be more difficult, she was usually in her quarters, but for some odd reason she was in the engine room. When the two entered the engine room, Dex pulled herself from under a console and looked up at the bald-headed lady and Rex. She knew too that she was a Reader. Slowly she got up, holding her back side. She pulled off her gloves and shook hands with the lady.

I'm Dexter. People just call me Dex for short. How do you like our ship?"

"It is nice. Now that I have answered your question, you answer mine. Did you pick up any passengers on Romes IV?"

Dex was quick to answer. "We picked up cargo to drop off here on the station. It's a routine run we make," Dex stated. "Now if you don't mind, I have to get this fixed before we blast off the station."

The bald headed lady who had purposefully not given her name to anyone so far watched as Dex got down on her back and slid under the console again. The lady looked down for a second and then back at Rex, who spread his arms out.

'That's it. There's only four of us here."

"Yes. I will inform the sergeant you may go as soon as you are cleared. I do not believe you are hiding anything on your ship."

"Thank you a…what is your name."

"I am not permitted to give you my name. It is for security purposes, so that no one comes to retaliate against us."

"A wise move," Rex stated.

They talked some more as they walked through the ship and soon arrived at the airlocks. Rex held out his hand for the Reader to hold until she could grab something through the threshold of the airlock and enter the hanger bay area of the station.

"Sergeant, the *Raptor's Claw* is clear for departure."

The Sergeant nodded to Captain Rex. "You may depart when ready, just get clearance with command." The Sergeant stated

"Thank you both."

"'Ray, run preflight checks! Let's get moving!"

"Aye!"

Rex and Raymond quickly got pre-flight checks done and contacted Omega One's command center and was granted clearance.

"Dex, are you ready?" Rex inquired over the intercom.

"Nothing I'm doing will interfere with takeoff, Cap. I just said that to keep her mind off me."

Rex laughed. "Yes. A busy worker is not distracted with other thoughts. Nice thinking." We're out of here."

The bay doors opened, the *Raptor's Claw*'s engines fired up, and Rex programmed the shuttle to head to Annapolis to take care of business. Rex figured that he could hide his ship with a few of his friends, shuttle over to Teranosis and take care of business that he had with Zydak. He would return to his ship and continue with the mission with the Clave Warriors and the Senators. He figured they would understand. In addition to this, he had promised Zydak he'd complete the delivery, and he always kept his word. More important, they had come too far in their relationship for him to get the impression that he was not dependable.

After they were well into their journey toward Teranosis, Rex called down to Langstrom, "Doc, you there?"

Yes, Captain," Langstrom replied.

"You're probably already doing this, but defrost them now."

"You're right. I already started the process which will take several days before they will be back to normal."

"Perfect. It will take several days to get to where we are going."

"May I ask where that is?"

"Teranosis."

"What's there?"

"Business."

"I heard it's a dive, a real hole in the after-blasters. You sure we should take them there?"

"I have some business to do there. You guys will be going to Annapolis."

"Oh no! Don't tell me! Not McCloud!"

"He's not all that bad!"

"You are forgetting how he was all over me the last time we were there! Please don't leave us there again."

"There's no safer place. Plus we can't risk being out in public on either place," Rex pointed out. "I won't be long; I promise."

"You had better not be."

"You never know; McCloud might have changed in five years."

"I seriously doubt that." Laughing at Rex, Langstrom continued to work on the restoring process of their passengers. "I'll believe it when I see it."

"You got yourself a bet."

"I never said I'd bet anything on this. You must know something I don't about ole McCloud."

"I don't know a thing. I only know that he learned a great deal from you the last time we came through."

"I'd be willing to give him some slack. Perhaps he has changed since I last saw him, but I'm not willing to put down terrons on it."

"Not willing to back your own opinion of the man, eh?" Rex inquired. "That's down right cowardly of you, Doc. Your impression of him is your impression, and you should back it up. Put your money where your mouth is, my dear."

"I don't …I'm not judging him."

"Don't back up now, Doc, You already put it out there. Might as well go for it. You could actually be right in your deductions of McCloud. Besides, it could make things more interesting for us. So…what will it be?" he asked while lighting up one of his cigars. "You are saying that McCloud has not changed since we last saw him, and I am betting that he has changed for the better. Now, to be fair, we must use Ray and Dex to say whether he has or not."

"That sounds fair to me," Langstrom stated.

"We will make our assessment after our visit."

"I bet twenty gold terrons," Rex stated. "That is low enough to make it friendly and high enough to make it interesting."

"That is suitable for me as well," Langstrom agreed. "I can't believe I'm doing this!"

Doc laughed, one of her genuine laughs that caused Rex to chuckle a bit.

"I know you like him deep down, Doc."

"I most certainly do NOT!"

'Your mouth says one thing, but the rest of you says another. There's no point in denying it, Langstrom. I know ya. You try to play it off, but I can see though the façade."

"There is no façade, Rex."

"Okay. If you insist on living in denial, then I can't do much to stop that. But I will say that the two of you fuss over one another like a married couple."

"We do not!"

"I'll let you know when you both start doing it again."

"I'm not going to argue with McCloud again this time. I'm going to ignore him," Langtrom stated.

"You can't ignore him!" Rex continued. "The day either of you ignore one another will be the day the universe collapses."

"I wish you'd stop playing matchmaker with us. It's never going to work out." She replied.

"On that note I'll leave you to your work. And I'm not playing matchmaker, Doc. I'm just stating what I've seen in the both of you over the years. Rex out."

Langstrom waited until she heard the coms system click off before she slammed down her instruments on one of the metallic tables. In fact, she did have feelings for McCloud, though neither of the pair would admit to anything remotely close to the pair being joined. Everyone else saw it in them, but the two of them would deny it with their last breaths. What frustrated Langstrom now was that Rex saw through her façade and read her from the pilot's throne like a book. If Rex could tell, then McCloud could tell as well. She was going to have make a stronger effort to hide her emotions.

While Langstrom struggled with her emotions, Rex chatted with Ray in the cockpit and let the auto pilot take over. He just sat in the big chair glancing at the controls every few minutes to make sure they were not heading into a star.

"Doc is going to have your head," Ray warned Rex.

"It's about time those two faced the music."

"Yes, but they shouldn't be pressured into it. Let nature take its course."

"I am letting nature take its course. I believe that this time around, McCloud will act differently with her. He'll try to please her. You'll see a complete turnaround from before.

/////

Meanwhile, streaking through space toward Star Base Omega, the Rebel patrol Beta, with ex-Clave Warrior Shatra aboard had an important mission to complete. Now a Commander in the Rebel forces, she sensed that Odan Amir was getting closer as they neared Starbase Omega One.

Shatra stuck her head into the cockpit of the shuttle, "Can't this thing go any faster! I have a bad feeling that they are getting further away as we speak."

"The shuttle is going as fast as it can now, Commander."

"Frig that!" She didn't like being one step behind Odan Amir. It had always been like that, even when they had been on the same side. "What will make it go faster?"

"We have too much weight aboard."

"Dump some of the cargo."

"We can't. We need everything we've brought with us."

Frustrated, Shatra left the cockpit and moved into the cabin, where she paced back and forth.

Her mind flashed back to a time before her decision to join the rebels. She remembered, how Odan Amir had always been one step ahead of her. It seemed that not much had changed between them, and they had not yet come face to face.

She plopped down with an audible sigh and looked at the rest of the patrol. "What's the plan when we arrive at the starbase?" Shatra asked.

"Premier HenRay, Commander. We communicate with *Omega One* command and inquire about any ships that have docked and the business conducted by the passengers. We also ask questions to find out if they had any passengers and where they were headed. Oh, yeah, the most important point is if they found anything during their search of the ship if one was conducted. It could very well be that the ship is still on the station."

"We hope it is, but I doubt it." Shatra stated." I believe that they have already departed from the star base. If they know what's good for them, they would not waste any time."

"Right."

"If the ship docked, there will be record of it. If they were off the ship and had business on the station, someone would have seen them."

Shatra shook her head at the crewmate. "No, we don't have time for some long, drawn out investigation. We need only to find out if the *Raptor's Claw* had docked there and where it was headed."

"We'd gain more information if we were to speak to people they came into contact with."

"That may be true, but as we speak, the ship and its passengers get farther away from us," Shatra continued.

HenRay would not back down. "We should not rush this search. If we take our time and get the facts, we minimize the chance that we venture on some wild goose chase. That would be a waste of time. We should also speak to the Reader that searched the ship. Perhaps, she missed something or she might be able to tell us something about the crew of the ship that will help us find them."

Shatra nodded, folded her arms across her chest, and sighed. It was a wise idea, she had to admit.

"Let it be so then. I want updates every hour that we are docked on the station."

HenRay nodded to her. "I will see that you are kept informed, Commander."

/////

Far from Starbase Omega One, on the outskirts of the Andromeda galaxy, Alpha and Gamma Rebel patrols departed into space and veered off in opposite directions. One headed to Rangolia and the other to

Sansadar. Both planets were inhabited by humanoids and aliens of several varieties.

Sansadar, the home planet of the Readers, had developed into a favorite place for vacationers. With its bountiful natural resources and rich mineral waters, including "Blue Rivers," a common drink throughout the galaxies, Sansadar attracted inhabitants of other galaxies for different reasons. Some came to trade in goods and services. Others found it a very popular place for tropical getaways. With its many beaches, mountain ranges and other unique places of interest, Sansadar provided a place to get away from all the stresses of life. It was a place that on any given day, one would encounter more than forty different species at a time, with each visitor meandering to and fro and minding the business that had brought him or her to this resort.

With orders to locate a specific ship, the Gamma patrol leaders knew that they had their work cut out for them. They would have to find one ship among thousands, and not only that, but find the crew and possible occupants of that vessel.

"Captain Zetos, we have been cleared to land."

"Then take us down."

"Aye"

The shuttle etched downward toward the planet and entered its orbital plane. Descending at an angle, the shuttle rocked slightly before smoothing out as it entered the atmosphere.

"This search won't be easy," Zetos thought aloud.

"No kidding. It will be like finding a space rat in the jungle," Mandus replied to his superior.

"What is the plan?"

"We find the ship first. We got the name of the ship from Commander Zolotan. It will be listed with flight command crews. They record every ship that comes and goes.'

"That's a good place to start. However, what about the crew? There must be millions of people on this planet. How are we to find a hand full from one ship manifest?"

"Same way anyone would. We ask around for the captain of that ship. Eventually we'll run into them sooner or later. We can also post a few of our party at the landing bay to be on the lookout for the crew of that ship. Who knows, we could get lucky as they might be aboard it."

"I like that idea. So who gets to stake it out, and who goes around asking?"

"Vern and Klevus will come with me," Zetos stated. "Mandus, you take Kyle and Sampson to stake out the ship at the landing port."

"Will do, Sir," Mandus replied while gathering his gear.

"When you do find them, let me know over the coms. We will be conducting the search of the ship together."

Mandus nodded as the ship powered down for the landing. Hovering over the landing port they had been assigned, the Rebel ship awaited the doors of the landing bay to open, allowing them to set down into one of the many cylinder shaped ports. After a graceful landing, the captain gradually powered down and shut off the engines.

Having issued out the assignments, the Rebel Captain Zetos, took his two men and headed out from the ship's ramp. They were heavily armed and geared for any event that they might encounter. Mandus and his team exited after the first group, careful to lock up the ship as they departed. They then headed to the planet's flight command center to get a listing of all the ships that had landed to see if the ship they were looking for had been there. They also needed to get the name of the Captain.

Meanwhile, Rebel crew Alpha went about their duty to search for the assigned ship and crew on Rangolia, a planet in a binary system. Rangolia was the opposite of Sansadar. It was not a popular space port and was more like a ghost planet, a place where people went to hide from everything and everyone. It was the kind of place one went to get lost.

With its barren terrain and very dry atmosphere, the dry heat from its two suns scorched the already sandy dirt, painting it a deeper reddish brown. One sun rose in the morning which made the morning bearable, but when the morning sun reached its highest in the sky, the second sun rose and sent all life forms into hiding. From then until the setting of the first sun star, living beings avoided being out. If one had to be outside for some reason, he would have to cover from head to toe to avoid being sunburned.

When the Alpha patrol approached the planet, without so much as a word to any command station or control towers, they landed their ship on the outskirts of the only thriving city on Rangolia, called Recca, during the hottest time of the day. The crew did not dare go outside to walk to the city. Instead, they waited until nightfall when one of the twin suns was on its descent making it somewhat cooler. The descending sun gave a fading light that disappeared quickly over the mountains in the south. With the setting of the two suns, it became much, much colder. Yet, Rebels were prepared for such surprises. Having locked up the ship, they exited and moved toward the city.

Raz, captain of the Alpha patrol, held up a long range scanning device, which was a hand-held gadget with a screen on one side and a camera lens on the other. As they walked along, Raz scanned ahead. "Estimated population of this city is just five thousand, give or take a few," Raz stated.

"I guarantee you that all of them have a price on their heads already, and our presence will not be welcomed. Rangolia is for people who don't want to be found by those in authority, meaning us."

"I say we disguise ourselves," Zac suggested. "Let us buy robes to cover up our uniforms.'

"Agreed," Raz stated.

With each step the patrol took, the fading light on Rangolia dimmed their path to the city. They quickened their pace. Before the second sun disappeared over the mountain top, the group set foot into the city and scurried into a store.

A lone clerk turned his head toward them and his mouth dropped open in stark surprise. He only had to look at their attire once to recognize that they were Rebel Warriors. For a moment he froze in fear. Never had he seen a Rebel Warrior on this planet before. What in the many worlds were they here for?

"C...Can...I...I... help y...y...you?"

Raz walked up to the counter where the man stood behind it.

"We need robes to cover our attire," Raz responded.

"Right you are. Tis dis way gentlemen, right dis way.'

The clerk came from behind the counter and led them to the rack that held the robes in different colors.

"Dese are what you might be looking for. Dis covers the entire body from de head to de toe," he explained, his accent obvious.

Raz nodded. "Thanks. That is just the thing."

Raz turned to the man once more. "We are looking for transport. Do you think we might find transport here?"

"Ye might try de tavern down de street dare."

"Which tavern?"

"Dare is only one tavern in de city dat will have wat de are looking for. Just go out de door here and turn to de left, and where you hear de music and noise is where de go. You can ask de bar man to point you to the pilots, and you will find transport dare. But I advise you to be careful who de ask. If de find you rebels, de might kill you. No rebels come dis way in so many yarns. I wish you de luck."

Raz and his patrol grabbed a robe that fit and pulled them over the official Rebel uniforms they were trying to hide. They approached the register and paid for them, each man from his own funds. Then they exited the store. The robes allowed them to walk out into the diminishing haze of light that was Rangolia's dusk and feel safe in their disguises. Walking the streets among other various beings of different species, the rebels blended in with the crowd of others who were hiding their identities.

The task at hand would not be any easier though. Finding the ship, the captain, and crew of the ship they were looking for would take a while. It would prove difficult to ask people who didn't wish to be found about people that didn't want to be found. Perhaps they could find their people a different way. If they were to pose as potential customers they might meet their quarry sooner than later. Eventually they came to a tavern that seemed to be the only place open in the city. Raz leaned into this group and whispered to them.

"Take my lead. We will pose as potential customers looking for transport from our pursuers. I think we'll find them faster that way."

"Sounds like a good plan," one of the group spoke while all nodded in agreement before entering the tavern through the swinging doors. Silence greeted them as the music abruptly stopped.   Every head turned to look at them. When they moved further into the tavern, the music started playing and everyone slowly returned to what they were doing before. Quickly scanning the room, Raz could see several things going on: a few star poker games, some quiet conversations where terrons and possessions were slipped under the tables. Even beings were traded right out in the open from one hand to another without a peep from anyone. All the black market deals went on behind the Rebel Alliance's eyes.

However, Zymon Keltor encouraged such shady deals, and he never raided places like Rangolia. Instead, he raided the smugglers and do-gooders that opposed his leadership. In turn, such beings that dwelled and thrived in places like Rangolia supported the Emperor because he let them operate without much fuss. Because the Rebels had given the Black Market a wide berth, allowing it to run without much supervision, the inhabitants there did what they wanted, and the others who came and went did what they wanted, as well. They never invaded others' territories. Now, circumstances brought the Rebel patrol here in search of a few beings that had left Romes IV a few days before.

Raz could only hope that their disguises worked and that they would be pointed in the right direction.

Chapter Seven

Desperate and Narrow Escapes

Ice cold was what Odan felt when he opened his eyes. He could barely see anything but a bobbing round thing moving into his field of vision, out and in, back and forth. Then after a few seconds he felt warm and cozy, so much so, that he almost fell asleep. He could see the round thing moving in closer and then he could hear something, muffled speech. The round things was talking to him.

"You...will...feel... cold...numb...for...a...few...hours...but...it ... will...go....away...I have...givvvvennnnn...youuuuu.mooorrrrphhhinnne... forrrrr...painnnn. Sleepppp...nowwww. Youuuu...willll...feelll... bettterrrr...soonnnnn."

Langstrom had done this to all her patients. She had shut down the cryo-sleep, taken them off the drug she had given them, and revived the adrenaline and the defibrillator. Then she had put them under heating pads and given them medications to warm them up. The defrosting stages were precise and required that she give the medication for reheating their tissue at specific times, at exactly one hour increments. She had allowed half an hour between each of the six passengers.

Odan Amir was in a deep, dreamful sleep, a deep, mind traveling sleep that if he had been awake, he would have been careful not to slip into. There Zymon Keltor willed many things within his mind better left locked up there. However, coming out of the cyro-sleep, he had no control over his mind and what it chose to broadcast at this point in time.

Behind his closed eyes he saw her, Shatra, standing before him on Remos IV, clad in her robes of the Clave. She had come with Clave leader

Atrious, and they were about to enter the great hall to discuss the matters that had come up concerning the Andromeda Galaxy. At the doors of the Great Hall, Shatra and Odan stood alone, talking.

"It is as I had thought it would be, Shatra. The Andromeda is on the verge of war, and it will bring the Universal Order with it if something is not done."

"What can be done but insist talks of peace? Shatra inquired.

"Zymon Keltor will speak of no such thing. He wants the entire galaxy under His control! He wants no dealings with the UO. He has refused to speak with me several times."

"Perhaps I could speak with him and have better outcome," She suggested.

"Perhaps, but I don't want you getting into things over your head."

"What do you mean? I could get him to speak with you. He will listen to me."

"All he wants from you is a night of pleasure, Shatra. I've seen how he looks at you."

"Who said I'd give him what he wants."

"I'm not saying you would. I'm just saying that it would not be a good position for you to be in."

"You don't think I could handle it?"

"You could and probably more. But it's just not safe. Your vows to the Clave would be challenged, and you'd have to choose. I would not suggest you be pushed to such extremes."

"You see further than I do."

"Keltor would seek for you to side with him, and being with the Clave, you won't be able to humor him. If you aren't careful, you'll find yourself in trouble."

"I see. You don't think I could stand my ground."

"You shouldn't put yourself in such a situation."

"Why are you telling me this now?"

"I've seen you with him, Shatra," Odan stated. *"If I have seen you, others have as well. I implore you to tread carefully."*

"Is that a threat?"

"I would never threaten you. I'm just suggesting that you watch your steps."

"I'll watch mine if you watch your own. I know you are just jealous of Keltor because he can have me and you cannot."

"No, Shatra. Please, don't think that. I care for you, that is the truth of the matter, and that is why I'm trying to help you now. Stay clear of Keltor. Please. It is for your own good. The war is on the verge of starting and you will need to find where you stand. Don't let it be on his side."

"We shall see."

Odan's eyes popped open wide and he sat up, rigidly and with great strain. A sharp pain nagged at his head as his mouth cried out the name.... "Shatra!"

Langstrom spun around in her seat at the computer and raced over to Odan's side with her scanner. His heart was racing and his breathing was steady, but a wheezing sound rattled in his throat.

"Breathe deeply, Master Odan," Doc cried out. "In and out, nice and slow."

Langstrom demonstrated how she wanted him to breath and he tried to follow her example. In a matter of minutes, all the buzzers and whistles that were attached to him quieted.

"Lie back down please."

"It was a dream?" Odan managed to say as he followed her direction. He reclined wincing with pain.

"Yes. When coming out of cyro-sleep, people sometimes dream strange things," Langstrom stated in her doctor-patient tone.

"This was more a memory than a dream."

"I'm not surprised. The training you Clave Warriors have with mind capabilities supersedes what is the norm for most. Instead of having just a dream, your trained mind would have a memory, something more constructive for your mind."

"Unfortunately, such a memory could be deadly for our mission. My dream could reach out to the person in my dream when I don't wish for it to be so."

"Can't help you there."

"Can't you give me something so I might stay awake?"

"Master Odan, you have just awakened from cryo-sleep, you need to regain your strength, which requires rest. I know it might sound silly but you do need to let your body recuperate."

"Can you not give me something that will keep me from dreaming or having these flashbacks?"

"Such drugs would do you no good now and would interfere with your recovery from cyro-sleep. Just lie back and relax."

"You don't seem to understand. The flashback I just had is just like a supersonic subspace connection to the person I dreamed about. This person is the enemy! She will try reconnecting with me and getting a fix on where I am. This will not be good for the mission."

Langstrom brushed Master Odan's hair back off his face and smiled at him. "Well, the only way I could think of not letting you fall asleep will be to keep you talking with me in here until you're fully recovered."

Odan nodded. "I'm with that then."

"Who is she?" Langstrom asked.

"Who is who?" Odan asked, not realizing that he had shouted out Shatra's name just minutes before.

"Who is Shatra? The woman you referred to, the one you yelled out to."

"You heard me then."

"It was pretty hard not to hear."

"Shatra was once a Clave Warrior like me and the other men with me here. But she was seduced by Zymon Keltor and turned to his cause and his ways. She abandoned the Clave at the most crucial time, leaving the Clave leaderless, divided and scattered.   It led to the destruction of the UO. She assisted Keltor in taking over the rule of the galaxies.

"I sense there is more to it than that."

"Oh, there is more to it than that. I loved Shatra, very much. But she would not listen to me, and I was too far from her to make a difference. We were bound by Clave law to keep things platonic."

"You think that things would have been different if you and she could have been together?"

"I know it would have been different," Odan stated.

"You can't be sure of that, Odan." Markel's crackly voice called out. "She would have turned on us regardless."

Langstrom left Odan's side to check on Markel's vitals.

"Love has a way of overcoming all obstacles," Langstrom interjected as if trying to convince herself that her words were true.

"Why are you discussing Shatra anyway?" Markel asked Odan.

"I had a flashback about her," Odan replied.

"This is not good," Markel replied. "Was there a response to your dream or flashback?"

"Not yet."

"Thanks to the seven stars." Markel stated. "Let's hope that she doesn't reply."

"I'm for that," Odan agreed.

Langstrom finished with Markel and went on to Justin, and then to Gorn, as they began to wake up a half hour apart. The last two to wake up were Cassandra and Seth.

"Did we out smart them again?" Seth asked as he used his elbows and forearms to hold his torso halfway upright at a forty-five degree angle, leaving his legs outstretched on the gurney.

'Yes, Senator," Langstrom replied. "The cryo-sleep idea worked like a charm. The Reader looked into one of the status units, but she didn't catch on because of the disguises."

Cassandra laughed or attempted to and ended up coughing instead. Seth also laughed.

"So we should be headed to Shangri-La now?"

"We have one more stop to make."

"This was not part of the deal," Markel exclaimed. "We already made one unplanned stop. Where are we going now?"

"Teranosis. Captain Rex must conduct business there, and then we are on our way to Shangri-La."

"All these stops were not part of our deal!" Markel stated. "Can't he do his business after we take care of the business we are paying him for?"

"Teranosis is on the path to Shangri-La."

"Any stops we make will give the Rebels a chance to catch up to us. We have a substantial lead on them now, which we need to keep."

"You'll have to speak to Captain Rex. I've only told you what I know." Langstrom said with a tone of finality.

"Would you please let him know we need to talk?"

"I'll let him know, but you should all be resting."

"I'll rest better once I speak with Captain Rex, Doctor Langstrom."

Langstrom nodded and strode over to the communications console, where she tapped a few controls and connected with the cockpit.

"Doc Langstrom to Captain Rex."

"Rex here, Doc. How are our patients doing?"

"Recovering well. One of them wishes to speak with you right away."

"I figured as much. I'll be right down. Rex out.'

Langstrom turned back as she disconnected the communication link and moved over to her patients.

"I've contacted the Captain. He's on his way down."

Markel nodded to her. "I thank you."

/////

Captain Maximillian Rex Faraday had figured that the Clave Warriors would wish to speak with him as soon as they were out of the cyro-sleep. However, he had no idea why. He assumed it was to talk about the mission in more detail, and he was ready to discuss this and was in fact, looking forward to it. When he entered the medical wing, he did not expect Markel's voice to be so loud, nor did he expect him to be asking him the question he was asking.

"Why are we not headed to Shangri-La at present?'

Taken back by the abruptness of the question, Rex looked to Langstrom who butted in.

"I told them we were headed to Teranosis for business," Langstrom admitted. "If I said this in error, I do apologize."

"No, you didn't. Yes, we are headed to Teranosis, and I do have some business there, but it will only take a few hours, less than a day's time to complete. We will be off to Shangri-La in the same twenty four hour time span, and it is enroute to our destination."

"Another stop will jeopardize the lead we have on our pursuers, Captain Rex. At present we have at least two days ahead of them, and I do wish to keep it that way. The more we stop the more they have a chance at tracking us."

"They won't track us. I can guarantee that. Our ship will be hidden within a large compound which will have a cloaking device on their shields. It will look as if we have disappeared."

"You do not understand who is following us, "Odan added "They can use more than regular tracking devices to pick up our trail. They could tap into our minds if they get close enough. This is what Master Markel is trying to explain to you, Captain. The one who is on our trail now is far more powerful than a Reader. She was once a Clave Warrior like ourselves before she joined Zymon Keltor's side. Now she uses the skills she learned from the Clave to do Keltor's evil works. The farther we are from her, the better chance we have of making it to Shangri-La," Odan said, trying to explain the urgency of the situation.

"I have already given my word to deliver this package on Teranosis. I plan to have the ship and the rest of you and the crew stay with a friend of mine until I return from my business venture."

'I don't like it!' Markel protested. "What if you don't return? What then?"

"Let the man do his job and be done with it, Masters," Seth stated. "He has said it won't take long, and we should hold him to that. I have a feeling that the lead we have on our pursuers will remain, especially if we disappear off the grid like he says. I think we can trust his friends as we can trust him. Besides we have little choice. We can't very well find a transport now in the middle of this dark cosmos."

"So far, we have trusted him and nothing has gone wrong," Cassandra added, giving Rex a wink of her eye. "Why stop now?"

"The Senators are easy to trust you, Captain. But they are young and naïve in the ways of the universe. I should hope you don't disappoint them."

"I would never dream of disappointing the lady and her brother," Rex stated. "And I thank them for their support in this matter. It is appreciated." Rex bowed slightly to them.

"So be it. Onward to Teranosis and wherever else you are taking us, but after this, I will take no more diversion. We are going to Shangri-La after this and nowhere else."

"Agreed. You have my word we will go directly to Shangri-La after this one stop."

Captain Rex gave a nod to Seth and his sister and exited the medical area, leaving them to recover fully from the cyro-sleep. A few moments of silence elapsed as the Captain left the area.

Then Seth spoke up, "Odan, tell us about Shangri-La."

"In order to tell you that, you must first be a Clave Warrior, or one in training to become one."

"You might as well tell them. We are, after all, taking them there, and we will have to teach them Clave ways if they are to be entering the mountain fortress," Gorn suggested.

"Yes, that is true."

Odan paused, as he tried to decide where he should begin. "Well to begin, Shangri-La is an oasis in space, a natural paradise. It is much like Earth was before all the people destroyed it. With its green grasslands, rolling hills, rising mountain ridges, garden valleys and plentiful oceans and seas. We loved it so much that we made a pact that we would take precautions to preserve it and its natural beauty. Thus we thought not to destroy the surface. We built our fortress into the mountains and tall trees. When the wars came about, the Rebels destroyed much of the forest and scorched the grasslands and meadows with their high powered laser torpedoes. Yet the mountain fortress remained intact. That is where we are going. There we can send out a beacon to recall all the Clave Warriors from all the galaxies and all the planets known to us."

"What was it like back when UO and the Clave were working?"

"When the Universal Order had power, our job was to enforce the laws, conduct peace conferences, and to maintain peaceful relations in the galaxies under Universal Order rule. However, Keltor's greed and desire for power led to wars. He wanted to govern all the galaxies and nations within them. He would not discuss anything else. He opposed the Universal Order's leadership and sought to dismantle it. And he succeeded. He knew that by killing your parents the UO would gradually lose its power, and the Clave would crumble. Your father was a Senator and the leader of the Clave.

Keltor, once a Clave Warrior himself, quit to pursue a career in politics. He knew that he could become more powerful than your father, if he represented a dictatorship rule, which is the way of the universe now.

He is the emperor and no one stands in his way. It is believed that with the return of Zeger's offspring and a reunion of the Clave Warriors, the UO and the Clave will regain the power it once had to take down the Emperor and his Rebel Alliance."

"Mm… I see," Seth stated. "Are we certain the mountain fortress is intact?"

"The one which we are going to is intact. It is how we came to get you on Earth." Justin stated.

"If you were followed, that particular gate may be watched," Odan warned. "Perhaps we should try the southern mountain range of Gilead Pass."

"Gilead Pass will be harder to reach," Justin stated.

"All the better. Then we will know that it has not been destroyed," Odan replied.

"He is right. Gilead Pass will be our best option. However, we shall have to persuade Captain Rex to leave his ship in the foothills."

"Perhaps we can hide it."

"Once upon a time we could have hidden it in the brush, but now, there is nothing but charred remains of brush that once was. There will be no hiding of this ship. It will stick out like silver in the sand," Odan added.

"I'm paying him enough where he can buy himself a new ship better than the one he has now. I doubt he will complain," Markel pointed out.

Langstrom moved closer to her patients and looked at them. "You all should be resting, which means your mouths should not be going on about your plans. There will be time enough to make such plans when you have fully recovered from cyro-sleep. Now, I would appreciate your taking my suggestion to get some sleep. Your bodies will thank me later.

"Very well, Doctor Langstrom. If it is sleep you want, then it is sleep we will do," Markel stated. "However, you forget that we have been asleep already for some days now."

"True, but your bodies will feel like you've been running some marathon. Believe me, I have done this kind of thing before, and they all say they feel fine afterwards, but later it catches up with them, and they wish they had listened to me about taking it easy. Now I'm highly suggesting you all rest now while you can, because you will not be able to later, more than likely."

"Don't worry then. We will rest," Seth assured her.

Surprised at Seth's words, everyone looked to him. Markel, Odan, Justin and Gorn gave Seth a nod and lay back on the beds, as did Seth and Cassandra. An uncomfortable silence lingered in the medical area, and Langstrom moved to her console and began typing. The only sound was her voice recording the day's report for the daily log she kept.

Chapter Eight

Awakenings, Fears, Reconnections, Flashbacks

Through the winding passageways of Romes IV's Ramada Castle, the Zeger Clan scrambled to evacuate. As minutes passed, the ground shook violently, yet the mountain fortress held fast. Running behind Premier Zeger and his wife were Odan Amir, Clave Master and other siblings of Zeger. Katia, Zeger's wife, held the twins in her arms. Then as they ran, a patrol of the Rebel Alliance broke through ahead of them. Katia turned and thrust the twins into Odan's arms.

"Take them to safety!"

Zeger himself turned. "Take Katia and the twins to safety, Odan! I care not where you take them but take them somewhere out of Zymon's reach!"

"But we can –

"Obey my order, Odan. Romes IV is lost! Zymon has succeeded! It is best to save who we can now!"

"Come with us!'

"I will stay and fight!" Zeger cried.

"And I will stay beside you, "Katia cried out determined to fight alongside her husband.

"No! Go with-

"You can't make me go! I will stay and fight beside you,"

"So be it. Go Odan. Take them somewhere where Zymon cannot find them."

"On my oath as a Clave Warrior, I will take them to safety…. somewhere where Zymon does not know exists. I will see to their safety and long life."

Odan had hurried through the corridors of Ramada and came to the Great Hall where he activated the gate to another galaxy. Before he disappeared, he saw Shatra trying to stop the gate from opening, but she had been too late. The look on her face showed disappointment and rage.

Shatra's eyes popped open and she sat up in her bed. She smiled as they walked to the port to look out to see the ship connecting to Star base Omega One. She would feel that she was on Odan's trail. She could feel him because his mind was close, but still too far away for her to get a solid connection. The slight connection she felt was just enough to know she was not far behind him.

Before long, Shatra was dressed and heading for the air locks of the ship that led to the corridor of the base. She wanted to speak with the patrol members who had searched the *Raptor's Claw* and also with the Reader who had been aboard the ship. After going through security checks, she moved to the command center where she was directed to the patrol leader who had overseen the search of the *Raptor's Claw*. General Zolotan had given her all the names of the five ships that had left Romes IV. Her feelings were telling her that Odan and the ones they were looking for were on the *Raptor's Claw*. So she was focused on finding out what happened during the searches.

"Greetings, Commander Shatra. It is a pleasure to meet you. I have heard so much about you, yet I have not met you face to face."

"What did you find on the *Raptor's Claw*?"

"Absolutely nothing except cargo which passed all inspections. Their ship was clean. No passengers."

"Are you certain of that?"

"We had a Reader scan the ship with the Captain. She scanned the entire crew of four, including the captain. Nothing was found to be amiss by the Reader of our patrol."

"I see," Shatra stated. "I shall like to speak to that Reader."

"I shall arrange it. At the moment, she is scanning another vessel. She is kept very busy on the station, and her name is kept secret, so that there is no violence against her."

"Tough job but someone has to do it," Shatra thought. "Make the arrangement. I shall be in a shuttle on the station. You shall bring her to me there."

"Of course, Commander."

Meanwhile, HenRay, the Captain of the Patrol assigned to follow the *Raptor's Claw*, followed a lead that led him to a tavern in the community level of the star base. The Captain traveled with two of his men dressed in the Rebel Alliance blue uniforms with the white stripes on the sleeve.

When they entered the tavern, the loudness diminished into silence and only continued as they moved deeper into the establishment. The trio walked up to the bar and ordered some drinks.

Then HenRay turned to the barman, "I'm looking for someone."

"Figured as much. You Rebels are always looking for someone."

"I can make it worth your while to point me in the right direction."

"Reb, I will do well to mind me own business, you got me?" the barman stated. "If I go flapping me jaws about de people in dis place, me customers that frequent here will make it hard for me to run me business. Right now I make me terrons off them because I keep me mouth shut. I can tell you nothing more."

The Captain put up a bag of terrons. "Here are nearly 500 terrons in this bag. I'm sure you could use it to fix up your place here. Perhaps hire some help that will put a stop to the scum running your business for you."

"That depends on what information you want."

"I'm looking for the Captain of the *Raptor's Claw*. I was told he visited your place not too long ago and did some business here with a certain Rymelion."

The barman held up his hands and slid the bag back to him, shaking his head. "Me can't help ye. Me not one to get meself on the wrong side of a Rymelion. Me like living, and me business is thriving because me get good business from the Rymelions. But me will tell you that the man ye are looking for was here and did have business with a certain Rymelion, but me will not tell you which one. There are about twenty here in the place as me speak. Me wish you luck in finding de right one. De don't like nosey Rebels poking de noses where de don't belong."

The information wasn't all that much, but it let the Captain of the Rebel patrol know he was on the right track. The trick now would be to find the right Rymelion and speak with him. However, getting the information they needed about the location of the *Raptor's Claw* would prove to be more difficult. Rymelions were known to be quite tight-lipped and easy to get angry, which he knew would force a change in their appearance. He knew when they changed form, that speaking further was out of the question. Stories had it that Rymelions were known to be carnivorous and would seek human flesh when enraged.

One of his men turned to him. "There is no way we are going to be able to find one Rymelion who would be willing to speak to us about this guy."

"Patience," he stated. "We will be patient and take our time."

"This is suicide!" The other officer said. "Twenty Rymelions we have to speak with? And who is to say that they will be forthcoming with the information we need. This is a wild goose chase, I tell you! And the joke is on us. We will end up dead as a falling star….lights out."

HenRay turned to face the bar and looked over at his two companions. "Truth be told, it won't be easy in any way, shape, or form.

However, we must try, at least, to investigate and inquire of this Rymelion where the ship was headed. I have a hunch this Rymelion knows."

"And I have a hunch that this Rymelion, whoever he is, will not tell us anything."

"A Reader will tell us all we need to know."

"How do we get a Rymelion to consent to being read by a Reader?"

"By Rebel Law," HenRay replied. "But first we must find the right one."

"This will take time. The more time we take, the farther they get away from us."

"We are looking for accurate information of the whereabouts of these people. So far, they have eluded all searches and patrols. It is as if they disappeared, when I know they have done nothing but outsmart us at every check point, even this backward star base! If our patrols are the best in the galaxies, why have they not been caught?" I suppose we have overlooked something."

"Darn straight we have! And as I sit here, I can't think of how they have done it." HenRay's frustration revealed itself in his voice.

"Perhaps they are not even on the *Raptor's Claw*. They could have taken one of the other five ships."

"No, Commander Shatra would not be tagging along with us for nothing. Even she thinks that they are on the *Raptor's Claw*."

"We need the name of the Rymelion Captain Rex spoke with."

"More information would be helpful," HenRay stated. "But we don't have the Rymelion's name. In fact, I think the Rymelions don't give out names very easily."

HenRay panned the establishment, looking over the array of species in the tavern. The smoke-filled bar and grill was packed with all types of humanoids and aliens from all galaxies far and wide. Star base Omega One's tavern was the meeting place where most business was conducted. HenRay's eyes landed on the face of a Rymelion sitting at a table in the very far back, almost separate from the hustle and bustle of the rest of the bar. The smoke and dimmed lighting covered his features, but HenRay gulped his drink down and turned to his men. "Come, I think I see one alone."

The trio of Rebel uniforms walked through the maze of bodies and tables until they reached the table of the Rymelion sitting alone.

"Greetings. I am called Captain HenRay. I was wondering if I might sit and buy you a drink or two."

The Rymelion looked at HenRay and slowly gestured his hands to the three open seats. "Last I heard, you Rebel sorts are free to do as you please."

"I'll take that to mean we can sit with you?"

"Do as you wish."

HenRay sat down, as did his two men. HenRay then raised his hands, and a waitress came over. "I'd like to order drinks for him and my two friends. Whatever he was drinking there is fine, and I'll have Blue Rivers."

The Rymelion laughed. "No alcohol for your blood?"

"I will admit that it is too much for me while I'm on duty."

"Duty eh…bleh! Get him a real drink that is still smoking when he drinks it!" The Rymelion ordered.

"As you wish," the waitress noted their orders and left to retrieve the drinks.

In response to the change of drinks, HenRay merely shrugged. "If you want not to drink alone, then I'll drink with you."

The Rymelion grinned, showing all, especially his razor sharp teeth that gave HenRay the chills for a moment.

"Now, what can I do for you, Reb?"

"I'm looking for the Captain of the *Raptor's Claw*. I heard from a source that he came to this establishment and conducted business with a Rymelion here. However, I don't know which Rymelion. I doubt I will learn the name of that Rymelion. I would rather know more about the human and the destination of the *Raptor's Claw*. Where was it headed?"

Zydak, leaned back, took a sip of his drink that was brought for him and sighed. "I wish I could be of some assistance. However, I do not know of the Captain of the *Raptor's Claw*. This human you are after, has he committed some crime?"

"He might have. He is wanted for questioning in relation to the smuggling of six passengers, who are Clave Warriors. This human is wanted by the Emperor himself."

"Ahh. I see. This is more political than criminal then?"

"Both," HenRay stated. "It is believed that these six will start a movement to overthrow the Emperor and bring back the UO and the Clave."

"As I said before, I know nothing of this Captain of the *Raptor's Claw*. If you value your life, I wouldn't go around asking much more about him. Most Rymelions aren't as friendly as I am."

"Thanks."

"Thanks for the drink. You'd fair better checking the station's ship records. They would have the last jump points of all ships that leave this place, and they would have a general course heading."

Nodding, HenRay rose to his feet and bowed his head toward the Rymelion. "For that, I thank you. I will be sure to look there and see for myself."

HenRay led the way out of the tavern and back up to the docking level where he questioned the flight control officers about the *Raptor's Claw*'s last course heading."

"Yeah, I remember the *Raptor's Claw*. It was a fine, medium sized vessel that checked out ok with interior and exterior scans. It even passed the Reader scans."

"Where was it heading when it left here?"

"It had a course heading towards the gate."

"Thanks."

/////

In another part of the station, Commander Shatra opened the door for the Reader who had scanned the *Raptor's Claw*. The two women bowed heads at each other. Then Shatra gestured with her arms for the Reader to enter.

"Come in and make yourself comfortable."

"Thank you."

"I take it you know who I am."

"You are Commander Shatra, the Emperor's right hand and advisor."

"That is right. You must know why I've called you then, if you are a Reader."

"You are here in search of Clave men and two young Senators."

"Yes, we were told to search for them on the *Raptor's Claw*."

"And you didn't find them?'

"We searched that ship….everywhere. I scanned the entire crew, but there was one that I could not scan."

"Who was it?"

"The Captain is an Angolian."

"What about the others?"

"Nothing. They were busy working."

"Could their working have been to distract them from possibly revealing a hiding place?"

"No. I don't believe so. The engineer was busy fixing the ship. The doctor was busy writing reports, and the security guard was busy at the entrance guarding the ship. I did ask questions of the doctor, but she didn't seem to be working on any science projects. There were no passengers. No one."

"They are on that ship…somewhere," Shatra stated. "They have outsmarted us twice so far. I will not tolerate another screw up!"

"I hope you don't blame me for-"

"Your lack of sensing them is not because of your abilities. It's not your fault. Fact is that they have managed to get the better of us twice so far. I have a strong feeling that they are on the *Raptor's Claw*, but they could very well be on any of the other five ships that left Romes IV. Therefore, we will stay here until we know for certain they are not on the other vessels. Then we will pursue the *Raptor's Claw* if it is clear that there is no other place they could be."

"I'm sorry if I failed the Emperor."

"You did not fail him. You did your job, and that's all you needed to do," Shatra reassured the Reader. "Finding them is our job. You may go now."

The Reader bowed and left through the doorway from which she had entered, joining her bodyguards in the corridor.

Shatra plopped herself down on her couch, taking in the ceiling-to-floor view of the station as ships docked and departed. In deep thought, she wondered how Odan and those with him had slipped past all their check points without being caught. Twice now, they have eluded the search efforts. What if they were not on any vessel at all? No. Her feelings were stronger now. She was certain that Odan Amir was on the *Raptor's Claw*. However, there was no proof of that. The searches and Readers had come up with nothing when the ship was searched. No passengers nor anyone else seemed to be hiding anything, according to the Reader she had confronted. Yet, her feelings were strong, and she was certain that she had felt a subtle distant connection that had been lost to her, a familiar presence. She had long since desired to be close to Odan again, as she had been in the past. Despite the restrictions they had placed on themselves, they still had feelings for each other, and they did not hide it when they were alone together.

She was sure that it was him. She had felt his mind; even now she felt him sensing her. Closing her eyes, she reached out to him as far as she could reach. Would his mind reach out for hers?

Her eyes closed, as a hand went to her mouth. Salty tears streamed down her face as she thought back in time, when he had warned her not to get involved with Zymon Keltor. She had been rude and defensive and did not listen. If only she could reverse time and redo every mistake she had made, she would give her right arm to make things right between them. Yet, it was too late for that. Perhaps she should have listened to Odan when he warned her against getting   too close to Keltor. Yet she did not become one of his many women. Keltor respected her far more than he did his other women and treated her like a queen. Because she had once been a Clave Master and knew their ways, she was valuable to him. He made her a Commander of his finest Rebel soldiers and made them his personal bodyguards. Yet now as she searched her soul, she could think of only one person that had brought out the goodness in her…

"Odan …" She whispered his name in her mind. And as she said it, she closed her eyes and she could feel him, but it was very faint.

Chapter Nine

Rebels, Neutrals, and Lizards

Erosodad, a planet among nine in a triple star system, was the only planet that could sustain life. The other eight planets were rich in minerals and ore, which were mined and the products sold at top terrons legitimately and illegally. Drake, the leader of Eronia, knew how to make a profit. He cared nothing about the Emperor and his laws. Privately, he wished things were as they had been when the UO and the Clave were running things. Then he could at least trust that his freighters would reach their destination without being boarded or stripped of their cargo. Now, he had to literally fight to keep his shipments intact and on time.

When he was not worrying about his shipments of ore and minerals, he worried about governing Eronia.

Eronia, a thriving city that covered the land and stretched within the depths of the ground underneath, used the tall trees and wire to create a transit system in the sky. The sky tram stretched all over the planet. Underneath the ground was a world subway that had several stops along its route. In addition, Travelers used shuttles for transport to and from different points within the city.

A lone, Rebel shuttle entered the atmosphere and gained clearance to land at one of the ports. Upon landing the Rebel patrol Delta exited the shuttle and were greeted by a host of security officers.

"Governor Drake sent you escort. We are to take you to him. Please, follow us."

"Why the escort?"

"It is for your own safety," the security guard replied, walking toward the exit of the landing bay. "Not too many folks around here like you Rebels."

"Thanks for the warning."

The security guards moved into positions around the rebel patrol who led them out of the building and into the crowded streets of the metropolis.

"Rebel scum!" exclaimed one unidentified being among the crowd.

"Looky Lou! It's the men in Blue! Twenty terrons says I can hit him in the nose with this brick!" another yelled.

"Go back where you came from, Rebs!" another voice rang out.

Projectiles flew at them, and the men of the patrol found themselves holding their arms up to deflect the debris. As they advanced, the projectiles grew more dangerous, graduating from paper and spit to rocks and mud. The security guards did nothing to stop the flying objects. They just moved them through the crowds at a slow crawl. Finally, they got to the building that was their destination. The projectiles ceased as soon as the doors swished open and they entered. The security detail led them to the lift and they ascended to the very top. The doors slipped open and the security detail led them out into what looked to be the dwelling place of someone very rich.   White carpeting, very comfortable couches, and a panoramic view of the entire city made a good impression on the visitors. Servants scurried to and fro performing their duties. One approached them.

"How may I be of service?"

"Get the Governor."

"Whom shall I say is here?"

"A Rebel patrol."

"I'll be back in a few moments. Please take a seat and make yourselves comfortable." The rebel patrol sat down and looked uncomfortably at one another. However, Talos, the Captain of the patrol held up his hand to calm his men.

"This is probably the leader of the planet. We'll have to get permission from him to search for the crew we are looking for."

"I doubt he will allow us to do it," Lan, one patrol member said.

"Terrons always change people's minds, Talos said.

"Terrons don't seem to be lacking here, Talos."

"True, but I'm counting on his greed to kick in."

"You think he will be greedy and take the bribe?" asked Lan.

"Most definitely, Lan. People in power always want more than they have."

"I beg to differ, Lan responded.

"I'll take that bet," one of the quieter officers in the patrol spoke catching the others completely by surprise.

"So be it,' Talos replied. "How much do you want to wager."

"Twenty terrons."

"You got yourself a bet then, Skar."

Presently, a man and two large aliens moved from another room into the room in which they were seated. Talos rose to greet them, as did the rest of the patrol.

Drake looked at each man of the patrol and gestured to the two aliens with them. "Leave us, but stay close."

Drake walked over to the bar and poured himself a drink. He looked over to his guests, "A drink to wet your tongues, perhaps?"

"Blue Rivers for us. We cannot touch the harder stuff as we are on duty," Talos replied.

A snap of his fingers and the servants hurried to get the Blue Rivers for his guests. Drake moved back to the sitting area.

"Please, sit down and relax."

The patrol sat down as they were told, and Drake sat down opposite them in a lone chair.

"I am Drake, Governor of Erosodad. What brings you to here, if you don't mind my asking?"

"I am called Talos. These are my men. We are looking for a ship and its crew and possibly six passengers," Talos replied.

Drake's face cracked a slight smile, for he found this rather amusing. He took a sip of his drink and crossed his legs.

"May I ask why you seek this ship and its crew and passengers?"

"The Emperor desires a word with them."

Drake shook his head. "No. That doesn't wash with me, Mr. Talos. If the Emperor wants them, nine times out of ten, he means to destroy them."

"That is not a fair conclusion. We were told to bring them back alive. Surely, if his intent were to kill them, he would have us to do his dirty work."

"Perhaps. However, I can tell you now that you won't find that ship or its crew among the thousands of people on this planet. There are just too many people and aliens here. It would be like searching for a single star in the midnight of space."

"So I take it you won't aide us in our search."

"I do not hide my distaste of you Rebels. Yet, I do realize that I cannot stop your search either. So I will cooperate only so far as to let you proceed with your search of the entire planet. I do wish you luck in finding your ship and its crew. Yet, I must forewarn you that many who reside on Erosodad came here to get away from Rebel influence. Erosodad is a neutral haven and will remain so. I want nothing to do with the Galaxy Wars.

"So we may search?"

"Proceed with your search. But this does not mean that I have taken sides with the Emperor and the Rebel Alliance, nor did I take much stock in the Clave and the UO, when it was running things. This planet has been neutral for a very long time even before Zymon Keltor took over. You might find a diverse mixture of peoples on this planet, all of them wanting nothing to do with the galaxy wars.'"

"You can try to hide from what is going on for a time, but eventually you will have to take sides. Thus it is best to weigh the pros and cons and decide early on, what is best for your people rather than to wait until you are forced to choose," Talos advised.

"I have already done this several times and have concluded that it is in our best interest to remain neutral. In this way, our freighters will not get boarded or delayed in transit because we will have enemies to worry about. Therefore, my letting you conduct your search makes my point clear. Any and every one that comes here can go about their business as long as it doesn't break any of my golden rules."

"What are the golden rules?" Talos asked

"Number 1: no killing. If you do kill someone on this planet, then you will expect the same treatment from those who knew the victim well, and you can expect me to administer judgment as I deem fair. Number 2: No destruction of property. In the event that you deliberately destroy property, then you must replace it or pay for it with interest. Number 3: No cheating in any of the gambling games. If you are caught cheating, punishment is decided by those who are directly victimized by your shady ways. Number 4: No stealing. If you steal, you will either be forced to return the item or pay for it. If you can't afford payment, then it shall be taken from your body in any way that the victim sees fit. Those are the rules and the people live by them here. Let me not hear of any of your patrol violating these rules during your stay here."

"We will abide by your rules while here," Talos agreed.

Nodding, Drake rose from his chair and moved to the ceiling to floor view of the city. "I will assign to you a security team. They will keep the peace as you conduct your search. As I said, the peoples here do not respond well to Rebels. The security team will ensure your safety."

"That won't be necessary."

"I insist," Drake stated. "You do not know these people. I do. I know what they are capable of. Security will not interfere with your search, I assure you. They might even be of some assistance."

"Very well then, Mr. Drake."

The patrol rose and bowed to Drake. The security team that had brought them to Drake's dwellings, escorted them to the lift and all descended.

When the doors slid upon, one of the security officers stepped up to Talos.

"I'm the Chief Security Officer. My name is Rusty. I will be escorting you through the city as you conduct your search."

"Right."

"Where would you like to begin?"

"Flight control. They must have a list of all the ships that landed here, and the names of the captains of those ships, right?"

"They do. Follow me."

In another part of the Andromeda Galaxy, the final Rebel Patrol, Beta, made its approach toward the system known as Andreazoo Belt which was surrounded by an active asteroid belt. Deep within the center of the belt, two planets orbited a lone bright, jumbo star, orange like a fireball. The planet closest to the sun was a barren, desert-like waste land, where the air was hardly breathable for most during the day. Most races stayed clear of it, but others found it isolated and quite peaceful. Hardly any beings ventured there since the pathway to enter the planet changed every second because of the asteroids constantly moving, making the approach dangerous for the average pilots. It was a place to hide for those who wanted no one to find them.

The other planet, Zenith, was more accommodating for nearly all types of species; thus it was filled with all sorts from almost every corner of the Andromeda. Mainly, Zenith was a paradise, an oasis among the stars that made it well worth the dangerous trip to gain its orbit. Not only was the planet a sight to see, but the inhabitants matched the beauty of the planet. The final ship that had left Romes IV had departed on a course heading for this system. The Rebel patrol prepared to search every planet including this one. If the Clave Warriors were not on this planet, they must definitely be on the other planet further out from the sun.

"We will check out this planet first. According to the life signs on this planet, it won't take us long to find out who is here," Captain Adam stated.

"The population is only about 100, even if it's that many," one of Adam's crew observed.

Adam took out a device and scanned the surface of the area in a circular motion. "The scanner indicated signs of scattered population, yet the majority lived in the city.

"Let us search here first," another of his crew suggested.

"Right," Adam agreed and barked out his orders to his men.

"Move out! Lando, you take point, and I will bring up the rear!"

The group of five rebel soldiers advanced forward toward the city. As they drew near, they found mostly empty streets, except a few people who appeared to be headed to nearby destinations. A door squeaked and startled the Rebels as they passed it. When they looked around, a rough voice bellowed out.

"Get off the streets you blasted Rebels!"

Adam turned and walked to where the voice had come from. "Why?"

"Come in here, quick!" a tall, lanky man cried out in a hushed command. "Hurry!"

The Rebels darted into the open door and looked about to find themselves in a general store.

"Who are you?" Adam asked.

"Derick. But people call me Rick for short."

"Why did you tell us to get off the street?"

Rick looked at them for a moment, before closing and moving away from the door and windows.

"Come in further away from the door, please," he insisted. "Believe me there is a reason for it, and you will soon find out what that reason is. "

"Why not just tell us why. We didn't come to learn about the crazy things that go on. We are here by order of the Emperor to search and bring to Regil Centuri the crew of the ship that left Romes IV nearly two to three days ago and came here. It is believed that they had passengers that are a threat to his leadership."

"Finally the old man is getting a little paranoid in his later days, eh?"

"His age is of no matter in this business."

"True, true. True that."

"You had better be glad we are on a mission."

"At least we know where we stand. I saved your life by letting you stay in here. Now you owe me."

"I don't see how that's true."

"Geana lizards come through here looking for people to eat. If you're not in by night fall, you are dead meat. There's only a few who can survive them."

"Who are those few?"

"Clave Warriors. They can communicate with the lizards' minds. I've seen it happen once. The lizard charged up to the Claveman like it was about to devour him, and the Claveman just raised his hand and spoke some words that made the beast stop and bow its head down to the sand in submission. The most fascinating thing I've ever seen!"

"You say there are Clavemen on this planet?"

"Not sure now. There were quite a few, but now I have no idea. I have not seen one in over eight years now."

"Aah! How long do we have to wait before we can go out?"

"Until sun up. You can sit on those chairs there to rest your legs. Store is closed. I will now retire upstairs with my family. Remember, don't open that door for anyone, not even someone in trouble. If you open it, the lizards will follow him inside. That will then be the end of all of us. Understood?"

"One question, Sir."

The man turned around, scratching his salt and pepper beard. "Yes?"

"Why not just kill the lizards?" Lando asked.

"Believe me, that's been tried several times. The bastards have hard outer shells that are resistant to laser fire. We've tried acid and all other sorts of things, but nothing seems to put a dent into them. The only sure defense against them is to run like hell, run like your life depended on it because it does. They will eat you whole, bones and all in the bat of an eye."

"If that's the case, why not just leave the planet to them?"

"Some of us have no way to leave and start up somewhere else. We just have to take necessary precautions to protect ourselves. We know that the lizards start hunting at sun down. So we go out during the day. It has been working for several years now."

"There's got to be something that will kill them."

"When you think of it, please let me know."

The store owner climbed the steps to the upstairs apartment, which was his home. The Beta team then sat down on the furniture that was for sale. A hush fell over the room as the patrol contemplated the information they had learned from the old man. Suddenly, a loud commotion outside sent chills down their spines, causing them to sit up and strain their ears to decipher what caused the noise. When they heard no other sounds from outside, they relaxed, closed their eyes and drifted off to sleep. A few hours later, a shrill scream of a woman's voice pierced the silence of the night, awakening the Rebels as if from a nightmare. All five bolted up at once, eyes wide from fear, their hands on their weapons ready to attack, but the scream lasted only minutes before silence again. The screams and cries went on through the night, and the team got little sleep. Mostly the

old man's words warning them about the invincible lizards being capable
of swallowing one person whole haunted them throughout the night.

Just before dawn, the lizards' footsteps scrunched against the
pavement, signaling their retreat from the town before daybreak, taking
refuge in the dark caverns and dense forests, leaving the town silent once
more. When the first rays of the sun hit the sand, the town woke up and the
people went about their daily activities as though nothing had happened.

The store owner descended from his home upstairs in the store,
opened up the window shade, and addressed his guests who were in
various stages of sleep.

You all awake?" he asked.

"Didn't get a wink of sleep," Adam stated.

"Newbies to the town normally don't rest the first night."

"Mr. Rick, I thank you for your warnings and hospitality."

"If I hadn't done it, I doubt anyone else would have. Like I said last
night, most people around these parts don't take kindly to Rebels."

"All the same, I thank you," Adam insisted. "Where might we find
the captains of freighters in these parts?"

"Tavern."

"Which one?"

"There's only one, The Blue Moon, down the street on the left. You
can't miss it. It is where everyone else spent the night."

"Thanks."

Adam led his team of four men outside and into the street. Blood
splattered sidewalks and paths marked the scenes where people who
had dared to venture out after sunset had been nabbed by those dreaded
lizards. As the patrol headed toward the tavern stepping over and around
the bloody messes, Adam shook his head in disgust as he contemplated
about ways those bastards could be destroyed. In the back of his mind, he
imagined himself in combat with one of them.

The Rebels walked into the tavern and found the place jam-packed with all sorts of sleeping aliens and humanoids who had sought shelter during the night. The bartender, who was the only one stirring, hustled behind the bar getting his business ready for the day. The large, burly looking male, wearing a white shirt and a brown vest turned toward them.

"We are closed until noon, and we are completely booked for rooms."

"We aren't looking for a room or alcohol. We are looking for a captain and its crew of a freighter called the Calypso."

"I don't know of anyone by that name, Mister. I got people coming in here by the hundreds, and I don't care to know anyone by name. I tend to keep my nose out of my patrons' business. If you think he's here, why not ask around for him yourself? You just might get lucky."

Adam eyed the big, bartender and nodded. He thought of pointing out that he had asked for the Captain of a ship named Calypso, not the name of a person but decided against it. He doubted that it would matter. He could read in his eyes that the bartender wasn't about to get into trouble by opening his mouth about his customers. He turned away from the bartender and looked to the sleeping aliens and humanoids. He doubted that they would welcome being awakened from their sleep to see a group of Rebels digging for information. Instead Adam turned to his men.

"Looks like this is going to take a little longer than we intended. We are going to have to wait here until they wake up."

"What do we do until then?"

"We wait."

They found some empty seats at a table in the back of the tavern and sat down. Adam looked at his time piece and noted that they had three hours to wait until the bar opened, and they had no idea when the customers would wake up. Many aliens had irregular sleeping patterns. They could be waiting for days.

Chapter Ten

The Shatra/Odan Connection

Having recuperated from the cryo-sleep, the two young Senators and the four Clave Warriors had been moved from the medical area to their cabins aboard the *Raptor's Claw*, where they began eating real food again. They talked and laughed as they enjoyed one another's company. After filling their stomachs with food and drink, almost everyone drifted into sleep again, everyone except Odan and Markel.

Sitting by himself, Odan could picture her standing far off when he closed his eyes, but she was close enough that he could decipher the features that made him know who she was: the long, reddish, brown hair, flowed as she walked toward him; the slim, shapely body which he had once held close. Shatra was not a woman that one would forget, at least not him. As she drew closer to him, he tried to calm his heart from beating so fast.

"You have not forgotten me," she spoke to his mind.

"I will never forget you, Shatra," Odan replied.

Odan embraced her in a welcoming hug, which she returned. Then he released her and stepped back a pace.

"You were right about everything, Odan."

"I was hoping that I would not be right concerning you, Shatra. But I see in your eyes that you have been swayed to Zymon's side."

"You left me here all alone with no guidance! What was I to do without you?"

"*You could have gone far in the Clave, Shatra. You didn't have to side with Zymon and destroy everything we had worked so hard to build.*'

"*The Masters would never have chosen me to sit among them, Odan. You know it as well as I do.*"

"*Patience. You should have waited for the right time. I would have sponsored you, supported you in your move to become an apprentice and Master,*" Odan shot back. "*If you had just waited! There was just too much going on at the time. The Clave was trying to stop Zymon's threat to take over the UO. We would have succeeded if the Clave had not been divided.*"

"*So you blame me for the fall of the UO?*"

"*You had a hand in it, Shatra. You cannot deny that.*"

"*Truth be told I caused the break in the Clave that lead to the break in the UO. The rest is history.*"

"*You can fix it,*" Odan stated.

"*I'm in too deep with Zymon, Odan.*"

'*It's never too late to turn things around. An opportunity will come for you to do just that. I hope you will take it.*"

"*I don't think I can.*"

"*Too much negativity I see in you, Shatra. Is all that training gone from your heart?*" Odan asked."

"*I don't know.*"

"*All you have learned from Zymon is negativity and violence.*"

"*It has worked. My powers are stronger! We are in control of the most systems now. Your return will not change things as you hope they will.*"

"*We shall soon see about that.*"

"*Why not give up. You know wherever you go, I will find you, Odan.*"

"*True. You have a connection with me, but I can control my emotions far better than you can.*"

"*Ha! It was easy to make this connection.*"

"It was only because I wanted to speak with you, Shatra. I wanted to see if there was hope in convincing you to rejoin us."

"Dreams, only dreams, Odan. "

"I see that you are unwilling to change your mind."

"Why would I side with the Clave? The Clave has done nothing for me! The Clave is dead, leaderless and scattered through the galaxies. They are divided and separated by their perspectives on how things should be run. To bring them back together would take more time than you would have to organize them into a working body to ever think of going against Zymon's forces."

"All too quick you are to forget who trained you, Shatra."

"I could have learned all those things anywhere."

"But not as well," Odan insisted. *"You were trained to be a Clave Master, Shatra, not a backstabbing, traitor who is selfish and thinks of nothing but terrons and what they will buy for you."*

"There is more to me than that!"

"You mean there was more to you than that. Now, I'm not so sure," Odan stated.

"I don't have to listen to this! I will hunt you down like an animal and when I find you, I will treat you like one!" Shatra cried out in frustration.

"Perhaps, perhaps not. Maybe you won't catch me, and then again, maybe you will," Odan taunted. *"The future is not set."*

Enraged, Shatra ended the connection, and Odan Amir opened his eyes. Blinking, he sighed, covered his eyes with his hands, and wept. Shatra, the one he knew, was gone to him. What was left behind was a stranger that he didn't recognize. The outward appearance was Shatra, but within was someone else. It wasn't the same lovely lady he once knew."

"What is it?" Markel asked, looking at Odan as he sat down beside him.

"Shatra has changed. She is not like the woman I knew. She is evil and corrupted into something I cannot describe. She is Zymon's evil-doer now, and her connection to me will not help our mission."

"We must use it to our advantage," Markel offered.

"How?" Odan asked.

We can lead her away from us."

Odan nodded. "This will work. When we reach our destination, I will travel in the opposite direction of where you will take the young Senators. I will go to the Eastern Fortress alone."

Markel nodded and glanced at the two young ones. "Will they come with us without you?"

"I will speak with them and let them know that we must split up."

Markel placed a supportive hand on Odan's shoulder. "Worry not of Shatra. She chose her own path. Unfortunately, it was not the right one. She does not see that, and she won't ever see that, Odan. Let her go and live the life she has chosen no matter how hard it will be because of her short-sightedness. You told her the way, and she chose not to go that way. What more could you have done?"

"I suppose nothing. I left her at a crucial time, Markel. I think had I stayed back, she would have stayed loyal to the Clave and the UO, and the Clave would still have control over the Andromeda."

"Don't blame yourself. You had orders from Zeger to leave with his children. You did your duty. No one faults you for that! Stop blaming yourself for this. It's not your doing."

"The masters—"Odan began but was interrupted by Markel.

"The Masters knew the Andromeda would soon fall. They put you there to protect the Senate Leader and his family. Zeger ordered you to take care of his children. You only did what you were ordered to do!" Markel argued. "Don't beat yourself up about this. It's time to let it go and move on."

Odan put a hand on Markel's shoulder and nodded. "You are right, my friend. You are right."

"Is this someone you loved, Odan?" Cassandra asked. "I don't understand. Did you leave her to take care of us?"

Odan and Markel had not noticed that the twins had entered the room. They turned to see Seth and Cassandra standing inside the entrance, not knowing how much of their conversation the two had overheard. Since they had come up from the medical wing to their cabins, Seth and Cassandra had not spoken much, except between themselves. However, both of them looked at him for answers. He had no choice but to respond to the question Cassandra had posed.

"You must understand that Clave Warriors are encouraged to care about the welfare of all living things, but we are discouraged from becoming so attached that we depend on them to satisfy emotions, desires or necessities. Back then, when I knew Lady Shatra, I was entirely dedicated to my vows of becoming a Clave Master. When I looked on Shatra, I only saw her as a path leading away from my goals and dreams. Truly I loved her, very much. She was beautiful! A part of me has regretted turning away from a relationship with her."

Odan closed his eyes and shook his head. "Oh, I loved her very much, but I also loved the life of the Clave, and I wasn't about to give up all that I had worked for to be with her. I figured that my parents would roll over in their graves a few times if I had made the same mistake they had made. So, I let go of my love and held on to the Clave, became a Master and the rest, you all know. I was ordered to protect your parents and they ordered me to protect you two, a duty that I have not strayed from in seventeen years.

"If she can 'connect' with you, then we should make plans using this to our advantage, like Markel suggested," Justin stated.

"When the Captain goes to the Teranosis, I think you should go with him, just to lead Shatra away from the twins," Gorn suggested.

"I'm not sure if this is a good idea." Markel pointed out a risk they would be taking. "What if Odan is recognized?"

"That is a risk we have to take. We can't take a chance that Shatra is not right behind us now. If she is, having Odan go with Captain Rex will lead her to Teranosis, instead of one of the moons, which is where the ship will go. We must protect the twins. Right now, to do this, we must keep this connection far from them, so that she doesn't see in her visions through you."

"Yes. It is wise to be cautious. I will speak with the Captain when I get a chance." Odan agreed.

"I don't like the idea of us separating from Odan!" Seth blurted out.

"Seth, it is dangerous for me to go on with the rest of you, knowing that Shatra has this connection with me. At any given time, she can connect with my mind, and it will take a great deal of concentration and time for me to shut down such a connection. During this time I'm trying to shut it down, she can see everything I can see, hear everything I can hear. I can do my best to block her, but I would never know when she will seek such a connection. It would be best that I not be near the rest of you until we find a way to shut this connection down, or rather until I find a way to shut it down myself."

Cassy looked to Seth and shrugged her shoulders and looked away from Odan's gaze. Then Seth looked to Odan. "You are going to leave us with…"

"You need not worry yourselves," Markel blurted. "We are Clave Warriors just like Odan. Our duty is to protect you both. We will let no harm come to either of you."

Odan sighed. "At some point, you knew that I wasn't going to be around. You both knew this, didn't you?" Odan asked.

"Yes. But__"

"At some point, you knew you'd have to trust Markel, Justin and Gorn as you would me, didn't you?"

"Not as soon as this," Cassandra replied. "You have to remember, we have no idea about anything that is going on around us, Odan. We have come from a place that is clueless about all of this, remember! Now you're asking us to put our trust into the hands of your friends that we just met a few days ago! Not only that, but we are going to meet a few more people we have no clue about as well! And we are supposed to just blend into all this as if we belong!"

"Cassy," Odan held up his palm to her, signaling her to calm down. "I know this is not easy for you but please, try to take this all in slowly."

"I've been taking things slow, Odan. We haven't said a word until now! The only reason I'm saying anything is because frankly, I'm scared out of my mind to see you leave us for any amount of time, even it if is in our best interest! The only reason I haven't flipped my lid is because you have been with us! You have made it all seem doable. Now you are asking us to do this without you around."

"I believe that you two can stand alone for a day without me here. I will only be gone for a day with the Captain."

"What if it's longer than that?"

"Heaven forbid if that be the case, but if that happens, then I'm certain you both will survive whatever comes. Markel, Justin and Gorn will then lead you both to Shangri-La, with or without me. The mission doesn't end because either Clave Warrior's life ends. Only your lives matter that much. You two are the life of the UO. You both must reach Shangri-La and breathe life back into the UO and the Clave."

"How? We know nothing of it!" Seth raised his voice in protest while jumping out of his seat in frustration.

Odan remained calm. "We will train you in the ways of the UO and the Clave from here on."

"What do we need to learn?" Seth questioned, still not convinced of his and Cassandra's role in this UO and Clave thing.

"I will teach you the ways of the Universal Order, and Markel will teach you the ways of the Clave."

Seth plopped down in his seat, sighed, and looked to his sister for some support. After a brief silent communication between the two, both nodded to Odan and in unison spoke. "We are here to learn, teach us."

Odan stood and positioned himself between the twins who remained seated. He squeezed their shoulders pulling them closer to him before speaking. He had never felt as proud of them as he did at that moment.

"You go to the ConClave where they will discuss universal affairs, such as world to world trade and world to world contracts."

"That sounds interesting," Seth warmed up to the idea that he and his sister could possibly continue the work that his parents had dedicated their lives to.

"Mostly you will be discussing how to take back what Keltor took from the UO. The UO was formed by your father. Leaders of other worlds joined forces to establish a governing body which guaranteed order for the universe. The Clave was formed thereafter to enforce the laws of the UO. Now, in order to restore the order and rescue the universe from the hands of the terrorist Keltor, we must get you two to Shangri-La," Markel continued.

"How will we get the word out to other nations?" Seth asked.

"We will spread the word as soon as we arrive on Shangri-La," Odan answered, pleased that Seth had begun to show more and more interest in the project.

"Why are we so important?" Cassy asked.

"You are the only two who remain of your father and what he built. Only you can bring back the Universal Order."

Chapter Eleven

Oasis on Teranosis

Diago, the seventh moon of Teranosis, was large enough to be a small planet and small enough to still be called a moon. It was larger than the other eight moons and was the only one capable of habitation. Various types of green vegetation and forests covered the surface. The natives, monkey-like creatures, lived above and below the surface of the planet. They welcomed immigrants who colonized and made Annapolis their home. These humanoids, also known as Angolian, and Sansadarian Readers, had established colonies that had flourished for many yarns. The leader of the colonies was an Angolian called Ruford McCloud.

A tall, heavy, muscular man hurried through the evergreen brush with his group of hunters, who had spread out to lure their prey toward the other group who would come from the north to cut off the unsuspecting rhinebuck that would serve as the main dish for dinner. The loud warrior cries and noises echoed throughout the valley as the hunters led the prey against the eastern mountain range. Soon, they would take their positions and take turns shooting at it.

Rhinebuck were difficult and dangerous prey when they reached adulthood, and this one was well into its years. However, the young ones were tastier than the mature ones. The people who lived here liked both. McCloud knew that the age of the prey determined how difficult it would be to shoot and subdue the darn thing. Experienced men let the prey run down to exhaustion before going for the kill, while greenhorns tried to kill the prey too early. If they made the mistake of making a move too early, the buck became enraged and the adrenaline and energy made it possible for it to stay alive longer. This is why McCloud hung back, letting the younger ones, run ahead. He knew that they would not catch the buck until sun down.

Just as the sun was descending, they managed to shoot the rhinebuck in the head and it dropped like a huge boulder to the ground. Every hunter gathered around the dying beast and waited until it took its last breath. Then they began to skin, gut, and carve it, putting chunks of meat into sacks and taking the hide to be cleaned.

While this was going on, a communication came over McCloud's com system.

"Command to McCloud."

Due to all the noise, McCloud didn't hear the first call. However, after clearing the connection of static and turning up the volume for another go at it, they succeeded.

"Command to McCloud!"

"McCloud here."

"Sire, you won't believe this, but the *Raptor's Claw* is requesting docking orders."

A large smiled spread across McCloud's face as one vision came to mind….Langstrom. "Make them comfortable until our return. Give them our best accommodations and break out our finest wines. We will have a banquet in honor of our guests."

"Aye, Sire."

"Let's hurry this up!" McCloud ordered the hunters. "We have to get back to entertain."

/////

Soon after talking with his comrades in the cabin, Odan Amir left to discuss his plans with Captain Rex. When he opened the entrance to the cockpit, Rex turned and was surprised to see Odan. He had expected it to be one of his crew.   Odan sat down next to Captain Rex in the co-pilot's seat after Captain Rex managed to conceal his surprise and motioned for him to do so.

"Ah, Master Odan. Is it?

"Yes, I'm Odan.

"What can I do for you?" Rex asked.

"Let me come with you to Teranosis." Rex was taken aback by his request. He was inviting himself on this mission to Teranosis.

"Why would I consider that?" Rex asked

"It's not up for consideration. I am coming with you. We have no choice."

Rex put the ship on auto pilot and turned his attention to Odan. "My trip to Teranosis was a one man deal. The business I have there is private, and I've been paid for it already. I never said I would include another person in on this with the person I made the deal with. I can't go changing things."

"Just let me take the shuttle with you there, and I can meet you back at the shuttle when you are done."

"Why the sudden change?"

"It is simply a precaution. We believe that an ex-Clave warrior is tapping into my mind and trying to track us by this method. If this is the case, our little excursion from the group will lead them away from our party and the rest of the crew."

'Ah, I see." Rex rubbed the stubble on his face. "Good idea then to have you go with me to Teranosis. All right then. So be it."

"Good," Odan replied, surprised that Rex had been so easy to persuade.

Odan rested a hand on Rex's shoulder, and then before he left the cockpit, he turned back. "Let me know when you are leaving."

"You bet."

Odan returned to the cabin where the other five passenger rested to find Markel in full gear demonstrating how to use the choice weapon of the Clave Warrior, while Seth and Cassandra watched, taking in every bit of information. Markel was engaged in a fight against a computerized avatar which shimmered from a holographic image protruding from a metallic sphere hovering in the air.

"Level One is all about defending yourself, correct posture and being able to read your opponent's moves so as to predict his attack."

Markel slipped on the metallic glove, which was the hardware of the weapon, snapping it into place, and making it a snug fit on his hand.

"Some Clave Warriors use both hands, but for Level one, you only need one hand," Markel demonstrated as he continued his lesson. "So where were we?"

"You were saying that the Level one was all about defending one's self, and anticipating the opponent's move and trying to predict what his next move might be," Cassy replied totally engrossed in this process.

"Quite right, Cassandra," Markel replied.

"Now, once you are suited up, you can activate the dummy."

Markel turned his attention to the sphere hovering beside him. "Activate Training level one, program 2."

Immediately the sphere beeped and an image of a humanoid enemy armed with a similar weapon appeared in a shimmering, florescent, blue light.

"Watch my movements. They are fluid and smooth almost like a dance. There is no chorography, just learned skills, not choppy or stiff movements." Markel pointed out. "You must focus on your opponent's movements and be ready to switch your stance according to the direction he takes the fight; you must be prepared, light and quick on your feet."

"Why don't we attack them?"

"I would say nine times out of ten, they will kill us, or they will kill you, but we will learn that later. For now, I want you to learn how to take care of yourselves. Blocking is a very important skill to master in order to fight with a weapon like this one."

Markel demonstrated how it worked. "This is what you do." He closed his hand into a fist and thrust toward the holographic image, and the image fell to the ground. When he retracted his hand, a lighted blade shimmered from the metallic glove over his hand.

"A kill is not authorized during Level one; please refer to your handbook, Rule number 7," The computer announced simultaneously, as the projected computer image disappeared, and a live image replaced dead one.

"It is not the Clave way to kill, either." Justin pointed out.

"True. Just wanted them to see and learn that the weapon is deadly," Markel added, turning to address the two young Senators directly. "Follow your hearts. If facing a Rebel, I would not hesitate to take his life because he would not hesitate to take my own. But it is really your call to take a life or not."

"I'd rather not," Seth replied in a voice that expressed disgust at the thought of killing another living being.

"Nor would I!" Cassy exclaimed equally horrified at the idea of taking someone's life.

"The choice is yours," said Markel. "It is good that you value life. "In the meantime, we must deal with what destroyed it, which will take more than a soft heart. It will definitely take a strong hand wielding a heavy, Kathra-sword."

Odan nodded. "Kathra is the weapon of choice for a Clave Warrior. It is, in fact, a metallic instrument with the ability to expand the will of the user. Meaning, whatever the wielder thinks, the Kathra projects into the hand of the user. If you think of a laser piston, it will put one in your hand. If you think of a sword, it will put on in your hand. You must then be specific about size, shape, and so on. He reached into his duffle bag, pulled out two hand devices, and walked closer to Cassy and Seth.

"These are for you. I made them for you. Here let me show you how to put them on.'

Odan helped Cassy and Seth put on the metallic gloves of the Clave and showed them how to make them fit properly, and nodded to Markel.

"Teach on, Master Markel.

"It is so important," Justin stated. "Those will be very useful when the senate is re-established."

/////

Meanwhile....

"*Raptor's Claw*, this is Annapolis Command, Governor McCloud is away on a hunting expedition, but he has left us strict instructions that we are to welcome you all warmly with the finest that we have. Please proceed to docking port A12. Our welcoming crew and I will meet with you and your party. Command out."

Having received instructions on where to dock, Rex proceeded to the port hatch that was now opening its bay doors. He opened up an interior communication link. "This is the Captain. We are now docking on Teranosis. Everyone prepare to disembark."

In the cabin, Seth addressed Odan. "I don't like this idea of splitting up, Odan. I don't like it one bit!"

Odan replied, "Not to worry. Seth. Think positively."

"I am thinking positive, and the more I think about it, the more I feel like something will go wrong, drastically wrong with this idea."

"Listen to me Seth. I know because I feel the same thing. Believe me when I say that this is best. It is best for the mission that I go this way, and you continue to your destination without me. It is a huge possibility that I may cause some critical delays that will ensure greater sucess of the mission. You and Cassy must get to Shangri-La and reunite the Order. If it is meant for me to be, I will see you there when the time comes. But for now, I must go this way to lead this Rebel scum away from you."

"I think I understand. Although I don't like it still."

"Don't worry about me, Seth. I can take care of myself pretty well."

At those words, Seth smiled. "You've lived this long, so I can't doubt you on that note."

They both laughed.

"I don't need to tell you to take care of your sister. She is very likable by those of the opposite sex. I know I don't have to say__"

"No, you don't have to say it!" Seth smiled and suddenly exploded into a belly laugh.

"You are growing wise in your youth, my boy. Keep her safe."

A single nod from Seth confirmed that he understood what Odan meant, and that he knew what was required. He would have to assume more responsibility when Odan left their company.

"Trust Markel, Justin and Gorn. As I told you on Earth, they are my friends, and they will not allow any harm to come to you. But do be on your guard when you reach Shangri-La, whether I'm there or not.

Seth nodded, and Odan knew he would not disappoint him.

Chapter Twelve

Senators Trained, Odan Distances Himself

The *Raptor's Claw*, etching its way through the endless darkness of space, travelling at hyperspace, dropped down to below light speed as they approached the system known as Teranosis. The ship headed on a course that would take them to the right side of the planet, which was where Annapolis was in orbit. As it neared its destination, Captain Rex made an attempt to raise Annapolis Command. He was hoping his old friend McCloud was available to speak with him personally.

"Annapolis Command, this is *Raptor's Claw* requesting docking clearance, over."

"*Raptor's Claw*, this is Lt. Jonas. Welcome back to Annapolis. We greet you with open arms. Upon entering docking port A12, proceed to dock in landing bay A11. I will be there to greet you in person. Commander McCloud is out on a hunting expedition and will be back shortly. I have already notified him of your arrival and he had order me to break out all the finest things for you and your crew."

Smiling, Rex answered back and chuckled a bit. So far, he was winning on the bet he had made with Doc and Raymond.

"We do appreciate everything." Rex stated.

"See you all soon. Annapolis Command out.' Jonas replied

"*Raptor's Claw* out." Rex replied

In the pitch darkness of space, the *Raptor's Claw* slowly glided on a course that would take it to the opening doors of the docking bay on the surface of the moon. Since the fortress was built underground, the landing port opened up on the surface of the moon to expose a huge lighted tunnel. The *Raptor's Claw* lowered into the opening, disappearing from sight, as the port doors closed behind it. The ship sank into the lighted tunnel and proceeded through to the end of the tunnel, which opened into a huge bay of ships of different sizes all docked in assigned areas identified by numbers. The Captain moved the *Raptor's Claw* slowly and parked it at docking bay A11, as instructed, shut down down all of the ship's engines and drives, and reached for his interior coms control.

"To all crew and passengers! We have now landed on Annapolis for an overnight stay. Please take clothes and things you many need as we won't be coming back to the ship for such things. They have a dinner planned for us, a sort of banquet, so be prepared for that. Captain Rex out."

The party in the cabin gathered their things as directed by Rex. Odan assisted Cassy as she would not know what was proper for a lady to wear to a banquet of this nature. All met back in the cabin, including the crew.

"Did you all get necessary items?" Rex asked.

When all nods and verbal responses confirmed that the crew and passengers were ready, Rex opened the doors of the ship and led the way to the landing bay. When they emerged, Lt. Jonas and a few security guards greeted them warmly as McCloud had ordered.

"What's with security?" Rex asked

"One can never be too careful, Captain. It is simply a precaution that McCloud has had to adopt after an attempt to take over our place here."

"Really. By whom?'

"Those bad ass Rebels, that's who," Jonas replied. "Who do you have traveling with you?"

"My crew, whom you know. However, this here is Seth, Cassandra his sister, Odan, Markel, Justin, and Gorn. I am taking them somewhere for a sizable price."

"Ahh, your ticket through the stars, is it?"

"On this go around, yes," Rex stated.

"So why are you stopping here?"

"I have some business on Teranosis and this is on the way to where we will be going."

"Kill two birds with one go?" Jonas asked.

"You know it! More profit this way."

"Come then. Let me take you to your quarters."

As Jonas led them through the fortress, he and Rex spoke freely, catching up on a lot of things. As they walked along, Seth turned around and noticed that Markel and Justin were directly behind them and Odan and Gorn were directly before them He looked at his sister as he realized that she had noticed as well that Odan and the others were keeping a watchful eye on them.

Before long, Seth and Cassy settled down in adjoining rooms. The others likewise settled into single rooms where they rested until the banquet.

Cassandra moved around her room observing the strange things on the wall and the interesting sculptures. A light rapping on the door which led to her brother's room interrupted her curiosity. Placing her hand on the silver panel, she immediately noticed that it turned white with the bright light and the door swung open, revealing her brother.

'What do you think so far?" Seth asked.

"I think we ought to hop on the fastest thing headed back to Earth!" Cassy cried out.

"Seriously, now, Cass," Seth prodded.

"I am being serious. We have no idea what this is all about and it feels like we are being brought into the middle of it without knowing the details. We don't know this Universal Order and we certainly know very little about this Clave."

"They are teaching us," Seth replied.

"I hope we learn it in enough time. How are we going to pull this off? They talk about us leading other leaders of nations against this Zymon Keltor who supposedly killed our parents and our brothers and sisters! I mean, we should want to! But, I don't know. Maybe things are better left alone."

"How can you say that?" Seth asked. "These people are being led by a dictator. They didn't elect Zymon into power. He took power over all the nations when he destroyed the Universal Order and the Clave. We are here to re-establish what he tore down."

"I know. I just don't think it will succeed," Cass replied.

"Come on, Cass. You have to believe it will. You have to have hope that we can do it," Seth urged

"Hope?"

"Yeah. When you believe something against all the odds. You just turn a blind eye to it and hope for the best outcome, despite what you see."

Cassy nodded. She sighed. "You're right. I don't like that Odan is leaving us with Markel and the other two."

"Markel, Justin and Gorn are not unlike Odan. They may be a bit younger but they have our best interest at heart. They won't let anything happen to us," Seth stated. "I think they are trustworthy. Besides, we can pick their brains for information about the Clave and the UO."

"I suppose we should learn all we can," Cass agreed.

"If you don't mind, I'll sleep in here with you on the couch there." Seth stated.

"You don't have to."

"I promised Odan I'd look after you." Seth replied.

Seth moved to the couch and lay down as Cassy stretched out on the bed. Within minutes both were sound asleep.

/////

Across the corridor, Odan Amir's door swished open, and he stalked out heading down a few doors to Markel's room. He rapped on the door, and Markel opened it.

"I am going to find Captain Rex before I get left behind," Odan said.

Markel reached out and put his hand on Odan's shoulder and pulled him inside his quarters, not allowing him to protest.

"Nonsense. You are just worried about Shatra finding out where we are."

"That and some other things, yes." Odan admitted. "This situation could get mighty ugly if she finds us, Markel. I tell you she's right on our asses, and if we don't watch it, we might as well turn ourselves in right this minutes to save time and save people from getting hurt."

"You were one to always worry too much," Markel scolded kindly.

"I have a right to worry. And you should be worried, too!"

"The Clave taught us how to use worry to our advantage instead of just worrying and panicking!"

"Right. You're right. We learned to use worry and doubt to prepare for the worst, but to hope for the best. Yes. To always hope for the best." Odan remembered his training.

"It didn't seem like you were hoping, Odan," Markel pointed out.

"I wasn't," Odan confessed. "I wasn't even preparing for the worst. I was just worried about the worst."

Markel chuckled a bit and placed a hand on Odan's shoulder. "I understand. She has an effect on you, but you must realize that she betrayed the Clave and led it to its destruction. She will destroy you too if she gets her hands on you."

"I know," Odan replied. "I think that is what I fear the most."

"You must resist her. Try to block her out. Don't entertain her with any conversation because that is what she wants... conversation so she can see, hear, and know where you are through the sounds about you when she's connected with you."

"Yes, I know." Odan shook his head. "I cannot believe I almost gave up the Clave to be with her."

"Well, may the gods be praised you didn't do that! People do strange things for love, Odan. You came out of love with your life intact. That's better than what most can say."

Odan and Markel laughed a bit at that statement, for it was true. He had dodged a fire- ball. How he had done it was beyond him now. He supposed it was because of his love for the Clave, and he knew it would be his love for the Clave that would do it again.

"My love for the Clave kept me from her before. I do believe it will be my love for the Clave that will keep me from her again. As long as I stay true to my beliefs, she has no power over me."

Markel patted him on the shoulder and smiled. "Now that's the Odan Amir I know."

/////

In the VIP quarters, Doc Langstrom examined two dresses that had been selected for her to wear to the festivities. The red one consisted of a bra and skirt with a shawl to cover the shoulders. The other black, silk, strapless dress would cling to her body down to just above the knees, tight fitting, but comfortable. After deliberating for a few minutes, she put the black one aside and opted for the red one which would also complement her red hair. Whoever had selected the dresses knew she would pick this one. In silence she wondered if McCloud had selected these two dresses for her. And why was she thinking about him?

"Oh, no! Here we go! I AM thinking about him! I MUST stop that, right this minute!"

Having taken a bath with scented oils and bubbles, Langstrom never felt so relaxed. She plopped down on the bed as it wasn't time to put on that dress yet. Instead, she tried to relax.

/////

Down the corridor, Dex was getting herself ready, as well. The dresses selected for her were different from the ones that had been chosen for Doc, but still very pretty. Dex selected a long, blue gown with only one strap over the shoulder. Her dress, a sleeveless, sky blue empire style, pleated from below the breast line, flowed elegantly downward, brushing the top of her feet. She had never worn the shoes like the ones that went with the dress before in her life. She usually wore boots that looked more like men's shoes. She wasn't comfortable wearing the dress and all that she had on under it. It was simply too much! She couldn't wait for all of this hoopla to end. However, when she saw a reflection of herself in the mirror, she could not help feeling pretty.

For the first time in history, Dex released her hair from the large braid and brushed it out. Her long locks cascaded down her back to her buttocks. The tight braid that had etched beautiful natural waves in her hair reminded her of waves of the ocean, no particular pattern, each row unique. To keep her hair from falling into her face, she took a portion from the front and pulled it toward the back, tying it with a leather band so that it flowed down around the sides. Dex knew nothing of makeup, despite having an assortment of makeup at her disposal. She did know of lipstick and applied it to her lips, giving them a more inviting, sexy look, but that was it.

/////

Raymond was a tough customer, but since he had been to Annapolis before several times, they knew how to accommodate him already. His clothes were set out for him, as well, just his size. There was a nice white shirt, trousers, and a decent, black robe that wasn't three sizes too big for him. This robe was designed for dwarfs.

For this occasion, Raymond trimmed his beard a bit, brushed his hair, and slicked it down after taking a bath. He looked and smelled fresh, which was against the norm. However, if he were to get a chance to dance with Naomi, the only dwarf female on Annapolis, he had to freshen up some. He cleaned his boots and put them on. He was ready. Ooops, one last thing. He wasn't going anywhere without his sword. After all, he was a security man, and he'd have to be secure and look the part, didn't he? He grabbed the blade and put it in his holster, strapping it around his middle. Although he had no intention of using the blade at such an occasion, one could never be too sure.

"It's better to be prepared," Raymond said to himself, as he looked in the mirror. He gave a single nod.

/////

McCloud bolted through the door of Rex's quarters without knocking and grabbed him in a big bear hug. This turned into the two men trying to see who could flip the other one over on his back, but the tussle soon broke up in laughter. The two friends could not hide the joy of their reunion.

"You've put on a few pounds, my friend," McCloud said.

"Only so you wouldn't fly me over your backside," Rex replied.

"HA! You've grown a bit wiser, I see," McCloud stated. "What brings you out this way?"

"Business as usual," Rex replied, as they both sat down in the sitting area. "Which brings me to what I have to tell you."

"What's that?" McCloud asked.

"I can't stay here, but I will leave my crew with you for a short stay."

"Short stay?" McCloud asked. "What the blazes is going on?"

"Well, I've got to go to Teranosis to drop off a package. That is business. My crew and passengers will need to stay here, and they need no Rebel interaction, if you know what I mean."

McCloud nodded. "I understand. Might I ask you something about them then?"

"Sure."

"If they don't want Rebels bothering them, then they must be against them, right?"

"Right," Rex replied

"Tell me, what nation are they from?"

"I will tell you because I respect you and because you need to know. They are Clave Warriors and two Senators. Their mission is to return to Shangri-La and bring back the UO and the Clave to overthrow the Rebel leader Zymon Keltor."

A slight smile spread across McCloud's face. "By the stars, this is good news! I hated when that Zymon Keltor took over from the Zegers and then UO. Keltor turned everything upside down. Now everything must be approved by him! I've been fighting him for years. He has tried to merge with me, turn this place into a Rebel colony, and make this an outpost for the Rebs. I have dodged him several times. The thing is when he comes through here with that woman...that X-Clave woman! Oh, she really gets on my worst nerve."

"Will rebel patrols come searching here while I'm on Teranosis?"

"Sometimes they do and sometimes they don't. I can never predict when they will."

"If they do, you send my crew and passengers on their way, and I will rendezvous with them on the other side of Teranosis."

"There are Rebels on Teranosis. You do know that, don't you?"

"No, I didn't." Rex's eyebrows shot up at the thought of Odan accompanying him to Teranosis. Suddenly, the whole idea of stopping here seemed wrong and pointless. However, he knew he had business here, but he guessed it could have waited. Yet then again he didn't want to disappoint his Rymelion business friend either. They were just going to have to be very careful not to get noticed.

McCloud saw Rex looking blankly off at nothing in particular and called him on it.

"What's on your noddle now? Must be a female. That look can only come from worrying about a woman or your work."

Rex laughed after shaking his head, "Work, my friend. I'm worried about going to Teranosis now that you tell me there are Rebs there. One of my passengers wants to tag along with me on this trip because of some reasons that concern the mission. But if there are Rebs down there, going there will also endanger the mission. I'm not too sure he would want to go, knowing Rebs might be there."

"Only one way to find out," McCloud replied. "Ask him. Ask him at dinner. My servants have gone to get them all. We will all meet in the banquet hall."

Rex nodded, as they left his quarters and moved through the underground fortress where dimly-lighted, motion sensitive orbs strategically placed equal distances apart allowed them to easily find the way to the banquet hall. Each one glowed when beings approached. He walked down numerous passageways, so many that Rex feared that he would lose his way; but having been there before, he regained his bearings.

After a long hike, the two friends walked into the banquet hall to see the place filling up. Rex spotted his crew and his passengers already seated and dressed for the occasion. He took his place at the head of the table there as Captain. He remembered that he needed to talk to Odan about their excursion trip. Immediately, Rex rose and motioned for Odan to come away with him to the side for a chat. When they had distanced themselves so that the others could not hear, Rex voiced his concerns about Odan going with him to Teranosis.

"Odan, I just heard from our friend McCloud that Teranosis has Rebels on the surface. I do not think it would be safe for you to come with me, knowing that they are there."

Odan frowned with disappointment, but sighed. "Rebels before us and Shatra behind. I would do better going forward, my friend. I endanger the entire mission by staying here with the rest of my party. I cannot risk drawing more attention to them with Shatra on my heels. I can hold my own against the Rebs on Teranosis. I will just have to blend in as best as I can."

"It's suicide, Odan. In the things that you wear you'll be noticed right off."

"I can change my raiment. I have brought other things to wear that are not definitive of the Clave. I will blend in," Odan stated.

"If you say so, then I guess I've done my part which is to warn you."

"I will be posing as your bodyguard. The Rebs won't suspect a thing," Odan stated. "I'm a good actor, believe me."

Rex chuckled a bit, "For your own sake, I hope you are."

The pair moved back to the table and sat down just as McCloud began to speak.

"Ladies and Gents, tonight we celebrate the return of good friends and the reuniting of old lovers. Let the music play and bring in the grub!"

McCloud clapped his hands, and the food that had been tantalizing them for some time now was brought from the kitchen: an array of rhinebuck steaks, vegetables of all sorts, salads, and dips. It was a feast that all would fancy. Everyone ate and ate again, more than they normally would eat. Then they danced with glasses of ale in their hands, swinging round about in happy circles, dancing and shouting, singing and laughing. Langstrom found herself in the strong arms of McCloud. Raymond had searched and searched and found his love at a faraway table and pulled her to the dance floor where they also danced the night away.

Then Markel, glancing over at Cassandra, rose from his seat and moved to where she sat and held out his hand.

"Would you care to dance, Cassandra?" Markel asked.

Cassandra's face reddened at first, because she didn't know any of these dances. She was from Earth and knew nothing of alien ways, especially how to dance properly.

"But I don't know how...."

"Dancing is something that all races know how to do, Cassandra. It is much the same as it is on Earth. Come. You'll learn."

Cassandra looked at her brother Seth, who smirked and nodded.

"What do you need his approval for?" Markel asked. "Where is your own brain?"

"In my head!" Cassandra replied, as she rose and took his hand.

"I should hope so," Markel chuckled.

As he led her to the dance floor and put his arm around her waist, she put her arm about his shoulders and held his hand. Then he led her in the dance that most people were now doing, which took them moving and spinning about the floor to the right. After a few spins and steps to the right, Cassandra found it rather easy to follow Markel and smiled.

"You dance very well," Cassandra complimented him.

"You're not so bad yourself. You catch on quickly. It will be useful in training for other things. But that will come later.

Justin and Gorn did not sit still either, they too found ladies to dance with. The only ones sitting alone were Seth, Odan and Rex.

Then a young lady with long blonde hair came to the table and looked at Seth.

"Were you going to sit this one out, Sir?"

"Oh, my Lady. I know not how to dance these fine dances," Seth replied.

"Do you want to learn?"

"I would like that."

"Then what are you waiting for. Come with me."

Seth followed her to the dance floor. It did not take long for Seth to find his feet, and they were dancing along with the rest. Joyous laughter and chatter echoed through the hall, and the Senators and Clave members forgot about Rebel patrols, Zymon Keltor, and the mission for a few hours, thanks to Rex and his friend McCloud.

Filled with dancing, eating and drinking, the revelers ended the festivities of the night.   Rex and Odan departed from Annapolis in a shuttle headed for Teranosis. Since the shuttle was from Annapolis, they were given docking instructions freely. They approached the planet and touched down at the crack of dawn.

Most beings were sleeping at that time, but the natives of Teranosis were known for partying well into the wee hours of the next mornings. Odan and Rex touched down, signed in, and took a hover car to the most popular joint on the planet, the Astrodome, the place where Rex was instructed to find this Rymelion female. Odan, having changed his attire in the cabin of the shuttle, now wore civilian attire, which made him look more like Rex's father instead of his body guard. Despite the sunshine signaling morning, the place was still hopping when they got there. They paid the transport and entered the establishment, paying the high price at the door for entrance.

The Astrodome was dimly lit but had light orbs which were motion sensitive throughout the place. As they moved into the main part of the place, Rex noticed the stage, dance floor, bar and tables. Odan took note of the Rebs and pointed them out to Rex. Rex nodded and began searching for his connection…the Rymelion female. As his eyes scanned the room, he saw the face that was on the picture he had of her.

"She's here. Come on."

Odan nodded and moved through the crowds toward the female. When they were close, standing right next to her, Rex took out the package from his dusters inside pocket and handed the package to her.

"This is from Zydak."

The Rymelion female had been in a conversation, but when she heard the visitor mention Zydak's name, she turned to him, surprised. Everything got quiet around the immediate areas about them as she looked at Rex and spoke.

"What is it?"

"My orders were to deliver, not to explain what's in it. To tell the truth, I don't know what's in it. I only know where it came from. Now I must go," Rex stated.

'You've got a lot of nerve coming here saying that!"

Rex didn't listen and turned and walked away as he had been told to do. Odan walked backwards from him, covering their backs while following Rex out. As they neared the exit, the Rymelion yelled at them.

"Wait! You cannot just deliver a package and leave without telling me what is in it! Wait until I open it so that I can respond." She opened the package and saw a picture and a note that read, *"Here is a picture of me holding our son. Because you deserted me while I was carrying him, you will never see him or me again. Zydak"*

Rex remembering the urgency in the voice of client, *"Give it to her and leave immediately,"* caused Rex to quicken his steps out of the tavern and away from the voice demanding answers and explanations. Just before he and Odan reached the ship, they heard a blood-curdling scream from the tavern. The Rymelion female screamed for others in the room to stop the two who had handed her the note. Because Rex and Odan had entered the place quickly and smoothly, no one had noticed them come or go so they could not connect them with the Rymellian's tirade.

What Rex did not know was that in the Rymelion's world, the men gave birth to their children. Zydak wanted this particular Rymelion female to know that he had given birth to their son whom she would never see. The cry from the Rymelion female exploded and echoed for miles. She later put a bounty ad on Rex because he was her only chance of finding Zydak and her son. Rex and Odan managed to blast off the planet before the officials could order the command center to deny take off. They calculated that they had escaped being detained by three minutes.

Chapter Thirteen

Romance, Partying, Reconnections

Back on Sansadar, the Gamma Rebel Patrol continued its search for the Captain and crew of the lone ship that had left Romes IV days before. Having met with the flight command officer of Sansadar, the three-man patrol had learned a lot from the commander.

"I don't think the Captain of this ship is who the Emperor is looking for, Mandus." Sampson said.

'Why do you say that?"

"Because the flight command officer said there were only two people on that ship, a human and an alien. We are looking for a group of six and a crew of four," Sampson replied.

"We still have to check it out to be certain."

"It's a dead end, "Kyle added. "Like he said."

"We have our orders" Mandus replied. "We cannot just let this slide because we think the numbers are not right. Like before, they could be hiding the rest of the crew and passengers."

"There's that," Kyle said.

"That could be possible," Sampson agreed. "But I doubt it."

The trio walked the streets of Sansadar, talking among themselves and finally found the docking port of the ship they were looking for. Since they were Rebel soldiers, they had been given the codes to unlock the entrance to the port. Mandus pressed in the code and the door opened. To their surprise, they were greeted by a tall, lanky humanoid.

"Can I help; you Rebels? He asked. "Looking for someone or something in particular?"

"Captain McNair, we are looking for Captain McNair."

"He gone. Come back when he here."

The door closed.

Mandus knocked on the door. The door slid open again.

"Wat you want?" He asked.

"Who are you? Do you ride with Captain McNair?"

"Me no answer questions! You ask Captain McNair. He tell you who is who. Now you go away, or I sic Mojo on you."

Behind the man, a huge, vicious-looking dog with its teeth bared growled and poked its head into the light beside the man's legs. "You go now before Mojo becomes angry from the knock on the door."

Mandus held up his hands and backed away, visibly shaken from the sight of the dog. "No more knock."

With a sigh, Mandus turned and looked around. He found a place with some shade from the sun to stand under, and he and his men moved there.

"We'll have to wait and watch for the Captain to come back," Mandus said.

Hours seemed to pass by slowly for the team, and then they saw a few men approaching the door.

"Hey! You there! FREEZE!" Mandus cried out. "Don't open that door!"

The two men who were headed toward the door looked around to see the three Rebel soldiers and froze with their hands in the air. Mandus approached them.

"Sampson, contact the Captain. Kyle, you watch the door so the dog doesn't get out."

"Aye!" they both cried out.

"Captain McNair, I presume?"

"Yes. That's me. What's this all about?"

"You left Romes IV some few days ago?"

'Yes. A routine run from there to Sansadar."

"Did you smuggle six passengers with you?"

"No. Negative. I did not." McNair stated.

"Who is your friend here?'

"One of my crew. His name is Pious."

"Is he telling us the truth?"

"Yes, he is telling you the truth."

"Excuse me, Mandus, Captain Zetos is on his way to search the vessel. He is bringing a Reader."

Mandus looked to the Captain of the ship. "How many crew members do you have, McNair?"

"Four."

"We count only three so far. One in there and two of you here. Where's the third?"

"Shopping for supplies," McNair stated.

"We have orders to search your vessel and to probe your crew with a Reader."

"It was searched before we left Romes IV," McNair replied.

"We have orders to search it again," Mandus stated. "Is this going to be a problem?"

'No. Search it. Although I do not have a clue what you are looking for. I've told you we have not smuggled any passengers anywhere. We are strictly a cargo freighter."

Running through the crowds of people, Zetos, Vern, and Klevus came up to where Mandus, Kyle, and Sampson were detaining Captain McNair and his crew. Behind the three of them was a bald-headed male with a dangling earpiece.

Captain Zetos stepped up to Mandus... "Report."

"Sir, we found the name of the ship, came to stake it out, and found one man in the bay area with a vicious dog. We did not go in, nor did we continue to question the man inside because of the threats he made concerning the dog. So we stayed out here until the Captain and his crew returned. We detained them and began asking questions while we made contact with you."

Captain Zetos turned to the Captain. "You can put your hands down, Captain."

"Thank you," McNair replied sarcastically.

"Captain, we are under orders from the Emperor to look for a ship with a crew of four and six passengers: four Clavemen and 2 Senators. Now, you could be the crew of four, but we have no idea. We've been ordered to search thoroughly when we find a ship in question, just to make sure it is not what we are looking for."

"Please do search it. I've already told your man here that we had no passengers when we arrived here to Sansadar."

"Then this will only take a few minutes. Can you control the dog inside?"

"Mojo will do exactly what I tell him."

When the door opened, Mojo burst out, ran up to McNair, and sat down. McNair said one word. "Stay." Then he turned to Zetos. "Go ahead and search the ship."

Taking off their backpacks, the Gamma patrol got the necessary equipment to scan the ship thoroughly. They were led inside the ship by one of the crew members. Four hours later, they emerged empty handed. Zetos turned to the Reader and nodded to him.

"Begin your scans of the crew."

A single nod came from the tall, slender bald-headed man who stood before the Captain of the *Minister,* looking into his eyes. The man didn't blink, look off, or turn his head, but stayed focused on him. After a few moments of silence, the tall, slender Reader moved to the man beside him, looking him in the eyes as he did the Captain. However, this man seemed not to like her intrusion. He tried to turn away from her but found that he couldn't. In the end, the Reader always won.

"Anything so far?" Zetos asked?

"So far no passengers that I can see that traveled with them."

"No need to probe the others then. I will believe the scans of these two that there were not any passengers," Zetos replied. He walked up to Captain McNair. "I am glad to say that your ship is clean, Captain. You may resume what you were doing."

"I would have told you that and spared you the hours of searching, but I realize that you had to do your job." McNair took out a cigar and lit it. "We done here?"

"We're done," Zetos stated. "You are free to go."

The Gamma patrol packed up its gear and headed back to their ship. They had come all this way for nothing, or so it seemed. Captain Zetos was now convinced that the *Minister* was not the ship that the party of six had employed. As this thought rolled over and over in his mind, his legs began to move faster and faster. The sooner the rest of the Rebel Forces received this information, the closer they would be to finding the right ship...the closer to finding the six passengers that had outsmarted them.

Captain Zetos led his team at a swift pace back to the shuttle. He then moved to the cockpit and prepared the ship for departure and hit the communications.

"Sansadar Command, patch me through to Rebel Leader Zolotan and Commander Shatra."

"Hold on one minute."

After a slight pause, the technician followed orders and made the connection. Immediately, the faces of Commander Shatra and General Zolotan flashed on the screen.

"General, Commander, I would like to inform you that we have searched the *Minister* and its crew with scanners, probes, and a Reader on

Sansabar, and found no evidence that there were passengers on that vessel when it arrived here. Therefore, we can eliminate them."

Zolotan smiled. "Good work. We now have four more reports to hear of. Return to base and take a few days off before returning to duty. General Zoltan out."

"Nice work there, Captain Zetos." Shatra stated. "I have a hunch that the party we are looking for has come out through Star Command Omega One."

"We'll soon find out," Zetos replied. "You can be certain that they did not come out through Sansadar."

"True, Shatra. Out."

Commander Shatra ended the link by pressing a button on her console in her VIP quarters on Star Base Omega One. The reports from the five patrols would be spilling in over the communications in the next few hours, and she would soon know which direction Odan and his party had gone. Although she already had her suspicions, she knew to wait for confirmation from the patrols to make doubly sure her mind wasn't playing tricks on her and that her connections with Odan were for real.

/////

On Rangolia, which rested on the outskirts of the Andromeda, Captain Raz and his patrol were inside a tavern, trying to gain information the old fashioned way, by word of mouth. The smelly, smoke-filled bar and grill was filled to capacity with aliens of all sorts and sizes: humanoids, non-humanoids, Rymelions, and Changlings. Just about any species of alien from the three known galaxies were present, including some that were unidentified. It was in places like this that one had to watch one's step and beware of one's mouth. Each could get one into trouble.

Raz sat at the bar and ordered drinks for the five of them, trying to blend in with the crowd. Then, after some time of sipping at the still bubbling liquid in the glass, Raz got the bartender's attention.

The bartender was a rather chubby human, wearing a white apron and a long-sleeved shirt. With a loud baritone voice, he spoke up, "What can I do for ye?"

"I'm looking for the Captain of the *Deringer* II, a cargo ship for transport."

The bartender then pointed to the left. "Over there. The table closest to the window. The Captain has his back to the wall and his boots on the table."

Raz nodded and flipped the man a few terrons for the information. The bartender quickly scraped them into his palm and deposited them into his apron pocket.

Raz then moved away from the bar and his four men followed him. They approached the table with the man sitting very comfortably with his boots on the table.

"Mind if we sit and talk business?" Raz asked.

The Captain of the *Deringer* II opened one eye, glanced at the five of them and then opened the other eye. He moved his hands from behind his head, his boots from the table, and sat upright. "Not at all, do sit down and make yourselves comfortable."

"We are looking for transport."

"I figured as much. Where you headed?"

"That would depend on where your last transport run took you?"

"It took me right here, gentlemen."

"Did you have passengers with you then?"

"Why you asking me that? I normally don't divulge private information about my previous runs."

"Alright. That's good. I just wanted to make sure we could trust you."

"I'm as trustable as the next guy. Probably more trustable than many. I live by a code of honor that many don't consider. It holds me fast to keep my word and to always do what's right and fair."

'Would that code be the Clave code?"

The middle-aged man leaned forward, putting his elbows on the table and his fingers intertwined.

"Something of the sort, you might say."

"Ahh," Raz replied. "We are headed to Star base Omega One."

A single nod came from the man. "My name is Dar, short for Dartan. You can call me Captain Dar. I have a crew of four, including myself. They are scattered throughout the bar here. If you don't mind us leaving in the morning, our ship is in docking bay 24A. My crew is a bit too tipsy for flight."

"Safety first, I always say," Raz stated. "We'll find accommodations and meet up in the morning, say two hours after sun up?"

"Deal."

Raz and his crew moved out of the tavern and acquired accommodations in the n*eares*t hotel. They ordered in food, ate, and crashed. Morning came swiftly, and before they knew it, they were heading to docking bay 24A.

"Captain, when do you plan to reveal to them that we aren't who we say we are?" Zac asked.

"Right now. We get aboard her, and then we take off our robes." Raz stated.

"Oh, hell, they are going to blow us to smithereens."

"They could if we are not prepared for that," Raz stated.

"I take it that we will be ready for that."

"Yes, we will," Raz replied.

The cylinder-shaped docking ports were lined up and stretched for several meters around the city. Finding the correct one, they knocked on the door, and Captain Dar opened it for them. "Welcome."

"Thank you," Raz stated.

Still wearing the robes, the five Rebel officers entered the landing bay area of the *Deringer* II. Raz looked at the ship and found it to be a fine, medium-sized freighter/cargo ship. As they walked closer, Raz could see

that Captain Dar had put a lot of work into making the ship more efficient
to run in the black market.

"Nice vessel you have here, Captain Dar."

"Thank you. I put a lot of work into her with my own funds. I didn't
buy her in this condition. I had to do a lot work on her before she looked
like this," Dar stated. "Go ahead and get aboard."

"Before we do that, I'd like to share something with you."

'"What's that?"

Raz looked at his men and nodded, "Okay boys, take off the cloaks."

The men took off the robes and dropped them to the cement. Then
they pulled out their laser pistols.

"Let's remain calm, and no one will get hurt, Captain. Call your crew
out here."

Captain Dar reluctantly spoke into his wrist piece and called his crew
mates out of the ship. One by one they came out to see the five Rebel
officers standing there with their lasers pointed at their Captain.

"Come out and join your Captain here, folks."

"What is this?" Dar asked. "We've done nothing illegal!"

"That's what we are here to find out, Captain." Raz stated. "A few
days ago, you left Romes IV where four Clave Warriors and two Senators
gained transport and managed to escape us. We have been sent out to
investigate the five known ships that left Romes IV that day. Your ship was
one of them. Now, the ship in question had a crew of four. Your ship might
be the ship because you have the same number of crew, but we need to
search your ship."

"Any passengers we might have had would be long gone by now, IF
we had them. But we did not smuggle any passengers. We had routine,
legitimate transport of cargo, nothing more," Captain Dar stated

'After we search your ship and ascertain that the passengers are not
still aboard your vessel, we will then detain you from further travel until

a Reader can scan you and your crew to make certain that you had no passengers traveling with you from Romes IV to Rangolia."

As Raz spoke to Captain Dar, the rest of Raz's team took their gear and searched the vessel thoroughly.

"Darn it, you Rebel scum, you are interfering with my livelihood! I need to transport cargo to make a living. If I don't make runs, I don't get paid; others will get paid. And I and my crew end up starving."

"It's not as bad as all that. You're exaggerating."

"Hardly! We have families to worry about."

"It won't take but a day for the Reader to get here. Until then I will notify Rangolia Command that your ship is grounded."

Captain Dar stalked off, grumbling curses under his breath.

"Zax, Roger, You two stay here and make sure this ship stays put."

Zax and Roger nodded, for they were finished with the scans. "The ship is clean, Captain."

Raz nodded to Zax and called for the Reader over the coms to put a rush on it. Raz and the other two officers took over guarding the grounded *Deringer* II at midnight, giving Zac and Roger twelve hours to sleep. Until the Reader came, that is how things would go.

Raz was asleep when the Reader came. Roger ran to his room and knocked. "Reader has arrived, Captain Raz!"

Raz was up and into his suit within minutes. He moved quickly but smoothly. His job would soon be over, or at least he hoped so. Inside the hotel lobby, he spotted the very short, bald-headed lady, who was actually quite beautiful. She wore a pair of high heels that made her somewhat taller; she still stood only about four feet. Looking down, he held out his hand to her.

"Greetings, Ms...."

"My name is of no matter. On these occasions we give no names to speak of," she replied smartly. "Now, where's this Captain and his crew?"

"Right this way."

Straight down to business, Raz thought. Good. He didn't have to direct her or get her focused on anything; she was ten steps ahead of him. Leading her and Zak through the crowds, they found their way back to docking bay 24A. When they knocked on the door, the guard opened it, and all of them escorted the Reader into the cabin of the ship where the four crew members waited for the Reader's arrival.

The short lady immediately started to do her job. She studied the Captain first, gazing directly into his eyes, then did the same for the remaining crew members, one at a time.   When she had finished, she turned to the Rebel Captain.

"Captain Raz, they had no passengers on this ship from Romes IV to this planet."

Raz gave a nod. "Thank you."   He then spoke into his wrist piece. "Rangolia Command, *Deringer* II is free to fly.   I repeat, *Deringer* II is free to fly. The grounding is lifted."

"Rangolia Command reads you loud and clear. Rangolia Command, out."

Raz turned to Captain Dar. "As you were, Captain."

"You give the Rebel Alliance a bad name, Captain Raz. You should have come clean to me in the bar!"

"We didn't want an incident with all those other aliens there. In the way we did this, we only let you know we were Rebels, which is how we wanted it done."

"What was it? FEAR? Were you afraid to confront us in the bar?"

"It wasn't necessary to let all those aliens know our business, Captain."

"I guess I understand now," Dar stated.

"Sorry I made you look like an ass in front of your crew, but I didn't have much of a choice," Raz replied.

"Apology accepted. Next time, if there is a next time, I'd prefer a little honesty up front."

"So noted," Raz stated. "Take good care of that ship, Captain. She's a nice one."

The Alpha Rebel patrol returned to their ship and powered it up for departure, while Raz reported in.

"Captain Raz to General Zolotan and Commander Shatra."

The shuttle's computer took a few minutes to make the links, and finally the digital display gave the images of both people.

"What is it?" Zolotan asked.

"Report," Shatra commanded.

"Sir, Commander. We caught up with the Captain of the *Deringer II*, searched her, and had a Reader scan the crew. The ship was clean, and they did not have passengers aboard their vessel from Romes IV to Rangolia."

"This is great news."

"How can you call this great news?" Zolotan asked.

"Because it narrows down where they might be. And it further confirms my hunch that they are headed towards Shangri-La."

"If that's the case, why not prepare for this possibility."

"Let's."

"Zolotan, out."

"Shatra, out."

Raz's eyebrow rose in interest. "Captain Raz, out."

Chapter Fourteen

Search for Senators Intensifies

On Erosdad, the Delta Rebel patrol and its assigned security team, led by Governor Drake, headed for the Flight Command Center for the entire world wide city of Eronia. They drew much attention from the crowds still on the streets at the eleventh hour, which many natives considered early. It was the beginning of what most would call the happy hours. As predicted by the Delta patrol members, projectiles flew at them, and the security team did little to deter it from happening.

Just as Governor Drake had said, there were various alien life in a mixture of humanoids from nearly all three known galaxies who did not care for Rebels. Erosdad was known for its planet wide city that never slept. Everything was open throughout the days and nights. In a full circling of all three suns, there were two different daylights. There was the rising of the two suns which was the hottest and then a period of darkness and then the rising of the lone star, which was the coolest and then a second darkness. A completion of both was one day. At the present time, the lone star had just disappeared over the sky scrapers in the distance.

Reaching Flight Control, the security team split, one part staying on the outside of the building while the other part went inside with the Rebel patrol to inquire about the ship that had blasted off from Romes IV a few days before.

The operator at the console searched for the name of the ship in the system computer. "We should have it right here."

"The Blue Star is the ship's name."

"Right," he confirmed. "I do recall that name, if you can believe that. It belongs to an old guy, although he doesn't look that old. He wears an old robe. Looks like an old Clave man. His crew wears the same sort of get up, too."

"Where's his ship located?" asked Talos

"Docking bay 101C, Building 44A. It's a high-rise on the dark side of the planet. Only the lone star shines on that side.'

"Where might I find the Captain and its crew?"

"You might try the clubs throughout the city. Yet there are several. You'd have to know what type of ship it is. If it's a freighter and they work under the table, then you'd find them in the darker clubs, trying to make contacts in the shadier places, the quieter places. If they are legitimate business, then they would be more open and deal business in the public places."

"We aren't sure about the kind of ship it is," Talos replied. "However, we will find them."

Talos turned to his four men. "J.C., you and Ryan stake out the ship. If anyone returns to the ship or if anyone is in the docking bay, let us know."

"Aye, Sir."

"The rest of us will check out the taverns throughout the city. This will take some time, at least a day or two. In the meantime, I will request a Reader to come here and lodge. When we need his or her services, he or she will be available."

"Sounds like a plan.' Ryan stated.

"Let's move out.'

The security team split their numbers to accommodate the division of the Delta Patrol, and as they exited the Flight Control center, they went in opposite directions.

J.C. and Ryan with their security escort moved through the city towards the nearest sky train, a rail system that picked passengers up at certain stations and transported them to various destinations throughout the city. As they boarded the sky train, riders already aboard glared at them with disgust. Some made quiet comments, while others spoke loudly.

"Rebel scum!" an unidentified voice rang out.

"Who invited you blue bellies here?" another yelled.

"Go back to your outposts and squeeze the life out of someone else! Don't think you can come here and do any of your mischief!" a female added her displeasure at the Rebels presence on the train. J.C. remained quiet as did Ryan. The security guards moved into a more protective position near the two Rebel officers.

"Why are you protecting them?" one man asked.

"We have our orders." The security man stated. "Just mind your own business. We have our own business, and you have yours!"

Finally, the train jerked to a stop, and the party stepped off into darkness. The security guards used orb lights that hovered and followed their every move, and lighted their pathway well enough for them to maneuver through the dark streets.

On the dark side of the city, the population in the streets was considerably fewer than they had encountered in the inner city. It was more like a ghost town. Occasionally, they heard footsteps, but saw no one. They were relying on the security guards' knowledge of the area to guide them to the right place. Hopefully, they would end up at the right high-rise where the ship was docked.

Finally, after a long hike through the darkness, entourage reached the landing bay of the 'Blue Star.'

J.C. knocked on the locked door of landing bay. There was complete silence. He knocked repeatedly for a period of time, pausing for seconds between each rap. No one answered. JC looked at Ryan, who saw his leader's face turn red and his breathing become heavy as he struggled to contain his anger.

"Darn it, Ryan! Looks like we are out in the cold."

"Yeah."

"We wait," the security guard insisted. "If this is home for them, you realize it will take days for them to come back here."

"Yes, I know. That is why I hope Captain Talos finds them."

Talos and his team of two men and the two security officers had found their way into one of the planet's most popular taverns, the Bottom's Up. They settled at the bar and ordered drinks. Talos asked the bartender if he had seen a man named Captain Baltar.

"Don't know anyone by that name. Sorry."

"He's the Captain of a ship called The Blue Star."

The bartender shook his head. "Sorry. A million people come through here, and I stopped trying to remember names a few decades ago."

An alien came up behind Talos and whispered into his ear, "You looking for Baltar?"

Talos turned and nodded at the hairy creature. "Yes, I am."

"Why you Rebs look for Baltar? He do troubled thing?"

"I just have to ask him questions. He's not in trouble yet."

"Baltar not here, but me know him very well. Me his first mate."

"Ahh. You travel with him then, do you?"

"Yes, we travel the stars together. We do much trading and deliver goods and services. Come, I take you to Baltar as long as you say he no in trouble with Rebel Alliance."

Talos turned to his team and smiled, "What luck!"

The team followed the hairy creature and moved through the city to a hovermobile. They squeezed into it and then took off toward the north. They got into the flow of traffic in the sky and meandered through the city. Finally, after what seemed an hour's drive, they slowed and landed in a high-rise parking facility.

"Me name is Santos. Come, Baltar is here."

The creature led the party through the parking docking area into the building, which appeared to be luxury suites. Santos rapped on the door twice and then once. The door opened, and a man holding a laser pistol greeted them. The team's hands reached upwards. Talos spoke first.

"We come in peace."

"Captain, it's okay. No trouble. Just some questions."

"Santos, what did I tell you about bringing strangers here?" Baltar asked.

"Sorry Boss," Santos said with a bit of remorse.

Baltar moved from the door and allowed the party into the apartment.

"Come in. Speak your peace and be off with you," Baltar insisted.

"Thanks," Talos stated. "I'm Captain Talos of the Rebel Alliance. We are here by order of the Emperor to ascertain whether or not your ship left Romes IV a few days ago with six passengers: 4 Clave Warriors and 2 Senators. If you did, then we need to find them, and we need to take you and your crew back to Romes IV for questioning."

"We didn't have any passengers from Romes IV, just cargo.... legitimate cargo, I might add."

"Well, then you would not mind a Reader scanning you and your crew to confirm?"

"I would mind, but I can't stop you from doing your job." Baltar stated. "So you said there were 4 Clave Warriors and 2 Senators on a ship from Romes IV, eh?"

"Yes."

Baltar's mind was racing. The news was what he had been waiting to hear for several decades now. Finally, after all these years, the Clave was doing something. He silently wished that he could be part of that group again. He needed more information.

"So a party of six left Romes IV, and you are hunting them down, I take it?"

"We are," Talos replied. "We will need to search your ship."

"Understood. I will cooperate fully. Yet my ship is way on the dark side of the city."

"No problem. We'll take a hovermobile there. I have two of my men in wait there."

"You all were not letting us get away, were you?"

"Not a chance," Talos stated

"Let me get my things, and we can be on our way."

Baltar got his things, and the group, now in two separate hovermobiles traveled through the sky traffic to the dark side of the endless city. Finally, they reached the location of the docked ship. As they had traveled, Captain Talos had called for the Reader and his crew to meet them there, as well.

When they were all at the docking bay, the lone star was just rising. The Delta patrol prepared their gear and searched the ship, with permission from Captain Baltar. Then after the ship was thoroughly searched, the Reader began her scans of the crew.

The Reader looked into the eyes of each of the four crew members, diving into their souls through their eyes and entering their brains. They traveled back through the visual images and found the trip they had made from Romes IV. After scanning all four, the Reader turned to Captain Talos.

"They had no passengers, but I found they are old Clave Warriors."

Talos raised an eyebrow, "We are not here to arrest Clave Warriors. "We are specifically searching for the 4 Clave Warriors who are seeking to overthrow the Emperor. These Clave Warriors here are not doing that. Our business is not with them."

"Then we can go free?"

"Yes, but I'd tread very carefully from here on out," Talos warned. "We will be watching you closely."

"Indeed," Baltar added.

Talos nodded to them, gathered his men and gear, and departed with his security team in one of the hovermobiles that would take them to their landing bay. After the Rebels were gone, Baltar and his crew headed into their ship.

"We had better find out what is happening and get the word out to other Clave Warriors that something is in the works," Baltar suggested.

Captain Talos and his men entered their ship that sat in the landing bay on Erosodad in the city or Eronia. They powered up the ship, requested departure clearance, and made contact with General Zolotan and Commander Shatra. Momentarily, the viewer was filled with a split-screen image of both officers.

"What is it?" They both said in unison.

"General, Commander, The *Blue Star* and Captain Baltar and his crew were scanned, and there were no passengers aboard their ship," Talos stated.

"That leaves one more ship, if I'm not mistaken," replied Zolotan.

"And that ship will come up empty-handed, as well. I am telling you that they have again found a way to outsmart our scans," Shatra stated.

"How can that be?" Zolotan asked. "They were hiding in the bulkheads, and we searched there this time around. They were not there!"

"They have done something far sneakier this time," Shatra observed.

"What could it possibly be?" Zolotan asked.

"I have no idea what it is. If we knew, we'd have them!" Shatra cried out.

"We will wait for the last report," Zolotan stated.

"Very well," Shatra replied. "Shatra, out."

'Zolotan, out."

"Talos, out."

/////

Far from Erosodad, on the other side of the Andromeda, in a system known as the Andreazoo Belt, on a planet called Andreazoo, the last of the Rebel patrols sent out by General Zolotan and Commander Shatra had survived the midnight by the generous hospitality of the General Store clerk and owner named Derrick. Now, they had gained information that they might find the Captain of the Callipso freighter in the only tavern, which was down the street a ways.

They now sat at a table, waiting for the rest of the customers to wake up so that they could ask them to identify the Captain of that ship. The five officers conversed in hushed tones to one another.

Gradually, the sleeping patrons woke up one by one. Then the bartender opened the bar   and the patrons resumed their drinking.

Adam rose to his feet after nearly all the aliens were up and walking around. "May I have your attention, Gentlemen and Ladies?"

"That would depend on what you have to say, Rebel!"

"I am looking for the crew of the Callipso. I just have a few questions to ask."

"Why you look for them? Have they broken any of your precious laws?"

"Not yet, but they might be involved in something the Emperor is displeased with. Right now they are just wanted for questioning."

"Lies!"

Adam slowly raised his palms. "No lies here. Five ships left Romes IV! One of those ships had six passengers who threaten the Emperor's reign. We are just here to prove that it's not this crew."

"And if it is?" A man asked stepping forward through the crowds. "You will just search my ship and ask your meddling questions, or will you force us to go with you to Romes IV?"

"Orders are to take you to the Emperor if you are who we are looking for," Adam answered.

"You and what army? Looks to me we outnumber you," the man replied.

"I don't want trouble, Sir. I just need to search your ship and ask that you accept a Reader scan for your crew," said Adam.

"I am the Captain of the Callipso. My crew are not here. I gave them shore leave. They have gone to Zenith."

"Then we go to Zenith," Adam asserted. "Recall them and say that we will meet them on Zenith somewhere. Let's get out of here before sundown. I don't believe I got your name."

"Sejes is my name."

"How many crew members do you have?"

"It is cost effective to have just four, including myself," Sejes stated, as he left the tavern.

"Two of my men will transport with you, and we will follow you to Zenith. Our ship is on the outskirts of this town."

"See you in the skies," Sejes stated.

The group parted and moved swiftly to their ships. Within half an hour they had reached their ships and were blasting off into the atmosphere. Then, they departed the barren lands of Andreazoo and headed toward the more popular planet called Zenith. Enroute, Captain Sejes contacted his crew and got them all together at the planet's space station, which was in orbit of the planet. Both ships docked at the space station and powered down. The three members of Sejes' crew met them at their docking bay, as did the rest of the Rebel patrol.

"If you will give us permission, we will conduct our search," Adam stated.

"Go ahead," Sejes replied with a hand gesture toward the ship.

"Race, contact the Reader Council and have them send a Reader here for a scan of the crew."

Race nodded and moved off to connect with the Reader Council as the search commenced.

"If you would believe me, I would just tell you that we have no contraband aboard nor passengers that are against the Rebel Alliance," Sejes insisted.

"I know. But, I have to conduct the search anyway."

Sejes shook his head. "What are you looking for?"

"Four Clave Warriors and two Senators."

Sejes stroked his goatee with his fingers, as he thought that information through. Was the Clave finally making a move? He glanced at his old friend Haus, who raised an eyebrow in interest.

Not too long after the Rebel soldiers searched the ship with their scanning equipment.   Then the Reader, a tall, thin lady with deep, blue eyes arrived. As all Readers, her head was shaved. She wore a tight, blue one-suit. She looked at the Rebels and addressed Adam first.

"You must be the Captain of this lot."

"I am," Adam stated. "Adam Allistar."

"What do you want to know from this crew?"

"If they had passengers traveling with them from Romes IV," answered Sejes.

The Reader looked to the four sanding near the ship and walked up to Captain Sejes. She looked into his eyes and dove into his mind. She did not expect what came next.

~You will not tell them we are of the Clave. ~

~No.~

~We had no passengers on our trip from Romes IV. ~

The Reader nodded at Sejes and moved to the next crew member. She did the same to each person of the crew and turned to Captain Adam.

"They had no passengers from Romes IV."

"Thank you for your services," Adam stated. "You are released."

"I told you we had no passengers!" Sejes exclaimed.

"It didn't hurt you for us to make certain, did it?"

"No." said Sejes, "but it did force a Reader upon us when one was not welcome."

"We do apologize for this inconvenience."

"An apology is all we get?"

"I realize that having a Reader is crossing the line a bit, but the Emperor is serious about catching the Clavemen and the Senators before they do some damage."

"That is understandable, but he doesn't have to step all over people to get at them."

"He thinks…"

"I don't give a hoot what he thinks. He doesn't have the right to force people to have their minds probed by Readers!"

"Is this going to be a problem?" We have nothing more to do with you. There were no passengers on your vessel; therefore, you are free to go," Adam stated.

One of the crew tried to step forward, but Sejes put out his arm to stop him and looked at his mate. "Stand down, Myles."

"Let's move out men," Adam ordered. "We're done here."

Adam waited until his men were walking through the air locks. Then he moved after them, moving backwards until he reached the port hatch. He walked through and followed his men to the lift, which took them up a few levels to their docking bay. They wasted no time in getting to their ship. Soon, Adam was on the coms, talking with General Zolotan and Commander Shatra.

"Are you certain they didn't have any passengers?"

"The Reader confirmed that there were not any passengers on the Callipso coming from Romes IV," Adam replied.

"This is the last report, Commander Shatra. I do not understand. They must have been on one of those ships. They had to have been on one of them!"

"It's the *Raptor's Claw*," Shatra insisted. "They have outsmarted us again, but I have felt the presence of one of the Clave Warriors that I used to know well….well enough to connect with him with my mind."

'Are you certain?"

"Yes," Shatra replied.

"We can't leave this to chance. Zymon Keltor will have both of our heads if we are wrong."

"I am not wrong! I know they are heading to Shangri-La. He is planning to recall the Clave. We must get there before Odan and his crew get there," Shatra insisted.

"Very well, then I hold you responsible for any errors," Zolotan stated. "We'll do things your way and prepare our forces to meet this ship at Shangri-La."

"Stick with me and watch the rest of the Clave that got away die," Shatra stated.

Chapter Fifteen

Desperation and New Alliances

Dancing, eating, talking and dancing, eating and talking again lasted for hours with no end in sight. Cassandra found herself captivated by Markel's stories of the Clave and the UO.

Markel noticed that talking to Cassandra did not require much effort. Normally, he didn't like to get involved with people connected to political issues, because what came out of their mouths usually benefited their own improvement or progression. However, Cassandra was young, not familiar with the ways of most politicians in the UO. Yet he had an idea that the UO would not change her innocence and her tendency to be fair play.

"I was assigned to assist in running the operations at Shangri-La," Markel stated. "The Clave usually had their meetings there every three moons."

"Three moons? Is that three months?" Cassandra's wrinkled brow showed her confused stare into Markel's eyes. She was referring to her own understanding of "moons" to be one month and questioning if this is what he meant.

"Not in Earth terms, no. It is the turning of the three moons on Shangri-La, which translates to about three years in Earth time."

"Oh. That's a long time," Cassandra stated, blinking in fascination.

"Not for the Clave. In the Clave, things take time to happen. It takes time to travel great distances, even with the keys to the gateways," Markel replied.

"What was it like at the meetings?"

"Crowded," Markel laughed. "There were many who wanted to be Clave Masters, so there were several apprentices. Yet there were few Masters. Your father was the head of the Clave Order. There was your father, Odan, Baltar, Sejes, myself, Antonia, Silver and Jade. Then came those that were one step away from becoming Masters who were on their first assignments. After them were younglings assigned to each Master. Each Master had about five younglings that they would sponsor. The apprentices to become Masters usually had a duty to perform under the watchful eyes of one of the Masters. After they successfully finished that duty, they would be tested and then placed as a Master in the order. They would be assigned to a particular nation's leader to mediate talks of trade, and other talks of setting up colonies and additional discussions of sending out exploration teams to different realms of space."

"I see," Cassandra stated. "So to start the Clave over again, what must we do first?"

"First we rebuild the UO. We gather together all the nations that oppose the Emperor and the Rebel Alliance, and then we will get volunteers to join the Clave. Most Clave Warriors that will hear of our re-entry into the Andromeda will know something is about to happen and will be looking for a way to rejoin. We will just give them that opportunity when we return to Shangri-La."

"If Shangri-La is guarded, will it be wise to recall the Clave there?" Cassy asked.

"We must retake what is ours," Markel insisted. "You will see. We will have enough Warriors to take back Shangri-La," Markel assured her. "The trouble will be getting there in one piece."

"The pathway there will be _____"

"Heavily guarded with Rebel forces. They know by now where we are going."

"Is this ship powerful enough to go against a Rebel ship?"

"Hardly." Markel shook his head. "Hopefully we can get to Shangri-La before a Rebel ship is aware of us. If not, I imagine that the road to the surface will be rather bumpy."

"Why can't we get some help before we go there?"

"That will take more time than we have. As we are now going, we are being pursued," Markel stated.

"One ship against the whole Rebel Armada?"

Markel smiled, "You think those odds are terrible?"

"They are horrible!"

"You have 4 Clave Warriors with you, Senator. That is more than enough."

"Unless you do some hocus pocus, I don't see how."

"What is hocus pocus?" Markel asked.

"Magic! What Odan did back at our house on Earth...that levitation trick?"

"Ahh. We have many tricks up our sleeves," Markel replied.

"Really?" Cassandra sat forward slightly. "Like what?"

"Clave lore is very powerful against the weak-minded. Most Rebels don't tap into using their entire brain capabilities. The Clave lore just exploits that known fact."

"An example would be?"

"Say for instance we come in a single ship like this. With our powers we can trick their scanners and make it look like we are several ships when we are just only one. At least it will give then false targets to shoot at instead of a single, clear target."

Cassandra laughed, "That is hilarious." She laughed again.

"Sometimes it works for a very long time," Markel chuckled as well.

Seth came over with his new-found lady friend. "Mind if we join you two?"

"Not at all," Markel replied with a smile as he stood up to greet the lady.

Once everyone was seated, Markel looked at the lady and glanced at Seth, "Who is this nice lady, Seth?"

"Oh! I forgot my manners. My sweet lady, Rebecca, this is my sister, Cassandra and Master Markel."

Rebecca smiled and nodded to Markel and Cassandra, "It's nice to meet you both. I've been dancing with Seth here for the last few hours. I thought we could use a break."

"Smart, isn't she," Seth chuckled.

Cassandra nudged her brother with her elbow to stop his untasteful jokes. "You needn't say such, Seth."

"From where do you originate, Rebecca?" Markel asked, taking a sip of his drink.

"I was born on Sansadar, but I'm a mixed breed of Angolian and Reader genes. My father was Angolian and my mother was a Sansadarian Reader. So I can read people quite well, but I was never fully trained to do so," Rebecca stated. "My mother died before she could teach me."

"Ah. You should learn to Read on your own then. It is a highly paid job these days," replied Markel.

"It is a highly paid job if you work for the Rebels. But I would not work for them even if my life depended on it. In fact, it's why I'm here working for McCloud. I will learn to read people and use it to assist him here."

Markel nodded and thought to himself that she was smart, as Seth had stated. At least she had a direction in her life. She knew what she wanted and was where she needed to be to get it. He wondered how many more there were out there like her, who wanted to use their talents for the opposite side of the Rebel Alliance. Markel hoped there were many... hundreds so that the UO and the Clave could be revitalized.

Markel looked at his time piece. 'It is getting late. I think it might be best that we say goodbye to the festivities for the night. We should rest so that when Odan and Captain Rex Return, we head be ready to head out again."

Cassandra rose. "That does sound like a good plan of action. We will need rest if what your prediction of what we will face is true."

"What did he tell you? Seth asked.

"Tell you later," Cassy replied.

Seth rose and saw Cassy's eyes lock with Rebecca's as they prepared to follow Markel toward to the door. Seth took Rebecca's hand.

"My dear, I must say thank you for teaching me how to dance these fine dances, and for spending time with me. I hope to see you again."

"I hope so, too," Rebecca stated. "I enjoyed the entire night."

"I won't forget you," Seth added before releasing her hand and running to catch up with Markel and Cassy. He saw them turn the corner down the corridor to the left.

"Hey! Wait for me!"

Seth caught up and the trio slowed the pace, while sharing their experiences of the evening.

"Do you know the way back, Markel, because I don't?"

"Another thing you will learn in the Clave is how to use your memory."

Cassandra smiled at her brother. "You don't remember do you?"

"Do you?" Seth asked

"Somewhat. But I still think I'd get lost." Cassandra stated "So far I think we are on the right path."

"All right then, I want you to tell me when you think we go astray."

Cassandra giggled, "No fair."

"Why?"

"You might try to trick us," the twins replied.

Markel chuckled, "Ah. Alright then. Tell me when you think we are there."

"Still no good. You still have the upper hand," Seth replied

"Now, here you two are learning. To get back to your rooms, you are now dependent on me to get you back there. Thus, you must trust me to lead you there, correct?"

"Yes," Cassy stated.

"But you told Odan. You don't trust Gorn, Justin, or me?" Markel stopped walking. "What are you going to do then?"

Seth looked at his sister and folded his arms, as he rubbed his bottom lip with his fingers. Then he said, "Trust you."

"Just like that?"

Cassy looked at Markel and nodded, "Yes, Just like that."

"So no more of this. I don't know if we can trust these guys with our lives anymore." Markel responded. "None of this, I feel uncomfortable with you, Odan."

Cassandra knew exactly who he was talking to now. He was referring to the time she had nearly cried to Odan when he had said he was leaving them for a day to go with Captain Rex.

"I'm sorry for my behavior then," Cassandra offered. "I was scared and … No more outbursts like that, Master Markel. We trust you."

Markel looked into her eyes and nodded. Placing his arms around both their shoulders, he continued walking. "I understand. Now, let's see if I remember the way."

/////

At midnight, Langstrom and McCloud danced into his quarters, and immediately the lights came on bright. McCloud's baritone voice blurted out, "Dim lights 60 percent."

The lighting in the room dimmed to a dull haze of light from the orbs that floated, hovering in the darkened corners.

"McCloud, I thought you were taking me to my room?"

"What does it matter, a rooms a room. Just as long as there's a door and walls, right?"

"No! No! No!"

"Doc, I have waited so long for Rex to come through here again with you aboard, and I have made so many changes to my personal life just to please you! You and you didn't even notice?"

Langstrom stopped moving and looked him straight in the eyes, "I've noticed, okay!" she replied forcefully. "I'm not blind. I see you are dressing more like a human and not like a hermit. I see that you care about your living space, and you took time to clean up your place here."

She looked around and sighed, "You….you look wonderful, and I love that you did all this to show me that you can be nice…and romantic."

"Then, why must I take you to your room?"

"Because in a few hours, I have to get back on the *Raptor's Claw* and fly away from here with my Captain and crew!"

McCloud looked down and sighed, "I was hoping you'd stay this time, Doc. I kept the doctor's position open for you, you know. We need a doctor. You could tell Rex that, and I'm sure he'd understand."

"He needs me on this mission, McCloud. He doesn't just need me; he needs help. He needs all the help he can get, and there's no one to help him!"

"What?"

"I know he makes it sound so easy, but the truth is that the Rebels probably know where we are headed, and they are most likely prepared for us wherever we go. The *Raptor's Claw* is no match against the entire Rebel Armada!"

"Jeepers! Is that what you guys are up against?"

"Yes!"

McCloud's eyebrows rose up, "That's serious."

"Very serious."

"You're right. We need to raise some help."

"How?"

"You promise to stay, and I'll get him some help."

Langstrom thought a moment. She thought about their passengers and their cause. She thought about Rex and the rest of the small crew and what a bind she would be putting Rex in if she stayed behind, leaving the ship with no science officer and no doctor.

"All right. Deal," Langstrom stated.

McCloud could not contain his excitement at this deal. He grabbed Langstrom, whirled her around, and held her tightly. He placed his lips on hers and felt a strong connection between them. Suddenly he released her, "Before we get carried away, let us seal this deal before you change your mind. I promised help for Rex. I aim to deliver. First things first: business. We will continue this celebration exactly where we are leaving off. First we get help. Then we celebrate."

"Who will help?" Langstrom asked.

"Any nation that is against the Rebels," McCloud replied. "The Sansadarian secretly despise Zymon and his Rebel Alliance. Most of our recruits will come from Orion's Belt Galaxy."

"Isn't that too far?"

"It is where you guys are going. With the Clave Warriors, you must be heading towards Shagari-La."

Doc nodded, "Yep."

"The nations that benefited from the Clave and the UO mostly were in that galaxy. Now that the Rebels have taken over, they have been at war with them. When they hear the Clave is coming back, they will come to help in droves."

"How do we get the word out to them?"

"We send a messenger."

McCloud led Doc to a room filled with computers and robotic AI Units. He selected one and began programming it to send word of the return of the Clave Warriors and the Two Senators. Then he sent the robotic messenger in a pod on its subspace journey at super-sonic speed.

Hopefully, it would get there before the *Raptor's Claw* traveled through the galactic gate.

"There! Help is on the way," McCloud stated. "And I just thought of something else."

"What."

"I and a legion of my men will come with you," McCloud added matter-of-factly.

Langstrom smiled, "Really?"

McCloud wrapped his arms around her and smiled. I can't have my woman going out there halfcocked."

Doc smiled, "No, we can't have that."

Chapter Sixteen

Shatra Breaks Through

Shatra stood looking out the ceiling-to-floor view from her VIP quarters on Star Command Omega One Space Station, her mind reaching out to connect with her old love Odan Amir. As her eyes peered through the dark midnight of space, she closed them and whispered his name in her mind.

"Odan."

Blasting off from Teranosis out of orbit and heading toward one of its moons, a shuttle, carrying Captain Maximillian Rex Faraday and Odan Amir made its approach for landing.

Just as it was about to receive its landing instructions, Odan turned in the co-pilot's chair, bent over and grabbed his head in both his hands.

"No! No! No!"

Captain Rex, fully engrossed in the instructions for landing, took a glance at Odan and became very concerned, so much so that he slowed the shuttle to merely drifting.

"Odan!' Rex cried out. "Are you okay?"

"No!"

"Who is that talking to you, Odan?" Shatra asked in his mind. *"Is that the Captain of your party?"*

Odan rose to his feet and rushed to the cabin of the small shuttle, bumping into the bulkheads and trying with all his might to push the intrusion of Shatra out of his mind. He was not prepared for her this time. He had not expected this abrupt invasion of his thoughts and actions…

~Trying to run won't help. You know that~

He remembered what Markel had told him.

"Do not entertain her with conversation. That is what she wants."

With a few deep breaths and time to regain composure, Odan began to build up his blockades, forcing her out of his thoughts. But he could still feel her, and he knew she was still there, lingering on the fringes of his mind. He opened his eyes, sighed, and calmed himself. With all his might, he forced himself not to think of her or anything that had just occurred. Forcing his mind to think on nothing in particular was difficult. So he thought of Earth and the home they had just left, how he had loved gardening and the sheer relaxation of pulling weeds. Another sigh and he felt confident enough to return to the cockpit. Yet, before he could move, Rex came out of the cockpit, looking in great condemnation to him.

"Don't tell me that what just happened was what we were afraid of?"

Odan waved his hand, "I successfully shut her out this time."

"You mean to tell me that she's able to …."

"If I had not closed my eyes, she would be able to see you as clear as daylight! I had to leave and regain power over my mind. I was not prepared for her intrusion just now."

Rex nodded, "I see what you mean. I see how this could pose a problem."

"I know how to handle it, now," Odan assured him.

"Do you?" Rex asked. "What I just saw back in there didn't appear like you had it under control!"

"The initial intrusion I was not prepared for, but further attempts I was able to curtail."

"She's going to try this again, isn't she?" Rex asked.

"She might. She didn't get much out of me this time except that I was with you, and that is all that she needs to know. I don't want her to know anything about the others.

"Okay. Is it safe for us to return and continue our mission then?"

"We have no choice." Rex nodded, "Come with me so I can keep an eye on you."

Rex and Odan returned to the cockpit of the shuttle and retook their seats. Odan eased into the co-pilot's seat, while Rex sat on the pilot's throne and guided the ship to complete its landing on Annapolis.

Meanwhile, back on Star Command Omega One, Commander Shatra hustled her teams together and headed out on course toward Teranosis, following their only lead, which was Shatra's intuition.

PART II

Chapter Seventeen

New Recruits for the Clave

The jungles of O'Sirus were thick and harsh. Plowing through them in search of a lost migrant worker seemed like a waste of time and resources, but the Stareans were caring of their workers and would rather save their lives than leave them to the local predators that crawled around in the jungles that thrived on the surface of O'Sirus. Somewhere near the high moon, a bright flaring light filled the dark sky and lit up the surface as if it were daylight. Everyone who was hunting down the lost migrant worker gazed upward and watched the blazing ball of light crash right near their location.

One command rang out of their leader's mouth, "TAKE COVER!!!"

The impact of the bright orange ball of light cleared an area of about 100 yards from where it crashed, breaking tall trees and jungle brush in its path.

When all was quiet again, everyone came out of hiding and moved toward the blackened space around the metal ball that sat in the center of a large crater.

The leader of the band, sitting on its mount, which was a large, burley creature with two lumps on its back, swung from the center of those two lumps, jumped from the top of the beast, and moved toward the crater's edge. Several of those with him did the same.

"What is it?" asked one of the workers.

"Looks like a life pod," the leader of the band guessed.

"But Master Jade, it couldn't be human. It would not have survived that landing."

'It's not human," Jade replied. "It's mechanical."

Jade moved into the crater toward the metallic pod that was still steaming hot from its burned entry through the atmosphere. Then, before he could get any closer, the pod opened, and out sprang a metallic robot. Jade stopped in his tracks.

"Master, be careful. It could be armed."

"Be still and quiet."

The metallic robot looked about itself and at its surroundings, making note of the humanoids and beasts. Then it attempted to communicate.

"Beep, beep, beep."

"What's that again?" Jade inquired.

The robot then spoke in the universal language that was known throughout all UO nations.

"I am AI number 53B3. I am a messenger sent from McCloud to inform you of an attempt to reestablish the Universal Order and the Clave Order with the aid of Odan Amir and Captain Maximillian Rex Faraday. He is carrying four Clave Warriors and two Senators to Shangri-La, as I speak, and I have been sent to spread the word and prepare those nations within the Orion's Belt Galaxy for the upcoming battle that will decide the fate of all lands."

"Unit 53B3, you have succeeded in your task."

"Then I am your property to do as you wish with me."

"And a valuable piece of machinery you are. Come along. We are searching for a humanoid in this jungle."

"If you are looking for a humanoid, he is about 30 yards forward and east of here. I saw one life form before I struck the surface."

"Mount up and move out!" Jade commanded.

They found the migrant worker in the exact spot that the robot had told them he would be and headed back to their compound a few hundred miles in the other direction. By daylight, the search crew returned home, exhausted from the ordeal.

The compound was built into the tall trees of the jungle, and the dwellers used the natural landscape to their advantage. Several levels of wooden platforms were suspended high off the ground and held up by strong vines wrapped around the large trees. Bridges and ladders made of wood and vines allowed access to and from the platforms. Nothing was made of anything unnatural, except the laser pistols, bows and arrows, and bombs. The wooden huts of different sizes, depending on the number of members in a family, were erected on the platforms.

Jade, once a Clave Warrior, had a family, even a large one, and his hut was very big. It encompassed two tall trees and rose up to three levels. His family consisted of three generations.

When he had settled himself in his bed, he tried to sleep, but the news that had come from the AI robot had kept him awake with suspense and intrigue. He was amazed that the Clave was finally doing something after all these years.

His wife, Jamila turned to him while they lay in the bed. "Something is bothering you."

"Did you read me to find that out?" Jade asked.

"No, I can tell when you are preoccupied. You toss and turn in your sleep and don't close your eyes to rest."

'Okay, I received some news about the Clave and the UO."

"What?"

She wasn't asking to know what the news was, but more surprised that the Clave was finally doing something after all these years of silence.

"They are making an effort to reform, and they have sent word by AI to get those opposed to Zymon Keltor ready for an attempt to take over control of Shangri-La."

Jamila sat up. "That is good news."

"I don't know about that," he replied. "I'm not the same man I was all those years ago, Jamila."

"What's different?" She asked.

"You, the kids, this place. I can't go back to that life. I have taken on a new life now, one that makes it impossible for me to rededicate myself to the Clave Order."

"They will need you. You were a Master! At least go back and tell them that you can no longer serve."

"What's the use in that?"

"At least they will know," She replied. "To not go will cause uncertainty."

"True. I could do what I can for them by spreading the word to the other brothers of the Order."

Jamila smiled, "Now, that's the Jade I know."

After talking with his wife, the two snuggled, made love and drifted off to sleep. In the morning, Jade rose up early, bathed under the waterfall, and moved through the many bridges and ladders, taking him to another large tree, where he was greeted warmly by another large family who lived next to his own cluster of great trees.

Norman, also a Clave Warrior, but not a Master, rose up from the bonfire in the far edge of his cluster. His family was roasting a large pig for their meals this day.

"Greetings, Jade," Norman stated. "What brings you hither?"

"The messenger." Jade replied.

"Ahh. I heard that some fool sent a message about the Clave and two Senators trying to start some mess."

"You don't believe it?"

"I didn't say all that," replied Norm.

"What do you think?"

"I think we should put the fire under our butts and get the word out."

"Then you do believe it?"

"The message came from an average smuggler named McCloud. From what I know about the Andromeda, McCloud is a trading post near Teranosis. If someone in the Clave were trying to get to Shangri-La, they would hire a smuggler, wouldn't they?"

"I suppose they would."

"To avoid the Rebels, they would stop at places like this trading post."

"Right."

"So it's likely that word about the mission of the party on this vessel would leak to the leader of the trading post, right?"

"Yes."

"So he would send word to prepare us, alerting us that the Rebels must know about this party's destination."

Jade nodded, "Which is why they are calling us to help them."

"They will need all the help they can get to go against the Rebel ships."

"They will need an army, which we don't have," Jade stated.

'We could get the rest of the Clave back together if we send word now, and I mean right now!"

"There is little time for that."

"But there is time for some to make it here," Nom insisted.

"We must do what we can."

"That is the Clave way."

"Send word in encrypted code to the other nations. Only those who are Clave will be able to decipher it."

Jade nodded, "Sounds like a plan, but we don't know when they will be coming."

"I gather they will be coming soon. You were always a good apprentice, worthy of becoming a Master before the fall of the Clave."

"You were always a good teacher."

"You never did learn to take a compliment."

"Nor did you."

The two laughed.

Then, Jade rose and looked about himself at the jungle, "I would so much like to see the others."

"Yes. Odan, Markel, and everyone."

"They must be ages old."

"Can you imagine Odan with white hair?"

Jade laughed, "No, but I suppose he has it now."

Both men looked up at the bright sky of O'Sirus. It had been several years since the Clave had assembled. Jade's mind flashed back to that dreadful day that the Clave shattered and with it the Universal Order.

They had been in an emergency session on Shangri-La, and Leader Zeger had called all Clavemen to the Assembly Hall in the Mountain Fortress called North Prime. A discussion over the Andromeda Galaxy was on the floor, and Odan was speaking about the unrest in the galaxy.

"The nations in the Andromeda are at odds on several issues concerning the galaxy's trade negotiations, minerals, water, and resources. Zymon wishes to represent all the nations within the Andromeda, while the Senators from the Andromeda, who represent each planet, do not wish for him to be the sole representative. Basically, Zymon wishes to take over management of the entire galaxy, rather than have the UO managing it."

This of course was not nearly what he desired. Zymon Keltor wanted much more than just the rule of the Andromeda. However, for the moment, he had lied to Odan just to get the Clave thinking that he still wanted to remain a part of the UO.

"This is not possible," Zeger replied. "Zymon knows that I will never agree to a dictatorship rule of any galaxy."

"If this body will not agree to his suggestion, he has stated to me that he will resort to using force," Odan replied. "Take note that I am the messenger and not the one sending the message."

"So noted" Zeger stated. "He is declaring war?"

Shatra rose, "Not in so many words, Leader Zeger. You do have a choice. Zymon merely wants to rule the Andromeda. That is all."

"You are behind him, Lady Shatra?"

"There is nothing wrong with his venture. All that it needs is a change in organization."

"I do not agree. I cannot speak for the nations of the Andromeda who must bow down to Zymon! I'd imagine they would not agree either."

"I am so sorry to hear that," responded Shatra. "If this is the case, then I will leave this order and take with me those that you passed over for Mastership. We will all work for Zymon Keltor."

"Shatra, don't be foolish!" Zeger shouted. "You don't know what you are doing!!"

"Oh, I do know!" Shatra cried out.

Odan shook his head in disbelief. "Shatra, please. Don't do this. It is wrong! You must see that!"

Shatra glared at Odan as she left the Assembly with half the Clave Order with her.

Blinking away a tear, Jade looked in the fire, as his hand clenched into a fist.

"You remember the day?" Norm asked.

"Vividly," Jade replied.

"It is high time to get a bit back," Norm replied.

"Yeah."

"Let's get the word out to the others."

"I'll send out a message."

"I will travel to Zatona," Norm added. "Be careful!"

"Not to worry. I still remember the old ways."

Chapter Eighteen

Clave Gains Support

Walking through the dry, hot reddish brown sand dunes of Zatona, Silver Downs clad in a black, hooded robe moved smoothly over the terrain. She walked a few more steps, turned to look behind, and kept walking. After another few steps, she turned again. Walking behind her at a much slower, staggered gait, a much shorter man struggled, trying hard to keep up.

"Come! We don't have much further to go. It is only a few hundred more feet."

"Only a few hundred more?" Jay Star called out in exhaustion. "Only?"

"If we stop to take a drink, you won't make it. It is better to keep moving and get there before the Dunetar track us down."

Dunetar, known as cannibals, were natives of Zatona. They usually came out to hunt during the night and tracked their prey. Jay looked off to the right and noted the twin stars on the descent. Sighing, he picked up his pace, if one could call it that, and fought to keep up with Silver.

"Silver, you said we'd make it to Ramatown before nightfall."

"I've done it before plenty of times. I must say, you've slowed me down this trip."

Silver looked back to see Jay running to keep up with her. Then she stopped and grabbed his arm.

"No running. Take out your water and drink a sip only. This will moisten your throat. I will hold on to you so you can stay with my pace. That is the only way we will make it to Ramatown before nightfall."

Jay tugged on the string that he had tied to his waist and pulled up the jug of water that hung on his right thigh. He took a long sip, and then Silver grabbed it from him, a few drops draining on his chin.

"Hey!" Jay cried. "I was drinking that."

"That is too much! I don't want you to vomit!"

"I'm not going to vomit. I promise," Jay replied.

"You will vomit by the time we get there. A sip is just enough to wet your hole, not a gulp that will sit in your gut and thrash about!"

"Sorry, but I'm thirsty!" Jay cried.

"When will you learn to listen to me? I am your Master, and what I say has reason and wisdom!"

"I'm sorry, Master Silver. I didn't think more would do me any harm!"

"It's your body; if you choose to abuse it, I cannot do anything now."

She grabbed hold of his arm and began moving at a swift pace through the rolling sand dunes. Upwards and downwards they traversed with no slowing down. Silver could see the effect the water was having, but she could do nothing now. She could no longer stop because only one of the suns now remained just over the mountains in the distance. She could see Ramatown now, and they would make it. However, Jay would be rather sick from the trip.

Some hours later, they moved into the city streets at a much slower pace. As predicted, Jay vomited. He ran to a darkened ally and threw up the water he had gulped down. Slowly, he rejoined Silver.

"You were right,' Jay stated while wiping his mouth on his sleeve.

"Perhaps you will take me more seriously when I tell you something now?"

Jay nodded, "I will, Master."

"Shh. Don't call me that here," Silver insisted.

Jay had forgotten that calling Silver Master would give the hint that they were Clavemen. However, if it wasn't what Jay said, it would be the way they were dressed. Both of them wore black, hooded robes that made them stand out from the other people. They looked like drifting monks.

Darkness fell on the city of Ramatown, and the crowded city livened up. Music played from the taverns which were the only establishments open after dark.

Silver led the way into one of the taverns and walked up to the bar with Jay following. She ordered an alcoholic beverage for herself and Blue Rivers for Jay. Then Silver scanned the establishment, looking for a certain face. After panning the entire room, she did not see the one she was looking for. She turned back to the front and gestured to the bartender.

"Sal, where is Baxter?"

"He hasn't come in tonight. But I expect him later on."

Nodding, Silver got Jay's attention, selected an unoccupied table, and sat down.

Jade had received clearance to dock his shuttle in landing bay 43A. He was on Zatona in the city of Ramatown. After locking up his shuttle, he moved through the crowded streets and into one of the taverns. He took note of Silver right off, sitting at a table with her apprentice, Jay Star. Jade moved to the bar, ordered a drink, and made his to the table where they sat.

"Silver!" Jade hissed loud enough so only they could hear.

Silver nodded in acknowledgment, and a broad smile lit up her face. "Jade! Welcome to Zatona. What brings you here?"

"I bring news. However, I'd rather speak more privately elsewhere."

Silver grinned and nodded, "Then we wait for a time. I have some business to take care of with a client."

Jade nodded, "Be free."

Jade watched Silver go. She was a very pretty lady with her dark, long hair and her tanned skin. She had always dealt with her brothers of the Clave professionally, no nonsense, and he respected her for that. Not many females made it into the Clave order, but Silver had always been the one that he respected most. Perhaps it was the way she handled herself, the way she walked and talked. She had this aura about her that demanded respect, and she got it from others by giving it where it was due. Of all the Masters, Jade knew why the Elder of the Clave had given Jay Star to Silver to bring up in the Clave ways. She was the only one who had the wherewithal to handle him and train him to become a respectable Clave warrior.

He looked to Jay Star, "Jay Star, last I saw you, you were a youngling about so high." Jade stuck his hand out showing how tall he had been.

"Yeah, I was a little squirt. But I'm bigger, stronger, and skilled now."

"Are you?"

Silver announced her return with a remark to their conversation, "Don't listen to him. He's full of hot air."

Jay turned to Silver, "You don't think I've grown and learned the Clave ways?"

"Shhhhhush!" Silver stated. "Be careful of your mouth. You just displayed your skills and your lack of discipline."

Jay's brow furrowed as he turned away from her and sat back, arms folding across his chest.

"If you are angry, you should be angry at yourself."

Jade chuckled, "I remember the task of bringing up younglings." He laughed again.

"Now, I'm a joke?"

"Hey, don't take it personal," Silver stated.

"I'm not," Jay replied.

"Jay, I can see how you've grown. You need not bring attention to it. It is very visible."

"There. You see. That is my point," Silver stated. "One need not bring attention to something that is already visible."

Jay nodded, "I guess silence is better."

"Sometimes, Jay, it is. You will learn," Jade added in an encouraging voice.

The doors of the tavern opened, and Silver's client entered. Silver rose to greet him and looked at Jade. "Stay here for a while. I'll be back."

Silver met her client, the humanoid Angolian, and motioned for him to follow her to an empty table in the back of the tavern on the other side.

"It is good that you are still with Silver, Jay. Many Clavemen didn't stay together," Jade whispered.

"I had nowhere else to go. Zymon, with his Rebel forces, raided my homeland and killed my entire clan. I had nowhere to go but with Silver. Plus, I wanted to stay with her and learn."

"It is good. You will find some use for it sooner rather than later."

"You think so?"

"I know so."

"Does this have something to do with the news you will tell us later?" Jade nodded.

"I can't wait to hear what this news is."

After a few moments, Silver returned with a bag in her hands. She did not say it, but the bag was filled with terrons. Being a Sansadarian Reader, Silver's services in the sector were paid at top terrons. She made a living with it, which kept Silver, Jay, and the rest of those with them well fed.

Silver returned to the table, but did not sit down, "Let's get out of here and go somewhere to talk.

Jade and Jay rose from the table and followed Silver out of the tavern into the dark but warm night of Ramatown. They found a hotel and shared accommodations in a suite so that they could communicate in private. Silver took the bed, while Jay and Jade settled in the chair and on the couch.

"What's the news?" Silver asked.

"A robotic AI messenger was sent from the Andromeda to inform nations within this galaxy of a movement...an action of four Clave Warriors and two Senators, heading to Shangri-La."

Silver tilted her head and dropped her jaw in amazement, "What did you say?"

"Yeah."

"Oh my! Is this for real?"

"Norman thinks so, and so do I."

"If that's the case, then the Rebel's probably know about it," Silver stated.

"True. That was our thought, too."

"They will need help."

"Right, thus the message."

"We have to get organized," Silver could not contain her enthusiasm. "Can we?"

"If there's time, yes," Jade added. "Norm and I will get the word out as best we can."

"I will do the same in the outer rim territories," Silver stated. "The outer rim will need to be notified. Most of the Clave fled there."

"Can you get out there?"

"It will be difficult. The Rebs patrol out there heavily."

"Try it," Jade encouraged her.

"I will. Jay and I will go."

"KEWL!" Jay cried out. "A real live mission!"

Silver smiled, "I think he's been bored to death on this planet."

Jade laughed, "You know kids. They like the action."

"Yes, I do recall," Silver agreed. "But mostly I recall the action leading to a bit of trouble."

"Minus the trouble! I'm not anymore! I won't get into trouble," Jay replied.

"So you say," Silver stated. "What about that time I had to save you from-

"Are we counting?" asked Jay.

"Yes, we keep good notes," Silver reminded him.

Jade just laughed, holding his belly as he lay on the couch.

"You two sound almost like an old married couple."

"Almost?" Silver asked.

We are married all right, married to the Clave."

Another belly laugh from Jade, and this time Silver laughed, as well. Jay was happy that he was able to get a laugh from Silver. That was a first for him.

"Jade, you mentioned there were two Senators. "Who could those be? I thought all the Senators were murdered."

"They were. These must be the lost children of Zeger. I recall Odan Amir had fled with the babies by order of Zeger himself. They went into hiding, and I suppose they are all grown up now and are back."

"Thanks to the stars!" Silver stated.

"KEWL!" Jay exclaimed. "I want to meet them."

"I'm sure you'll have a chance. Let's get some sleep. We have a long few days ahead of us," Silver suggested.

"Night," all replied in unison, as the orbs of light were ordered to the corners of the room leaving the blackness of the night.

Chapter Nineteen
Mal Organizes Volunteers

On the outskirts of the Orion's Belt Galaxy, on a planet known as Andoria Five, an event was scheduled to begin. A five day fight in an arena where there could be only one winner. Although it was usually a fight to the death, that decision was left up to the fighters; after all, it was their lives at stake.

After the fall of the Clave, many of the Clavemen who were not yet Masters, fled to Andoria and became fighters to earn a living, stay in shape, and to sharpen their skills. Three members of the Clave who made that choice were Reese, Kal and Troy.

The trio had become renowned fighters, winning every fight they had been a part of. However, they had never been asked to fight against each another. They had specifically requested that they not be pitted against each other. Since they were fighting well and attracting audiences, their managers listened and set it matches up so that they would not battle against their friends.

Silver had heard about Reese, Kal and Troy a while ago, and she had seen them fight. However, her agenda this time was not to watch them battle in the arena, but to persuade them to rejoin the Clave. Silver and Jay made their way through the crowds of the great city to the Arena and purchased tickets. They would watch them fight and then speak with their comrades in private.

Finding their seats in the crowded arena, Silver and Jay waited for the fighters to enter. First up was Reese against a Rebel Fighter, who was twice his size.

"That Reb looks bigger than Reese," observed Jay.

"Not to worry, Reese will take him," Silver answered.

"You sure?"

"Yep."

"How do you know?"

"You'll see." Silver replied with a smirk on her face.

The bell rang and the fight began. At first it looked like Reese was losing the fight, but halfway into the first round, Reese landed some hard blows to his opponent's face and abdomen. Then, a swift, roundhouse kick to the side of the head, and his opponent dropped like a sack of potatoes.

Jay looked at Silver. "How did you know?"

"I know Reese."

"But that doesn't explain how you knew he'd win."

"Shh. They are bringing out Troy."

The announcer introduced the next two fighters. The bell rang and the fight began. Troy was strong. He had a tall, muscular build and came out throwing punches and spinning roundhouse kicks, front kicks and sidekicks with ease. This series of attacks overwhelmed the opponent. Even though he tried to fight a good fight, he, too, went down in the last seconds of the first round.

Kal and his opponent entered the ring, and the announcer introduced them, and the bell rang to start the fight. However, unlike the preceding bouts, this fight promised to be more evenly matched. Kal tried to go for the knock out, but realized after taking a beating, that he could not get it. He slowed his pace and went for a different plan of action. Throwing combination punches to his opponent's body and face, Kal danced around forcing his opponent to chase him in search of a good punch. After a few rounds, he could see his opponent growing tired and landed more punches to the face and head area with a few unexpected kicks to the body. Finally he delivered a round house kick to the side of the head, and his opponent dropped to the canvas. Although it had taken longer, Kal came out the winner.

Silver rose to her feet and motioned to Jay. "Let's go."

Making a path through the crowds, Silver and Jay headed to the back of the arena where the fighter's dressing rooms were located. They got up to a certain point before they were stopped by a large Rymelion.

"No go further!" The Rymelions cried out.

"I'm here to see Reese, Kal and Troy. We are old friends."

"No go through!"

Then Troy, who was coming down the corridor, saw them being hassled by the guard. Troy ran down and looked at the Rymelion.

"Zac, it's okay. They are friends of ours."

Zac growled, nodded, and backed off.

Troy turned to Silver, embraced her and held out his hand to Jay.

"By the stars! It's good to see you Silver. You look fantastic, and Jay, you're sprouting up like a weed!"

"I'll take that as a compliment," Jay replied.

The trio walked to the dressing rooms and opened the doors. "Lady on the hall!' Troy cried out.

Reese and Kal emerged from the showers wearing their boxing robes. When they saw Silver and Jay, their faces erupted into broad smiles as they rushed to embrace them.

"So, what brings you to Andoria?"

"I've got news concerning the Clave. I thought you might be interested."

It grew very quiet as they moved in closer to where she stood with Jay. Reese, who was the oldest of the three spoke first.

"What news?" he asked.

"Jade and Norm received a robotic, AI message from the Andromeda Galaxy that a lone freighter ship with 4 Clave Warriors and 2 Senators is headed to this Galaxy. Their destination is obviously Shangri-La.'

Reese smirked. "Now that has got to be Old Odan Amir. No one else would even attempt such a feat."

'If we organize, we could help them out when they get here. We could fight the Rebs in this sector and take back the Belt"

"Possibly," Reese stated. 'But we'd have to find as many fighters as we can get our hands on in a limited amount of time."

"Jade and Norm agreed to get the word out as best they can and round up some of the old gang. I told them I'd come and talk to you guys."

"The two Senators must be Zeger's two kids, the girl and the boy. The babies that Odan took with him into hiding."

"I wouldn't know, but I guess that is the case," Silver replied.

"We'd be able to bring back the UO with those two at the head of it," Reese added. "Old Odan is a smart man. Alright. I'm in," Reese stated looking to his two younger friends. "What about you guys?"

"Master, wherever you go, we go," both answered in unison.

"So, it's settled then," Silver replied. "The meeting place will be on Zatona. In three days. We'll get organized there. I must go to another planet where I will solicit help from some other friends there before returning home to Zatona. We will need some ships also.'

"Good thinking. By the Gods I hope this works. It's been too long without order in these stars," said Reese.

"That makes both of us. Come on Jay, we have to alert others about the plan."

Jay bowed to Master Reese and then gave a brotherly embraced at the shoulders with the other two.

"Safe travels," Jay said.

"Safe travels," all replied as they departed.

Chapter Twenty

Clave Recruiting Thrives

Other inhabitable planets existed farther west of Andoria, one being Deran. However, few believed it to be true because of the abundance of water on the surface and very little visible land, most of which was swamp, marshlands, and a southern mountain range. Alien beings questioned how any form of life could possibly survive on Deran. What they did not know was the obvious; those who chose to live on Deran lived under the water.

Deep down, far below, submerged in the caverns and caves, the water did a strange thing with the air that was caught up from the core. This natural air forced the waters outward through warm pockets within the caves, which is where the living beings resided. They were not just ordinary people. These inhabitants had chosen Deran to hide from the Rebels who didn't know how to live on Deran. They learned how to survive and live off the planet and at the same time avoid the Rebel Patrols. They mostly ate fish which were readily abundant due to the geography of the planet. Occasionally some of them ventured topside to hunt birds for variety in the diet. Fresh water springs dripped down into the caves and created pools of warm and cold waters for the inhabitants. These were used for bathing, washing and drinking.

When the Clave shattered and divided, most of the younger Clavemen and women traveled to Deran. Knowing that there would be no Rebels that would come calling on Deran, one of the Eldest members of the Clave led the establishment of an outpost. Rumor was that the old man was still alive mentoring the young who looked up to him as a father figure.

The underwater caverns were a maze of winding and twisting tunnels that emptied into larger caves and caverns some of which had multiple tunnel entrances and exits. The Clave Warriors that had lived there for all these past few years knew the maze quite well.

Even Mal, the eldest member of the Clave, knew those pathways and could maneuver through them even though his eyesight had dimmed the last few years. As a precaution, Devin, a Clave Warrior who turned down Mastership to serve Mal, led him around despite the old man's grumblings that he still could see well enough to pass through the tunnels without falling.

When they entered the dining cavern to find it crowded with many of their brothers and sisters, the loud chattering voices died down to a complete silence. Only the rushing waters of the waterfall could be heard splashing against the rocks below. This showed the great respect Clave Warriors and their descendants had for their elders who had guided them to a safe haven from the Rebels.

"Carry on, brothers, sisters! I am just here to eat like you all," Mal teased, giving the diners permission to continue in their conversations and feasting.

Gradually, the chattering rose to its original level. Devin walked to the front of the cave and fixed a wooden platter of food for Mal and placed it in front of him on the table. After making sure Mal had been taken care of, Devin served himself and sat next to Mal who ate slowly chewing with the few teeth he had left. Between bites, he looked about the cave with his limited eye sight, straining to identify anyone he recognized, but he turned back frustrated that he could not make out any faces. A slew of curses flew from his mouth in a whisper, but Devin had heard him and knew why he had uttered them.

"You shouldn't get yourself worked up like that."

"What do you know about it?" Mal spat out angrily.

"I know a lot about it. I understand you want to socialize with the younger ones and your vision prevents that sometimes. Why not just ask me to find whoever, and I can bring him or her over to talk to you?"

"Are you going to wipe my buttocks, too? You're not always going to be around me, you know. I should be able to do some stuff on me own," Mal argued. "I have some vision left, but not enough to make out faces."

"Ask me. Who were you looking for?"

"Anyone," Mal growled. "Anyone would have been just fine!"

Devin nodded. Mal was frustrated with his lack of sight. Of course, there were procedures he could have done, but that would mean he'd have to leave Deran. Beyond Deran, he was wanted by the Rebel Alliance. If he left, he'd most likely be caught before a procedure could happened. It was a risk he'd not take.

While they ate and talked, one of the younger brothers rushed into the hall with Silver and Jay in tow. Devin turned to see them and smiled as he rose to greet them.

"Master Mal, it is Silver and Jay coming for a visit,' Devin exclaimed.

Mal wiped his face and hands with a rag which served as a makeshift towel and rose to greet them. Silver rushed to Mal's side and embraced him.

"Master Mal. It is good to see you!"

"You seem well," Mal stated.

Silver then released her embrace, held the hand of her former Master, and nodded, "I am well, Master." She took Mal's hand and pulled Jay's hand to take Mal's. "This is Jay Star. You remember him. You assigned him to me. He's my apprentice."

Mal pulled the hand of Jay toward him, and the two embraced in the Clave manner, right shoulder to right shoulder. "It is good to see you, young man. Last, I saw you, you were but a youngling."

"I know. I've grown up a bit."

"Indeed."

Jay left it right there. He'd say no more. He had learned his lesson about tooting his own horn among the older brothers. Jay then kissed the hand of Master Mal and led the old man back to his seat.

"We don't mean to disturb your meal, Elder Mal," Jay apologized. "Please finish your grub."

Mal laughed, "Very observant, this one is."

Silver smiled, "Sometimes he says the wrong things, but this time, I agree with him."

"You do?" Mal stated. "Why's that?"

"It am taking a great risk coming out here, but we managed to avoid the Rebel patrols."

"Why would you take such a great risk, especially to come here?" Mal asked.

"We have received a message from the Andromeda," Silver stated, "a very interesting message from a trading post owner."

"What was the message?"

"That a smuggler is bringing four Clave Warriors and two Senators to Shangri-La in hopes of rebuilding the UO and the Clave."

Suddenly, Mal started to cough and was nearly choking until he grabbed some water and drank it. Then he coughed some more and gradually started breathing correctly again. "What... (Cough cough!) "What did you say?"

"Four Clave Warriors and two Senators are enroute to Shangri-La to rebuild the UO and the Clave."

Blinking in disbelief, Mal turned to Silver. "Odan," he whispered. "It's about damn time!"

"You believe it?" Silver asked.

"Of course, I do. "Odan is bringing back Zeger's children to rebuild the UO. With it we will rebuild the Clave Order," Mal replied.

"What do we do?" Silver asked.

"We make ready!" Mal exclaimed, as he stood and raised his hands in the air. It was as if this news had restored some of his youthful enthusiasm about life. "Brothers, Sisters! Hear me!"

Quiet settled throughout the cavern straight away as all eyes focused on Mal who panned the room with an authority that only the older Clave members recognized.

"By the stars I have great news! Finally, after all these years of hiding, the time has come for us to strike and take back what is ours! I have prepared you all for the coming of this day. We have worked hard to build the ships and beef up our storage of weapons. Soon, we will go head to head against our enemies; we will conquer them and once again walk the paths of Shangri-La!"

Loud cheering erupted from the young men and women in the room.

"After you finish your meals, be ready to hear your orders from your leaders."

In unison, they all responded, "Yes, Master Mal!"

Mal nodded to them, "Carry on brothers and sisters."

He did not sit down, but looked to Devin. "Come, we have work to do." He then turned to Silver. "Are you going to stay here and help?"

"Yes, Master Mal," Silver answered eagerly.

"Good, we must organize. We need to plan how we will meet the ship that is smuggling Odan and the Senators to Shangri-La and how we will keep the Rebels from shooting down their ship."

Silver nodded as Devin took hold of Mal and led the way, with Silver and Jay in tow. Mal talked about the situation as the party exited to a more private cavern where they could map out their strategy.

"I've been preparing for this very day for years, and now it has finally come to pass! Now that I find myself without proper eyesight to get into a star cruiser and fight the Rebels, I tell you, it makes me want to just...."

Mal's voice trailed off there for a few moments as he looked at Silver, Jay, and Devin. After a brief pause, he continued his thoughts.

"No matter. I'll just be the one organizing. First, Devin, you're going to have to leave my side and pull your weight in this."

"Master Mal, I must insist…"

"Hogwash! We need every Claveman and woman in a star cruiser or a star ship to go up against the Rebel Armada. We must take over Orion's Belt and then retake the Andromeda."

"I doubt we have enough to do both galaxies," Devin replied.

"Perhaps not right away. But soon. At any rate, we will take back Orion's Belt from Zymon and establish order in this sector. We will revitalize the UO with the new Senators, the offspring of Zeger and bring back the Clave, as well. I have never been so excited since the old days when we made contact with a world for the first time."

"Those days were special," Silver added. "I remember when I was given the task to be the liaison for Sansadar."

"Yes. Representative for the Reader," Mal stated. "Many nations were afraid of your kind when your nation joined the UO."

"There was no reason for fear," Silver replied.

"We know that now. We know that your people take Reading minds very seriously," Mal stated.

"To read a mind without permission is rape. It is very simple, actually. Unless you are invited, you don't do it," Silver explained.

"I've always wondered about that," Devin stated, "Do Readers read minds in casual conversations, or don't they?"

"They are not allowed to," Silver explained.

"Surely, there are some exceptions to the rule, aren't there?"

"That would depend on the situation. If one's life is in jeopardy, then perhaps there is cause for the Reader to do so…. IF a life is at stake. But usually, there is no situation like that."

Devin asked, "What about…Confidentiality? Privacy? What if what you have read must be kept secret and you're asked to do so by the one you read?"

"Then we are silenced, and we would take it to the grave," she said.

"I see," Devin replied. "Quite honorable."

"Sansadarians are honorable people."

"Enough," Mal bellowed. "There is no cause to question Silver's loyalty."

"I wasn't," Devin explained. "I just wanted to know—"

"Yes, yes. For another time. We have business to attend to first. As I was saying, Devin. I will not take no for an answer. I want you to lead a legion of our finest Warriors in the star cruisers. I haven't forgotten your skills with those small, one-man fighter ships."

Devin nodded this time. "I will do as you wish, Master Mal. I will take the *Avenger*, a large starship, to battle the Rebel star fighters. I will deploy from that ship maybe two to three patrols of star cruisers and four legions to go against the Rebel vipers. In the meantime, Silver, you and Jay rustle up whatever help you can muster from other planets and get them to attack with us. The only way we are going to defeat them is if we fight together.'

Silver nodded. "Jade and Norm are spreading the word, and Jay and I will stop at other planets on the way back to get the word out."

"Good! Good! When they cross over through the gate, we will be ready for them!" Mal exclaimed. I don't need to tell you to be careful who you talk with, do I?"

"No, I know the Rebels will be around," Silver replied.

"Where will you go first?'

"Artica."

"Articans were once loyal to the Clave and the UO. However, rumor has it that they swayed to the Rebel's side. You think it's wise to confront them now?" Mal asked.

"Articans thrived with the Universal Order in power; they would want to return to the old ways, instead of bowing down to Zymon. If they heard of a plan to retake the Belt, they would jump at it," Silver argued respectfully.

"Perhaps. Yet, if they entertain Rebels, you could run into trouble," Mal continued.

"I suppose you wish to look past them?" Silver asked.

"If they want to join us, they will hear about it and make up their own minds. I'm not going to have you risk your life to go there and ask them to join us! That would be foolhardy," Mal replied sharply. "No, my dear, go to Tatoway. Truman York will fight with us. I know his people will not forget us."

"Trueman York's people are only a few hundred. Artica has thousands," Silver added.

"Must you persist with this?" Mal asked.

"No, Master Mal. It's just that we need all the help we can get to go against the Rebels successfully, Sir."

"Artica is not a safe choice at this time! Their loyalty is in question. I'll hear no more about it! Now, you have your orders to go to Tatoway."

"Aye, Sir," Silver knew when to stop protesting with Mal. "Come Jay."

Jay and Silver left the company of Master Mal and Devin and followed the lead of one of the brothers to their ship. Pressing a button of the remote on her belt, the ramp leading into the cabin of the shuttle lowered, and they climbed inside in silence and prepared the ship for departure.

When the bay doors opened, they could see the long tunnel which was the same one they had taken to access the landing port. The tunnel led up through the mountain range, which was under water, and opened up at the surface in the marshland. The doors they had entered parted and the ship blasted out of the ground and into the atmosphere of Deran.

"What was all that about back there?" Jay asked.

"Just a difference of opinion," Silver assured him.

"Mal doesn't seem to like the Articans."

"He used to like them, but for some reason, he doesn't now," Silver replied.

"I wonder what changed his mind."

"Me, too. But I guess we'll never find out now. I've been ordered not to go there."

"You've been ordered not to go there. But he didn't say anything about me," Jay looked at her smiling.

Silver gave him a smirk and shook her head. "No way, Jay. Mal will have my head."

"It could be my first assignment! To find out if they are still with the Clave!"

"You're not ready for something like this," Silver insisted.

"You're the one who said we needed all the help we could get. We need them, don't we?"

"Yes, we do," Silver agreed.

"Then why not drop me off there; you go to Tatoway, and I go to Artica. I will find out if Artica still wants the UO and Clave rule or not. I can do this. I know I can without getting caught."

"Jay, if you get caught, you're on your own, you realize that? I will be the only one who knows that you are there."

"That's how we are going to keep it," Jay said.

"What's your plan?"

"I will go there and act like a drifter, get a job and hang around some. Then I'll ask around about the Rebels and the UO and see what the natives say."

Silver agreed, "It sounds good, but we don't have that much time."

"A few days. I know," Jay stated.

"Alright. I will take you there. After I meet with the Tatoways, I will come back to Artica to look for you. I'll give you three days."

"If you don't see me, I will probably be in the jail," Jay teased.

"Don't say that!" Silver scolded.

"Alright, but you never can tell."

Jay glanced at Silver and smiled but didn't say anything more because he could see she was not in a joking mood. Pleased that she was allowing him to do this alone, he did not want to cause her to change her mind. He also knew she was risking a lot to allow him to spy on the Articans. She had already been told not to go there by Elder Mal, but she was just as curious as he was as to why Mal would not call on them for help when it was most needed.

"Weren't the Articans like our closest allies?" Jay asked.

"Yes, they were which is why I wanted to go there and clear the air with them," Silver stated, glancing at him for a moment. "Instead of me, it will be you."

"How should I approach it?"

"Carefully. We don't know what's happened. Your task will be to find out what happened and then find a way to rectify it in the time you have there….three days."

Jay's eyebrows shot upward. "That's not a lot of time to go fishing."

"Welcome to the world of diplomacy."

"Yeah. Thanks."

"There was a strong connection there before with Senator Rufus' daughter, Elaina. See if she's still around. She's your best bet to find out what went wrong."

"I remember her. She was …"

"Yes. Baltar struck out on his own. If I'm not mistaken, he runs his own smuggling/freighter and cargo business in the Andromeda."

"I see. Could that be what went wrong?" Jay asked

"It might be part of it, but there would have to be more to that story. It couldn't be that relationship by itself was enough to sever the bond between the Clave and the Articans."

"Right."

"That is your task. Find out what went wrong."

"I will. You can count on me."

"You have three days so pace yourself. Go with the flow of the people about you. If they are willing to answer your questions, then no problem, but if they are hesitant, don't push."

Jay nodded. It was good advice. He would have to hold himself back for this mission. He was the gung-ho type of guy that powered ahead. He gathered he would learn patience on this mission.

"You're right," Silver stated. "This trip will be good for you to learn how to be patient with people. Remember, don't speak of the Clave around Rebels or Rebel supporters. You know what to look for don't you?" Silver asked.

"Gold coins instead of terrons, blue uniforms and their vipers."

"Right. If you see them in abundance, just wait for me; don't even try to get anyone's attention. The more I think about this, the more ridiculous it sounds."

"We need their help, don't we?"

"Yes."

"Then it's not ridiculous. It's necessary."

Silver nodded. "Go in the back and get weapons, extra water, and whatever else you'll need."

"Right."

"Take an extra cloak. It might be cold down there. We are coming into orbit now."

Silver guided the shuttle into orbit and contacted Artican Command for landing instructions. Then, after a few loops around the large planet, they were given permission to land. After about half an hour, Jay, with his gear, emerged from the mid-sized ship, and just as it had come, it took off again, leaving Jay on the surface to take care of the business at hand.

As he exited the landing bay they had been assigned, Jay looked both ways. The twin suns beamed down making it unbearably hot, sweltering hot even. Jay draped the extra cloak on his arm, turned to his right, and walked slowly down the street.

The city streets were roughly crowded with people and creatures of various species. Jay spotted the patrol of Rebels right away. Hover mobiles moving at various speeds passed him on the streets. Some sat parked along the streets waiting for their owners to return. The city had solved the problems of pedestrians and hover mobiles clashing in the streets by building crosswalks that allowed the hover mobiles to pass under a bridge while the pedestrians walked over the traffic. Then the cities passed a law forbidding pedestrians to walk in the streets. Jay took note of this and followed the crowds to the bridge, crossed over, and went into the nearest tavern for a drink. He was totally unnerved having seen a patrol of Rebels right away.

The tavern was lightly crowded. A few people played star poker at a table to the right, while another game of some sort going on at a table to the left. Ignoring both games, Jay strode to the bar.

"I'll have Solor," Jay stated.

Solor was an alcoholic beverage, yet it was not as strong as most of the alien drinks.

The barkeeper poured his drink and spoke up. "Anything else I can do for you?"

"Do you have rooms?"

"Last one is up in the back. Last one on the right. You want it?"

"I'll take it. How much?"

"Fifty gold or forty terrons."

Jay counted out the terrons and paid the bar keeper, taking note that the man had mentioned gold first. "Thanks."

It's per day?"

"Yes."

"I'm looking for a job for a few days."

"I need a cleanup man to go around and collect the glasses after people drink out of them, to prevent them from throwing and breaking them. I have to buy new glasses all the darn time. If you could save me money on that alone, it will get you a handsome price. I'll even let you stay for free and give you 40 terrons a day for it."

"Deal. I'm only going to be here 3 days."

"If you save me glasses for three days, then I'll make it worth your while to do that job."

"Very well then. It's a deal. Shake on it?" Jay held out his hand, not remembering he was wearing his glove with the metallic overlay. He blinked and realized that he might have given himself away. However, the bartender didn't say anything except to introduce himself. The metal parts of the glove were covered by leather that interlaced between his fingers, palms and forehands.

"I'm Buck. I'll introduce you to the ladies we have taking orders when they come around. You can get started after you stow your gear up there in the room."

"Thanks. I'll be right back down."

Jay walked up the winding staircase to his room on the second floor. He put his gear on the bed, left the room and closed the door. Then he returned to help out in the tavern.

Chapter Twenty-One
More of the Same

Silver nearly turned the shuttle about five or six times on her way to Tatoway. For a Clave Warrior, the feelings she was having about leaving Jay on Artica II were too profound to be just normal everyday feelings. These were visions, and she was quite sure that Jay was about to get into some serious trouble. However, on the other hand, if he were to be a skillful and wise Clave Warrior, he might avoid getting into trouble at all. As she entered the atmosphere of Tatoway, she pondered this further and then tried to figure out her own way to break the news of the return of the Clave leaders to Shangri-La without alerting the Rebels.

Tatoway was known as a neutral planet but had secretly supported the UO and the Clave for several eons. The planet allowed Rebel patrols to enter and exit the planet at will. Silver noticed the presence of a number of them moving about the streets of Totaway when she landed. She silently cursed her luck in this regard. They would check her out, no doubt about it. They would surely inquire about her business on Tatoway. *"Rebels are so darn nosy with their darn questions,"* she thought.

One of the patrol strode toward her as she was looking into a shop window.

"You there! Come over here."

Silver looked about herself and at the Rebel patrolman in bewilderment. "Me?"

"Yes, you!" He bellowed in the most unfriendly tone.

Silver walked over to him. "Can I help you, Rebel?"

The Rebel's eyebrows narrowed as she said <u>Rebel</u>. He could tell she didn't approve. "What is your business here on Tatoway? I've never seen you here before!"

"I just came to buy some things from the markets and see the sights. I heard Tatoway has some lovely sights and that the sunsets are beautiful with the triple stars."

The man grunted. "Oh yeah. It is a sight to see, I suppose. So you are just visiting?"

"And shopping" Silver stated. "Plus I know a few people that live here."

"Who?"

"Hannible."

"Oh, the General Store owner?" The man asked.

"Yes."

"Ahh."

The patrolman smiled. "He's a nice man. Very well. Proceed with your business, Miss…"

"Silver."

Silver cringed as she told him her name, but she had always been told by Elder Mal that the truth is always the best option rather than lying. The man nodded and smiled again.

"That's a beautiful name, Miss Silver."

"Thank you," Silver stated smiling. "See you around."

Silver casually made her way back to the General Store of Hannible and walked inside. Turning she glanced back to see if she was being watched, and just as she suspected, she was. Hannible came toward her and embraced her out in the open, smiling and laughing.

"Girly, I haven't seen you in many moons gone by now. How many?"

"It's been far too long now, Hannible."

"Where is Jay?"

He's taking care of some business for me," Silver stated. "But, Hannible, we need to talk."

"Yah, yah! We talk about all things, Come, come in and have some chocolate, the expensive kind. I pay, you enjoy!"

"Hannible!" Silver grabbed his arm, looked him in the eyes, and whispered as the patrons in the store turned to them to see her eyeing them. She whispered and mouthed, "Serious talk."

"Oh. Something come up?"

Silver nodded. "I'll tell you later. Not now."

It was then that Hannible understood. It was Clave business, of which he had once been a part.   He gave a slight, single nod of his head and went back to his customers, assisting them with buying things in his store. Silver browsed the aisles and then disappeared to the back of the store where Hannible had a makeshift kitchen and dining area for himself and his staff, which was just his family. When he closed the store up in the front, he joined Silver in the back.

After washing his face and drying it with the white towel hanging by the sink, he took a seat at a small table across from Silver.

"You looked serious when you said my name back there. You almost scared me to death. I almost lost my composure," Hannible admitted.

"This is serious," Silver replied.

"It has to do with the Clave; that much I can tell."

"Yes, you're right about that much," Silver replied. "For being half Sansadarian, you've got that much right."

"What's the rest?"

"We've been sent word from the Andromeda that four Clave Warriors and two Senators are headed this way. They aim to re-take Shangri-La."

"By the Stars! It's Odan!"

"That's what Master Mal said," Silver commented.

Hannible smiled and chuckled. "After all these years, he's bringing those kids back to re-take the Belt!"

"Well, we need to help him," Silver insisted.

"Not to worry. I'll get the word out on Tatoway. Everyone who needs to know, will know, and will be prepared. Just give us a meeting time and place."

Silver gave the meeting times as instructed by Elder Mal. Then, the duo left the General store and moved through the city to Hannible's dwelling place, a nice hacienda. Hannible's wife had prepared food and was pleased to see Silver. A guest room had been prepared for her, as well.

As all the lights went out in the Hannible's home, Silver rose and looked up at the last sun setting over the darkening sky. She thought about Jay and wondered how things were going for him on his first night away from her guidance …

Meanwhile, on Artica II, in the tavern called Spartica, Jay was collecting glasses after the customers drank their liquor, so that they would not throw the empty glasses against the walls of the establishment. Everything was going great, and he was making friends; he was even making tips after the waitresses made their own tips. This had been unheard of. Buck was impressed with Jay's abilities to keep up with the glasses and the flow of the customers. He was even surprised that the customers had not started trouble with Jay as they had done the other busboys. Jay also went around and emptied the ash trays and wiped the tables down, keeping them relatively clean for the next customers. Everyone was noticing the work that Jay was doing and liking it.

One of the customers, a tall man, wearing a nice, clean outfit looked up at Jay as he came to the table to wipe it.

"You got a good sense of this job, my boy," the man stated.

"It's really nothing," Jay replied. "I just see what needs doing and I do it."

"Yes, but most people would have to be told what to do. You just do it. It takes a good eye for things like that. How about I give you a better job than this cleaning of tables?"

Jay chuckled. "My first day and you want me to take another job?"

"Just give it a thought."

"What?"

"I work for the Artican Government here. We are doing business with the Rebels."

Jay held up his hands as soon as he said Rebel, "I can stop you right there, Mister. I don't want to be a part of anything involving the Rebels."

"Why not? They pay in gold, not terrons."

"I know, but I don't care. I would rather not say. Now, if you don't mind, I have more work to do here."

"You're a foolish boy."

"Your opinion is yours."

"You'll reconsider after doing this job for a few days."

"No, I don't think I will."

Jay then turned after emptying the ash tray and setting it back on the table.

"Do excuse me, but I have more tables to wipe down before I'm done here." Jay stood up straight, looked the man in the eyes, and walked away.

Silver's words came back to him when he said those things to the man. "When you want to make a point to someone, you look him or her in the eyes, stand up straight, and give him the most serious look you can." She had coached him well. He didn't have to turn and look back either; he had made his point clear.

At the end of the night when the place closed its doors at 3 AM, there were no broken glasses, and, as Buck promised, he gave Jay 40 terrons plus a healthy tip for keeping order in his place. Jay smiled and put the money into a pouch without counting it.

"You're not going to count it?" Buck asked.

"I trust you."

"You, my friend, are a man of honor. I like that. I wish you were staying for a longer time, like permanently," Buck stated with a smile.

"Perhaps one day," Jay replied. "But right now I have promises to keep."

"I understand."

"I heard something about the government here, and I was wondering if it were true."

"What did you hear?" Buck asked.

"Is the government here really siding with the Rebels?"

There was a moment of silence, and then Buck reached under the counter, brought out a laser pistol, and pointed it at Jay. As his face distorted to one of surprise, Jay held up his hands toward Buck.

"Woe!"

"NOW, I don't like you anymore!" Buck exclaimed.

"What!"

"Why did you ask this?"

"One of the customers told me that the government is siding with the Rebels! I was just wondering if it were true, because I had always thought that the Articans were supporters of the UO and the Clave!!!"

Buck looked at Jay, lowered the pistol, and glanced at Jay's hands, noticing the gloves for the first time, really noticing them.

"By the stars....You are Clave."

"I don't know whether to say 'yes' or 'no' now, but, yes, I am," Jay stated.

"What did you say to that customer?"

"That I wanted nothing to do with the Rebels."

Buck laughed. "Good! Now, I like you again."

Jay sighed. "I ...You scared the living daylights out of me."

"Why scared?"

"There's a rumor going around that the Articans are not supporters of the UO and the Clave anymore. I was sent here to find out the truth and to get all the men and women I could find to support four Clave men and two Senators coming from the Andromeda Galaxy to fight for Shangri-La."

"Holy Moly! When?"

"The exact time is unknown, but we imagine it to be soon. The meeting time is a few days from now. Is there still support for the Clave here?"

"You bet your bottom there is," Buck stated. "You'll want to talk to the Princess."

"Yes, Silver did say I would want to talk to a lady."

"I'll take you to her in the morning. For now, get some rest. You worked hard tonight. We'll get up early and travel to her place."

Jay nodded, "Thanks."

Jay wiped a few more tables down before climbing the stairs and heading toward the last room on the right side. He took off his shirt and hung it over the bed post. Then, he lay down on the bed, letting out a sigh. As he lay there, he suddenly felt as if he were being watched and not from afar either. He still had his gloves on, and at any moment, he could call upon the Clave words to conjure up a weapon of sorts. However, not knowing who was spying on him, he was hesitant to utter the old Clave words. Instead, he started talking to the walls.

"You can come out of your hiding and speak directly. I know you are there," Jay insisted. "It's not easy to hide oneself from a Claveman."

There was a rustle in the closet, and the door opened to reveal the man who had offered him money to take a job with the government.

"You would have done well to take the job and be rid of the competition," the man stated. "I've been sent to off ya for a tidy sum."

"How much?"

"Three thousand gold pieces."

"I'll give you five thousand in gold if you tell them I'm dead and give them this as proof." Jay took off his left hand glove and threw it to him.

"Hmmm. I will make money for lying to them?"

"You lied to me. Why not lie to them, too?"

The man chuckled, "How'd you find out I was lying to you about what I said before about the government?"

"I asked someone I trust."

"Ahh. Okay. We'll see who was lying to whom."

"You weren't lying?"

"That is for me to know and for you to find out."

"Why can't you just tell me?" Jay asked.

"You wouldn't believe me," he stated.

"What are you called?"

"Rasko."

"Alright then, Rasko. I will find out if you were telling me the truth tomorrow."

"If I were you, I would read very carefully."

"Yes. I know." Jay held up his hand, pointing at him. "I don't understand why you didn't just kill me? Why did you ..."

"I like the way you handle yourself. If you are wise, you will live longer than tomorrow, perhaps even last the few days that you are to be here. But, to do that, you'll have to learn a great deal about the politics of this place in a limited time, and that will take a very wise man indeed. I think you might be wise enough to handle it. If so, you'll see me again."

"Hmmm," Jay thought. "I realize you say this for my own good and that I must go through this discovery period on my own, right? Nodding, the man said, "Right."

"Okay," Jay stated. "Then I will soon understand why someone sent you to kill me?"

"Yes, but I can't go tell them you are dead just yet because you will go out tomorrow.

See, I must wait to kill you....later."

"I just said I'll pay you not to do that, more than what they will pay you to kill me."

"I know. I'll have to wait till you leave."

"Oh."

"Until then, you find out what you need to," Rasko stated.

"Where do you come from?"

The man smirked, "Around."

Rasko walked out and left Jay feeling very uncomfortable. It was after he had left that Jay noticed that there was no lock on the door. He put a chair under the knob and decided that the only way he'd get a little shut eye was knowing that if someone came through the door with the chair there, he'd hear and wake up. He lay back down and fell asleep right away. He didn't wake up until he felt a hand shaking him.

"You there," Buck stated. "Wake up, sleepy head."

Jay couldn't believe that he had not awakenend when Buck entered the room with the chair against door.

"Why did you put the chair here?"

"Someone was in my room last night."

"Ahh," Buck stated. "Sorry about that. There are no locks on my doors. It is policy. Fire hazard."

"I understand. Life hazard for me."

"Yes, I understand. Come on, freshen up, and then we go to see Princess."

"Okay."

Jay cleaned up and before long entered an empty tavern. The chairs had been placed with the seats on the table tops and the legs pointing to the ceiling so that the floors could be swept and cleaned of all the debris for the early morning revelers just before daybreak. His eyes traveled to the counter where Buck sat sipping coffee. Buck pointed to a mug that he had filled for Jay and motioned for him to join him; they spent the next thirty minutes talking and getting to know more about each other. When they finished their coffee, Buck looked at his timepiece and jumped up.

"We had better get going if we are to reach our destination before nightfall."

"Thanks for the cup of coffee and for giving me a job and a place to stay for my short visit," Jay expressed his gratitude as he rose and followed Buck outside.

"We have a long trip, but we will make it there by sundown," Buck said as he led Jay outside the tavern to find two chestnut brown Calamazoo animals which Buck had prepared for the trip while Jay was getting dressed. The Calamazoo was a cross between a horse and a camel. Its head looked like a horse complete with a mane hanging about its neck, but its body resembled only half the size of a camel and with a single hump on which the rider sat. The two men mounted the creatures and headed out of the city.

The Calamazoos increased their pace, as they entered the desert. They reached top speeds, heading toward the mountain ranges in the distance. This explained why Buck had chosen this mode of transportation instead of a hover mobile. The Calamazoo could move fast and required little water since it stored water in its hump. Before Jay could guess the speed, they had reached 50 mph in only a few seconds. Jay looked behind them to see only two dust walls as he held on to the reins to keep from falling. Jay smiled. He liked the Calamazoo.

Following the lead of Buck, they came to a large settlement in the middle of the desert. It was an agriculture habitat, and there was a very large green house on the property. Several robust guards, who seemed to know Buck very well, greeted him.

"Comrade Buck! Welcome!" one of the guards shouted.

"Thank you," Buck replied while dismounting. "I'm looking for the Princess."

"Lady Elaina is inside. I will notify her of your arrival, Sir." The guard lifted his communicator to inform the princess of Buck's presence.

"That will be good." Buck then turned to Jay. "Dismount."

Jay nodded and got down from his Calamazoo. "These animals are very cool."

"They do their jobs well," Buck stated.

The guards came and escorted them through the yards to the entrance of the main house. Servants and all sorts of officers and people were milling about, and Jay kept his eyes open for Rebels. Presently, the two guests were escorted into a large room where few people were gathered.

Princess Elaina rose and rushed over to greet Buck; however, her eyes immediately locked on Jay. She looked at him and smiled, noting his cloak and his attire. He looked like a Claveman to a "T."

Jay also took note of her rare, dazzling beauty, as if she were a precious gemstone on a chain. Suddenly, his eyes focused, and he found himself staring at her. He could not look anywhere else, nor would his eyes blink or move from her beautiful face. She was more sparkling than the twin sun on the horizon. It was not until Buck nudged him that Jay turned to look at him and raised his eyebrows.

Jay leaned to him, "You didn't tell me she was so beautiful," he whispered.

"Greetings, I am Princess Elaina Rufus, Senator Rufus' daughter."

Jay bowed, taking Elaina's hand and kissing her knuckles in the old way he had been taught to respect royalty and stood at attention. "It is an honor to meet you, Princess Elaina Rufus. I am Jay Star, at your service."

She smiled again, "Indeed. Come have a seat with us. What brings you out this way?"

"I have wonderful news for your ears only, your highness," Jay stated walking toward the viewing windows with his hands behind his back. "I am here on a specific errand, you see."

"Oh?"

"Yes. I would require your ear for a few moments alone, of course."

"I'm sure that can be arranged," she stated with a slight smile.

Then Jay nodded and sat down as he had been instructed. "Fabulous."

"You are quite assertive aren't you?" Elaina stated.

"I tend to get business out of the way and then move on to the pleasure," Jay stated, winking at her.

Elaina chuckled, "Right. I like that."

"Sounds like you and I can work well together, "Jay replied.

"Excuse me, but we haven't been introduced."

"Oh yes," Elaina stated. "Sir Jay Star this is Bernard Rufus, my cousin."

"I see. Greetings, Sir Rufus," Jay nodded to him. "You belong to an active family."

Buck nudged him and gave him an angry look, but Jay shrugged and shook his head. Then he sighed, nodded, and sat back.

"Whatever do you mean?" the man asked.

Elaina looked to her cousin and shook her head at him, "Never mind, Bernard!"

"Your Highness, do forgive me," Jay pleaded. "I don't mean to pry."

"All is forgiven," She said. "However, I think that it is best we speak in private."

Elaina held out her hand to Jay who allowed her to lead him into another room, where the door slid closed behind them. She turned on music to prevent their voices from being heard outside before she began speaking.

"You are risking a great deal to be here, Claveman."

"It is out of great respect for the Articans and the Rufus' clan that I come at all, Lady Elaina. The Clave is on the move, and we have great need of Artican support. I have come to find out if rumors are true that your people have sided with the Emperor."

"These are difficult times. The Emperor pushes my father to side with him."

"Surely, he hasn't," Jay exclaimed, taking a desperate step forward.

"No. Not as yet. But what is so important that you would risk so much to come and seek us out?"

"Word has come from the Andromeda that four Clavemen and two Senators are coming to retake Shangri-La. The Clavemen in this sector are gathering to lend them aide."

"There will be a great battle then," Elaina stated.

Jay agreed, "I imagine so."

"So, what Master Mal predicted is coming true. Odan is returning."

"That's the word. "We would like the Articans at our side."

She lifted her head as she turned to him. "I cannot promise you all the Articans, but I can promise you those that are with me, will be with you. Just tell me one thing."

"What?"

"The message that came from Andromeda, did it come by Baltar?"

"I don't believe it did. Master Jade came and told Silver and me, and he didn't mention that name."

Nodding, Elaina sighed. "Very well. I will gather as many of my people that will come with me, and we will travel with you in our ships when you are ready. However, we must avoid the Rebel patrols who are monitoring our system now."

"Silver will be here in two days, coming from Tatoway with as many people as she can get from there. Can you gather your people in that amount of time?"

"Yes. Stay here for the night. I will send out messengers to get supporters. By the second day, they will be here. When your lady friend Silver comes, we will be ready to travel."

"Silver is my Master. She is over me in the Clave. She is not my girlfriend. I just want you to know. But, this sounds like a good plan." Jay stated.

Chapter Twenty-Two

Help At the Gate Organized

Under the ice-capped peaks of the Southern mountain range on Deran, which was only one of the few land masses on the predominately water world, Elder Mal, who had envisioned this battle years ago, had built a fortress and stock-piled a variety of military equipment. His arsenal included UO star cruisers, one and two- man star vipers and fighters, and hundreds of different kinds of ammunition for any and all types of war vessels to man an all-out war of the worlds. He had foreseen the coming of this battle in his nightmares as he sat awake and daydreamed about the return of the Clave Warriors who would restore the Universal Order someday. He somehow knew that he had to prepare the rest of the Clave despite their unbelief. Therefore, he planned this in secret with very few others knowing what exactly he was doing. He told some people, those he trusted. One of those people was Devin, his friend and guide, who had led him by the hand since he had lost his sight. He had also informed Odan Amir and Markel Amar.

Devin now stood by him in the loading bay area of the fortress. From the balcony, they observed as the army loaded all the military equipment onto all the ships. It was a massive operation.

"I want you to take one of those cruisers and lead the convoy to the gate," Master Mal ordered.

Devin nodded. "As you wish. Won't you come along?"

"No. I will be overseeing things from here on our long range scanners. If we need more assistance, I will send more ships."

"Ahh!" Devin responded.

"I would suggest you take the Avenger II. Its Captain is a fellow named Yegar Son. He is a well-tempered Claveman and won't take your presence harshly. There are some who are territorial, but he won't mind."

"You sure about that?"

"Yes," Mal assured him.

"Good."

"He will welcome you aboard.

"But I really want you to take charge of those fighter pilots and manage them well against the Rebels," Mal added. "We need to be effective against their pilots."

"No problem," Devin replied.

"The ships are looking good. I just hope we get to the rendezvous point on time,"

"We will, Sir. We will."

As Mal and Devin looked down at the five large space cruisers being loaded with supplies, men, ships and ammunition, Master Mal wondered if it were enough to go against Zymon's Armada of Rebels. He knew the Rebel Armada was a million strong, whereas the Clave were only a ragtag fleet of a few hundred. In the past they had fought and won with worse odds. He thought of Silver and wished he had sent her to Artica to verify whether they were going to side with them or not. They really needed their old allies on their side again, like old times. He surmised it would have been best to find out the truth. Yet, he sighed and shrugged it off. He had told her specifically not to go there, warned her to stay away. In silence now he regretted it.

"Something bothering you, Master Mal?" Devin asked.

"Eh. I just remember having told Silver not to inquire of the Articans of their support."

"Yes?"

"I should not have forbidden her to go there. We need them."

"It's not too late to inquire of Senator Rufus."

"Perhaps. It's been a while since we last spoke."

"Then he may welcome your call," Devin replied, glancing at him.

"Maybe." Mal said, still looking down at the ships below. "I'll give it some serious thought.'

"Begging your pardon, Master Mal, but it's not a perhaps situation anymore. It's a do or die situation now. Either we get them on our side, or this last effort of the Clave to rebuild the UO or the Clave Order will die without the Artican's assistance. This must be a combined effort of all the races that oppose the Emperor and the Rebel Armada," Devin argued.

Mal turned to Devin and nodded. "You are right." Placing a hand on Devin's shoulder, he continued. "I am glad that you will be in charge out there. You have the heart for this mission. It is a do or die situation. I will make contact with Rufus using an encrypted message. If he responds to the old code, then I will know of his support."

"Once we have gathered everyone a few days from now, we should focus on when to strike."

"Yes. We must be there at the right time, or else we'll fail them," Mal reiterated.

"Is there a way to monitor the gate to watch their status?"

"Yes, but the Rebel patrol will see that we are watching. It will be very difficult to get readings on that area without being seen or noticed."

"Hmmm." Devin thought. "There must be a way."

"If you think of something, let me know."

"Perhaps a probe?"

"AI Bots?" Mal asked. "That might work. They are small enough to go unnoticed…"

"But efficient enough to do the job required," Devin completed the words.

"Have it done," Mal ordered, pleased with Devin's quick solution to the problem.

"Yes. I'll get some of the men on it and have them set it up and positioned."

"Brilliant," Mal said with a smile. "Brilliant. In this way, we'll know when that gate opens and what will be coming though it before it arrives."

"Great minds think alike." Devin said with a smile.

Master Plan to Assist Raptor's Claw

In the darkness of space, a rag-tag fleet of mid to large size ships crept trough the endless midnight, heading toward the rendezvous point, Deran. As the ships played follow-the-leader, each ship's science team had their eyes glued to their instruments, trying to spot any Rebel patrols that they might have to outrun or hide from.

They flew in a zig-zag formation across the chasms towards the outer-rim territories, using the neutral planets dark sides as cover. Only Clave Warriors could travel through space in such numbers unnoticed. It was as if the will of the Universe was on their side. Jade and Norm led the fleet onward and reached Deran with no Rebel interactions. Their fleet entered the atmosphere of Deran and headed toward the Southern mountain range. They contacted the command center and supplied them with the access code, the secret password, which had been told to Silver and passed on to Jade.

As Jade and Norm exited the Millennium Star, a Freight and Cargo Cruiser, they were greeted by Master Mal and Devin.

Jade grabbed hold of Master Mal's right shoulder with his own right hand and smiled as Mal did the same. "Master Mal, it is good to see you again after so long!"

"Jade! How is the family life?"

"Wonderful," Jade replied, releasing his hand and shaking Mal's hand, kissing it as a sign of respect.

"Hmmm. I respect your decision to come back despite your family. It is a hard choice. I must warn you that the Rebels may try to utilize them against you." Mal warned him. "I hope they are well hidden."

"They know not to get caught," Jade answered.

"Good," he said, patting his shoulder. He then turned his attention to Norm. "Norm!" he said, as they grabbed each other's right shoulder with their right hand, in the old Clave tradition.

"Brother to brother."

"Brother to brother, in all things," Mal repeated. "You haven't aged much, Norm."

"Ha!" Norm protested. "More than you think."

Both men laughed. "This assignment you gave me, Jade, has put more grey on my head than you thought."

Mal laughed. "I thought he would."

"Hey, I didn't do anything, honest," Jade said holding up his hands in denial.

"Enough of these jokes." Mal stated. "We have serious business to discuss."

"Have you figured out a way to know when they are coming?" Jade asked.

"We've got that under control." Mal answered.

Jade nodded. "Good. Before, we had no way of knowing when they were entering through the gate."

"We'll send out a robotic probe, like the one they sent up, but this one will remain at the gate and take readings of the area and report back to us when the gate is in use," Devin explained.

Jade nodded. "Ingenious!"

"We are setting it up as we speak. All we are waiting for now is getting everyone here so that we can get organized to leave."

"Who do we have still out there?"

"Silver and Jay have gone to the Tatoways," Mal stated.

"What about the Articans?"

"I told her not to go there. It is undetermined if they are still with us or not."

"Shouldn't we find out? We will need their support," Jade inquired. "The Articans are a formidable force in this system."

"I know it. But it is rumored that they are with Zymon now."

"Are you certain?"

"I am certain enough not to go assuming at this desperate time. We cannot take such a great risk with what we have. We have only a small number as it is, and I think it is just enough to beat the forces Zymon will put forth against us. If we take the Articans, and they are secretly with the Rebels, they will sabotage our efforts and ruin our plans," Mal explained his hesitance to contact them .

"I see," Jade replied. "However, if they are with us, having their number will help us to overtake Zymon and his Rebels."

"I know it would," Mal stated. "The risk is too great to go for what could be true."

"You sure?" Norm asked.

"For now, yes." Mal stated.

Chapter Twenty-Four

Rebel Patrols In Pursuit

Reese, Kal and Troy were sitting in the cockpit of their new spaceship, admiring all it had to offer when their scanners began blinking and an annoying siren pierced their ears. Troy looked at the instrument panel as he shut off the siren.

"Rebels, coming in at ten o'clock, fast."

"Frack!"

"Lose em! We can't let them know where we are headed!" Reese cried out.

"No kidding!" Kal replied at the pilot's seat, moving the ship controls hard to the right, making his way toward the nebula. The Rebel ships quickly determined where they were being led and commenced firing on them, knowing that they would get lost in the murky chasms of the nebula. However, they didn't break their pursuit.

"Cripes, if we get stuck in here, we might not be able to get out," Troy exclaimed, "and that won't be good."

"No kidding!" Kal replied. "It's not my plan to get stuck, but to either lose them or eliminate them. I'd rather lose them, but if they persist, I will have no choice but to eliminate them so that we may continue on our path to Deran."

Laser shots streaked past the ship as it zipped toward the nebula at top speed. The smaller ship blasted after it, trying to gain on it, getting closer and closer, decreasing the range, the laser blasts finding targets on the ship's hull.

"They are hitting the hull. Can't this thing go any faster?" Reese asked.

"It's topped off now," Kal cried.

"Pray we make it before they get a lock on us."

Just as the pursuing ships honed in on them, the ship disappeared into the nebula losing the pursuing vessel. The Rebel pilot cursed and slapped his hand on his joystick in frustration. Turning away from the nebula and coming out of it, the pilot reported back to headquarters what had transpired. The patrol remained for another 20 minutes before leaving the area.

Inside the nebula, Reese, Kal and Troy ran their ship in tight circles and scanned beyond the nebula where they had entered and took note that the Rebel's had departed. They waited another few minutes before departing the nebula and continuing to Deran.

Jumping into hyperspace speed, the brand new ship zipped into a line leaving a flash of fire light behind, marking the spot of exodus. The three day trek through the Orion's Belt would bring them to Deran in the Outer Rim territories.

In the ship, Reese, the eldest, commented on their situation. "At least we were able to make it to jump speeds."

"By the skin of our teeth," Kal stated. "We better hope we don't run into Rebs on the other side of this jump."

"Don't go jinxing us," Troy, the youngest of the trio yelled.

"I'm not jinxing us. I'm just saying that they could have reported our ship to other rebel patrols," Reese stated. "In other words, we need to be on the lookout for them."

"So noted. I will be keeping an eye out on the scanner," Kal stated.

"Ahem!" Troy cleared his throat. "That's my job as your co-pilot."

"You know what to look for?"

"Of course," Troy stated.

"I think that Kal should keep a look out for the patrol and you should handle the communications, Troy."

"But-"

"Understanding takes time and patience, young one. Kal has seen the reading before and knows what to look for, Troy."

"Yes, Master Reese," Troy responded. "I understand."

"It is nothing against you personally. We just don't want to overlook something because we think it is something else."

"I understand."

"Good," Reese replied.

Kal looked at Troy and could tell that he seemed offended in some small way. He glanced at him as he kept his eye on the instruments. Reese went into the cabin of the ship, leaving the two alone.

"Not to worry, Troy," Kal stated. "Reese will come around and trust you with important things sooner than you think."

Troy turned to Kal. "Why not now?"

"He thinks of you as a youngling, Troy. He still thinks you need protection."

"Yeah? When will he get the idea that I'm grown?"

"When you prove to him you don't need him anymore."

"How?"

"It will happen naturally. Don't worry about it. Might be sooner in coming than you realize."

"Yeah, well, I wish it will come even sooner! I'm tired of him treating me like a little kid!"

"Calm down! He'll hear you and that won't be good."

"I don't care if he does hear me. I hope he does hear me!" Troy cried out.

"Troy, just be patient."

"Were you patient?"

"No. I was just as upset and anxious as you are. But I had no one to calm me down either, and I wish someone had kept me from mouthing off to Reese when I did because he prolonged my time from happening maybe another year or so."

Troy turned to him. "What?"

"Yeah. I got pissed off and told Reese off, and he waited another two years before reporting to the council about me."

"Wow!" Troy exclaimed.

"See. Take my advice. Be patient. Let this go and wait your turn. It will come soon enough."

"Okay," Troy sighed. "Thanks."

"That's what I'm here for. To guide you."

The ship sped on its path with no more Rebel entanglements, arriving at its destination three days later. An alarm announced its arrival, and Kal quickly shut it off. He also disengaged the hyperspace and the auto pilot so that he could take over the controls to guide the ship toward the predominately water world before them.

Reese moved from the cabin into the cockpit of the ship and sat down in one of two chairs directly behind those occupied by Kal and Troy, and gave Kal instructions.

"Type in this old code. Deran Command, GM Reese on Falcon X requesting docking clearance, over. Encrypt it."

Troy nodded and did as he was instructed. "Done."

Troy pressed the headphones closer to his ears and waited for a response. Seconds later, he turned his head and reported what was coming through.

"Deran Command has received our message and is granting us clearance to follow exactly these coordinates S 235 and L 500. Landing port 22A"

"Acknowledged, Deran Command, advancing on those coordinates. *Falcon X*, standing by," Troy replied.

The Falcon X arched toward the planet and entered orbit, curved around the dark side and entered the atmosphere at an angle. Then gravity grabbed the ship causing it to drop, and Kal started the engines again. After they had entered the stratosphere, he blasted the jets forward, and the ship zipped into high speed, forcing its occupants against the backs of their chairs.

"Take it easy there, Kal," Reese cried out

"You always hated flying, didn't you?" Kal replied

"Especially when you were at the helm."

"Why is that?" Troy asked.

"He's a bit too fast for my taste," Reese retorted.

'Naw, he's just a slow moving turtle," Kal teased.

"Not in the ring," Reese explained.

"Okay, that is one place where you seem to move," Kal conceded. "But that's only because your ass is on the line."

Troy chuckled. "If my ass were on the line, I'd move too."

Reese laughed. "Now that's my boy."

Troy rolled his eyes. "Master Reese. I'm not a boy. I'm a young man now. I can hold my own in a ring, so I should be considered a man now."

"Eh. When I was your age, I was still considered a youngling by Master Mal."

"Alright. I'll take your word for it, Sir."

"You shouldn't rush old age, Troy. It will come soon enough, and you will wish it hadn't come when it comes," Reese advised. "It comes with a lot of baggage!"

"Does it?" Troy asked.

"Yes."

"I told you," Kal reminded Troy. "Patience."

"Listen to your brother."

Troy nodded. "Patience is something I will learn."

"Good." Reese put his hand on his shoulder. "It is better you do."

The ship touched down on the landing bay of the Southern Mountain Range of Deran, where the highest Mesa provided a landing platform for ships. When the ship had come to a complete stop, landing personnel moved it under cover to hide it from the Rebel Control.

Reese, Kal and Troy looked up to see Master Mal and Devin approaching them.

"Welcome, Master Reese."

Clasping Master Mal at the right shoulder with his right hand, Reese hugged his blood brother Mal.

"My brother, it is good to see you again."

"My younger brother! You look well!"

"How are your eyes, brother?" Reese asked.

"Not so good. I see a little, but not enough to join you all in this trip."

Nodding, Reese kissed his brother's hand, and he slipped out of the Clave hold. "Silver told us that we are meeting here."

"She was telling you the truth. Jade and Norm are here, as well."

"Ahh," Reese stated with a smile. "Good. I haven't seen Jade in a long while."

Mal turned to Kal and Troy. "You two were but young boys when I saw you last."

"We are older now, Master Mal," Troy piped up.

"Indeed! You have grown up into fine young men. I cannot believe how fast time has passed."

This made Troy smile and look at Reese.

"Don't say anymore, Master Mal. You will have him throttle me."

Laughing heartily, the party moved into the mountain fortress and through the corridors, chatting lively while remembering how their lives had been when the Cave Warriors reigned and kept order in the universe.

Chapter Twenty-Five
Clave Warriors Re-Awakened

Forty-eight hours Earth time was calculated differently on other planets. Of course, it was the celestial orbs moving around the stars at different speeds in different rhythms to different drummers, and each strummed their own little songs. Therefore, it took the equivalent of two days in Earth time for the Tatoways to round up supporters and gather them all in the caves of Dead Gulch, which lay 45 miles west of the city in the Southern Mountain Range at the edge of the Dead Forest.

In the darkness of the night sky, lighted only by the large pale moon, Silver and Hannible held up torches to see who was coming up the pathway.

"It's Jon. I see his red hair," Hannible stated. "Jon over here."

The people with Jon turned and walked toward Silver and Hannible. When they got closer to the light, they ran.

"Sure you weren't followed?"

"There were some Rebs in town, but they paid us no mind. Besides you told us not to come in great numbers. I believe we're the last."

'Then we only have about 300, Silver."

'That's enough. "I hope we have enough ship space to take this many."

'We got that covered," Hannible assured her.

Silver entered the cave and positioned herself in the center of the crowd. She raised her hands to quiet them.

"Thank you all for coming on such short notice. We shall depart
this night and make our way to the gathering. Soon we will be among
others who share our goal which is to see the Emperor fall from power
and Universal Order restored. Bring only what you need. The Clave will
provide food and water there."

Hannible stepped forward. "We have six ships. A quick division puts
fifty people in each. It will overload a few but we will do what we can.
The ships are hidden in the meadow behind the mountain. Follow our
lead."

With the torches, Silver and Hannible led the Tatoways through
the mountain tunnels into the valley behind it. After an hour of loading
and organizing the six medium-sized ships, Silver boarded her ship with
Hannible and began powering her vessel up. The others followed her lead.
In compliance with the rules of the planet, Silver called in to Tatoway
Command for departure clearance, which was granted without delay.

The six ships blasted off and up into orbit, circling once before
entering the blackness of space and changing course, heading for Artica.
The mid-size ships flew in a diamond formation, leaving enough room
between each for their thrusters.

Meanwhile, on Artica, Jay and the Princess sat on the balcony of the
Rufus home and gathered about them were all the Articans that Princess
Elaina had invited to join Jay and herself to support the Clave, a total of
about 5oo men and women.

"I still can't believe this many people have come and with their own
ships," Jay spoke in amazement.

"This is a serious situation. No one in this sector likes the Emperor's
rule right now. Most nations are being forced to deal with him, or else
someone dies or loses something important. The Emperor hits people
where it counts, you see. Like my father for example. The Emperor has
made threats on my life to persuade my father to side with him."

"That doesn't really give him a choice. Surely he'd rather protect you," Jay responded.

"Yes, but he can't be with me at all times. But I've thought of a better thing. I'd feel much safer with the Clave than here on Artica II."

Jay smiled at her. "Very wise. The Clave would see to your protection, I assure you."

"I hope they assigned you the task," Elaina stated.

"Really?" Jay asked.

"Yes." She smiled at him.

Then Jay saw a familiar sight. He pointed into the sunlit sky. "Silver is here with the Tatoways."

"Six ships?"

"Wow." Jay stated. "Looks like we have our own little army." he stated.

Elaina smiled. "Seems so."

The pair watched as the six ships touched down and landed a short distance from the Rufus estate. Then Jay and Elaina descended to lead the Artican 500 to meet Silver, Hannible and the Tatoways.

Before the mansion was the courtyard where everyone had gathered. Silver walked up to Jay and Elaina with Hannible at her side.

"Jay! Looks like things worked out here."

Jay smiled and nodded. "So far, so good." Jay turned to Elaina. "Princess Elaina Rufus, this is Silver and her companion; I'm sure she'll introduce us."

"Yes, Your Highness, this is Hannible. He owns the general store on Tatoway."

Princess Elaina held her hand out and Hannible kissed her knuckles. Then, Silver glanced back at the 300 who had traveled with them.

"We have three hundred men and women who have come with us from Tatoway to support the Clave. How many of the Articans will come?" she asked.

Princess Elaina smiled and gestured to the crowd. "We have five hundred with us. If we get clear of Artica without any Rebel entanglements, we should be okay until we reach our destination."

"Then I say let us depart now before the patrols on the planet get wind of this gathering." Jay suggested.

"I agree to that," Silver added.

"So be it." Princess Elaina raised her hands and waited for silence before she spoke up again. "People, we will now board our separate ships again. Let us all do this in an orderly fashion. We head now to the gathering at Deran. Good luck and God's speed."

The volunteers followed her orders and boarded the ships, five, large Artican cruisers and six Tatoway mid-size freighters. It took nearly an hour before every ship was loaded and ready for blastoff. After contacting Artican command for departure clearance, the ships formed a convoy into the endless midnight of space, heading on a course to Deran. Eight ships traveled at light speed, but the overloaded ones could not make the jump to hyperspace speed. In addition, the convoy was too large to make a jump into hyperspace while keeping the ships together. This of course would make them very visible to Rebel patrols.

As the eight ships inched through the chasms of space, the passengers took the time getting to know one another. Jay had opted to travel with Princess Elaina on one of the larger Artican ships, while Silver traveled on her own ship. Silver, having noticed Jay's admiration of the Princess, had smirked at him and indicated her disapproval. She had moved closer to whisper a reminder to him of the Clave rules regarding romantic relationships and to also bid him bon voyage.

"Don't get too close."

"Meaning?" Jay had asked.

"Don't start anything you can't finish," she replied.

That had been plain enough for him to understand. She had reminded him not to get too close to the Princess and start a relationship with her because Clave Warriors were forbidden to start romantic relationships. It was considered to be distracting for those involved, taking them away from their duties.   Jay already knew this. As he glanced at Princess Elaina, he wondered if he had been trying to start a relationship.

"The mere fact you're on this ship says it all," Jay said to himself.

"Jay?" The Princess called to him.

Blinking, Jay turned to her and raised his eyebrows. "Forgive me, I was…"

"Thinking?"

"Yes."

"A terron for your thoughts?" she prodded.

Jay smiled. "I can't say."

"Oh. Clave business?"

"In a way, yes," Jay replied.

"When Buck brought you to meet me, I must say I was struck by your manners. You act so much like Master Mal."

"In a way, he's like my Idol. I have always looked up to him and have admired him as someone I wanted to emulate. I watched him when he greeted dignitaries and friends. I listened to what he said and how he said it, and paid close attention to his gestures and mannerisms. Then Silver taught me more. She taught me why I should do those things so that I would understand it all. Now it's a part of me."

She smiled. "I know that the Clavemen are forbidden to have relationships, but what about friendships?"

"We are encouraged to love people so much that we would risk our lives to save them. In the course of doing that, one acquires friends, I suppose. There is no rule against friendships, but there is a rule against romantic relationships."

"Why is that?"

"One can become obsessed with their lover to the point where they are distracted from other things…other duties."

"Oh," Elaina uttered, obviously disappointed by this information. "What if there is no obsession?"

"If there is true love, then there is a possibility of one being overly protective, overly zealous, overly jealous, overly anything really."

"There's something about you that –"

"I know," Jay interrupted.

Sitting at a small table in the cabin across from one another, gazing into each other's eyes, Jay let his hand fall on top of hers as he spoke. "I sense it too, Elaina." As if drawn by an unbreakable force he shook his head and leaned forward to kiss her hand and squeeze it.

"Things are much too complicated at the moment, your highness. This upcoming battle is sure to shake up this sector for a long time. And I'm still concerned about what I heard back on Artica."

"What did you hear?"

"That the Articans are siding with the Emperor.'

"My father would never do that! He was a Senator of the UO."

"If your lives were threatened, he would," Jay pointed out.

"My father is not a passive man. He would fight back!" Elaina cried.

"Not if he couldn't count on your safety," Jay added.

"Now he can."

"But he doesn't know that. Anyway, where was your father when we were making those plans?"

"I'm not sure. He had business to attend to."

"He didn't say where he was going? He will then miss you when he returns."

"I left him a note."

"Good, I hope he doesn't send the Rebel Armada after us."

"Don't be silly!" Elaina scolded. "You had better take that back!"

"Alright! I take it back," Jay readily recanted."

"I can't believe you just said that after all I've done to support this endeavor!"

"I'm just a bit edgy," Jay confessed.

"More than a little!" she emphasized.

"It's this trip. It's taking so long! I mean, if we were going at hyperspace, we'd be there by now."

"We can't go that fast. Some of the ships are overloaded with people and supplies."

"I know. It's good that we have such a turn out, but I'm more concerned about the Rebel patrols finding us."

"Space is too vast and wide, Sir Star."

The Princess had barely finished that statement when Buck came running up to them.

"Mate! Come with me! We need to arm the cannons!"

"What's happening?"

"Rebel patrol spotted us!"

Jay and the Princess jumped up and ran with Buck to the armory to find that volunteers had already taken positions in front of the three cannon control panels because of the over-crowded ship. Buck took control.

"Those of you seated here, move to the inside of the ship! We need to use the cannons! We are being attacked!"

Suddenly the ship rocked violently, sending the Princess and others standing crashing to the floor. Buck quickly activated all three panels. Standing on a roller platform with a 150 degree swivel, a skilled shooter could fire at selected targets in front and on both sides of the ship. These platforms had been positioned so that they would not collide with each other while they were being operated. Jay hopped on the platform, grabbed the controls and button that would fire the laser balls.

The Rebel ships were fast and furious. They struck and zipped away like vipers. Three Rebel ships flew by their side in formation and Jay blasted one of them.

"Yee Haw!" Jay cried. "That's one for me."

"Who's counting?"

"Me!" Jay laughed.

The Princess then downed one. "One for me then. We're tied!"

"Don't leave me outa dis!" Buck responded in the Artican dialect.

When the lone rebel craft circled in front of the ship, Buck fired and blasted it to pieces. "Woo hooo! One a piece."

A report came to the three that there were no more Rebel patrol ships in the area. Jay powered down the cannon, closed the panel and headed to the cockpit to speak to Silver. He knew the Rebels would return.

"Connect me with the lead ship."

"This is Silver, go ahead."

"Silver, this is Jay."

"Jay. I'm glad you guys are okay."

"Those Rebels will be back with bigger and more ships, Silver. We've got to get out of here!"

"You know we cannot make the jump to hyperspace."

"Let's try it," Jay stated. "We have to try. Our lives depend on it now. If we stay here inching along, we will be crow's meat!"

Silver sighed and thought for a moment. Perhaps Jay had a point. It wasn't like they were heavily overloaded, just a few extra people. They could make the jump…take the risk. Sometimes, risks had to be taken for the greater good.

"Alright, we'll try it."

Jay looked at the pilot and the pilot shook his head. "This is a crazy thing we going to attempt."

"It's the best thing we can do right now, or do you want to wait for the Rebs to come back with a Cruiser?"

"No. I guess you're right."

"I thought you'd see it my way," Jay stated. "Now make your calculations, and I'll come back to check them. They have to be spot on accurate for this to work out."

Jay went back into the cabin

"Everyone, listen to me. We've decided to make the jump to hyperspace. I know we said before that we couldn't do it, but if we don't try, we are going to get killed by the Rebel patrols. We have to try to get out of here and make it to Deran. Please find a seat, strap in, and make yourselves comfy. Don't get up for anything. Go to bathroom now, please."

The crew of volunteers scurried to quickly comply with Jay's orders, as he returned to the cockpit where he checked the calculations.

"Excellent!" Jay exclaimed.

"I confess. Silver suggested we do the calculations together. We did them as a group from our current course headings and positions in our convoy."

"Smart."

"That lady, Silver is rather bright."

Jay took an empty seat in the cockpit, but it wasn't the copilot's seat. Someone was already seated there, a young man about his age.

"Hello there." Jay introduced himself.   "I'm Jay Star."

"I know. I'm Malcom Conner. People just call me Conner."

Connor's brown skin and black, puffy hair shaped into an afro momentarily surprised Jay.

"I've heard about the Clave from my relatives, but I never knew it to be a reality. My uncles, aunts and my father swore it was true. Now I believe it."

"What do you think?" Jay asked.

"If you are for freedom and democracy, then I am for that."

"The Clave is for the will of the people. Whatever the people want is what the Clave will enforce, and will die trying to fight for that which is just and right. They will sacrifice all for that which is true, fair, honest, and what is the good for all nations, not just one or two."

"It sounds good. But is it really practiced?"

"It is," Jay replied. "Or rather it was before the Emperor overthrew the UO and the Clave and established his dictatorship."

Conner nodded. "So this gathering is to reestablish the UO and the Clave?"

"At long last, yes," Jay confirmed.

"Cool!" Conner exclaimed.

The countdown for the convoy to make the jump into hyperspace speed started over the communication system. Amazingly, before they knew it, all ships were traveling at top speeds, ten times the speed of light, and in a few hours they would be just minutes away from Deran.

Chapter Twenty-Six

Odan's Revelation Concerning Shatra

T he cave was smaller than most, but large enough to hold the gathering of the Clavemen that had come together from far and wide in the Orion's Belt Galaxy. Master Mal sat in the middle of the orbbed-lit cavern with Devin at his side. He was just about to speak when word of Silver and Jay's convoy came by messenger from the command tower through the communications.

"Master Mal, They have eight ships which are heavily loaded with Tatoways and Articans. Princess Elaina is among them."

"Good gracious! I told that woman not to go there!"

Jade smiled. "Perhaps SHE didn't go there."

Mal raised a white-haired eyebrow and smiled. "Jay," he chuckled. "I see your point. In this case, I'm glad they disobeyed me."

Reese laughed as well. "Usually, when a youngling disobeys the orders of a Master, the consequences are not good at all. However, this one time would be an exception.

"I suppose we'll wait for Silver, Jay, and whoever else is with them, so that I will not have to repeat myself," Mal announced the delay of his speech. After a pause, he continued.

"It is rude to start something before all the players are present. Silver did work very hard on this."

"Yes," Jade added, speaking up on her behalf. "She risked a great deal."

After a few hours, Master Mal received word that the eight ships had arrived and had safely landed in Deran. Silver, Jay, Buck and the Princess debarked first and were immediately escorted to the gathering of the Clave Warriors. The Princess who was considered an honorary member was allowed to attend in the place of her father, Senator Rufus.

When Master Mal's attendant saw the Princess, he guided him over to greet her.

"Master Mal, Princess Elaina Rufus is before you."

Mal stuck out his hand and grabbed Elaina's hand. 'Yes. I know this hand anywhere. It is the prettiest girl in the Belt."

Elaina smiled. "Master Mal, you shouldn't say such things with other women present. They might get jealous and try to off me."

"Nonsense!" Mal replied. "Since they know how important you are to this movement, they'd do no such thing."

Mal, still holding her hand, tugged at it as he moved deeper into the room. "Come and sit here with Silver. She'll protect you."

Silver rose as Master Mal approached her and Jay.

"I know Jay her underling," Elaina stated.

"Yes. I'm sure you two have met. Why don't you sit with him during our meeting?"

Jay smiled, took her hand, and guided her into an empty chair, then he stood behind her, folding his arms and standing at ease.

Devin, who was never far away from his master, gently escorted Master Mal to his seat. Slowly they walked together side by side as Mal began speaking.

"Now that we are all together here, I thank you for coming on such short notice. This is a wonderful turn out for an important cause. It proves that the Clave lives on in spite of common beliefs to the contrary!"

Mal paused as cheers and applause exploded in the meeting room. After several minutes of celebration, he raised his arms signaling for quiet. Immediately the audience responded to his request and he continued.

"I must thank Silver and Jay for going to Artica and contacting Princess Elaina. Without her support, we would have 500 fewer Warriors."

"Here! Here!" Jade shouted.

"Also, it was his first assignment away from Silver, who traveled to Tatoway while Jay investigated the Artican's support for the Clave."

Loud clapping and whistling echoed throughout the cave, and many of the Clave Warriors rushed over to give Jay a pat on the back or express words of praise which he greatly deserved for his hard work.

Mal stopped and raised his hands to return order to the room.

"Now, we will move some of the people from the overloaded ships to the cruisers and use those ships to assist in the attack of the larger Rebel cruisers."

He paused for a moment and Jade spoke up.

"What about fuel?"

"We've thought about that, and we've decided to load only one cruiser with enough fuel to reload the entire fleet twice. However, it will move slowly and be vulnerable to attack. Also, it cannot make the jump to hyperspace because of the weight. Therefore it will need protection of perhaps one cruiser and a few large ships."

"Can we spare that much?" Reese asked.

"We will have to. We can't have our fuel suddenly exploded or taken from us by the Rebels. We'll have to overly protect it. Unfortunately, this also means that we won't have fuel at the gate right away. Most likely, it will arrive perhaps a day or two days later at top speeds."

"Can we last that long?" Silver asked.

"We'll have to try," Jade replied.

"If you find your ship running out of fuel, you could make a dash toward the refueling ship, but that will just lead them to us."

"No. It's best that we stay and fight until you arrive," Norm suggested. "We must maximize our resources."

"Princess, what is this rumor that I hear about your father joining Zymon Keltor?"

"My father has not done any such thing," Elaina exclaimed.

"Forgive me for asking, but I have to be certain. You realize that our efforts will not be double crossed."

"Not by me," Elaina replied. "You know I'm for the UO and the Clave, and I always will be. My father, if he is swayed, it would be because our lives are threatened and he fears Keltor can get to us."

"You know that would never happen," Mal stated.

"To be quite honest, Master Mal, before Jay's arrival, we hadn't seen anything of the Clave except Buck here. I think my father was beginning to get a bit edgy."

"I see," Mal stated. "I take it he doesn't know of your coming here."

"No. But I left him a note."

"I will send him word to join us."

"Thank you," Elaina could not control the joy she felt at the news that her father might join her and the others in this endeavor.

Mal sighed and then spoke up again. "That is all I have to say. Let us all take the remaining time to get some much-needed rest before we board our ships and prepare to head out."

"Master Mal, how is the robotic probe doing at the gate?"

"It is doing what it's supposed to. No Rebel patrol has seen it or noticed its frequency yet, which is good for us. Besides, I believe our computer experts encrypted it."

Laugher erupted, and the crew filed out of the cavern.

"Have a good rest people," Mal ordered, for he knew that the upcoming days would require it. In the deep darkness of space, a small, metallic, sphere-shaped object floated, landing on the black nothingness surrounding the stars. Then, in a sudden burst of movement and a flash of bright, white light, it thrusted forth, beeping and blasting alarms off as it picked up activity from the anomaly that was awakening about it. The triple stars glowed brighter than ever before. The mass of space between those stars swirled clockwise. Lights all over the robotic probe lit up and streamed data to Deran, encrypted so that only they would understand it. Yet the tremendous anomaly was not something that could be hidden for long....

/////

At Deran, the data streamed in and was passed on to Master Mal. Once he reviewed this information, the ships moved out from Deran, blasting off the planet, making orbit, and making the jumps to hyperspace. Before the ship from the Andromeda Galaxy would make it across the gate within the next hour, they would be there in full force to fight the Rebels.

Chapter Twenty-Seven

Passage Through Gate To Shangri-La

Odan stood with Cassandra in her assigned quarters looking out the ceiling to floor glass that gave a spectacular view of the landscape of the Moon's enormous valley that rested below the mounting fortress. As he stood there, he was sure to shield his mind from Shatra. He could not have her homing in on these two.

"We are getting closer to Shangri-La, are we not, Odan?" Cassandra asked.

"Yes. As we do, I must say that things will get more complicated. Your roles in this will become more evident as this time comes closer."

"Just what is our role in this, Odan? I have yet to understand it." Seth spoke, his voice filled with uncertainty.

"Once people see that Zeger's children survived, and that there are remnants of the UO still alive, many will once again rally behind us and form a resistance to Zymon's dictatorship. Eventually, he will be outnumbered and over powered."

"As the UO was?" Cassandra asked.

"The UO wasn't outnumbered but betrayed by Shatra and Zymon Keltor. They cooked up the plan that destroyed the UO and the Clave. The Clave knew nothing about it until it was too late."

"That's not entirely true, is it Odan?"~ Shatra's voice reached out to him but Odan quickly closed his mind again with a harsh slam of his inward mind walls.

"You okay, Odan?" Seth asked.

"Oh. Oh yes. What were you saying?"

"You said the UO wasn't outnumbered but betrayed by Shatra and Zymon Keltor."

"Right. That's right. They cooked up a plan before we knew what was happening. When we caught on to it, it was far too late to do anything except save you two and prepare for the worst while hoping for the best. We did. We also went into hiding deliberately to make it difficult for them to get rid of all of us."

"Do you think that those who survived will come to your aide now?"

"If they knew what I'm up to, they would."

"Why not send word?" Seth stated.

"The whole idea is to avoid the Rebels, not to bring attention to ourselves," Odan explained.

"But they already know where we are headed and why. What is the point of keeping it secret anymore? We might as well prepare for the worst and hope for the best."

"I think that word of our coming may have already traveled by word of mouth through the grapevine, so to speak."

"You think other people have spread the word?"

"Yes. I have a feeling that we won't be alone when we go through the gate."

"I hope not. Otherwise this will be a short attempt to retake Shangri-La," Seth stated.

Odan turned from the view and looked at the twins he had known since their births. "It will not be an easy thing when we go through the gate. The battle will be intense. We will know right away if we are outnumbered or not."

"What shall we do?"

"Keep your chin up. Even when it looks like the end, hope for the best." Odan stated "We have a lot of people on our side."

"Now, what do you want us to do when we get to Shangri-La?"

"Ahh. As Senators, you are leaders of the UO, which is a democratic body from each nation or world. You both represent Romes IV. As leaders of that nation, you are to direct or give orders to any people from that nation to act in whatever way toward anything that defies the laws of Romes IV's previously written democratic constitution, which states that no man will rule over all people and make himself Emperor or King. Keltor has broken the rule of the constitution, thus, the law must be enforced, which is to capture him and bring him to justice under the Romes IV court."

"Now I get it!" Cassandra and Seth exclaimed at the same time as if something had just clicked in their brains.

Odan smiled. He recognized that the twins' innate powers were beginning to kick in.

"Good."

A rap on the door interrupted them and Captain Rex Maximillian Faraday stuck his head in the door."

"Let's mount up folks. We need to head out!" Rex bellowed in his deep masculine voice.

"If you hadn't come, I was going to come hunting for you, Captain," Odan stated. He turned back to Cassy and Seth. "Are you two packed up?"

"We didn't bring much to pack," Cassy reminded him.

"Yes," Seth added. "Remember we were practically kidnapped and whisked away before we knew what was happening."

"Get your things quickly. Timing is important if we are to accomplish our mission safely."

Cassandra moved quickly, gathering her belongings and outfits and stuffing them into the bag. When she looked up, her eyes met Seth's eyes, and she saw that he was smiling.

"Are you ready for this?" he asked her.

"I suppose I'm as ready as I'll ever be," Cassandra replied. "Let's go."

The twins moved to Seth's room where Cassy waited for him to gather his things. They opened the door to find Odan, Markel, Justin, and Gorn in the corridor outside their rooms. The whole party joined the crew of the *Raptor's Claw,* who awaited them down another corridor.

As they came around from another intersection of the corridors, they could hear Captain Rex's voice booming, as he checked the controls and his time piece. "One thing I know is that we had better get a move on rather soon!"

Markel spoke up in a calming voice, "Then by all means let us get moving. I hope we aren't slowing anyone down."

"No. I don't mean that," Rex replied. Smiling, he tried to cover his irritation. "I merely mean that the longer we stay here, the greater the chance that we might run into Rebel troops. Odan knows what I mean."

"Indeed, I do," Odan concurred, remembering what had happened on the way to Teranosis.

"All the more reason to leave now," Justin added.

"Right. Let's stop talking about it and go."

Rex led the way and moved the party down the corridor to the landing bay where the *Raptor's Claw* was moored. Langstrom smiled as she and McCloud stood with their arms wrapped around each other's waist. Rex saw them and gave Langstrom that "I told you so! I won!" smirk. Langstrom smiled shyly and looked away. She had lost the bet, but she had gained a lover. She was happy to lose this bet with Rex. However, she knew Rex was not one to win a bet quietly.

"Look what we have here! McCloud and Langstrom Together?"

"Watch your mouth there matey," McCloud warned. "You're liable to get it full of your own foot!"

"Oh? Pardon Me!" Rex said sarcastically.

"Be nice, Captain Rex," Langstrom interjected, her eyes pleading to Rex for mercy.

"Fine!" Rex relented, "but I won!"

"No kidding! Yes, you did."

Rex smiled. "Told you so."

"Yeah, you did," Langstrom stated. 'But now we have work to do."

"And I'm coming with you," McCloud's voice surprised both Rex and Langstrom.

"What?"

"You're going to need some help."

Rex looked to Markel and Odan, shrugging. "Is it alright?"

"Let them come," Markel stated. "We will need all the help we can get."

"That is fine," Markel nodded.

"How many?" Odan asked.

'How many can you spare?" Rex asked McCloud.

"About a thousand."

"That's plenty," Markel replied.

"Get them ready to move out. We will be leaving shortly."

"Right." McCloud turned to his men barking orders. The men darted off down the corridor to get the one thousand ready for a quick departure.

The *Raptor's Claw* party and now the McCloud group prepared for departure. McCloud's people scrambled to their ships, while the *Raptor's Claw* party headed to the docking port and scurried up the open ramp into the cabin.

After the captains checked their flight patterns, they revved the engines.

The landing bays' alarms sounded, alerting everyone that the bay would decompress. People not boarding a vessel hurried to a port-hatch to safety. The bay decompressed, reducing everything to zero gravity. Anything not locked in place floated. The two ships powered up and were skillfully controlled by the best pilots, Captain Rex and McCloud. The *Raptor's Claw* shot through the parting doors of the landing bay first. The large cruiser carrying one thousand star fighters aboard, along with its own firepower, followed under the command of McCloud and his crew.

McCloud's voice rang out over the frequency, "Command, this is McCloud. Batten down the hatches and prepare for the worst. If we get visited by Rebel forces, try to avoid direct contact with them because if they board, they may have Readers with them who will be able to detect that Rex and his passengers and crew were here."

"Roger, boss."

"Make up anything…the swine flu or something like that."

"Affirmative."

"Don't just say 'affirmative' and send them right to us," McCloud warned. "It would be very bad to have them attacking from both ends. Enough said?"

"Enough said, Sir."

"Good."

The ships blasted into the midnight of space, heading toward the triple stars and the gate leading to the Orion's Belt Galaxy. Master Markel held the key for that gate secure about his neck. He looked down at it as he sat in the cabin.

"It's been a long time since I put this gate key to use."

Odan smiled, "Orion's Belt, oh, yes, I can remember a time that I envied your having that key."

Markel chuckled. "Really?"

"It was not long after I was given the one to Andromeda."

"But why?"

"It was because of all the problems the Andromeda was experiencing at the time: Keltor and the Nations were squabbling over who was going to lead what. Oh, I was too done with it!"

Markel chuckled. "It often tickled me when grownups acted so much like children over something so insignificant."

Odan smiled. "OH, yes!

The fact that Zymon hasn't changed in all these years is what's so funny to me. I can bet you he still has the 'me me me' complex."

Markel covered his mouth and got a full belly laugh out of that. He laughed until tears flowed out of his eyes. "My planet, damn it!" Markel mocked Zymon's voice. He laughed again. "Yes. I believe it."

"That's why problems still exist," Odan pointed out.

"But we're here to fix the problem, are we not, Odan?"

"Not just to fix it, but to eliminate it!" Odan exclaimed.

"Wait. What do you mean, Odan?" Markel asked.

"I mean what I say….eliminate the problem."

"How?"

"How else?"

"We aren't here to kill anyone in cold blood,' Markel whispered.

"Not killing anyone, but killing a belief in someone's rule will take a lot of persuasion over a lot of people, Markel. This must be a history making event in all galaxies for it to be effective." Odan explained. "I imagine that the word has already traveled through the grapevine in the Orion's Belt and here in Andromeda. But it must have reached other galaxies by now also. If not word, the news of an imminent event about to take place, the Clan of the Clave Warriors returning to re-establish UO. By the time the UO is in control and running, most nations will know, and they will come to see for themselves. When that time comes, we will have eliminated all of the Rebel Alliance, and hopefully Zymon Keltor will be captured and imprisoned."

Markel sighed. "For a minute there I thought you…"

"You thought I had flipped my lid?" Odan chuckled. "No. I just can't wait until this is all over and done with."

"Same here." Markel agreed.

"Let's go tell them where the jump point is." Odan rose and led the way to the control room.

"Right." Markel replied, unstrapping himself from his seat belt.

The pair walked through the sliding doors to the cockpit where Captain Rex and Raymond sat chatting away. When the door swished open, both turned, thinking it was one of the girls of their crew. Markel and Odan, dressed in their robes, appeared to be floating toward them.

"Hey! What brings you two up this way?' Rex asked.

"You need to know exactly where to go; a course heading that will take you to the entrance of the gate," Markel stated.

Odan explained, "You must fly this thing spot on if we are to make it through without any scratches.

"I can manage that," Rex said.

"I'd pass that thought on to the rest of the pilots," Markel added.

"Will do. Now what are the coordinates?"

"Punch in 233.234L and 532.123LA." Markel replied. "Keep directly toward that heading, and when you see three stars as bright as can be, let me know."

"What if I miss it?"

"You won't miss it." Odan stated. "It's very noticeable."

"Oh." Raymond nodded. "Sounds easy enough."

"It gets more complicated after that."

"How do you mean?" Rex asked.

"Going into the gate will take precise timing," Odan added.

"Yikes!" Rex cried. "What about the others?"

"We'll just have to give them the directions. "Just relay the coordinates to the other pilots for now."

"Right," Rex replied and activated the communication system to the frequency that would contact the convoy of ships following them. "*Raptor's Claw* to Annapolis Parade, over!"

"Annapolis Parade reads you loud and clear, check back, over!" McCloud replied.

"Punch in these coordinates to follow 233.234L and 532.123LA."

Rex relayed the coordinates to McCloud's ships, which were carrying the volunteers he had recruited to assist the Clave Warriors. To Rex, it was turning out to be a bit more than he had bargained for. He had never picked sides in the political debate that had ripped the galaxies apart, but he found himself leaning to one side now. He liked the side he was on, but he wasn't sure where it would take him or where he fit into it. Perhaps, that was yet to be determined.

"About how far is the gate entrance?" Rex asked.

"It is a few hours from this location," Markel answered. "At this speed we should be there in three hours or less," Markel estimated while looking at the control panel where Rex was sitting...

"Just a glance at this thing told you that?" Rex asked.

"I am an experienced pilot, as well. I need only a glance at your instruments to make an estimated time of arrival to our destination."

"Not bad," Rex stated while punching in the numbers for the computer to make an approximation. "Let's see what it really is."

The computer took only a few seconds before it beeped. "Three hours and ten seconds," Markel smirked.

"There is a three percent margin of human error, I forgot to mention," Markel said, chuckling at Rex," who had a look of amazement over the fact that he had estimated so close to that of the computer's.

"Right," Rex laughed. "I'll have to remember that next time. And you're the one who expects me to fly this baby precisely on target?"

"Well, as best as you can," Markel explained.

"Listen to me son. No one is perfect except the Almighty God, you got me? So don't go expecting things from people that they can't possibly deliver."

"You're right. Only God is perfect." Markel nodded in agreement.

"Glad we are on the same page," Rex stated. "Now, I don't feel like you are bossing me around."

"I wasn't trying to boss you. I know. I understand. You're in a leadership position, and it comes naturally."

"That's true, Markel. You took the words right out of my mouth. As Captain, I get the same thing," Rex admitted with a straight face.

"You should have better things to say about us, Boss," Raymond interjected.

"Butt out, Raymond!" Rex yelled.

"You're making us look bad," Raymond replied, pointing a finger at him.

"Not as bad as you're going to look!" Rex responded.

"Oooooh! I'm shaking in me boots, Boss," Raymond teased.

"You better be!" Rex stated.

"Now you're bossing me!"

'You forced me."

Feeling the situation escalating from teasing to the next level, Odan spoke. "I suppose we had better leave you two to it?"

"Yes, that would be best," Rex replied. "Raymond and I can handle things from here on. Although it might not look like it, we are quite competent."

Markel and Odan laughed as they exited the cockpit. They had three hours and ten minutes to kill. Odan turned to Markel and put his hands behind him as he walked.

"I think it's time to train the children how to use their minds, but I want them to use you, Justin, and Gorn, not me. Shatra is too close and intuned to me. I don't want to risk her connecting with me," Odan said.

"Good idea," Markel agreed. "I think the children know us well enough to attempt mind links with us."

The pair walked back into the cabin to find the rest of their party sitting around chatting with one another. Cassy and Seth were talking with Justin and Gorn, and they were playing Star poker.

"....I think you are getting the hang of it, Seth. It seems you'd be a wise player," Justin caught Seth off guard.

"Wow. Thanks for the compliment!" Seth blushed not expecting such an observation. "So, if I get a red star, no matter what, I win?"

"Yep. Nothing beats the red star. There are only two in the deck."

"Cool. Told you, I'm lucky!"

Odan and Markel approached them and interrupted the game. "Excuse us, but there are more important things than star poker."

"Like?" Seth asked.

"Clave business," Odan stated sternly.

"Oh, yes," Seth replied, setting the cards on the table. "What's up?"

"You both need to practice your mind skills."

"With you?" Seth asked.

"No. Not with me, but with Markel, Justin and Gorn. Since I'm not going to be with you guys most of the time, you both need to learn how to connect with them better."

"Why not with you, Odan?" Cassy asked.

"Because it would be too much of a risk right now. The enemy is too close to us, for me, to allow myself to be that vulnerable and open minded to be receptive to your thoughts. I'm sorry, but it will have to be Markel, Justin, and Gorn. However, this will sharpen your skills and let us know if you can connect with others yet."

"Sounds interesting. I'm curious whether or not I can connect with them," Cassandra added.

"You should be after all this time being together. After a few days in close quarters you would be able to," Odan assured her.

Nodding, Cassandra glanced at Markel. "It should prove interesting."

The five moved to a secluded section of the cabin and settled themselves for the task of mind connections, leaving Odan alone to concentrate on keeping his mind clear of all things. Odan sat on one of the chairs and sighed, focusing on his mental barriers, shutting out what

Markel and the others were doing. Instead he focused on making sure Shatra did not invade his mind. It would be too dangerous for the mission.

"*What shall we work on?*" Cassy asked Markel using her mind voice.

Markel focused on her.

"*We shall work on multiple mind connection.*"

Cassandra stared into Markel's eyes.

"*Now, concentrate on me. Just let your mind slip into my thoughts,*" Markel instructed her.

"*I feel you,*" Cassy cried unable to contain her excitement over this new experience.

"*Now you come in, Seth,*" Markel said. "Look into my eyes."

Seth stared into Markel's eyes and concentrated as Cassy had done.

Cassy could feel his entrance to the mind link.

"*Welcome,*" Cassy relayed to her brother with her mind.

"*Good. Very good, Cassy,*" Markel praised her. "*Now Justin and Gorn will come in as well, and we can talk a while.*"

Justin and Gorn were used to mind connection, so it didn't take long for them to dive in. Before the twins knew it, Justin and Gorn were in the mix with them.

"*You will find that using your gloves will take some mind connection as well,* "Gorn pointed out.

A Clave warrior must be in tune with his glove," Justin added.

"*Most definitely.*" Markel remarked.

"*What do we do now?*" asked Seth.

"*We talk to each other using our minds only,*" Markel answered.

"*Tell us more about the Universal Order,*" Cassy suggested.

"*The UO consisted of the Senators and a few Clave masters who met occasionally to discuss strategies to keep peace and to ensure safe and easy traffic flow through the gateways.*"

"*How will we start things back to the way they were?*"

"Just by your presence, the UO will re-establish itself and seize power from the tyrant who murdered your parents and turned the entire universe into a dictatorship."

The twins listened intently, their minds focused on all the information Justin, Markel, and Gorn transmitted to them.

Meanwhile ...

Heading toward Teranosis, the Rebel Fleet, led by Commander Shatra, now consisting of two Star Cruisers each holding 500 star fighters aboard, traveled at hyperspace speed. Commander Shatra sat in the command throne of her cruiser, the *Hydra*, looking at the view screen with a grin on her face. She could feel Odan Amir. He was not far ahead of them now.

"They are close, oh, so very close," she thought. *"If we continue at maximum speed, we can catch them."*

"Are we going as fast as we can go?" Shatra questioned the pilot.

"Yes, Ma'am."

"I want to be within range to fire before they make the jump through the gate. If they go through the gate, we are going to have to go through it with them," Shatra warned.

"But what if it closes behind them, we'll be crushed."

"We'll have to take that risk, Captain. The Emperor's regime depends on us destroying that ship and the people on it."

"I thought they were only wanted for questioning?"

"You thought wrong," Shatra replied. "The Emperor doesn't need to know anything from them. Take my word for it. He will thank us."

"If you say so, Commander."

"I do say so. Now get us into range!" Shatra ordered.

"Aye," the captain stated, "just as soon as we find a few ships to chase," the captain laughed. "You know the reports were that there were no passengers on any of these ships. What makes you think the people we are looking for are on this ship?"

"Believe me, Captain, when I have a hunch about something, I'm usually right. I'm willing to bet my life that the people we are searching for are on the *Raptor's Claw*, and I have staked my life on it. The Emperor doesn't play games. He is counting on me to find these people, and I will, before they cause any damage. All you have to do is get me to them before they cross over into the next galaxy where they can do that. It is by your subordinates mistakes that they have gotten this far as it is."

The Captain frowned a bit. He didn't like being blamed in front of his crew where the blame for the lack of progress was on a lot of shoulders. It was not his fault alone. However, he said nothing to this and turned his head back to the viewer. He thought better of replying to that.

"Get me engineering," the captain barked.

The operations officers on deck responded. "On screen, Captain."

The face of the engineering officer appeared on the viewer. "Captain, Sir. How might I be of service?"

"I know we are going top speed, but is there any way to make her go faster, Simon?"

"No way possible. She is putting out all she can right now, Captain."

The Captain glanced at the Commander who gestured her approval with her hands, saying nothing more. He nodded to the screen and thanked him. "Very well, Simon, Thanks for that."

"Hopefully we will get to them in time," Shatra replied, trying her best to break into Odan's mind.

Chapter Twenty-Eight

The Clave Battles the Rebels

The hours passed by quickly as Markel, Justin, Gorn, Cassy and Seth conversed using their minds quite well. Over the past few days, they had grown close, and what Odan predicted before they started this practice session was true. They didn't have any trouble connecting with each other.

Odan sat concentrating on keeping his mind clear. The door to the cabin swished open, and Raymond peeked in, his short arms holding the door ajar, and announced, "Pardon me, but Odan, Markel, we are approaching the 3 stars now."

The group of five who had been communicating with their minds stopped and turned their heads in unison to Raymond. Then Odan rose to his feet.

"Come brothers, we must open the gate,"

Markel, Justin, and Gorn followed Odan up the ladder. Finally, the six of them were crammed into the cockpit, with Rex at the helm, Raymond at the copilot's seat, and the Clave Warriors behind them.

Odan, Markel, Justin and Gorn got themselves into a half circle, pulled out their medallions, which were the keys to the gates, joined hands, and began speaking the old lore.

Suddenly, before the ship, the three bright stars flashed one after the other, and a white light lit up the vortex in the center of the triangle of the three stars. The parade of ships headed for the vortex and slowly entered one by one.

No bumps or rough rides. The trip through the gate was as smooth as a ship sailing over calm seas. However, the crew and passengers had not anticipated what they met on the other side…

McCloud, aboard one of his ships tailing the *Raptor's Claw,* thought and was prepared for a large battle before they passed through the gate. He had been sure the battle would be on this side of the gate, but as they continued through the threshold, he realized that the battle would be on the other side in the Orion's Belt Galaxy, which was a far better place for the battle to begin. He suspected that the Clave would have more support there.

"Have all fighters prepared to blast off as soon as we cross over?' McCloud barked.

"They know, Sire. All fighters are standing by for your permission to proceed."

"No, tell them to go ahead as soon as we clear the gate. They don't have to wait for my word. They just have to wait until we clear the gate. I don't want to waste time here."

"Very well, Sire."

"Sir, long range scanners picked up a fleet of enemy ships tailing us."

"How far away are they?"

"They will not make it to the gate before it closes, but they have spotted us."

"Great. We got them coming behind us. Get me the *Raptor's Claw.*"

After a few moments, the communications technician turned around and nodded to McCloud.

"Rex, did you see the fleet behind us?"

"Yes. We've beat them to the gate. They will have to get through another way," Rex replied.

"They have their ways of getting through the gates?" McCloud asked.

"It will take them longer, but, yes," Rex confirmed.

"We have quite a number of ships ahead of us though."

"I hope they are friendly."

"Most of them are, but some aren't. I believe we are in for a battle getting to our destination," Rex warned.

'Well, we didn't come along for nothing. Why don't you slow your speed and let us pass you, taking point."

"Probably a good idea," Rex agreed.

The *Raptor's Claw* came through the triple star pattern first and slowed down turning to the right and allowing the ships from Annapolis to take the lead. Then the first laser fire came from the *Imperial Star* ⬚⊏⊐⊐⊐⊐⊐⊐⊐⊐⊐⊏, flashing out and hitting one of the ships from Annapolis. That ship, in turn, fired back at the same destroyer and thus began the intergalactic war.

Laser fire blasted out from every ship, lighting up the darkness with colorful hues of red, green, white, and blue. Occasionally, an explosion of a ship added color to the fireworks display. Blackness temporarily disappeared, as tiny lights of the star fighters and the fire light from their thruster engines replaced it. Their lasers were smaller, but no less damaging, as they connected with targeted ships which exploded upon contact.

As the fighting raged on, the gate from the Andromeda galaxy re-opened, and the two star annihilators from the Empire sailed through the gate hours after the *Raptor's Claw* and the Annapolis party. They blasted through at the most opportune moment, exactly when the enemy was in need of fresh fighters. However, the Clave and its entourage of civilians and other forces who opposed the Emperor's dictatorship held their own quite well. Thankfully, they had people who had mastered the art of war and the use of lasers and shooting. Plus, they had Clave Warriors from back in the old days with them, skillful fighters who were doing their best to lead the men and women to victory.

Chapter Twenty-Nine

The Battle Intensifies

Light years from the Andromeda Galaxy but just a gate jump away, three stars lit up the Delta Quadrant, queuing everyone in the vicinity. Rebel or not, the gate was about to open and the battle of the universe was about to begin.

General Devin, who was named general by Master Mal, was put in charge of the resistance efforts. He contacted all the ships: "All fighters, launch! All medium-sized ships, prepare to engage enemy cruisers! All large ships stay out of firing rage and maintain a perimeter for fuel loading and repairs! Let's meet the approaching brothers with as much help as we can. General Devin out."

Some responded positively while others simply did as they were told. Jay and Silver led a platoon of six ships. Master Mal watched from the control room of one of the large ships through the large viewer, as the small fighters began appearing as blips on the view screen. Then the enemy's star trooper ships began spilling out of the cruisers. On the large viewer at the helm, the lasers lighted up the darkness, reminding Odan and the twins of Fourth of July firework celebrations back on Earth. Occasionally, a fireball connected with a ship, shattering it into innumerable tiny pieces floating into space.

The first through the gate was the Annapolis fighter vessels which immediately took aim and fired at the rebel cruisers. The *Raptor's Claw* sailed safely in the middle of its convoy.

General Devin gestured to the communications technician, who nodded and immediately opened up a line. "General Devin to *Raptor's Claw*, come in please."

Rex glanced at Odan, who nodded, giving permission. "This is Captain Rex of the *Raptor's Claw*! We read you loud and clear, over.'

"We got your message," Devin continued.

'So we've noticed," Rex stated. "It's good that you guys are here, or this mission would have ended very quickly."

"Roger that. I think for the most part we were prepared for this one."

"They aren't going to stop coming. You know that, don't you?" Rex asked.

"Yes. But we are ready. Now that we have the brothers back, we can organize again," Devin replied.

"Cross your fingers. I heard that some had crossed over to the Emperor's side."

"Perhaps some have, but they wouldn't ship up here. They wouldn't be able to hide their thoughts," Devin replied.

"I see." Rex agreed.

"We'd know by what they do, say, and think."

"Ahh."

"Let us combine our efforts and take care of these cruisers, shall we?"

"The name of the guy leading the team from Annapolis is McCloud. McCloud, you listening?"

"To every word, my friend."

"Good. Then let's organize ourselves.'

Following orders given to him by General Devin, Jay maneuvered his patrol through the fire fight. Meanwhile, Master Mal noticed his aggressive action and skill with admiration. *"He could be a fine leader in the Clave."*

"Delta Patrol, stay in formation!"

"Roger that, but everything is moving so fast it's hard to keep up with all this."

"Just stick to your wingman, and everything will be fine," Jay demanded. "Your job is to look at aft scanners and side scanners to make sure something doesn't blindside us."

"Thanks for telling me what to do. I didn't know."

"You must be a civilian," Jay inquired.

"Yes. I am from Tatoway," she answered.

"I'm Jay, a Claveman."

"My name is Pricilla."

"Well, Pricilla, do we have any enemy fighters on our tail?"

Pricilla checked both long and short range scanners on the display. "We've got a group of six on our course headings."

"Delta patrol! This is your team leader! We will split the patrol into two triangles in mark-3 seconds! Delta 5, you will lead your tri with Delta 4 and 6 to the right. We will turn to the left. Both will circle toward the center and then shoot the opposing team's enemy ships!"

"Roger!" Pricilla confirmed.

"Split now!"

The six-man patrol broke their formation and split into two triangles, one to the right and the other to the left. Making a sharp turn toward each other, they positioned their ships so that they could target the Rebel ships which were zeroing in on their convoys' tails without hitting each other.

"Delta patrol, resume formation!" Jay ordered.

"Nice move there, Jay," Silver chimed in.

"Master Silver! You watching me?"

"I'm too busy watching my own tail to worry about yours. I just happened to be in the area and noticed it."

They both had a laugh.

"You two need to concentrate on your mission," Master Mal injected. "Enough of this kind of open talk and gibberish on the lines!" Master

Mal was getting annoyed with all the talking that was going on over the frequency they were using for organization and to communicate with one another.

"Aye, Master Mal. All team leaders order your team to maintain frequency silence unless absolutely necessary, meaning life or death situations," Silver instructed.

No one spoke over the frequency again. There was an eerie silence over the line.

"That's better," Mal stated. "Now then. I only want to hear team leaders as they organize attacks on the trooper fighters. Please focus on plans to take out the landing bays on the cruisers. That means getting a patrol in close and causing some damage to the landing bays, but you'd have to somehow get through their shielding. I will leave that to my Clavemen."

"Which team do you wish to assign to that task?" Jay asked.

"Since you're asking, your team is just as good as anyone else's," Master Mal replied. "Have a go at it."

Jay chuckled. "As you wish, Master Mal." He smiled while turning his ship toward one of the cruisers. "You heard him, Delta team. Let's go get 'em where it hurts!"

The six ships in Jay's Delta team sped through space, zipping past other ships, weaving through the maze of enemy fighters and friendly ships, heading toward the lead Rebel Cruiser. It was the one that was receiving the most fire from the Clave Destroyers and Starfighters at the moment. If they took out their landing bays, they would not be much help to the battle any longer.

"Silver, I'm going to need some back-up for this operation."

"I'm right behind you with my own team," Silver assured him.

"Well, I didn't know if you were paying attention."

"I got your back, Jay."

"I don't know why I doubted," Jay stated.

"Explain it to me later. We have a cruiser to blast away!" Silver turned the focus to the business at hand.

Twelve ships now zipped in and out of the maze of ships and debris. Finally, they zeroed in on a Rebel cruiser, which immediately fired at them as they came into range.

"Here we go, people, ready or not!" Jay regretted doubting whether Silver would back him on such an important mission. No one responded to his words, for they had been silenced by Master Mal. Yet, it was with good reason. Excessive chattering over the frequency could result in confusion.

"Delta team going in!"

Jay angled his ship toward the landing bay of the cruiser, as laser blasts whizzed by his wings, finding no target. The other ships in his patrol followed his lead in formation.

"Delta, change to prime formation. Let's hit the same target and break a hole into the shielding, then come about and do it again. Then we can concentrate on hitting the landing bay. Hopefully, they won't catch on to what we are doing," Jay informed his team of the master plan.

The star fighters in Delta patrol angled their ships, lining up one behind the other, but leaving enough space for after-thrust and turbo-thrust. The pilots zeroed in on the cruiser's side landing bay. When they soared within range, the large cruisers spotted them and shot lasers at them.

"Sir, when do we start shooting at the shields?" one of his team members asked.

"Just hold on for a few more minutes; we aren't close enough to cause any damage yet."

"Those cruise gunners are getting close to our trajectory, Sir. They will pick us off soon," Pricilla warned.

"Maintain course and cut the chatter! Follow my lead. We will get as close as we can and then cut to the right or left. Let's split into a tri patrol and meet up when we come about," Jay ordered.

As the six Delta ships zoomed closer to the cruiser, the lasers fired from the cruiser lit up the darkness, coming dangerously close to their targets. When the ships were moments away from the shields, Jay fired his torpedo and banked to the right.

"Fire your torpedoes one at a time on that same target!" Jay shouted.

The five ships followed Jay's orders, hitting the target without suffering a loss. The cruiser locked on the last fighters and fired. Instead of banking to the left, the ship zoomed forward, crashing full speed into the landing bay. The previous torpedoes had penetrated the shields, allowing the last ship to enter, causing a huge explosion on the end of the landing platform.

"Sir, I am afraid that we lost Pricilla!"

Jay gasped in a moment of surprise. He had only known her for a short time, but had recognized her courageous willingness to fight for the return of the Clave and the return of Universal Order. Sighing and shaking his head, he uttered a silent prayer and continued his duties as the leader of Delta Patrol.

"After she was hit, she directed her ship straight at the target! Your idea to punch a hole in the shields worked, and her ship finished the mission to destroy the landing platform. They won't be using that one for some time."

"Get into formation!" Jay ordered. He did not want to lose another ship. "We'll make a second run for it. Hopefully, we can get through this without losing another."

Master Mal's voice chimed in, "Nice work, Jay. I would like Silver's patrol to join yours and continued to do what you're doing. We'll have the rest of the patrols to do the same. If they cannot launch or land their ships, at least we can keep adding fresh fighters to the mix."

"Yes, Master Mal. Sounds like a plan."

"You don't have to say it, Master Mal, I followed Jay anyway," Silver interjected. "I knew he'd need me," she joked.

"You two are quite a team. See what you two can do," Mal complimented the two. He recognized that Silver had trained Jay well.

"Aye, Master Mal," both replied in unison.

Chapter Thirty

Clave and Volunteers Rendezvous

Commander Shatra watched the view screen as the battle of the universe raged on. In all her days, she had never seen such a battle as the one going on before her eyes. She thought of what Odan had told her so many years ago about the nations going to war and being so divided that there would be a war that would end all wars. Was this it? It certainly looked like it encompassed many nations.

Am I on the right side? Will the Clave overpower the Emperor and retake control of the galactic power? Am I putting my efforts in with the wrong man? The Emperor is in power now, but will he be able to fight off Odan and all the nations' leaders?

Shatra knew that if Odan made it to Orion's Belt, he would gain support of the Clave men and women who remained undercover there. Low and behold, here they were to back him up, along with a host of civilians from other nations, some free and some not free from the Emperor's rule. Odan had somehow gotten the word out to these people, and now the numbers had grown larger than the emperor could contend with. They couldn't just board their ship and put them under arrest. To get to Odan now meant they would have to get through a host of Clave Warriors in star fighters and many star annihilators.

She had failed to get Odan as the Emperor wanted, but the game was not over. She assumed the captain of that ship was taking them somewhere. Where exactly that was, she didn't know, but she was determined to stick around and find out.

"Get us out of here before we get hit so bad we can't get home or something!"

"What?"

"You heard me! Our plans have now changed. Our previous plans were to get them before they reached the Belt. But that failed! They've already passed through the gate! So now our mission is to follow them to their destination."

General Zolatan looked her way with a questioning expression on his face.

"This isn't over with," Shatra barked. "We still have a job to perform! Those offspring of the previous Senate Leader, Zeger, are on that ship, and if they survive and start rebuilding the senate, Emperor Keltor's reign won't last very long. Believe me, once the Senate starts up, so will the old Clave. It's all a matter of what you want. Do you want dictatorship or a democracy?" Shatra asked.

"The current regime is working fine for me," General replied.

"Back us away from the battle, but keep close enough to be within communications range. We want to be in the loop, but we don't want to be in the battle, at least, not yet."

General did as he was told, and their ships gracefully backed away from the battle without attracting much attention, except Master Mal, who made note of it but said nothing.

Darting through enemy fighters, Reese led his patrol of six fighters through, firing lasers and picking off a few enemy ships as they zipped by. Sensing enemy fighters on their tails firing back at them, Clave fighters performed clever maneuvers that allowed for the opposite wing men from the other tri to fire and take out the tail. However, it was a trick that was getting old. Just how many times would the enemy fighters fall for that loop trick? Once, twice before they stopped and did something different?

Kal led his patrol toward a cruiser's landing pad and tried to punch through the shield to get to the unprotected hull close to the landing. They could then send a torpedo through the hole in the shield and blow up the landing bay. On another Cruiser, Troy led his team to do the same thing. It was what Master Mal had ordered.

Jade and Norm commanded two-manned fighter teams which Master Mal had ordered to damage the engines of the Rebel cruisers. This required two men: one to fire at the target, while the other piloted the ship. The shooting had to be accurate, or they could blow up not just the engines but the ship and the entire sector. In spite of the danger of this mission, it was a risk they had to take in order to come out ahead.

Hannible, a Claveman from the old days, had opted to remain on the *Star Annihilator* to look after Master Mal, whose physical disability prohibited him from active duty. Time had taken toll on his body, but his mind remained sharp as ever. He moved slowly on his wooden leg which he joked would never be a replacement, but it would have to do for the moment. Also, he had a serious vision disability which concerned Hannible most. Even though he had a seeing-eye bird named Jewels that sat on his shoulder and accompanied him wherever he went, Hannible insisted on being there in case Master needed a service the Jewels could not provide. That meant going to the war zone with him.

"Looks like we are coming out on top, Master Mal," Hannible expressed his excitement on what he had observed thus far in the battle.

"It looks that way, but I believe I saw a cruiser back off into the shadows over this way," Mal pointed to the direction that Shatra had ordered her general to exit the fight area.

"Perhaps they don't want to fight."

"No, they want to stop Odan," Mal frowned, squinting to make eye contact. "This battle is just the tip of the iceberg. I'm afraid that we'll be fighting the Emperor for a very long time."

Chapter Thirty-One

Odan's Haunted Communications

The *Raptor's Claw* zipped past several star troopers, spinning upside down to avoid the laser fire that zipped toward the ship. With Raymond and Seth manning the guns on either side, the ship was holding its own against the host of star troopers trying to take hits at the *Claw's* shields.

Suddenly, the ship rocked violently, causing everyone inside to scream.

"Don't panic!" Rex exclaimed, pressing down the intercom to talk to Seth and Raymond. "Come on, you two, keep 'em off of us!"

"I agree!" Seth replied.

"Agree? No, no. That's what you do."

"I am doing that!" Seth yelled.

"You do it better then!" The ship rocked again.

"Yes, Master. You want to trade places with me?"

"Not exactly," Rex replied. "You'd get too many scratches on my baby."

"According to you, I'm already doing that."

"Yeah. Just try to hit them better, Okay?"

"Roger."

In the cabin of the Claw, Cassandra sat gripping the chair as tightly as she could. Every time the ship rocked, she shuddered and held on tighter. Seeing her discomfort, Odan rested his hand on top of hers to comfort her.

"Don't worry. We are going to be alright," Odan whispered.

"Are you sure?" Cassandra asked.

"Quite sure, my Dear," Odan spoke with authority.

After much firing on both sides, one cruiser's nose suddenly pointed downward, losing complete control. As it disappeared into the blackness of space, a gigantic fireball illuminated the darkness where the cruiser burst into thousands of burnt particles, spewing debris onto other ships still engaged in battle. The Rebel fighters responding to the loss of their ship and crew blasted a Clave destroyer, sending it to join the fiery grave of the Rebel cruiser. Master Mal, watching all of these developments, directed Clave ships that had been assigned to refuel on the downed destroyer to the landing pad of another one nearby.

Suddenly, as if the loss of one star cruiser was enough, the Emperor's Rebels backed off, heading away from the sector, leaving the Clave Star annihilators and rag-tag fleet of various ships behind.

Master Mal nodded his head and looked to Hannible, "All ships stand down! I repeat, stand down! Return to your various docking bays. The battle is ours, for the time being."

"What about the *Raptor's Claw* and its mission?" Hannible asked.

"We'll meet them and discuss what our next step will be," Mal replied. "Organization to rebuild the Clave and the UO will take combined efforts of many, not a few."

"Agreed," Hannible said with a smile.

Slowly but surely, the Clave ships left the area. Yet, Master Mal knew that they were being followed by at least one star cruiser. He did not dare take them to Deran or to Shangri-La. Therefore, he had the ships form a circle and meet up in one location.

Chapter Thirty-Two

Unsuspected Clave Warrior Volunteers

The largest hall in the star annihilator, *Callipso II*, wasn't large enough to hold all who wished to hear the words concerning the Clave and UO's next move to retake Orion's Belt Galaxy. The seats were all taken, and there was standing room only. Master Mal stood at the podium with Odan and Master Markel.

"Brothers, Ladies, friends. Please, listen to me…listen to us. The time has come for us to join together and fight for freedom from Zymon Keltor's dictatorship of the nations."

There was applause.

"However, we must be organized as we were before. We must rebuild the Clave and the UO. Our starting point is with Senator Zeger's Children, Cassandra and Seth Zeger, who have traveled here from their safe haven to join our efforts in taking back the nations from this tyrant, Keltor. Here they are."

Mal gestured to Cassandra and Seth, who rose and unhooded themselves. The crowd cheered, whistled, and applauded.

"However, rebuilding the UO will have to come after we have brought peace and harmony to this galaxy and others. Therefore, it is more important to rebuild the Clave first. We will accept new people into the Clave and assign them to those who are already Clave Masters or who will become masters shortly. These masters will no doubt have a lot of underlings because many newcomers will be joining the Clave. We do need all the Clavemen we can get. Therefore, I encourage you to join now before we become more selective."

"Master Mal!" One man yelled, rising from his seat. "Will we be trained by these Masters?"

"Yes. If you allow yourselves to be trained, you will be trained," Mal stated. "Some of these Masters might be younger than some of you who join our ranks. Believe me, the young ones are just as knowledgeable as the elderly ones. They are even better because they are quicker in their minds and skills. They will teach you to be quicker."

The man sat down, nodding his head.

"The next thing is the mission to Shangri-La. It was my mission to revitalize Shangri-La."

"Shangri-La is highly patrolled by the Rebels," one man cried out. "They routinely check the planet and send patrols to the surface.

"No matter. We have enough people and fire power to deal with them, especially if we maintain support of all the nations as we have during this battle. They could not overtake us if we stay this strong."

"So we go down to the surface and just take back the planet?"

"We take a star annihilator or two, and when they send their cruisers and patrols down to check, we fight them off just as we did today," Mal explained.

"Alright," Odan agreed. "We need to watch out for Shatra, Master Mal."

Master Mal turned his head to Odan and frowned.

"There seems to be some misunderstanding between us. Shatra has never been our problem. She was your underling, Odan. She became evil-minded and changed sides…went to Keltor. You must face her, not us."

"Then I think my knowledge of your plans to take Shangri-La might prove to compromise the plan. She's connected with me. She can get into my head and know things."

"Your being here then is not safe. You must go. Don't come back until Shatra is no longer a threat."

"Surely you don't mean for me to—

"You either bring her back to the path, or eliminate the threat of her revealing Clave secrets, Odan. She's already taught them about the gates. Although I don't think they can get through them without her, she must be key to them getting through."

Odan sighed. Master Mal was right. He knew that Shatra needed to be dealt with. He wondered if she could be brought back after so many years of corruption. It was hard to tell. He had been away from her for so long that he had lost touch of her mind. Yet now that he was back, she seemed to have direct contact with him despite the passage of time. He had no clue whether or not she would follow the path back to the Clave. His departure to Earth had been abrupt, and he had not been able to give her a proper farewell. A Master usually doesn't abandon his underling, but it was an emergency situation. She had no one to guide her during the takeover of Keltor's Rebel Alliance. He imagined that she had gone to Keltor out of spite. If so, she might not be turned back. At any rate he needed much time with her alone, away from the pressure this new war presented.

It was then that Odan knew what he would do.

Odan turned to Markel, whispering in his ear, "I need to take care of Shatra before we head to Shangri-La."

Markel nodded and turned his head to him, whispering back as he interlocked his fingers and rested his elbows on the armrests, "Agreed."

"I will head to Ottoway. You are the only person I will tell that to. Keep the Senators safe, Markel. I leave them in your care. If I don't come back, you will know what's happened to me."

"Do you think she will follow you?"

"She will."

Odan rose to his feet, and as he headed for an exit from the hall, Seth rushed to him from his seat.

"Odan!"

Odan turned back, "Seth, go back."

"Where are you going?"

"I have some business to attend to, Seth. I have to do this on my own," Odan stated. "Stay with Markel, Justin, and Gorn. They will take good care of you both."

"It's the one chasing us again, isn't it?'

Odan nodded. "They will continue until I do something about it. Now, go back and listen to what's going on. You're a Claveman now. You need to pay attention to what our mission is."

Seth nodded once and placed a hand on his shoulder. "Good luck, Odan."

Odan smiled slightly and placed his hand on Seth's shoulder as the Clavemen did in the past. Good luck to you."

Odan turned, hooding himself as his robe swayed through the walkway, and exited the hall. Seth's eyes watered, as he watched him go, and he returned to his seat. Cassandra leaned over and whispered to her brother.

'Where's he going now?"

"Same problem as before. The one following us from the other galaxy followed us here and will follow us whatever we do. Odan is going to perhaps lead them astray."

"Well, I hope he's successful."

Cassandra and Seth focused their attention to the podium. Master Markel was speaking about their plan of action.

"…we need to gain orbit of Shangri-La as soon as possible before they get wind of our next move and beat us there," Markel stated.

"What is the plan to make repairs on things that need to be working when Rebel forces come after us there? We need to have at least some basic things working like shielding and artillery," Justin called out.

Master Mal nodded, "Master Justin, I agree. Why don't you set up a group of engineers who will organize themselves to do just that?"

"I will do that with pleasure, Master Mal."

"This is what I like to see, people volunteering for things that need to be done. We will send three ships to Shangri-La to orbit the planet. I will put Master Markel in charge of that entire operation. The rest of the ships will return to Deran to refuel and repair damages. General Devin will be in charge there. Those of you who wish to be Clave Warriors will be instructed to remain on the star annihilators that will maintain orbit of Shangri-La. Master Mal will decide which of you will enter apprenticeship training. The remainder of our volunteers will follow us to Deran. That will be the safest place for you all now. To divide would be suicide at this delicate time," Mal stated. "Until another time, we have concluded talks."

Chapter Thirty-Three
An Old Dilemma Settled

As Odan Amir blasted away from the star annihilator, *Ares*, where everyone had gathered in one of the many star fighters, his memory on how to fly the viper came back to his mind.

"Like riding a bike," Odan said to himself and chuckled.

It was an Earthly thought to have. He hadn't said such a phrase since he had taught Cassy and Seth how to ride a bike on Earth. His hands moved over the controls and very swiftly he found his thrusters and shot forward.

"Wooooo! Good heavens! This thing can really scoot. I remember how much I enjoyed flying these things." He chuckled again and set course for Deranium, a binary system, which was quite uninhabited and in the outer-rim territories.

/////

Commander Shatra had noticed the lone star fighters blasting away, and she sensed that Odan was in that ship. She turned to General Zolotan. Before long she was blasting away from the star cruiser, following the path of the lone star fighter.

"Alright, Odan, where are you taking us?"

Chapter Thirty-Four

Shangri-La Ground Invasion

Captain Rex walked through the corridors of the star annihilator named *Ares* with his crew, Raymond, Dex and Langstrom. For some distance, they walked in silence, each of them knowing what the other wanted to discuss, but none of them wanting to bring it up. As always, Rex spoke up. He was, after all, their leader and Captain.

"Well, we're almost at the end of this mission, gang."

"Are we?" Langstrom asked.

"Yeah. Once we get our passengers to Shangri-La, then our contract is fulfilled. We get the rest of our payment, and we're free."

"And leave them in the middle of this war?" Dex asked. "How could we do that?"

"You just turn and go, Dex," Rex stated.

Dex stopped walking, which caused the others to stop. Rex turned to her.

"What?' Rex asked.

"You are going to have to go without me," she said.

Before Rex could answer, Langstrom walked over and put her arm around Dex's shoulders. "Me, too. I can't leave these people to fight out this war alone. They need all the help they can get, and they will need a doctor to care for the injured."

Raymond looked at Rex, "I hate to do this to you, Bro, but I want to stay, too."

Rex threw his hands up and let them fall. "For Pete's sake! Fine! We'll all stay and help out!"

Squealing and laughing, the girls darted forward and embraced Rex. "I knew you had a heart in there somewhere," Dex teased.

"Yeah? You guys weren't making it easy."

They had not been expecting an audience, but people who were in the corridors clapped and welcomed them. Rex and company raced to Markel's quarters to inform him and the others of the good news.

Markel's Quarters were handsomely large, complete with an extra room for entertaining guests. At the moment, that was the crew of the *Raptor's Claw*. Cassandra, Seth, Justin and Gorn. After allowing them to enter and take a seat, they talked about the battle and how things seemed to have gone their way for the moment.

"That's the thing with Keltor; you can never predict what he will do next. He may return with more fighters and ships than we can handle."

"That's just what we were thinking, and we know you need all the help you can get," Rex stated.

"But I suppose you all are ready to dash away to get back to your lives of smuggling things here and there, right?" Markel asked.

"That's what we are trying to say, Markel. We don't want to go. We are staying. All of us," Rex informed him of their decision.

Markel's face lit up like a flashlight when he digested the good news. His lips immediately broke into a broad smile. It was as if he had been hoping that Rex and his team would stay with them. He had watched them operate and knew their skills would help them immensely.

"I had hoped you all would stay, but I wasn't going to ask. But now that you have said it, I welcome you both with open arms. We can use your skills very much. So do you all plan to be part of the Clave or the UO?"

They replied in unison, "The Clave."

Markel laughed a bit at their answer. It came at him so loud that he felt overwhelmed for a second. "Very well. I will assign you all to myself as your Master. It would be best that you know the person who is to be your teacher."

"Sounds good," Rex stated. "So what do we do now?"

"Go down to deck 45 and tell them that I sent you to get apprentice packages which will include two robes, two pairs of Clave gloves, a Clave weapon of choice, and eye shades to protect your eyes from the beams the weapons create which can be blinding. Then pick up a pair of black boots, two laser pistols, and one laser whip from the check stop. You'll pick up other things along the way, of course, but for now, those are things that you need. Oh, yes, your clothes must be khaki pants and a white shirt, a belt to be worn with the pants, and a long leather duster. All of this will be in a duffle bag."

"I suppose we should go down there then."

Cassandra clapped her hands and walked up to Rex, "It is good that you are joining the Clave. I am very pleased."

Rex smiled. "Thank you, your highness."

Seth held out his hand to Rex. "See you around, Mate."

Rex and Seth shook hands, and both Cassandra and Seth waved to the crew of the *Raptor's Claw* as they departed. Markel sat and turned to address the twins.

"You will be meeting numerous national leaders. I want you to become familiar with them. Talk to them about what is going on in their systems. Ask them what the Clave can do to help them once it gets organized."

"We will," Seth stated.

The door buzzed, and Markel simply directed the computer to open it. Hannible, Silver, Jay, Jade, and Norm entered, all dressed like Clave men and women, except Hannible. Norm's long, grey, braided locks hanging down his back signaled that he was the senior in the group. Markel jumped up and grabbed Norm in a genuine bear hug. The two had been close in the days before the Clave.

"Look what the lizard dragged in!" Markel cried out and laughed.

Norm laughed as well. "The tastiest morsel in the sector, I hope."

Markel chuckled. "It's a matter of opinion, I suppose. How the heck are you?"

"Just fine. And you?"

"Couldn't be better after that showdown out there."

"Target practice?" Norm asked. "Are you still counting?"

"1506," Norm stated.

"I beat you by 4 points," Markel teased.

"No way."

"Anyway, we came to say something, remember?"

"Right." Norm replied. "You can say it, not me."

"I'm afraid that I cannot rejoin the Clave, but I will help the UO all I can."

"Why not?" Markel frowned. "We need all the Masters we can find."

"I know, but I have a family now. I can't leave them and go running around the universe. It wouldn't be right. They need me as much as I need them."

"You went and started a family after Keltor scattered us?"

"Yes. I thought that we'd not come back like this in a zillion years!"

"You didn't believe Odan then?" Markel asked.

"I didn't know what to believe. I was a young apprentice, unsure of my decision. But I don't regret having chosen to start my family. I will do what I can to help, but I can't rejoin because it will violate the rules."

"So noted. And I am sorry. You had such a bright future in the Clave, Jade. But now your future is on another path. I wish you well."

"For that I thank you."

"You should have traveled with the civilians. It is to be just Clave men and women on these ships, plus the Senators," Markel stated.

"I could take a shuttle," Jade suggested.

"No matter now. You're here. We can still use you, can't we, or do you wish to return to your family right away?"

Markel was a bit cold with Jade, but the news of his decision not to rejoin had struck him, and he was just a tad bit more serious than he previously was.

"No, I don't have to rush home. I did come to fight in this battle and help out."

"Yes. Well, I don't quite understand why you tell me that you can't rejoin when you seem to have already joined in a sense, Jade."

"I couldn't just sit back and do nothing. I had to help out when I knew you needed all the help you could get. I HAD to come."

"Ahh. I see. So you abandoned your family to rejoin us here now?"

"I guess I did."

"Are you planning to continue fighting with us?" Markel asked. "You know the rules of the Clave."

"Yes. I suppose I plan on staying here."

"You have a task then."

"What, Master Markel?"

"Send word to your wife that you won't be coming home and that you've rejoined the Clave."

"I will, Master Markel."

"Good."

Markel looked at the rest of the Clave men who had entered his sitting room.

"Silver and Jay! The last time I saw you two was the last meeting of the Clave before it broke up!"

Jay was holding the Princess's hand. He released it and then bowed to Markel, "Greetings, Master Markel."

"Greetings, Master Markel." Silver addressed Markel, bowing her head. "Last time I saw you, Justin and Gorn were younger and you had hair."

Markel laughed. "Quite right. Hannible, what should I do with her?"

"Promote her? She's the only one who noticed the change in your new hairdo."

Laughter broke out in the room, and it took a few seconds for it to subside so that Markel could respond to Silver's observation concerning his age.

"Indeed! But who is this handsome lady here?"

"Master Markel, this is Princess Elaina Rufus of Artica," turning to Princess Elaina, "Princess, I present to you, Master Markel."

"Greetings, Princess Elaina," Markel said holding out his arm. "I shall introduce you to the rest of the people here."

Markel led the Princess to Cassandra and Seth.

"Princess Elaina, May I present to you, Lady Cassandra and her twin brother Sir Seth. They are the children of-..."

"Zeger's children!" Princess Elaina ended the sentence and held out her hands to them both.

Cassandra shook her hand and curtsied, and Seth took her hand, smiled, and bowed, while kissing her knuckles. He stood and greeted her warmly. "Greetings Princess Elaina, Seth Zeger at your service."

Elaina smirked slightly, "You remind me of your brothers. They were confident and friendly like you."

"Thank you, Princess."

When the Princess sat down, everyone else found a seat. Markel sat next to the princess on the couch, while Jay sat on the other side of her.

"You knew our brothers and sisters, Princess?"

"Yes, I did. They were very good friends of mine, But..."

"But what, Princess?" Seth prodded.

"Keltor found where they were hiding and took them away. They are believed to be dead now. No one has heard heads or tails of them."

"What if they are not dead?"

"When the Clave is more organized, we can possibly try to find and rescue them if there is proof they are there in Zymon's compounds," Markel said.

Cassandra looked to Seth and nodded. Seth took her hand and placed his own over hers. "Don't worry. If they are alive, we'll get them out of there soon."

"I'm greatly sorry for this news, but there was little we could do to stop the Rebels," Elaina explained.

"I understand," Seth changed the subject. "We must concentrate on Shangri-La now, and at the right time, we'll worry about freeing all captives of the Emperor later. One thing at a time."

Markel nodded. "Very wise of you, Seth. We must make plans for retaking Shangri-La now."

Grabbing a remote control from the table, Markel pressed the "On" button, and a map of the planet Shangri-La appeared on the view screen revealing all of the fortresses for everyone to see. Using a lighted pointer, he proceeded to update the map, marking some of the fortresses with a red "X."

"From what I recall, the fortresses to the south and west have been destroyed, but the Northern and Eastern ones are still intact. We need the engineering team to go to the Southern and Western fortresses, while we get the other two up and running. I believe we will still be able to hold and defend the planet with only two operational."

"What if they invade with Warriors? What if they are already at the Northern and Eastern fortresses?"

"I don't see them wanting to make this a foot battle. So far they have only attacked us in space, not on the ground. However, it could lead to that down the road."

"If we go to Shangri-La, they will come there and fight," Jade pointed out. "The Rebels will follow us, and the battle will be on land because we will take it there, not them."

"True."

"Then we can expect them to come with fully loaded cruisers, complete with star tanks and transformorados. You get those transformorados on your tail, and you can forget a peaceful ending," Hannible interjected. "Those things are designed to destroy things, people, and everything they come into contact with."

"Then the thing to do is not let them get down to the planet," Markel stated.

"How?"

"We board the cruiser and take the transformorados out before they can get down here."

"Now, who's going to take that suicide mission?"

"I'll go!" Jay volunteered first.

Princess Elaina chuckled. "Now, how did I know you'd go for that?"

Both Jay and Silver smirked, "See what I had to deal with all these years. By the way, Master Markel, I am recommending that you promote Jay to Master status."

Markel looked at Jay, whose mouth slightly opened as he stared at Silver in surprise.

"He's learned all he can from me, and he is ready for the last test."

"I am ready for the test." Jay echoed his teacher, still not believing what he had heard.

"I'll confirm with Master Mal and get back to you. Now, we must continue our plans?"

"Yes, let's," Silver agreed.

Jay sat overwhelmed with joy and gratitude toward Silver for saying he was ready to become a Master. He wondered what had made her say that. Was it his last successful mission to Artica alone? Had that been what made her make up her mind that he could handle himself as a Claveman? It probably had something to do with it, he thought. Yet, for the moment, he'd not know until he could get her alone to ask her why she recommended him. Then again, why bother asking her that. It would just show he's not ready. She had said he was ready for the test, and he was ready for "it," whatever "it" was.

No apprentice to a Master knew what the test was. They just knew one existed. Before one became a Master, he or she had to take a test and either fail or pass it. There was a long list of people who had failed the test and another shorter list of people who passed. Not everyone could be a Master. One had to have the right temperament and the right combination of attitude, skills, knowledge, and understanding. In addition, one had to carry it all well and not be too power hungry. The test would reveal all this. Most apprentices feared the test because it revealed too much about them. Therefore, many refused to take it, choosing to just remain warriors instead. Warriors were apprentices who refused to take the test to be Masters, but who wished to serve and still be considered a part of the Clave. There were a lot of them, and they mastered a trade in the brotherhood. They either chose engineering, swords, lasers, weaponry, chronological and other records, mechanics, medicine, science, or some other area of expertise.

Jay took his eyes away from Princess Elaina for a moment to admire the new beautiful face in the room. Lady Cassandra was also very beautiful; however, she seemed different. There was something about her that he could not identify. As he admired her, he saw her brother looking directly at him.

Jay averted his eyes for a moment and smiled at him, but Seth did not smile back. He just looked at him and glanced at his sister, who looked back at her brother. Cassandra's eyes followed her brother's eyes to Jay. Jay gave her a nod. Cassandra acknowledged him momentarily before returning her attention to Master Markel, who was discussing their plans to retake Shangri-La.

Chapter Thirty-Five
Cassandra and Princess Elaina Bond

Deranium, a binary system in the outer-rim of the Orion's Belt Galaxy, was a habitable planet; however, not many people wished to live there because it was so far from the main stream of activity. It would take a day to get there and a day to get back, traveling the major trade routes. Yet, there were a few people who chose to live in such places, people who didn't like much company.

Known for its wild animals and wilder civilians, Deranium was not a hot spot for honeymooners. It was a place for hunters and people who liked a little target practice, yet many laws existed to protect the creatures on such planets. Odan chose to connect with Shatra here to keep from being followed. Only a Clave warrior could come to such a planet and survive. Clave men and women had a way of talking with the animals and creatures, reasoning with them and coming to some understanding. Odan hoped she had not forgotten how.

Zipping into the atmosphere of Deranium, following only the instruments and his instincts, he guided his star fighter into a clearing of a meadow where the tall grass did not interfere with his landing. Most of the animals in the vicinity of his ship quickly retreated into the forest.

He turned on a homing device so that she'd find him quickly. Then, he gathered some supplies and stuffed them into a duffle bag: food, water, weapons, and a first-aid kit. He checked the bag, saw that everything was intact, and swung it over his shoulder before setting out to find shelter.

Hours passed before Odan found an empty cave in the foothills. A blanket of snow covered the area around him as far as he could see, but he spotted no wild animals. He built a fire at the mouth of the cave so that he could cook his food and make beverages to warm his chilled body. Then he heard a ship fly overhead and land where his ship had landed.

"There she is," Odan said to himself. "I knew she'd come."

Odan sat down, drank his warmed water, and waited for Shatra to show up. It didn't take very long, an hour or so, and she walked up to him, her long, reddish-brown curls hanging down her back and shoulders.

"You were waiting here for me?"

"Yes."

"Where are the others?' Shatra asked.

"Not here with me," Odan stated. "It's just you and me."

"Playing it safe, are you?'

"No. What we have to do is between us, not the rest of them. What they have to do concerns the universe, not me or you."

"Oh, but it does. Keltor wishes to rule the universe; therefore, what they wish to do does concern me."

"Then I'm sorry. I didn't bring them for that. WE need to talk, you and I, first."

"About what? According to me, there's nothing to discuss."

"Yes, there is, Shatra. I am here to apologize to you for leaving without telling you what I was doing. But I didn't have time. I had orders from Zeger to protect his younglings, and it was a desperate time. We were under attack, and I could only take those children to safety. I told no one where I was going, save Markel."

"I was your App…"

"Apprentice and you should have come with me, yes. But you were thousands of light years across the galaxy, Shatra. If I had delayed, those children would have been assassinated or something," Odan stated.

"You left me no messages."

"I could have, but again, I didn't have time to leave one. My hands were full of two babies, two crying babies, mind you, and I had to take them across the galaxies and through the gates without being noticed. That was a tall order. I figured you would do well until I returned," Odan said.

"Without any guidance? Without a Master to lead me?"

"All the Masters knew of your predicament, Shatra. They would have looked out for you had you stayed with the Clave. But you were so impatient...so restless that you had to defy the leadership of the Clave and cause trouble and disrupt things by dividing the Clave in half! Why in the stars of the heavens did you do that?" Odan cried.

'I was angry. I wanted you as my master because I wanted to become a Master myself! I thought it was the best way to become one."

"You were right about that. But I was out of the picture for a spell, and it ruined your plans, didn't it?"

"That was only part of it," she mumbled. "Then, there was you and my feeling for you."

"You know darn well that that would never be, Shatra. Did it take so long for you to forgive me for that?"

"You've explained it to me. I understand."

"Now, there's the matter of you being on the wrong side of this war. This greatly concerns the Elders of the Clave and the re-establishment of the UO."

"They should be concerned!" Shatra exclaimed.

"It's not too late for you to come back to the Clave, Shatra."

"Alright, I hear you. I accept your apology."

Shatra shook her head, "it is way too late now, Odan. I'm in too deep."

"Nothing is impossible to change, Shatra." Odan took a step toward her with his hand out. "It's never too late."

Shatra's eyes glazed over with moisture; she turned her head away and wiped her eyes. "It's too late for me. I belong..."

"With the Clave!" Odan finished the sentence for her. "Your foundation is with the Clave. You can come back and start where you left off. That much I can promise you."

"They'd never let me become a Master."

"You judge yourself too harshly, lady. Perhaps not these first few moons, but eventually they would have to make you a Master because there is such a short supply of them."

Shatra looked down at her feet and sat down, warming her hands at the fire. "It is very tempting, now that you're back."

"This is where we both decide, Shatra. We either both leave together, or only one of us departs from this planet," Odan stated.

"What is that? A threat?"

"A fact, actually. You can't go back to your ship without proof that you've eliminated me, and I can't go back without proof that I've eliminated you. Either you come with me to rejoin, or we battle things out here."

Shatra looked across the flames of the fire into Odan's eyes, stared at them, and saw the pain. He did not wish to do what he was saying. It was as if he were a robot doing some dastardly task on the orders of someone else.

"Who sent you to kill me off?" Shatra asked.

"You must see what a danger you are to the Clave and to the UO? You also must see what an asset you could be if you were to rejoin our ranks. At this juncture, Shatra, I would suggest you rejoin."

"You don't think I can take you?"

"I don't think either of us wishes to find that out," Odan admitted. "I certainly don't. I would rather fight the enemy. However, if you're the enemy, then so be it. I will beat you down as a Rebel deserves."

"You must have known that I would not surrender," Shatra stated.

"You....you are not a quitter. That's why I thought you'd give the Clave another try. Perhaps I was in error."

"You left me with no choices but to go to Keltor's side, Odan. I was young and impressionable. I could do nothing but follow his guidance after you left me. He treated me like I belonged with him. The Clave shoved me aside after you left."

"It was a delicate time, Shatra, and you were a young apprentice. The Masters were focusing on the wars," Odan explained. "Oh, what good is it to argue this out when you have made up your mind!" Odan cried, turning on his light-whip. "You either come with me, or you don't leave this place. The choice is yours!"

Odan headed toward the entrance, facing Shatra and walking sideways, keeping his front facing her as she turned on her light-whip.

"So it's come to this?" Shatra asked.

"Such as it is, I regret it already."

"Why?"

"You are supposed to be the example to the females, Shatra. For a long while, there were no females allowed in the Clave. You came along, broke that rule, joined, and became an apprentice. You were to become a Master, the first female on the Elder council. It was going to happen, but you were so impatient…too eager…too greedy for power. Now, you have that power but no control nor guidance. You have an evil leader that wants only power and to rule the universe. I told you a long time ago to separate yourself from him, but you didn't listen."

Odan spun the light-whip in large circles over his head as the whip's whistling sound reverberated throughout the cave. He then let his arm fall straight before him pointing at Shatra.

Shatra raised her left hand, which had the metallic glove on it, and a white light appeared in her palm as she raised it and met the whip, blocking the blow that would have struck her body. She slashed her whip at Odan, but he too, was quick to block her attack. Surprising Shatra, Odan grabbed hold of her light-whip with his left hand which had the metallic glove on it, and yanked, pulling her off balance. She fell forward, landing in the snow on her stomach. Odan swished his light-whip, slashing her on the back, causing Shatra to cry out in pain.

"Arrrugh!"

"You should have rejoined. We always made a good team, you and I. But now I must eliminate the threat against the Clave and the newly forming UO. Having you on the wrong side is detrimental to our goals. You will undermine our efforts at every turn if you were to be left alive." He slashed his light-whip again as she was getting up off the ground, and it knocked her backward so that her back was now in the snow. She cried out again in pain. The laser whip, now kicked up to full power, cut through her clothing and penetrated deep into the skin.

'Ahhhhhrgh!" Shatra cried out. "Please, I rejoin!"

"This is best, Shatra. In this way, no one will be worried if they have to trust you or not."

"Please."

Odan wiped a tear from his face. He knew one more blow in the chest with the light-whip would take her life. He circled with his arm, his light whip in the air.

"You should have listened to me long ago, Shatra."

"Noooo-------!

Odan let the whip fall forward with the drop of his arm pointed toward her chest. The blow lifted her from the ground and lit up a perimeter around her with electric discharge.

Odan gathered his light whip, switching it off. Then he walked through the snow, wiping away the tears falling down his cheeks. He had not wished to do this, but there was no choice for him. The Clave order expected it of him. He stepped up to her still frame and could see the smoke rising from her chest area. Then, he squatted and grabbed her hand, taking off the metallic glove. He looked at her face, reached his hand up and closed her hazel eyes.

Suddenly, Shatra grabbed his arm. "I didn't think you'd do it."

"Oh, Shatra. Why did you make me?"

"I can't go back. Everyone would hate me for causing the rift in the Clave before."

Odan nodded, "they would have gotten over that in time."

"No….they wouldn't. Tell me, why did you meet me here?"

"You don't remember?"

"Yes, I do, but why?"

"I just wanted you to recall our friendship and consider that before you made up your mind," Odan stated, brushing her hair back.

"Odan?"

"Yes?"

"Kiss me goodbye."

A last request didn't seem inappropriate, so he leaned in and kissed her on the lips. When they parted, she smiled. "I knew you loved me."

"Very much, Shatra…very much."

She held his hand until the strength left her, and she inhaled for the last time. Odan picked her up, took her into the cave, and buried her with dirt and rocks. He said some words over her grave, and then returned to his ship. He set fire to her ship and watched it explode. Then he climbed into his, did his flight checks, and blasted off the planet.

PART IV

Chapter Thirty-Six
Keltor Receives Bad News

Deep within the spiral galaxy, known as Orion's Belt, in a Tri-Star system, twin planets encircled the three stars. The triple stars sat in a triangular pattern, and the twin planets encircled them in separate orbits, one being closer, which was Sandune. The one farther away with bearable weather patterns was once the Clave stronghold. However, now it was occupied by Keltor's Rebel Alliance Troopers. Aside from what was destroyed during the last intergalactic war, Keltor took what was left on Shangria-La and used it against the Clave now.

At present, three star cruisers orbited Shangri-La with several star fighters on call to take to flight, along with several ground patrols. Keltor knew that if the Clave were to be reborn, they would seek to take back Shangri-La.

Meanwhile, enroute to Shangri-La were three star annihilators of the UO and the Clave led by Master Markel. All sat in his quarters making plans.

"We must consider that they have Shangri-La heavily guarded," Markel surmised.

"Should we send down a patrol to set up ways to sabotage them?" Jay asked.

"In sabotaging them, we'd ruin our own systems which would then need repair," Jade stated. "Whatever ground patrol we send will have to be able to take them on and retain whatever territory gained."

"That would be best," Markel agreed.

"Not to mention making it to the surface," Seth mumbled. "They probably have their big ships in orbit."

"That is most likely. We'll have to fight our way in, Senator Seth, and that means taking our time to get past their defenses before we get to the surface and then dealing with their ground patrols, fighters and what not. This is not going to be easy at all." Markel emphasized the difficulty of this mission again.

"We should call for back up," Cassy suggested. "I don't think we have enough people power."

"We have enough here, Senator. We're just going to have to make it work," Jade said, trying to reassure her. "Believe me, we've fought against more numbers with less and won."

"That is reassuring," Cassandra beamed.

"I say we take on the cruisers first, hit their landing bays, hit their vulnerable points, damage, cripple or destroy them, and then proceed to the planet. Then we'll concentrate on taking on the ground patrols on foot, with some direct contact; using our light-whips will be most effective. I imagine there might be some damage to our working equipment, which comes with the territory of war. We must use any means necessary to take back our fortress."

"So shall it be then," Jade agreed.

Cassandra connected to Seth's mind; and when he received her message, he turned to face her and mouthed the words, "I am so excited to be a part of this!" Nodding to indicate he agreed, he put his index finger to his lips, communicating for her to be silent.

"I would now suggest we all get some rest. We'll be needing it," Markel insisted.

Princess Elaina rose and walked over to Cassandra, "Care to come with me to my quarters for some tea? The both of you?"

Seth walked up and nodded, "I would be delighted, your highness."

Cassandra agreed. "Yes, that sounds good to me, too."

Chapter Thirty-Seven

Silver Seeks Reinforcements

Deep mahogany everywhere! The bed spread, the curtains, carpet and the furniture all that dark, redwood definitely signifying royalty.

"Lights 80 percent! Temperature 75 degrees!" Princess activated the computer to set the controls in the room. Seth and Cassandra shivered because the controls had been shut off automatically when Elaina left earlier that day. Gesturing for her guests to sit in the two, extra-plush armchairs in the sitting area of her quarters, Princess Elaina tapped a few commands into a wall panel to order something to warm them up. After a few moments, the Princess joined them, placing herself gracefully on her own chair, adjusting the large, fluffy pillows around herself until she felt comfortable.

"So, how do you like it our here, so far?" the Princess asked.

"I haven't really had time to assess how I like it," Cassandra answered. "We've been so busy trying to save the universe with Odan that we took no time to assess anything else."

"Truth be told," Seth added, "we were taken from our hideout and thrown into this mission, knowing nothing about what we were getting into, only that we were important to the outcome."

"Indeed you are," She stated. "You don't know how important, but you will soon."

"Mind telling us?"

"You are the link between two great groups: The UO and the Clave. Your father was once that powerful link until he was murdered. Now that you are here, you will learn the ways of the Clave, and you will be UO Senators, rather than leaders of the UO."

"What about me?" Cassandra asked.

The robots approached the table speaking in a different language to the princess. One robot stood about 6 feet tall and had arms and legs. It looked almost human, except for the fact that he was made entirely of metal with wires and circuits. The other robot was shorter, about 5'5" tall with a flat table top on its head instead of hair, which carried a tray with a tea kettle, three cups and saucers, spoons, sugar, and cream. To serve the Princess and her guest, it scrunched down so that its head disappeared into its neck, which disappeared into its shoulders. The downsizing process stopped automatically when the table top was low enough for the Princess to take the tray.

The tall one spoke, "If you need anything else, just ask. I'll be right over there by the control panel."

"Thank you, now, go." She turned back to her guests. "Both of you will hold that seat together," the princess said, answering Cassandra's question.

"Where do you fit into the grand scheme of things?" Seth asked.

"I'm a Senator's daughter, and I'm going to be Senator when he retires, which is in a moon's time."

"A moon?"

"You don't understand what a moon is?" the Princess asked.

Both Cassy and Seth shook their heads.

"It's when … It's when your world goes around the sun once and you see the moon."

"A year?" Cassy blurted out.

"I guess so," Elaina stated, "A year, you say?"

"That's what we call it."

"I see."

The princess poured all their drinks, and they each picked up their tea cups as the steam swirled above the cups in white misty circles. Cassy took a sip and set her cup down. She had never tasted tea like this before.

"What is this flavor of tea?"

"Rangoon," the Princess stated.

"So what exactly do the Senators do?" Seth asked.

"We all make the laws that people live by in the universe, and we enforce them with the Clave Warriors. The Clave is like a Universal police."

"So what nation are you from?"

"Artica," the Princess replied, her voice expressing pride for her home planet. "We are very much supporters of the UO and the Clave.

"I see," Cassandra stated.

"Odan said we were born on Romes IV," Seth stated.

"It's true. I was just a little knob myself, but I was around when you guys were born. Your parents lived there. Then the war started and..."

"It's allright, we know they were killed by Keltor," Seth stated.

"I'm sorry," the princess replied. "I didn't mean to bring it up."

"It's okay," Cassandra assured her. "It's bound to come up in conversations."

"We're used to it," Seth reiterated.

"Yes," Cassy said.

"I don't know what I'd do if Keltor killed my father."

"Would you want to kill Keltor to get your revenge?" Seth asked.

"No. I'd just want justice to be done."

"Meaning you'd want to see him pay for the crime?"

"In some way, yes."

"I don't know what I will do, yet he did kill our parents?" Cassy said. "Perhaps nothing."

"Why nothing?"

"Whatever goes around, comes back around, you know," Cassy admitted. "It's only a matter of time for things to be made right."

"I like your answer," Princess Elaina said.

"Well, that's probably what I'd do."

"What team are you going to be on, Seth?" she asked

"Star Fighter patrol," Seth answered.

"So am I," Cassy said. "I'm a pretty good shot."

"I'm going to be on the ground," Elaina stated. "I wish you both luck with those vipers."

"Thanks, same to you on the ground there," Seth replied with a smile. "So, tell us more about the UO."

"What do you want to know?"

"Everything," Cassy stated.

"That would take a long time to explain. I'll start, but I will probably have to finish at another time."

"Sounds good," Seth nodded in agreement.

"Long ago, there was much chaos and disorganization in the universe. Declarations of war and too many no fly zones were constant. Total confusion and distrust! Finally, your father managed to get every group in the universe to send one representative from each nation to a meeting to discuss the problems. The results of this meeting were phenomenal. That was the beginning of the UO."

"What of the Clave?" Cassy asked.

"The Clave was already formed by that time. The Elders were asked to perform the duties of enforcing the laws, protecting the Senators and maintaining peace in the galaxies," Elaina continued. "See, the shoes you are walking in are very large."

"Yes," Cassandra agreed.

"The reason I asked you to come and have tea with me is to get a sense of what you are like."

"Why?" Seth asked.

"So I'd know what to expect when the Senate meets."

"That's a good idea," Cassy agreed.

"Yes, I'm glad I did," Elaina stated. "I see there won't be a problem with us."

"You certain about that?" Seth asked.

Elaina looked at Seth and smiled. "Very certain. You two are not two-faced, disloyal, or crooked. You wouldn't say one thing and do another."

"No! We wouldn't!" Cassy exclaimed.

"Then I can count on your support in the Andromeda?"

"That depends on what we are supporting," Seth stated, folding his arms across his chest.

"Indeed, it would," Elaina agreed. "Well, enough of this talk then."

"Whatever makes you comfortable, Your Highness," Seth teased with a smile.

Tea time continued, but the reason they were there with the Princess was clear to them both now. The Princess had come clean with her purpose and had explained to Cassy and Seth what they had to look forward to.

"If she had to case us out, then there must be some issues within the Senate that need to be dealt with," Seth thought. He made a mental notation to put this issue on the back burners to deal with after all this ruckus with Shangri-La was handled.

Cassandra was simply enjoying the Princess' company and was starting to make friends with her.

"...I really like your outfit. Is that specifically for royalty?" Cassy asked.

"No. I'll make a point to get you the fabric," Elaina stated. "It is exclusively in the Orion's Belt; that much I know."

Cassy smiled. "I'm starting to see the fashions and appreciate the styles around here."

Elaina laughed. "I hope you aren't just using me as a model."

"Definitely!" Cassy stated.

"Now I am blushing."

Suddenly, Seth rose to his feet. "Do excuse me ladies, but I must get some rest for our big encounter coming up soon. Cass, you should too. But," he held up his hands. "I'm not telling you what to do. Do as you wish. I'm going to get some shuteye. Honestly, I hate to dash off like this, Your Highness."

"No, no! You are right. We all should get some sleep as Master Markel suggested."

Cassandra finished her tea and stood up. "Yes. Seth, hold up. I'll come with you. Your Highness," she said extending her hand, "Thank you for inviting us here for tea. We've had a beautiful time talking with you, and the tea was out of this galaxy! I mean it was very tasty."

"You are both welcome. Perhaps when this is all over with, we can meet again?"

Seth turned to her and took her hand, stooping to kiss it again. When he released her hand, he also expressed gratitude for her hospitality. "I thank you for the heads up about the Senate, also. Now, I know better what to expect."

"Anytime," Elaina stated. "You two be careful out there. Although I doubt very seriously that they will let you both go into battle."

"We'll see," Seth stated. "Until another time, good night."

Cassandra and Seth entered the corridor and took the lift to the 32nd floor where they entered their adjoining rooms through Cassandra's door and opened the door to Seth's room. After sharing a few details of their adventures, they settled down on their own beds and drifted off to sleep.

Chapter Thirty-Eight

Premonitions, Bodyguards, and Precautions

As the great star cruiser, *Draco* entered the orbit of Shangri-La, General Zolotan sat down in his command seat on the bridge and sighed as he looked at the time piece on his wrist. What Shatra had gone to do was a waste of precious time, he thought. But he could not convince her of that, nor did he try to. He just went along with whatever she said because she had the backing of the Emperor.

The doors to the bridge swished ajar and one man entered and walked directly to General Zolotan.

"Patrol leader Darkon reporting, Sir!"

"Did you find Commander Shatra?"

"We found her ship burned and a shallow grave site made in haste, Sir. We dug up the grave and found Shatra dead."

Zolotan frowned a bit and nodded. He sighed and refrained from saying what he was thinking, which was the, "I told you so," speech. Instead he told the soldier to make ready for battle. He knew that Emperor Keltor would take vengeance of her death. Although he was not certain, he felt there was something between Commander Shatra and Emperor Keltor…something special…something unspoken, but it was clear that they kept it private. It remained a rumor in the ranks of the Rebel Alliance, and now it would forever be a secret. General Zolotan felt it was deeper than just a fling. In fact, he felt Shatra's death proved just how much she loved the Emperor.

"Who did it?" Keltor asked.

General Zolotan could hear the rage in Keltor's voice, and he did not wish to make the man any angrier than he already was. He scratched the stubble on his chin and thought for a second. Then the voice of the Emperor came again, louder this time.

"Who!" Keltor screamed.

"It was that Claveman she was going on about. O… something."

"Odan?'

"I believe so."

"You don't know?'

"No one was there with her, Sir. She went alone."

"How could you let her go alone! You Idiot!" The Emperor screamed. "She was the most valuable person we had against the Clave! She was going to be a Master, and she knew all the gateway combinations! All those secrets died with her!"

"I'm sorry, sir."

"Odan will pay. I want all forces to head for Shangri-La and prepare for war. They might have won at the gate, but they won't get Shangri-La back! Shatra will not have died in vain. Keltor, out!"

Keltor's image faded into a blue haze of light, then into a foggy mist, before the screen went black. General Zolotan severed the link and leaned back in his high-backed chair. In truth he had not wanted Shatra to go by herself, but she had left without giving him a chance to order a patrol to go with her. He did send a patrol after her, but by the time they picked up her trail, it was too late. At least, that is what the report he was now reading indicated. They did not get there in time to see anyone leaving the planet or in time to save Shatra.

Zolotan stormed out of his office to the control room, plopped down, and started barking orders to his crew. "Helm, new course heading! Set course to Shangri-La, hyperspace speed! Communications, get me interior coms!"

The communications technician followed orders, "Interior coms open all decks! All hands prepare for a jump to hyperspace! I repeat, prepare for a jump to hyperspace!"

On all decks of the ship, the entire crew rushed to an open seat, and seatbelts clicked all over the ship as the crew prepared for the jump. When all decks reported they were ready, the communication tech nodded to both the General and the helm.

"All set to go!" Coms notified the general.

"Proceed with the jump."

"Aye, General."

In the blackness of space, the star cruiser zipped into a speed greater than light speed, leaving just a streak of white light in its wake, almost like a falling star. After the cruiser reached hyperspace and it was safe for all to move around, the General notified everyone to return to their duties.

The short trip to Shangri-La would take them only a full day, at the rate they were traveling. General Zolotan ordered his crew to rest before they reached their destination because rest time would be nonexistent once the war started. Zolotan noticed that Emperor Keltor was contacting him again. "Yes, Your Majesty," he answered.

"I've been doing some thinking, Zolotan," Keltor said. "I need someone to replace Shatra as Commander of my royal guard. I hope you will take on the responsibility."

"It would be an honor, Sir," Zolotan replied.

"I am putting you in charge of things at Shangri-La. Whatever happens, don't let them take the planet."

"We will attack them before they reach it. We will cripple them so much that they will abort their plans to take back control of the planet. However, if they insist, we are ready for them on that front, as well. We have ground troops there and three cruisers in orbit as we speak."

"Good. Good. I like to see someone who is ready for a change. I look forward to hear that you have defeated them."

"Aye, Sir."

"Keltor out."

Zolotan pulled up a large globe protruding from the wall behind him into the empty space between the wall and his desk. It was a replica of Shangri-La. The globe rotated as the normal planet would, showing land coverage, sea levels, water, and mountain depressions. With a lighted stick, he began planning the Rebels' defense against the Clave.

Chapter Thirty-Nine

Silver Encounters Scrutiny

Master Markel and Master Odan sat looking at a florescent image of Shangri-La. It was an enhanced, miniature image of the planet in a lifelike simulation with all the elements it possessed.

"At least she's out of the way," Markel stated. "We don't have to worry about her and the gates anymore."

"Yes, Clave secrets are safe," Odan stated with a sigh.

"You did the right thing," Markel said. "She would have ruined our efforts to get control of Shangri-La and other planets."

"I know. It's just that…"

"I know you loved her, Odan."

"Love is not the word for what we had. It was beyond love, without anything physical to mess it up. She wanted to be physical, but I would never allow that."

"Is that why she…"

Odan cut him off, "partly, but the main reason was because I left her without saying anything. I was her Master, and she had no one to guide her to become a Master, which is what she desperately desired."

"She was lost the day you left then."

"I guess you could say that."

"That's why she divided the Clave and dismantled the Universal Order. Since her plans were ruined, she wanted everyone's plans ruined, as well?"

"I suppose that was her initial thought."

"I think we are going to need Master Mal's destroyers to assist us in our attack." Markel changed the subject seeing how much it hurt Odan to talk about Shatra.

"I agree. You need to send for them in secret….not a communication, but a person-to-person telegram, like we used to do in the old days."

"Yes," Markel agreed. "They won't be expecting that."

"How soon could a messenger get to Deran?" Odan asked.

"In a day and a half."

"Then we would need someone who knows the system and someone who could use it to his or her advantage," Odan pointed out.

"I believe we will most likely have to fight off the star cruisers and fighters before we get close to the planet and still be able to deal with the Rebel ground troopers and their war machines."

Nodding, Odan then pointed to the Northern mountain range. "They may not know about this because it was shut down due to the severe weather there. Many blizzards and snow storms made it difficult to run that base, but with a little effort, I think it can be done. It might still be closed up; I don't think Shatra knew about it."

"Hmm." Markel scratched his chin. "Interesting. We could use that to land and set up a station."

"Perfect."

"I'm still trying to think of whom to send to Master Mal."

"Silver," Odan suggested.

"Silver and Jay, or just Silver?" Markel asked.

"No. Just Silver. Jay is a Master by himself now. He has done his own mission, and he is just waiting for the test."

"Silver is a good choice. She knows the area well, and she can fly her butt off."

"Well, then, it's settled. She will go."

Markel moved over to a com link and switched to an interior com. "Master Markel to Silver. Silver to the control room. Markel out."

Silver's eyes popped open when she heard her name being called over the interior coms. She hopped out of the bed and slipped on her one-suit and robes. Then she freshened up a bit before heading to the control room. When she stepped off the lift onto the control room floor, she saw Master Markel and Master Odan studying the image of Shangri-La.

"Silver reporting as ordered, Master Markel. Greetings, Master Odan."

"Silver, as we get closer to Shangri-La, we will need more destroyers to fight off the Rebel Cruisers. We want you to personally deliver a request to Master Mal for more firepower from those residing at Deran. Can you do this without being detected?"

Silver pointed out the danger of being followed and having the Rebels learn about Deran.

"Yes, but we have no other way to communicate this need without giving up location. If we send someone that we trust and who can avoid being followed, then we are safe."

"I can do it. I will double back to be sure that no one is following. I will deliver the message to Master Mal and impress upon him our need for additional help if we are to retake Shangri-la." Silver then pressed her fist to her chest, "For us all."

Markel smiled. He hadn't heard those words in ages, but he returned them to Silver, "For us all."

Chapter Forty

Keltor Opens Gate to Shangri-La

Cassandra awoke, sweating and panting, as if she had been running a marathon. She remembered her nightmare vividly, as if it were reality. Seth walked in and stood by her bed. "You saw it too?" Seth asked.

Cassandra nodded. "We have to tell someone. Now!" she cried.

"Get dressed," Seth said, returning to his room to do the same. "We'll find Odan and explain it to him. He'll listen."

"He's back?"

"I felt it when he returned," Seth said.

Cassandra found a one-suit and a matching robe before rushing to the bathroom to freshen up. Within minutes the twins rushed down the corridors of the star annihilator, looking for Odan. The ship's computer guided them to the control room floor. When they arrived and stepped off the lift, a security guard halted them.

Everyone in the control room turned to the two young Senators. The guards grabbed Seth's shoulders.

"Please Sir, no civilians on the control deck."

"Do you know who I am?" Seth asked. "If you did, I doubt you'd be saying that or putting your hands on me in this manner."

"Sir?"

Odan came forward and placed a hand on the guard's shoulder. "I think you had better stand down, Lucus. This is Senator Seth Zeger."

"OH! Senator, Sir! I am most sorry! Please do accept my apology! The control room is yours!"

Seth smirked and looked at Odan, "Never mind, Lucas. I just wanted to speak with Odan here."

"Right you are. Go right ahead. I'll excuse myself at your permission, Sir."

"You're excused."

Cassandra coughed to hold back her amusement. The entire encounter to her was rather funny. Yet her smile faded when she returned her gaze to Odan.

"We have bad news," Cassandra stated.

"What's the matter?"

"Do you recall when you said we must remember our dreams and nightmares because they are sometimes visions of past or future events?"

"Yes, did you both see something?"

Cassandra looked at Seth, and the two turned back to Odan, nodded, and replied in unison, "Yes!"

"What was it about?"

"The upcoming battle," Seth stated.

"We don't have enough ships to take them on."

"We know. We've sent Silver to ask Master Mal to send us more star annihilators."

"Phewwww!" Seth stated. "I hope they get back in time before the fighting starts."

"We don't recommend fighting until that backup gets here," Cassandra added. "Otherwise, we will fail."

Odan nodded as Master Markel joined the trio. "What's up?" he asked.

Odan turned to Markel, "The twins have foreseen doom to our side if we don't get the backup from Deran before we start fighting."

Markel nodded. "I have foreseen the same."

"I'm glad we aren't the only ones," Seth chimed in.

"Not to worry, Seth. Master Silver will return with the forces we require," Markel assured her.

"I hope so," Cassandra said.

Master Markel diverted their attention. "Have you two seen the control room of one of these ships?" Markel held out his arm to Cassandra, when they indicated negatively by shaking their heads, "Let me give you a grand tour."

Swept away by Markel, Cassandra smiled as he showed the side of himself that she had grown to know so well during their transit to Shangri-La in the *Raptor's Claw*. Seth rolled his eyes and leaned over to Odan.

"He just likes my sister," Seth whispered. "He has liked her since he met her on Earth."

Odan chuckled. "She resembles your mother, and he liked her, as well."

"Is that why he treats her as someone special?"

"I think so. He treated your mother like this. But you should know Markel is a ladies' man. He treats all ladies like that."

Odan and Seth followed Markel and Cassandra, as Markel explained different stations of the room to Cassandra. Both twins paid close attention and made mental notations about each one. They had a feeling the information might come in handy before long. Finally, the last station led them back to the lift where Lucas took his job very seriously.

"And you know Lucas here because you met him on your way in."

"Yes," Cassandra replied with a smile. "I believe he was doing a good job."

Lucas blushed, "Thank you Senator Cassandra. That's a fine compliment. I thank you."

"Continue to do your job," Cassandra complimented him.

"Carry on Lucas," Seth added. "It was good to meet you."

"Yes, Sir. It was very good to meet you."

Odan thought for a moment and grabbed Lucas' shoulder. "I have a very important assignment for you, my man."

"Sir?"

"I want you and three more Clavemen whom you trust to accompany the two Senators at all times to protect them. I'm too preoccupied. I should have thought about this sooner. The Rebels might try to attack and end the movement before we even get it started by eliminating the two Senators. Your job is very important, and you need to trust the people you pick to do their jobs well."

"I will be very selective, Master Odan."

Lucas summoned three more men to the control room. They arrived within minutes, carrying laser pistols for all of them. Seth turned to Odan, "What is going on?" he asked.

"Bodyguards for you and your sister."

"Do we need them on a ship filled with Clavemen?"

"Yes," Odan replied. "Don't question, just try to understand. There is a reason why I do this."

Markel turned to Odan, "Very good idea. Yes, they need it."

"Need what?" Cassy asked.

"Protection. Bodyguards," Seth stated.

"Lucas?" Cassy asked.

"Right," Odan replied.

Cassandra smiled. "That's great!"

"You might consider having more than just four men for this assignment, Lucas."

"I hate to cut this short, but we do have work to do before we engage the Rebels," Markel remarked. "Although it was a nice break having the two of you on deck."

"It was nice to finally see the control room. Thanks for the tour," Seth replied.

"Yeah, where everything happens," Cassandra added. And thanks for the bodyguards. Now we can go about the ship feeling safer!"

"Just be careful you two," Odan warned. "Just because it's the Clave doesn't mean squat."

"We'll be careful. Odan," Seth assured him.

"We'll make sure they are careful," Lucas added.

"Now that is the kind of help I wanted," Odan breathed a sigh of relief.

Before following Lucas into the lift, Seth called Odan aside and whispered in his ear, "I trust that we no longer have to worry about the threat you mentioned before." Seth was referring to the problem of Odan and Shatra.

"It is taken care of," Odan assured him. "We can proceed now, knowing without a doubt that the enemy no longer has that edge against us."

Relieved that Odan was now safe from the possibility that Shatra could read his thoughts, Seth grabbed Odan into a big bear hug before joining Cassy and the bodyguards.

Once on the lift, Lucas turned to Seth. "I should introduce you to the other three."

Seth waved him off. "I only want to speak with you, Lucas. My sister and I will only speak to you. You will be in charge of the guard. Nothing personal against the other three, I just don't want any misunderstanding. It's better if orders come from one man, and that will be you. You will report to me. Leave my sister out of the gory details. If you need to speak to her, you let me know."

"Very well, Sir."

"As for the guards, they are to be seen, not heard."

"Right."

"As for how to run the guards, I leave that to you."

"Thank you, Sir."

"That is why you were chosen," Seth reminded him.

"Yes, Sir."

The lift door swished open, and Lucas stepped out first with one of the other guards. Both looked down the corridors before motioning for the two Senators to exit. Then the remaining two guards stepped out close behind the twins. The party marched down the corridor to the twin Senators' quarters where Seth addressed Lucas.

"Lucas, you and another will guard my sister's door all the time, while the other two will guard my door. That is all that I will ask of you."

"Consider it done, Senator."

Nodding, Seth felt more at ease. He turned to Cassy, "Good night Sis."

"I hope you are not ordering Lucas about. He knows what he's doing," Cassy said.

"No, My Lady," Lucas stated. "Just men talk."

Seth smirked and laughed, "That's all."

Cassandra looked at both of them and shook her head. "I don't know whether to believe you two or not. I hope you weren't fussing over me."

"Don't kid yourself," Seth mused and headed to his door. Now, you go that way, and I'll go this way."

Cassy looked at Lucas. "Goodnight, gentlemen."

"My lady." Lucas said bowing.

Cassandra entered her quarters and disappeared behind the swishing doors.

Chapter Forty-One

Silver Secures Requested Reinforcements

Silver blasted off from the UOD *Ares*, heading on a direct course to Deran. She planned to make one stop for refueling on Artica before making the final leg to Deran. It would not be easy as Rebel forces would recognize her ship as a Clave ship on sight. She would have to stay clear of Rebel ships and mostly do things in the shadows. Silver knew from experience how to remain unseen.

She recalled a time in her past when she had to fend for herself, when she was a little girl...an orphan. On big transport ships where she used to steal her way aboard, she would approach patrons and ask for a bite to eat. Many patrons would invite her to sit down and join them, while others would brush her off. She was thankful to those who helped her. She surmised it was her smile that won them over.

Silver estimated that it would take her one or two days to get to Artica and then another day and a half to get to Deran, without any Rebel patrols spotting her. Now in hyperspace, she relaxed and enjoyed the ride. The alarm would tell her when she was getting close to Artica.

She must have been exhausted because when Silver opened her eyes, the alarms were buzzing and Artica was looming in the darkness before her. She blinked, rubbed her eyes, and put her head gear on.

"Artica Command, this is Silver Ashstod, I wish to dock and refuel my ship. I need docking instructions and clearance."

"Your ship is not in our registry as one allowed to dock at our port. Please hold in orbit while we check with the registry authority."

"Frack!" Silver whispered. "Aye. Maintaining orbit."

She had not thought about her ship being recognized by the command tower as a Clave vessel; and since Artica was a neutral planet at present, they may not allow the ship to land, which meant there were already Rebels on the planet. Silver sighed as she completed her first orbit of the planet. Then the voice she was speaking to came back.

"Command to Silver."

"Silver here."

"Proceed to landing dock 31A. You may refuel and spend as much time as you need on Artica."

"Thank you. Proceeding to dock 31A as ordered."

She angled the ship out of orbit downward into the atmosphere of the planet. Slight turbulence made the entrance a bit bumpy, but she maintained control of the ship and landed safely. With the grace of a swan and the skill of a prized fighter, Silver placed the viper perfectly on a landing platform that lowered into the hanger. Immediately after the landing, the control center lowered the platform with the ship on it down under the surface of the planet.

Silver got out of the ship as it was being lowered. The minute she set her feet down onto the platform, she was greeted by Rebel forces.

"Freeze!"

"Where'd you get this ship, pretty?"

"I won it in a game of star poker. Isn't it a dandy?' Silver smiled. "I think it's worth a few thousand rubles, don't you?"

"No one's ever seen this type of ship before," another officer replied

"I got it from this strongly dressed fellow. He said it was all he had to offer into the pot. He lost, I won."

"I don't buy your story, lady."

"It's the only one I have for you."

"What's your business on Artica?"

"Refueling and a bit of relaxation in the tavern. No trouble from me, I promise," Silver responded, trying to keep her composure.

"I can't arrest you for having a strange ship, but I will arrest you the first thing you do wrong in this city!" He said.

"I guess you won't be arresting me. I don't plan on getting into trouble. In fact, I plan to be far from it if there is any."

Having no reason to retain her, they let Silver go on about her business. In the darkness of night, she walked through the semi-crowded streets to the tavern, headed straight to the bar, and ordered a drink.

Loud music exploded throughout the room, while different species frolicked on the dance floor. Gamblers played all sorts of star poker, and smoke filled the air forming like a foggy mist covering the entire place.

Silver took her first sip of the drink and sighed deeply. This whisky made most humans who drank it get stupidly drunk. She had to watch her intake. One shot would be way too much.

A human-like being strode up to Silver, "You by yourself, Pretty?"

Silver turned to the voice, "Looks that way."

"Want some company."

"How much do they pay you to say that?"

"I don't work here, pretty. I come here for a good time like you do."

Silver chuckled, "I came to relax. You can either join me or go somewhere else."

"Ahh! There is something nice about you after all. I will join you then."

"Do you need transport? I have a very fine freighter that will take you anywhere you wish to go."

"I have my own ship, thank you."

"Ahh. A woman of power and smarts."

Silver chuckled, "What's your name, Superfly?"

"Greggor."

"Well, Greggor, I'm Silver. It's nice to meet you."

"Likewise, I'm sure."

"Bartender, another round for the lady and me!" Greggor yelled to be heard above the music. "So what brings you this way?"

"The wind."

Greggor exploded with laughter and sipped his drink that the bartender had set on the counter. He put his elbow on the counter, leaned his chin on his hands, and gazed at Silver.

"You're very mysterious lady, and that is turning me on."

"Oh dear, I better stop being so mysterious then."

'Seriously, what do you do?'

"Live, move, and have my being. Seriously, right now? I can't say. It's a secret."

"Now you got me interested more."

"I don't mean to be harsh, but I'm not here for long. I 'm just here to refuel my ship and continue on my way."

"I see. So you came down here for a few drinks."

"To pass the time, yes," Silver stated.

"Nothing wrong with that," he said. "Another time then?"

"If fate chooses for us to cross paths again, I would not complain."

The man smiled, "Well, alright then."

Silver gulped down her whisky, turned, and strolled out of the tavern. When she returned to her ship, she found that it was already refueled. Therefore, she prepared to depart, making the   preflight checks, noticing if some things were out of order. She boarded her ship and contacted command for clearance...

Some hours later, Silver was blasting out of the orbit of Artica toward Tatoway. She would head that way and then change course toward Deran later when she had doubled back to make sure she wasn't followed.

With half the trip over and with only one run-in with a Rebel patrol on the surface of Artica, she thought it wasn't that bad a run so far. As she continued, she came close to the orbit of Dunezar and noticed a Rebel patrol coming out of orbit. They had seen her and were blasting turbo thrusters to catch up with her.

"Unidentified vessel, please identify, state point of origin and destination."

Silver quickly thought to herself. She now knew she'd have to land on Tatoway. This patrol would track her there. "I am called Silver, and I am coming from Zanzadar on a course to Tatoway," she stated.

"Your ship is not recognized in the directory."

"It is a new ship. I don't know why it's not listed," Silver replied.

"Very well. I'll make note of it for future reference. It is a nice design, your ship."

"Thanks."

Silver continued toward Tatoway and landed on the surface there. She stayed there for a few hours. In the middle of the night, when she blasted away from Tatoway, she did not see any Rebel patrols lingering around. She engaged hyperspace speed and would be in Deran in a couple of hours.

Chapter Forty-Two

Odan Prepares the Twins

The entire Rebel Alliance Armada departed Caprica I and set on course toward the gate of the Orion's Belt Galaxy. One thing Shatra left behind was the medallion that had been given to her by the Clave before she had split the Clave apart, the key to the gate of the Orion's Belt Galaxy. The only person now who knew how to use the medallion was the Emperor, once an ex-Claveman himself. He knew the words to say to open and shut the gate. He had heard Shatra repeat it over and over, so he just had to copy what she said. Hopefully, it would work.

Keltor now sat in the throne seat on the control room floor watching the stars whiz by on the view screen. There were ten ships with him and possibly ten on the other side. The Clave would be over-powered, outnumbered and crushed. He was hoping for a quick victory.

Then, he saw it. The three stars came closer and closer in the viewer. All the ships of the fleet slowed out of hyperspace speed and continued at below light speed, traveling toward the gate now. Keltor rose, took the medallion into his hands, and uttered the words he had heard Shatra speak many times before. A flash of white light radiated and the space within the triangle circled to the right. The gate was now open. The ships passed through, all ten of them.

In the Orion's Belt Galaxy, the fleet appeared through the triangle of stars and zipped into formation. Then the Emperor ordered them to head for Shangri-La.

Chapter Forty-Three

The Clave Battles Rebels

Geneneral Devin, up late and going over some things, noticed a blip on the radar. He moved over to the scanners and noted it was one of their own ships. He ordered the technician on duty to contact the ship.

"Deran Command to approaching vessel! State your identification and point of origin and destination," the technician addressed the pilot of the approaching ship.

"This is Silver coming from the frontier fleet to bring a message to Master Mal, priority green and urgent!"

Devin scratched the stubble on his chin and nodded, "Give her clearance."

As the technician obeyed orders, Silver followed instructions and placed her ship on the landing deck perfectly. General Devin managed to meet Silver from three decks down from the landing deck by taking the lifts and sprinting to arrive just as Silver climbed out of the ship onto the ladder leading to the metallic deck. She took off her helmet and gave it to the ship mechanic before turning and smiling at Devin.

"Master Devin!"

"Silver! It's good to see you again. But why have you risked so much to travel here ....?" Devin asked.

"Believe me, I know how risky this trip was. However, it was necessary."

"How so?" Devin asked.

"Master Markel believes we will get clobbered if we don't show up at Shangri-La with our entire force," Silver replied. "I happen to agree. Enroute here, I saw no cruisers out, just patrols from the planets. My guess is that every cruiser is being routed to Shangri-La."

Devin nodded and sighed. "I see."

"And if you think about it, having more than enough back up will be safer than not having enough," Silver added as the duo walked through the corridors and continued their discussion.

"That's true," Devin agreed.

"And if we really did need help, it would be too far away to do any good. A whole day at hyperspace. That's too far!" Silver stated. "It would need to be closer."

Devin nodded as Silver spoke for the fleet. "If this is going to work, we need to bring our best at the onset."

"Yes, that is correct. I'm not the one to convince, Silver. Master Mal is the one to persuade. He will have the last say in what the fleet does here. That will have to wait until tomorrow."

"Wake him up. The fleet is close to Shangri-La. They will be within radar range in a day and that is all we have to get there."

"Very well, follow me."

Master Mal sat upright in his bed sensing someone approaching. He stood up, hands stretched out, feeling his way to the door. Then suddenly, the door swished open.

"General Devin, what do you want at this crazy hour!?"

"It's not his fault, Master Mal. I'm the one demanding to talk to you."

"Silver?"

"Yes, Master Mal. It is I, Silver."

"What is it?" He found his way into the sitting area of his quarters and sat down into his rocker. "No, no, don't tell me. You are here to ask for more star annihilators and fighters for back up."

"How did you know?"

"When you get as old as I in the Clave, reading minds comes second nature," He smiled. "Now Master Markel seems to think we are going to need more forces there."

"Yes."

"He's right. The gate to the Orion's Belt opened not too long ago, and Keltor came through on a cruiser to personally attend to this matter. I felt that the ancient lore was inappropriately used."

Silver's eyebrows raised. She wondered how he felt all that when she had felt nothing of the sort.

"Believe me, my dear when you have as many years in the Clave as I, you know what to listen for and what not to."

"I guess so."

"Now, General Devin, Prepare all ships for departure to Shangri-La at hyperspace. Hopefully, we'll get there before the entire Rebel fleet does."

Chapter Forty-Four

Dodge My Fire!

At the frontier of the Clave Armada, all the newly enrolled apprentices spent the rest of the time enroute to Shangri-La for advanced training on Clave law and the Clave way of life. They were to learn how Clavemen walked, talked, fought, slept, ate, learned, and advanced in the order. It was a lot to swallow in just a few days, but time was crucial, and the new recruits had to master basic skills if the mission were to be successful. It was a crash course, and they would get more in-depth training on how to use the light whip and other gadgets of the Clave later. The light whip, exclusively a Clave weapon, was used only in defense or in some cases to eliminate a threat.

Another device the Clave used exclusively was the shadow communicator which displayed a view of the person connected with a glowing white haze of light. Not only could one talk to the person, but he or she could also see the person he or she was connected to. However, many Clavemen and women seldom used this device, having abandoned it for modern weaponry. In the olden days, when the Clave and the UO were in control, this device had been the weapon of choice.

Seth and Cassandra, exhausted from their days of training, sat in Seth's sitting room examining their new weapons, a light whip and a shadow communicator. Master Markel told them to leave the communicator on standby when he had dismissed them for the night.

"I'm beginning to like the way of the Clave, Cass," Seth stated. "But I really do miss Jess."

"You never know, we might have to go back there," Cassy reminded him of the seriousness of their mission.

"Yeah. Not if we win."

"I don't think there is a winning in this. I just think it will be a win THIS time, but there will be a NEXT time unless we get Keltor."

"Yeah, I guess you are right about that," Seth stated with a sigh. "I wonder if Keltor will bring Earth into this thing."

"Now that he knows it's there, he just might."

"We have to make sure that Earth is protected," Seth added.

"We will. When we re-establish the UO and empower the Clave again, we can order them to keep the key to the gate of Earth locked up," Cassy explained.

"I hope so," Seth stated.

"You, Odan, and I will make sure of it."

"Yes."

Suddenly, both of their shadow coms lit up and the glowing figure of Odan came up from the crystal panel on their arms.

"Come down to my quarters, you two." Odan directed.

The figure of Odan disappeared in a hazy fog and the light went down into the device. Seth jumped up and held out his hand to his sister and the two headed to Odan's room which was a short distance down the corridor, armed guards in company.

Odan's room was very spacious and extremely plush, but Cassy and Seth didn't pay much attention to the décor. Curiosity as to why Odan had called them, consumed their minds blocking out everything else.

"There you are," Odan stated. "Come in and take a seat."

Cassy sat on the couch while Seth settled into the comfortable high-backed chair. Odan sat down next to Cassy.

"Well, now, I know this trip has been a little unexpected, and we haven't had much time to do that much talking about it, but I figure now is a better time than any."

"You brought this on us rather suddenly, Odan. I'm still trying to swallow that, but I understand why you did what you did and why you didn't tell us much until now. We probably wouldn't have believed you just like we didn't believe you when you told us a few weeks ago."

"I'm glad you understand why I had to wait to tell you. I was waiting until you would be able to accept it better, but I suppose no time would have been any better."

"Nope," Cassy retorted.

"I asked you here so that you can tell me what you think of all this now."

"I'm concerned about Earth," Seth replied first.

Odan turned and looked at Seth and nodded. "I am as well."

"Now Keltor knows about Earth. Won't he try to go there?"

"He might. Many will try once they get knowledge of it. Yet that is a concern for another time. Right now, we should focus on Shangri-La."

"How are we going to defeat a whole Armada?'

"Simplicity," Odan stated. "Greater forces overlook simple things, thus we focus on the simple things, capitalize on them and defeat the enemy."

"I don't see how…"

"Keltor has too many ships…too much to focus on at one time. He will miss small important things that are key to winning a battle. WE will focus on the small important things and use them to defeat him and his big ships."

Seth smiled. "I see. Just like the Vietnamese in the Vietnam War on earth?"

"Similar. They used the land against their enemies. We will do that and more," Odan replied.

"Then we stand a chance."

"I believe we do even when they out number us," Odan stated. "But it's time to get some shut eye."

"Thanks for bringing us here, Odan." Seth began. "We would never have known our true heritage if you had not told us."

"I was going to tell you. I was just waiting for the right time, but Keltor beat me to that, forcing me to tell you before I thought you were ready, but that's no matter. You're both younger than I would have liked, but you are old enough to lead the UO and the Clave to victory." Odan expressed his confidence in the two.

"I'll take your word for it," Cassy responded.

"Me, too," Seth added.

"Now, you two get back to your rooms and get some sleep."

The pair hugged Odan and returned to their quarters, tucked themselves in for much needed sleep.

Chapter Forty-Five

Security for Senators

RED ALERT! The ship's computer repeated. The loud ear-shattering siren made many silently wished it would shut down, but it did not. It kept on going while those aboard dashed to their battle stations. A reddish haze filled the corridors of the star annihilator, as Malte, pulling on his left boot scrambled out of his quarters to find his sister just exiting her quarters as well.

"What the heck is going on?!" Della shouted.

"I don't know, but we were told to report to landing bay and our assigned ship if the alarm went off."

"Right."

Jogging through the crowded corridors, Malte and Della, two unknown people in the new Clave forces, took a lift and descended to the level on which their assigned fighter ships were located. When the door swished again, they found themselves on the landing bay and saw many of their squadron scrambling to their ships. Malte gave his sister a thumbs up and shouted to her.

"Good luck!'

"You too!"

"See you when we get back!"

"Yes!"

Still running across the deck, each climbed the metallic ladder to his ship while their mechanic gave them pre-flight check data and a helmet. Della took the helmet, put it over her head and snapped the thing into place, attaching the wires with the rest of her gear. She climbed into

the cockpit and shifted into a comfortable position. Then she pressed
the button for the protective, glass door to close over her. She flicked
on her engines, lights and other instruments: radar, communications,
and scanners. Plugging in her helmet she could see the display on her
visor. She pulled the mic into place on her helmet so she'd have good
vocals with command. Everything that she was taught in training, she
remembered and put into action. Then she checked her equipment by
looking at her display on her visor where almost everything glowed in
bright, neon green on a black background. A few different colors appeared
randomly, but green dominated the display of the lettering.

Della heard the first voice and the only voice she'd hear.

"This is Master Jade. Blue Squadron, that's everyone on this landing
bay, report in."

It took only a few minutes for all the fighter wings to respond before
he contacted command.

"Command, this is Master Jade reporting all Blue Squadron are
present and accounted for. We stand ready to blast off, over."

"Fire when ready."

"Blue Squadron, follow my lead. Maintain formation. Then break
into Tri-wings."

Then Jade blasted off, and all thirty ships in his squadron followed
his lead out of the landing bay into formation. Other ships launched from
landing bays throughout the destroyer and orbited as well.

When they had blasted out about one league, everyone saw the reason
for the red alert. Three Rebel cruisers were in their path. The squadrons of
30 ships each advanced toward the cruisers and blanketed the blackness
of space before them. Then the cruisers launched their fighters and
everything equalized and the opposing fighters just sat in space, looking at
one another, not moving.

After a long eerie and dark silence, the two opposing forces just
hovered in the darkness of the chasms of space waiting for some unspoken

cry of war to begin. Finally, it came from Keltor, who stood in the observation lounge of the lead cruiser and was able to see an Armada of Rebel fighters through the ceiling-to-floor window. He pressed the communications button on the desk beside him and uttered the dreaded cry of no return.

"Advance Red Battalion! Fire when ready!" Keltor cried out.

"Aye, Sir!" came the reply.

Seconds later, the Red Rebel fighters began their advanced toward the Clave fighters, and Master Jade sprang into action.

"Blue Squadron! We're up first! Let's take this bunch and cut them down to size meaning fewer of them and more of us."

Leading the fighters from the Clave, Jade blasted forward hitting his thrusters and angling his ship off to the right toward the approaching ships. His squadron followed his every move, so it looked like a wave of the same motion floating through space. In just a short time, the squadron had become used to one another's flying. Master Markel, watching this from his radar, smiled as he could see this in reality how it would look. Silently he thought they were just showing off.

Jade quickly got serious as they got closer to the battalion coming at them. *"There are many ships to deal with,"* he thought to himself.

"Break into Tri formations now!"

The ships following Jade jumped and slid into their Tri formations, having one lead ship and two wing men. Seth and Cassy turned out to be Jade's wing-men. Jade decided to stick to the present course for the first strike.

"For the first strike, remain in Tri's but maintain present course so that we hit them going from this front position. Then we will break off and scatter! Got that?'

Everyone replied that they understood. And as they got closer and closer, the magnitude of this battle settle on Seth's mind.

"Just a few weeks ago, I was home on Earth going to school and living the good life, and now I'm here in the middle of a war, about to get blown away by some aliens!"

"Don't be so mellow dramatic, Seth. They are Rebel scum and they asked for it."

"I supposed you're right about that. They started this one, coming at us with a full battalion like that. Who do they think they are?"

Cassy laughed as did Jade.

"You two stay close to me!" Jade ordered. "Odan will have my head if I lose you two out here."

"Yes, Sir!" Cassy said.

"Who else do we have here?" Jade asked.

"Captain Rex."

"He's not alone by the way," Dexter stated as she angled her viper to keep in formation of her lead ship. "We decided to stick around."

"Much appreciated. I will find some way to repay you guys for your assistance in all this. If it weren't for your willingness to assist us, we'd be caught by those Rebs by now," Master Jade acknowledged.

"Things have a way of working out, Kid," Rex stated. "Perhaps I've found my calling."

"Jade, you guys got a few on you, stop yapping and get firing!"

"Roger that."

"Let's shake em up a bit, guys."

Doing all sorts of flying maneuvers, dips, dives and hair-turns, Jade, Seth and Cassy managed to confuse their pursuers enough to strike a few of them out of the cosmos. Then, another Tri-wing formation came barreling through blasting away enemy ships about them.

Master Jade was quick to give thanks, "Hey there, thanks for that aide! Who was that?"

The voice that did not sound familiar to Seth or Cassandra, but Jade knew it but couldn't quite place it at the moment. Was that Master Rex?

"Rex? Is that you?"

"Never mind about that, just consider us even. You saved my hide, now I saved yours."

"Point taken. We'll talk later."

"Yes, I think it best since we are quite busy fighting fighter ships at present," Rex stated.

"But it's good to hear from you, and it will be even better to see you after all these years."

"Indeed."

And so the war for Shangri-La began, Clave fighter against Rebel fighter, and the cosmos exploded with laser fire. Although the first few encounters were orderly and clean, the latter bouts were not so. At the spur of a moment, another battalion was launched by Keltor's men, and the Clave responded with a launching of one of their regiments. Again they were outnumbered, but willing to defy the odds against them for the greater good.

Chapter Forty-Six

Doubts of the Raptor's Claw Crew

Master Markel stood in the control room, watching the battle, and he rubbed the whiskers forming on his chin. He was quite sure that they were outnumbered about three to one from the beginning of the onslaught. He was certain that they'd lose a few in the star fighter exchange going on at the moment, but he remained hopeful that they would not lose too many of their good Warriors in just the pre-surface battle of this war. What they needed was more forces.

"Any sign from Silver yet?"

A technician looked at and checked the long range scanners and shook his head. "Nothing yet, Master Markel."

"Keep looking. The moment you see them and they are within communications range, you get them on the viewer!"

"Aye, Sir."

Markel was hoping that his men could hold out until Master Mal and Silver arrived, that is, if they were coming. He was sure they were, having explained the situation to Silver. He hoped Master Mal would see things the way they were. After all, it had been his call to separate the forces from the beginning. Or perhaps there was some unforeseen reason why he was delaying the reinforcements. Master Mal was known for his gift of seeing the future and thus conduct his actions in relation to upcoming events. Some did not understand his ways. Markel was one of them. However, in the end, he knew that Master Mal, elder of the Clave, had the best interest of the Clave and the newly formed UO at heart.

All he could do was wait for Master Mal to show up and literally save them from their fate, which was not looking good at the moment. As time passed, more and more ships were eliminated on their side as well as the other, but they were taking a beating.

"Do we have a backup battalion ready?"

"Aye, Sir, but they were to be launched only if another star cruiser came on the scene."

'We'll stick with that," Markel stated. He didn't want to change the plans just yet and foul up what was already working to the best of his knowledge.

Then several explosions erupted on one of the star cruisers of the Rebel forces, and the ship exploded, severely damaging the cruiser beside it. This was the break the Clave desperately needed.

Markel turned to the communications officer and gestured for him to send out a command.

The officer's hands flew over the controls, opening all command channels. Markel stepped into the view of the camera revealing his face on all other ships' viewers. "Focus all fire on the crippled ship!" Master Markel barked out!

In the darkness of the cosmos, laser fire from the UO star annihilators and the Clave star fighters focused on finishing off the crippled cruiser. Trying to escape the barrage of fire, the ship attempted to move out of firing range, but it was much too late. Within minutes, it exploded into a zillion fragments which floated to their final graves in the blackness of space.

Then, from the direction of the gate to Andromeda Galaxy, six cruisers and a host of Rebel starfighters appeared in range on the scanners led by General Zolotan. All hopes the Clave had celebrated from the edge they had momentarily gained from the destruction of the two Rebel cruisers vanished when they saw the enormous fleet coming closer.

Markel looked to the communications officer as he tried to keep his men's minds on task. "Open a channel to all ships!" Again, Markel's face appeared on the viewers in all ship command rooms. Regroup your star fighters and prepare to engage the new threat! We'll hold them as long as we can. Help IS on the way!" Markel bellowed more as a reminder to himself than to the men and women serving with him.

The Clave star fighters retreated to an invisible line and formed into their squadrons. It was painfully obvious that they had taken casualties, several of them, but they would forge ahead still. They were Clavemen and simply would not quit, no matter the odds. At the moment, it looked almost impossible, yet, Markel knew from experience in the Clave that one could never doubt the brotherhood's faithfulness. No matter what, they would fight until the very end and fight even after that end until no one was left standing.

"Remember who we are. We are Clave and we fight until it's done!" Markel cried to the men and woman fighters in the starships and vipers.

Although there was no response, he felt he had lifted a few hearts, eased a few rookies' minds, and created a sense of calm. He could imagine how the fighters felt and hoped his words had reassured and encouraged them.

The second wave of the battle began with Zolotan's men blasting out in new ships and fresh pilots to fly them. The two sides engaged each other in the endless depths of space exchanging laser fire. The Clave, no longer in Tri formations, since they simply did not have enough ships to provide that kind of spread, resorted to two-wing formations which left some vulnerability unchecked. There wasn't a third man to watch the other side and rear, therefore the second ship would have to cover nearly 180 degrees while the lead ship did the same. That was a tall order while trying to fly, aim, and shoot down ships simultaneously. Yet, those who flew the starships had mastered these skills and were counted on to perform their tasks. Some were better than others who were new and just learning. At any rate, those left in the dual wing formations were lucky to be alive.

As the battle raged on, Markel's brow furrowed when it looked as if they would lose. He had no other weapons to command against the Red Rebel fleet. His belly trembled at the thought of the reality that the mission would be lost after the first engagement with Rebel fighters. Even then, he maintained hope that help would arrive in time to save them and rescue their goal of delivering the universe from the hands of Keltor, a tyrannical dictator, and restore Order and peace among the planets.

Suddenly a communications technician cried out.

"Star annihilators, six of them, coming into range, Master Markel!"

"Open a channel."

"Aye, Sir, with pleasure," the tech replied as he pressed the controls and yelled into the mic. "Channel Open!"

On the viewer, an image of Master Mal appeared with Silver at his side on the viewer. "Did someone call for reinforcements?" Master Mal joked.

Markel smirked and exhaled a sigh of relief. "Yes, Sir! I've ordered all fighters to focus on the four cruisers remaining. So if you would join us, we'll have this knocked down in no time, and then we can get to the surface."

"Roger, Markel!" Master Mal replied.

"Master Mal," Markel said with his head hanging downward somewhat. "I'm sorry I failed you Master."

"No. Did you know they were going to bring so many cruisers? No. This is not a time to place blame. We must carry on and defeat them together. No fault here! Understood?!"

"You are in charge here. Markel. Lead them to victory!" Master Mal ordered.

"Aye, Master Mal." Markel turned to the communications officer. "Open a channel to all ships including the new ships that have arrived."

When all channels opened so that everyone in the Clave fleet could hear, Markel regained command and optimism. "Now that we are all together, let us show them how the Clave really functions. All fighters target landing bays and engines. All Gunnery on star annihilators aim your fire for the nearest cruiser's hull. We need to break down shielding so that our Warriors can get closer and cause some real damage."

Once everyone knew the plan, the ships set out on their individual missions. The star annihiators moved in closer to play the dance, "Dodge my fire!" in the midnight of space. The sky exploded into chaos, yet some organization to the madness remained. When it looked like ships would collide, at the last possible second, some Clave pilots made hairpin turns to avoid a collision. Seconds, inches and odd angles during such situations revealed the skills of true Clavemen. The ability to function effectively in such chaotic situations and make it look simple was a skill not many possessed. Such abilities separated the average from the gifted simply by the way they piloted their ships.

Fighter pilots either flew their ships by the seat of their pants, or they could refuse to command authority over the controls and make the ship an extension of themselves. Most star fighters out there now were confident pilots. The timid and inefficient ones had been picked off.

The battle raged on for hours until a star cruiser was destroyed. It fell out of its sleek line as if it had been derailed like a train. Then, it exploded into countless specks of fiery debris into space.

Markel motioned to the communications technician, who instantly opened a channel to all Clavemen and women. "Star Fighters! Focus your attentions on the next cruisers approaching! One down and three to go! Let's finish them all off!"

There was no response to the command, only action. The star fighters zoomed toward the remaining enemy cruisers, directing their laser at the hulls in an effort to penetrate the shielding. Seeing that the first cruiser had been annihilated, Clave destroyers returned to the aide of the star fighters.

/////

After a long and grueling battle, Keltor surveyed his depleting armada and the armada of the Clave. He surmised that his enemy was outnumbered, but they were strong. Although he had many warriors, they were weak and unskilled. If only Shatra had survived, she would be able to tell them how to fight them.

Keltor sat down and prompted his communications officer, "Open a channel to all ships."

"Yes, Emperor. Channel open Sir!"

"All ships, retreat to the surface!"

/////

Immediately the Rebel cruisers turned tail, their course heading, Shangri-La.

"Sir, the Cruisers are retreating toward Shangri-La! Shall we give chase?"

Before Master Markel could speak, the communications technician spun around.

"Incoming communication, Priority One! Deemed urgent from Master Mal.'

"On screen!"

The glowing image of Master Mal as he would normally appear showed on the viewer. It was deathly silent. "Well done, Master Markel. They have retreated. Yet now we must plan how we will attack the surface. Let us join together again on my ship. Bring the Senators."

"Yes, Master Mal." Markel bowed his head and thrust his fist to his chest.

"Master Mal out."

"Markel out." As he said these words, he made a slicing motion across his neck with his finger to cut the channel. "NO, we do not pursue. Coms report to all ships that we will be maintaining current positions for the meantime. Have them prepare a shuttle for a few passengers only and a security detail. We will meet in the landing bay in one hour. You can find me in the Observation Lounge."

Chapter Forty-Seven

Clave Ground Invasion

The twin Senators representing Romes IV now stood looking out of the large viewing window of the Observation Lounge, their eyes focused on the Rebel forces retreating.

"Looks like we've won this battle," Seth exclaimed.

"For the moment." Cassy added.

Then a voice addressed them from behind as the doors swished open.

"Were you two thinking this to be an easy task?"

Cassandra took a step closer to Odan. "It looks as if we've won the star fighter battle and the bout with the cruisers and destroyers."

"They will take this to the surface of Shangri-La now," Odan stated.

"Can we beat them there?" Seth asked.

"Of course!" Master Markel answered as he stepped into the room.

"If we execute the plan we've made, we will retake control of Shangri-La and begin to rebuild. Keltor won't give up his efforts to stop us, but we will have re-established our presence. Sooner or later the whole galaxy will come to know of it. You will then begin to see a swell of people coming to the UO for safe haven from Keltor and his Rebels."

"It's going to be a busy time," Odan added.

'Busy?" Cassy asked.

"Busy for the Senate and busy for the Clave. Both organizations will have to work together to take power from Keltor. He has enjoyed being a tyrant for a long time. He will not relinquish it easily."

"What happens now?"

"We must get ready for the ground campaign," Markel replied.

Odan turned to address Markel. "The twins should not go down to the planet until we have taken possession of it."

"Agreed. But we will leave them with a regiment of men to protect them."

Odan nodden in agreement. "I would imagine that would keep them safe. One of the Masters should be in charge of their safety."

"Hmmm. I think Silver and Jay would do a splendid job."

"Indeed they would."

"Better yet, let Jay do this for his test."

Markel concurred, "It is an enormous responsibility."

"Yes."

"It is settled then. Jay will play bodyguard for the Senators."

"That would include Princess Elaina," Odan suggested.

"Yes."

"Very well."

"Send for him," Odan ordered while addressing Seth and Cassy. "Not to worry, you two. You'll be in good hands with Jay."

Seth recalled that Jay was the man who had looked at his sister with goo goo eyes before. He sighed and rolled his eyes.

"Is there a problem, Seth?"

"No. This Jay character is a ladies' man is all. He's holding hands with the Princess and trying to look at my sister all goo-goo eyed."

Odan chuckled. "Your sister is pretty, and men will often look at her."

"Well, not when they are looking at someone else already."

"I see your point," Odan stated.

"Don't be so quick to judge a man. Jay is a respectable fellow. You respect him, and he'll respect you.'

"Alright Odan. But one false move and I swear!"

"Don't swear!" Odan replied. "If he does anything wrong, then you're entitled to give him your mind, but until then, be cool."

"Very well." Seth knew that Odan was right.

Odan chuckled a bit as he left the lounge. He was proud of Seth trying to look after his sister in such a way. It showed that he cared for her well-being.

Markel moved to a communication's console and called for MIT Jay. (MIT stands for Master in Training) Jay's voice could be heard across the room by Seth and Cassy as Markel spoke with him.

"We need you to be in charge of the Senators' safety while we run the ground campaign. It is an enormous responsibility, for without the Senators, this thing will crumble."

"Understood, Master Markel. I will do my best to protect them."

"You will have one regiment of Clave Warriors at your disposal, plus the Senators' bodyguards at your command. At the moment we are aboard the *Ares*. Come aboard, pick one of the ships to reside on while the ground campaign is running its course."

"Aye, Master Markel. I will be there shortly."

"We will all be in the Observation Lounge."

"Very well. Thank you for this opportunity."

"Tread carefully, Jay. This mission is very important to you. Markel out."

"Jay out."

Markel turned back to the twins who were looking at him with blank faces.

"I wonder if we are doing the right thing."

Seth strode forward and folded his arms across his chest, "What do you mean?"

"Not sure if we should leave you two up here or not. Those Rebs might try to do something stupid like capture you three Senators and end this war."

"Well, if you trust this Jay character, that won't happen."

Markel nodded, sighed and turned to Seth, "Yes, you're right. I do trust him to do this, but it is a tall order for one so young."

"Then put him with his Master, Silver," Seth stated.

"He's a MIT. That would be an outright insult."

"Better that than a quick ending of this war. Believe me, I am not saying this because of my distaste of the man, but there is too much riding on our safety up here. We must be secure. Perhaps another regiment of Clave Warriors would be in order, as well."

"Can we spare them from the surface?"

"If they are needed we can send them down," Seth replied.

"True, that is." Markel stated looking at Cassandra. "Very well, I will assign another regiment to Jay, and I will have Silver oversee his charge of the situation."

"Now that sounds like a plan," Seth stated. "I feel more comfortable already."

Presently, they were joined by Jay, who appeared very pleased with himself. However, some exchanges of words between him and Master Markel at the entrance, and his demeanor changed.

"I thought you said I'd be doing this mission alone?"

Seth strode forward then and declared, "It was my call, Jay. I asked for more security because of the situation. If the Rebels get anywhere near the Princess, myself, or my sister, the war will be over and all our efforts these past few days and weeks will have been for nothing. I can't leave this to chance. It's not that I don't trust you, I just want more than one master at the helm. I am happy to have you with us. Yet I think having your former Master, Silver, someone you've worked with before, will be in order here. Since this is to be you leading us, Silver will only be observing and providing support to you."

Jay nodded, "I understand."

"This is good for you?"

"Whether or not it is good for me is of no matter. I will perform the duties laid out for me," Jay stated.

"Good. Then, perhaps, you could call your Master to the Observation Lounge."

The doors swished ajar and the Princess entered the Lounge with her escort. She walked over to where Seth stood talking with Jay.

"Greetings," Princess Elaina stated. "I hear we are going to ride out the storm on the ship."

"You heard right," Seth responded.

"Silver and I will be in charge of security, remarked Jay." "You can rest assured that you may sleep well."

"I would hope so," Elaina replied.

"Excuse me Princess, I have to call Silver to the lounge as ordered," Jay stated, walking off to the communications console.

Cassandra approached the Princess and bowed to her. "Princess, it is good to see you."

"And you. How are you?"

"I am well, Princess. Thanks for asking."

"What do you think will happen while the battle goes on down there? Are we in jeopardy up here?"

"Of course, we are. The Rebels may try to capture one or all of us. That's why the security. It shall not be a dull moment up here at all."

'Oh." Cassy's eyes cast downward as she reflected this news.

At every turn since they had arrived to the alien nations, they had been running away from their pursuers. Even now they had to protect themselves from them. There was nowhere to exhale and enjoy a moment's peace, she thought.

"Not to worry, Cassandra, there will come a time when you will be able to breathe in and sigh with comfort."

Silver was aboard the *Calypso* with Master Mal, looking at the layout of Shangri-La. Devin and others pointed out strategic locations and conversed with Master Markel, who was on the command ship *Ares*. She overheard her name being mentioned and walked toward the viewer.

"Silver," said Master Mal, "we need you to report to the *Ares* and hook up with your old friend, Jay, to oversee him on his MIT test which will be to safeguard the Senators during the battle on the surface. The rest of you will remain on one of the ships while we go down there. You are to observe and give support to him only, not tell him what to do."

Silver nodded. "I will do this."

She was happy to help Jay during his test. Yet, she also knew her limitations in that same regard. She could only support him, not tell him how or what to do in any given situation that emerged. He was the decision-maker or else the test would be null and void. However, another trick up her sleeve was that she could explain things to him or suggest things. Sometimes a suggestion expressed in the right tone could change one's whole outlook on a matter, especially between Jay and herself. The two knew each other well, having been together for so long.

After bidding farewell to Master Mal and to Master Devin, who was now General of Clave forces, she gathered her few possessions from her temporary quarters, stuffed them into a duffle bag, and headed to the loading deck. Silver settled into the small ship again and performed the usual preflight checks before requesting clearance from the flight commander.

"Leaving us so soon, Silver?" the Claveman asked.

"Just going to another ship to get involved with another mission."

"Always something going on with you Masters."

Silver smiled and nodded. "There's never a dull moment."

"I suppose it keeps you on your toes then?"

"It does."

"Be careful out there. Those Rebel patrols could be anywhere."

"Understood."

Silver knew that the Rebels had retreated, but she appreciated the reminder. She was so excited about Jay's test to become a Master that she wasn't thinking about the possibility that the Rebels could still be monitoring them. Minutes later, the doors to the landing bay opened and she blasted out of the hold, arching towards the UOC *Ares*.

Chapter Forty-Eight

Odan Encourages The Clave

Deep in the bowels of the *Ares*, Maximillian Rex Faraday, Dexter, Langstrom, Raymond, McCloud and his crew were gathered around their ships, preparing for the trip to the surface as ordered by Master Markel. They were talking amongst themselves about Seth and Cassandra and the Clave Warriors who had brought them here.

"They've forgotten about us," said Rex

Langstrom shook her head. "No, they have not. They are just busy."

"We are about to go risk our lives, and they don't even care!" Rex cried.

"Come on, Rex, they do care. They are Senators! They are running this show with the Masters! How can you expect them to just …to just come down here for us little guys?"

Suddenly they heard footsteps approaching and a very loud voice talking back.

"You better take that back!" Cassandra cried.

"Yeah! Seth reiterated. "We don't like that kind of talk."

Rex, grinning from ear to ear, jumped up, raced over to greet Cassy, lifting her off the floor embracing her fondly. He then embraced Seth, patting him on the back. "It's good to see you both!"

"I second that," Raymond said equally excited to see the twins. Tugging on Cassy's dress, he got his chance for a hug. "We were afraid you'd forgotten us little people," the dwarf joked.

"Awe, Raymond, we would never forget you guys. You helped us and kept us from the Rebels. You got us here. You are our best friends," Cassy looked to them all. "Don't ever think that we'd forget you, ever. You're in the Clave now and definitely our close sisters and brothers."

"We came to wish you well on your mission on the surface, for we will not be joining you down there," Seth stated. "We'll be staying up here."

"That's not smart!" Rex exclaimed. "They are bound to try to capture you guys."

"We'll have protection," Cassy stated. "Two legions of Warriors and Jay and Silver will be with us leading our security."

Rex nodded. "I hope that's enough."

"It will be," Seth said. "It will have to be."

"How do you like the Clave so far?" Cassandra asked Rex.

"It's a sight better than the smuggler's life. Three squares per day, plus anything you want in between. Before we either had to pay for our victuals or hunt for it ourselves on some god forsaken planet. Plus, we are part of a group, and the fellowship takes away the loneliness of a smuggler's life."

That statement caused whistles and responses to erupt from the rest of the crew.

Casandra smiled, happy that her friends did not regret their decision to stay and fight with the Clave Warriors. "The Clave suits you well. I'm glad you've settled in."

"There's no dying while I'm around," Langstrom exclaimed, putting her arms around McCloud.

After a choir of laughter subsided, Seth chuckled and could not resist the urge to push the dagger in deeper. "Looks like she's got you locked up, McCloud."

"That's the thing. It's one thing being locked up with a woman you hate, but if you love her, you don't mind it so much."

There was more laughter and knee slapping. Seth smirked and shook his head, remembering Jess. He understood the man's words to the tee. He would love to be locked up with her.

"I know what you mean."

"Aye, then you know love, then, lad," McCloud stated.

"Very much so. I'm happy that you held on to yours though."

Seth unfolded his arms, placed a gentle hand on his sister's shoulder, and spoke softly into her ear. "Time to go sister; Silver and Jay will be waiting for us."

Cassandra looked to him and gave him a nod. "Yes," she agreed and turned back to Rex and his friends. "I'm sorry to cut this short, but Silver and Jay are probably waiting for us by now. We must get back upstairs."

Rex embraced and kissed Cassy on the cheek. "Thanks for coming down. And don't be strangers."

"We won't be."

The bodyguards surrounded Cassy and Seth and escorted them off through the corridors of the ship. Rex watched them go.

"Those kids are great," Rex stated.

"It was good of them to come down here."

"At least they don't forget their friends," Raymond remarked.

"Told you they were just busy," Langstrom reminded them that she had been right before.

"You always tell us so," Rex admitted his error in thinking negatively about the twins.

"You always put me in a position to do it."

"Can there be just one time where you don't say that?"

"Next time I won't say it."

"Bet you will, out of habit."

I can bet you I won't."

"How much?"

"Hold it!" McCloud stated, "Now you're betting she won't say something she has no control over?"

"Yep."

"I'll take that bet," McCloud cried. "Because I can't believe you'd bet against something she has control over. She can stop herself from saying that."

"I don't believe she can."

"Done deal then."

They shook on it.

Chapter Forty-Nine

Increased Security for Senators

inal preparations were underway for the newly formed
Clave's launching of the ground invasion of Shangri-La.
Despite heavy casualties during the last two battles, they
still had an impressive, intimidating number of Warriors to contend with
Keltor's Rebels.

All the landing bays were a buzz with activity, people scrambling
here and there getting things ready for the last and final battle that would
determine if the UO and Clave would again rule in the Orion's Belt
Galaxy. Once it started there, there would be no stopping it as others
would learn of the revolution and the re-establishment of the Universal
Order and the return of the Clave Warriors. It would expand, and crush the
Rebel Alliance, and bring Keltor under arrest.

Finally when all preparations had been made, the ships headed
toward the destination like swarms of angry bees. They advanced toward
Shangri-La in the midnight of space with the star annihilator *Troy* escorting
the fleet. Like fire-flies, they blasted closer and closer to the surface.
Suddenly Rebel patrols and a Rebel cruiser started firing into the Clave
ships who returned fire as they continued to the surface. Star fighters
swooped in and gave cover fire to the shuttles as they continued to drop
down into the atmosphere of Shangri-La's gravitational pull. The star
annihilator *Troy* fought head to head with the Rebel star cruiser exchanging
laser fire, making it look like an electrical storm instead of a fire fight.

Master Markel's ship touched down first, followed by other shuttles.
Immediately Markel began barking out orders to set up command stations.

Amid exploding shuttles that were not able to dodge the fire from above, others landed safely, and the fighters disembarked, and set out on their many tasks. Several hours passed before all the shuttles landed, but the Clave Armada's ground crew was organized and operational on the surface of Shangri-La. According to plan, they had landed at the Southern compound, which was now deserted because the Clave neglected to repair it when it was last damaged. Master Mal had decided against it at the time, because of weather complications. However, now, it was summer on Shangri-La, and the weather in the Southern Pole was not strikingly freezing as it had been before. Thus, it was great weather for fighting, and even better weather for making repairs to the Southern and Western compounds.

The dry, brown ground crunched under the weight of his boots as Master Markel studied the pad in his hands and pointed east. "Send six legions of men out in Range Rovers, East. If they encounter the enemy, they are to engage them and call for backup."

"Aye, Master Markel."

The Clave Warrior hurried off to communicate the orders and spread the word. Markel continued moving and talking. "You engineers get the command center up and running as soon as possible."

Engineers rushed off to carry out their orders.

"Troops, stand ready for your orders to depart the area."

Markel climbed up on a bolder and raised his hands in the air. He pressed a button on his wrist piece, making his voice blast louder. "All ground troops advance!"

In the valley of the Southern Plain, one sea of black robes inched Eastward, as another advanced Northward. In front, the foot soldiers set out behind ten rows of Range Rover Riders, straddling big-wheeled buggies which could travel over the rough terrain with ease. Then the air-jet men and women flew overhead in jet powered contraptions that allowed the pilots to fly without bulky machinery. They were called air-jets and were controlled by joysticks. Pilots could control the air-jet with one hand and use their weapons with the other hand. It was not for everyone, of course, only those who were ambidextrous.

As Master Markel moved into the damaged compound, he saw that it was already being repaired.   As he walked deeper into it, a familiar voice called out to him. He could recognize that voice anywhere. Before he turned he spoke the name softly to himself, "Odan."

"Markel, everything seems to be well organized."

"For the moment. I've come to see exactly what needs to be done in here."

"Allow me. You should be out there directing things."

"Yes, but when you want something done right, you know the way it goes."

"No, you find someone you trust to do it right. Right now, I am that person. You go back out there before those troop don't know what to do with themselves."

"I suppose you're right."

"You know I am. People are probably looking for you right now," Odan said as he gestured with his hand pointing toward the exit.

"Find out what the engineering crews need to work on."

"Right."

Odan set to work, looking among the damaged equipment for anything that showed signs of life. He accessed the opps console and was lucky enough to find it working. The screen lit up and showed a report of red flags on several systems. Odan read the flashing words quickly:

Main frames I and II – malfunctioning; faulty power cells in levels 3, 2, 1 and below levels. Air ventilation obstructions in ducts 32 thru 39; weaponry systems, faulty electrical wiring and shortages; faulty power cells in unit 3, 5, and 6; power source to main system, depleting in power to expire completely in 24 hours....

Odan read it over putting it to memory before shutting off the console. Then he went to find Markel.

Meanwhile, Master Markel had returned outside to the command station and just as Odan had mentioned, there were people looking for him to give directions. Markel gave orders to the commanding officers who carried them out. Soon, the hourly reports were coming in from the ground troops sent to the northern and eastern compounds. So far, no one had come into contact with ground oppositional forces. This was foreseen, in Markel's eyes. They were far from the other compounds and it would be some long hike before the opposing forces would meet. Most likely about midnight, they would begin to hear something of substance.

Odan found Markel and reported on the condition of the southern compound according to the information he had received moments before.

"The command center has extensive damages to the main power grid and the main frame computers. It's going to take a while to get them up and running, Markel."

"For the moment, we have time for those repairs, but when the battles get started, I'm not going to be able to oversee their progress," Markel replied.

"Leave that to me," Odan volunteered.

"Alright. That sounds like a plan."

Markel stood looking off to the North. Odan regarded his gaze and questioned it. "You look as if there's trouble brewing."

"I don't like how things are unfolding," Markel stated. "The men will encounter the enemy when they are in need of rest. I should order them to stop and rest before confronting the Rebels."

"That's a good idea," Odan agreed.

Markel walked off a short distance and tapped his communicator to make contact with Justin and Gorn, who were in charge of the northern and eastern troops.

"Master Markel to Masters Justin and Gorn, come in."

"I read you," Justin's voice came through.

'I hear you, Markel," Gorn's voice followed.

"Around a quarter until high moon, take a break from the march."

"Will do.'

"We'll need it."

"That's what I figured." Markel stated. "Rest the men for the battle."

"Right," both Justin and Gorn responded in unison.

"That's all I wanted to say," Markel said. "And good luck."

"Thanks."

Odan folded his arms across his chest. "Feel better about the troops?"

"Yes. They'll be ready now."

"There's another thing we have to worry about, Markel. At some time or another, the Rebels will get around to attacking us here. We need to come up with a way of defending ourselves."

"We have the air support, and we have the regiments of troops here, meant for backup."

"We can't use them."

"Well, if we really need to, we can send for the legion that we have topside with the Senators, but I'd rather not."

"We can't use them either."

"We'll have to use the troops down here…half of them."

Odan nodded, "If it comes to that."

"They'd have to break through our forces to get to us."

"That's a lot of open space, and they could slip by our troops unnoticed."

"Whose side are you on?"

"Ours," Odan stated, "But we have to think ahead about these things."

Markel sighed. "I guess we do."

"It is why the Clave is known for being prepared for everything."

Markel placed a hand on Odan's shoulder and nodded. "I'm glad you are here."

Chapter Fifty
Ground Battle Intensifies

As the shuttles and star fighters left for Shangri-La, those who stayed behind on the *Ares*, the three Senators and Master Mal, watched the ships disappear into the depths of space. They watched the largest destroyer, *Troy*, follow the shuttles and ships toward the planet.

"Well, herein begins another battle for peace in these sectors. It's a terrible thing that one must fight for peace," proclaimed Master Mal.

"If not that, what is there left to fight for?" Cassy asked.

Mal turned to her, "A good question. Perhaps Love."

"Ahh." Seth said. "Yes."

"I like the way you two think." Mal noted their levels of maturity though only seventeen.

"Sorry to interrupt, but I would rather you all move to a more secure location." Master Mal turned to see Jay whose hands were gesturing toward the doors.

"As you wish, Master Jay," Mal agreed.

The party moved out the exit doors and down the corridors. Soon they entered the VIP suites, which consisted of several rooms joined by a single community area. "This is where everyone will be staying until the battle down there is over. So I suggest you go to your other rooms and get things you need and move them here. Nothing major, just clothes," Jay instructed.

Everyone nodded, even Master Mal, who was mainly observing Jay while he ran things.

The doors opened and in walked three gentlemen of superior build. One of the men stepped forward.

"Master Reese at your service, Master Jay. Reese smiled at him.

"Thanks for coming so soon and upon such short notice. I will need to spend much time in the command center, so I need you three to secure these rooms."

"Not a problem. We'll get it done."

"Then, I'll leave you to it."

Master Reese turned to introduce his companions. "Well then, people, I'm Master Reese. This is Troy and that is Kal. As you have just witnessed, we've been assigned to secure this area; therefore, no area is 'private.' We will be moving in and out of all rooms on visual patrols without prior notification."

"Hold it! What if I am taking a bath?" the Princess Elaina exclaimed.

"You can take it, but someone may be checking up on you while you're taking it."

The Princess sighed. "There are some things that are meant to remain private!"

"Alright when you take your bath, we will post a guard, and no one will enter."

"That's better," The Princess replied. "The same for Cassandra."

"The same for the Senator," Reese answered.

Silence was deafening for a time. Then Reese began talking again. "Before you all go into those rooms, we will search them out for anything that might harm you. Keltor would love to eliminate you three and be done with this war. So, let us do our jobs before you go moving in."

They divided into three groups, led by Reese, Troy and Kal and searched out the three rooms. After about fifteen minutes, they emerged comfortable that the area was secure.

"You may enter the rooms and move in," Reese announced. "The rooms are clean and safe. We've put devices to monitor sound and motion, so minus your own bio signatures, there should be no others."

Seth raised his eyebrows, "You have this well in hand."

"You can rest assured that all will be secure here, Senator," Reese asserted with confidence.

"We'll have to share the three rooms among the four of us."

"Let Cassy and me share a room, and the three of you have your way with the other two rooms."

"The two ladies should have a room each," Mal insisted.

"So shall it be."

"I was only offering because there are more of you than us women," the Princess stated. "It only makes sense."

"I agree," Cassy stated.

"Fine. If they so wish for us to be so accommodated, then so be it," Master Mal gave in with some frustration,

The Princess grabbed Cassandra's hand, and they headed to one room, guards in tow.

The men watched them go.

"She did have a point," Seth stated. "There are more of us."

"No matter. They wanted to be together in there."

"Why?"

"So they could talk about us," Seth offered with a grin. "But guess what? We get to talk about them, too."

Reese laughed as did the others. Master Mal shook his head. "These are young games that the old have no time for."

"But you don't forget how fun they are."

Mal laughed then. "No, no! They were fun. Yes, indeed! I have not forgotten anything.

"That is good. Then you have a chance to go back and visit."

Mal shook his head. 'No, this was a long time ago. Too long ago for her to remember."

"You'd be surprised what people remember, Master Mal."

Seth added, "Especially girls."

"Perhaps."

"What was her name?"

"Isabella."

"We'll make a point to go and visit her when this war is over to see if she remembers."

"Exactly."

"Alright," Mal stated. "To Zune we go after this."

Chapter Fifty-One
Keltor's Back-Up Plan

Emperor Keltor, desperate to eliminate the Senators now, played the only card he had left to play. He called upon the Centurion Assassins to fix his problems with the Clave uprising. He summoned them and described the mission he had for them.

"I want you three to kill the Senators and any of the Masters that are in charge of operations of this uprising of the Clave."

"This will cost you much more than the usual amount. To kill a Clave is no easy task," the leader explained.

"I know it. I am willing to pay whatever you ask."

"Three million terrons," he replied.

Another leaned forward. "Each."

"That's expensive!" Keltor exclaimed.

"No pay, no kill."

"Alright, consider it done. I will pay each of you three million terrons, but for that amount, you will kill them all!"

"That is fair," they said in unison.

"Use whatever means you must," Keltor added.

"We will." They rose together, tapped their wrist devices and shimmered out of sight before his eyes until nothing remained where they had been standing.

"They really creep me out with that," Keltor mumbled.

"Sire, do you think they will be successful?" asked Keltor's attendant.

"We shall soon find out who is better, the Clave or the Centurions. My money is on the latter."

"I hope for the sake of your Empire that you have chosen the winners."

"Centurions are undefeatable. One of them will be successful if not all."

"Perhaps you should send out more?"

"Three is enough."

Chapter Fifty-Two

Surprise Attacks

On the surface of Shangri-La, Clave ground forces moved closer to the proposed battlefield. The power-filled meal along the trek had renewed them for the battle. The hearty meal and a good night's rest made them more determined to push forward with their ultimate goal: to make the universe free for all again.

The eastern lands consisted mostly of forest and tall brush. If one were to drop to their knees and crawl, they could be invisible for a while. Though it was a cowardly thing to do, it might be a wise choice if one's life were at stake. Dropping down to hide or take up a strategic vantage point might be in order,

As they advanced through the thicket, slicing the brush limbs back with blades of iron, they soon came face to face with their enemy.

Justin, leader of the eastern troops yelled only these few words: "Alright men, they are upon us! Attack on sight!"

Charging ahead the troops followed orders and engaged in the first battle on land. Light whips struck out, and lasers blasted from one side to another between the brushes. Soon the battle field became a blur of confusion as both sides clashed and fought. Yet, the Clave slowly but surely made a steady progression Eastward.

As the night sky transformed to daylight, the Rebel troops retreated. Justin commanded his remaining men to regroup. He ordered a head count to determine how many had fallen. Throughout the night, 104 of 1000 men and women had been killed. After the dead were gathered and buried properly, Justin spoke to the rest of his men.

"Everyone fought well last night. We will camp here and seek them out again tonight. We will advance tomorrow, pursing them when they retreat. Does anyone have anything to add?"

"I thought our goal would be to pursue them and advance after them today!" one warrior shouted.

"They would expect that and be prepared for it," Justin stated. "Let them think we will battle them here throughout. Tomorrow, we will surprised them. Our goal is to deplete their numbers as best we can before we reach the eastern stronghold. I think it is better for us to battle out here than at the stronghold."

Silence. He made sense. No one said a word.

"Make camp." Justin ordered.

Justin found a lone spot in the camp by the fire and tapped his wrist communicator.

Back at the southern stronghold, Markel tapped his wrist communicator in response to it having lit up and vibrated, letting him know there was a communication waiting. In a shimmering light of blue, Justin's face appeared.

"Justin! Tell me good news."

"We engaged the Rebs last night as planned."

"Casualties?"

"104"

"So many?"

"I know. But these younglings are fresh from training, Markel. Only half remember what they learned from us."

"But still. 104. Wow."

'I doubt it will be like that tonight."

"Let's hope not."

"We will move forward as planned. I'm going to send out scouts tonight."

"Be careful with that."

"Right."

"Send someone who knows what they are doing."

"I know. Justin out."

Justin wondered which of his men he could send as spies. Suddenly the images of Rex and Raymond the dwarf entered his mind. He would send them together to spy on the enemy. From his experiences with Maximillian Rex Faraday and Raymond, the two would be perfect for the job.

Justin walked around the camp, stopping at the individual camp fires to speak to the men and women, until he found the two he was looking for.

"Rex, Raymond, I have a job for you both."

Rex and Raymond moved closer to Justin, leaving the comfort of the fire and their small group. "Yes, Master Justin. How can we be of service?"

"I'd like you to scout ahead of us and check up on the enemy. See what they are up to tonight and report back before dawn."

"Will do, Master Justin," Rex stated

"I like those orders!" Raymond agreed as he grabbed his battle ax.

Justin smiled, and spoke to some of the other groups briefly while moving on through the troops until he had gone through the entire battalion. Then he turned in to get some sleep.

Rex and Raymond gathered their gear for the scouting mission and headed on foot through the brush

"When we get closer, we'll use sign language," Rex explained to Raymond.

"Good Idea," Raymond said trotting alongside Rex to keep up. Raymond's bow and arrows posed a challenge for him too, but he had insisted on bringing them. At first Rex opposed the idea, but Raymond argued that a silent weapon might be useful in picking off single targets without alerting an entire camp. Having mastered the skills of archery,

Raymond had a feeling that with his short body and his skills, Rex would be surprised when he saw him in action.

Plowing through the forest was easier because the enemy had paved the way. However, they avoided moving too fast to avoid making noises. When they came to a ridge overlooking a large valley, Rex and Raymond dropped down to take cover behind the greenery. The enemy had camped not far from their very own base site. It was quiet, too quiet. Rex looked behind them and saw nothing. Then he pulled away and signed to Raymond that they needed to get closer to hear what was going on. Carefully and stealthily, the two spies climbed down the ravine and moved in closer, careful not to attract attention and be spotted by lookouts.

Snaking their way through to the camp, they stopped behind a large tent where they heard voices. They eased up closer on the dark side of the tent, staying out of the light of the fires. Raymond watched for anyone coming, while Rex listened.

"We must attack them before light. They will be expecting us to attack at dawn."

"It's a good plan there to attack before dawn."

"Then we get the men ready for another charge."

"I expected them to pursue us. It looks like they will hunker down here and battle things out here until the end."

"Then we'll end it here."

Rex turned and motioned for them to head back and warn Justin. Running back through the maze of tents, they came to the edge of the camp and saw two lookouts moving on the side. Rex motioned to Raymond for them to go another way. Moving toward their own camp as fast as they could go, they detoured and climbed up another part of the ravine.

When they were far enough away, Rex tapped his communicator.

"Justin, this is Rex, over!"

Back in the Clave camp Justin lay on his tarp looking up at the starlit sky, when he felt his communicator go off. Tapping it he rose.

He saw Rex's face and smiled, glad that he had remembered how to use the communicator. "What news?"

Still out of breath, Rex managed to speak, "Rebs will attack before dawn. I don't know if we'll make it back in time to prepare for that battle, Master."

"Before?"

"They said it would surprise us."

"Indeed. Good work. We'll have a surprise for them alright. Don't worry about getting back here in time. Rest up and see if you can get a sniper point."

"Rodger that."

Rex and Raymond looked at one another and grinned. Of course, being a sniper meant being sure to hit the enemy and not one's own men. Yet most snipers had good vision and Rex and Raymond were excellent shots. Rex got his laser rifle out and examined it, as did Raymond.

"It would be best if we are on opposite sides of the battle."

"Right. I'll go this way to that big tree and take a limb," Raymond stated.

"I'll head for those rocks up there."

Both man and dwarf set off in different directions armed with weapons. Raymond climbed up the tree with ease, and Rex found his way upon the rocks quickly. Once comfortable with their weapons readied, they just waited.

Justin had taken the news and alerted all his troops. He got them up and ready for battle BEFORE dawn, and they were now moving toward the enemy's camp. When Justin was satisfied that they had gone far enough, they took up hiding positions in the brush and trees.

Just as the enemy had said they'd do, they tiptoed back through the brush, thinking they were sneaking up on the Clave Warriors.

Then Rex and Raymond began firing their sniper shots taking out several of the rebel troopers one after another. Panic struck the Rebels momentarily before their commander ordered his troops to proceed despite the sniper shots. Then Justin cried out a battle cry, and the Clavemen came out of their hiding spots surprising their attackers, causing them to turn and run. However, many stood and fought. This time the battle favored the Clave, and the Clave pushed the REBs back to their campsite. The Rebel commanders sounded a retreat, but the Clave pursued after them, taking over the Rebel base camp.

When there were only stragglers left, Justin called off the pursuit, and they regrouped at the Rebels' campsite, where the Warriors and their leaders celebrated.

Justin reported the good news to Markel.

"We've scattered the eastern Rebel force. They are no more. We march on to the stronghold come daylight."

Markel sighed. "That's good to hear. You've all done a great job, Justin."

"Many thanks will go to Rex and Raymond. I will recommend them for recognition at the gathering."

"I shall like to hear THAT story from him."

"He will tell it with much enthusiasm."

"If he doesn't, the little guy will have his big toe for dinner!"

They both laughed.

"How are things coming on the northern front?"

"They had much farther to travel. Nothing as of yet," Markel stated.

Justin nodded, "I hope they have as good a night as we have had. If they need assistance, we could lend a hand."

"Noted," Markel stated. "For now just hold the fort there."

"Understood. Justin out."

The florescent blue haze view of Markel disappeared and the flickering light of the fire filled Justin's eyes. He sipped his beverage as he thought about the next day. They would have to prepare for anything. Therefore, he sent out scouts to comb the area ahead of them for any sign of the Rebels regrouping. The reports came back that there were no signs of reforming Rebels. On the eastern side; things had quieted down.

Chapter Fifty-Three

Keltor Plan Uncovered

C assandra stood in front of the massive window of the room she shared with the Princess with her arms folded and her eyes glued to the shimmering image of Shangri-La below. A Clave Warrior approached her.

"It is not safe to stand by the window, Senator Cassandra," Troy warned.

Cassandra turned only her head, "My friends are risking their lives for us while I sit up here, twiddling my thumbs! And you come and tell me that standing by the window isn't safe? What about what they are doing right now? It's beyond not safe!"

Seth approached the two and put his hands on her shoulders to comfort his sister. "Easy. She's a bit worried about Rex and the gang."

"Rex?" Princess Elaina piped up. "You don't need to worry about him. He can take care of himself in any situation."

"That doesn't mean we shouldn't worry about them," Cassy retorted.

"True," Elaina replied. "You care deeply about Rex and his crew?"

"Yes, I do," Cassy admitted.

"We do," Seth confirmed the close bond that had developed between the two of them and Rex's crew.

"I can tell you they will be fine. Fighting and fire fights are not foreign to them. They were smugglers and fought most of their lives. They know a lot more about it than some of the others," Elaina tried to calm their fears. "Yet, I understand why you worry. Not hearing from them after all this time is quite nerve-wracking."

Troy ushered Cassandra and Seth away from the window, and they continued their conversation with the Princess in the common area of the suite.

Outside the suite, a Centurion landed in the corridor, with no warning, and the Clave Warrior guards opened fire immediately. The Senators heard the commotion, and the guards acted quickly to protect them.

"To your rooms!" the guards ordered the three Senators!

The girls headed to their room, Master Mal was secure in his quarters while Seth darted to his which he shared with other Clavemen. The fire fight continued in the corridor while Reese called for backup from the command center, alerting them of the intruder.

"There are three of them on the ship, Reese! Hunker down and keep the Senators safe while we try and get rid of them out here," Jay replied.

"One is right outside our door!"

"I know. We have Clave Warriors enroute to you now. If they get in just hold them! Whatever you do, don't let them get to the Senators!"

"Very well," Master Jay."

The link severed as the fire fight outside the door of the suite continued. Several times, Reese felt like going out there to help in fighting off the assailant, but he had to obey his directives. He was told to protect the Senators at all costs, which meant, standing just where he was, just outside their doors between the enemy and them.

"Keltor would call upon the Centurions!" Kal yelled.

"It was his last resort," replied Reese. "But it will fail!"

"How can you be so sure of that? Centurions are the only thing that can match us!"

"If you believe that, then we're done," Reese countered.

"I don't. It's only what people have said."

"Now we will prove it once and for all that the Clave warrior is more skilled than the Centurions," Troy declared.

Suddenly, Reese, Troy and Kal did not hear any more blasting outside the door. They looked at one another and Reese held up his hands and stretched forth with his mind. He closed his eyes. Then he opened them

"Take cover!"

All three of them jumped behind furniture in the room while the door blasted open. The Centurion entered slowly, looking around. Raising his weapon, Reese struck out with his laser whip hitting the Centurion on the chest. Electric sparks danced all over the Centurion for a few seconds, then the whip retreated. The Centurion recovered quickly and raised his laser pistol, firing at Reese, barely missing him as he ducked. While the Centurion aimed at Reese, Troy, who was on the other side of the Centurion, used his laser whip and struck the Centurion in the chest. Again electricity danced all over the body of the Centurion, and this time the Centurion cried out in agony. The Centurion aimed at Troy and when it did, both Reese and Kal used their Laser whips and struck the Centurion on the chest. The Centurion fell to the floor, his body smoking and smoldering. However, Troy was hit badly.

Reese ran to Troy's side and held him in his arms. "Troy."

"It's bad, isn't it?" Troy whispered, gasping for each breath.

"Command! We need a medic fast!"

"Roger!" Jay answered. "Who's down?"

"Troy."

"It's too risky to do a site-to-site transport. They might home in on the coordinates."

"Agreed," Reese stated.

"Jeepers. This sucks! The way to you is blocked by fire fights with the other two Centurions!"

"You are understood. Reese out."

One of the suite doors opened, and the Princess dashed out, making her way to where Troy lay. She took her hand and placed it on the wound and spoke in her own tongue. She closed her eyes, concentrating on healing Troy's wound. Her hand gradually glowed a pinkish color and then turned white, as she slumped over him, passing out.

"What just happened?" Cassandra asked.

"I believe Elaina saved Troy," Reese answered.

Troy's eyes opened, and he smiled as he felt something heave on top of him. "Why do I feel like someone is ……."

'Because Princess Elaina is passed out on top of you, Troy."

"Did she?"

"She healed your wound."

"She could have died doing that. Is she alright?"

"We don't know yet."

Troy moved his arms and wrapped them around Elaina's still warm body.

"She's still warm!" Troy yelled.

"That's a good sign," Reese replied. "We have to hurry and be prepared for another strike from those Centurions."

Troy sat up and brushed Elaina's hair from her face. "Princess Elaina?"

"Are you well?" Princess Elaina asked.

"Yes, I thank you for saving my life."

Elaina smiled, "That was my first save."

"You could have been killed trying a stunt like that!"

"My father told me I'd know the time, and I did. But he was right, it takes a lot out of you. I'm still very weak. I don't think I can walk."

"Well, I can."

Troy rose with the Princess in his arms and carried her to her room, laying her on the bed. He then exited and joined the others.

"Senator, I don't think she should be alone."

"Right," Cassandra said, dashing into the room.

"As soon as she is able, we should find other accommodations. This doorway has had it," Kal stated.

"Give her some time," Reese advised, walking towards the blown out doorway. Peeking around the corner he saw the fallen and shook his head. "I'm glad we have a legion of men on this vessel protecting them, and not just us three."

"Do you think the other two Centurions will get this far?"

"Depends on the skills of those in opposition. Right now, we should prepare for the worst case scenario, which means we should hope for the best and prepare for a fire fight." He pointed to four Clavemen who were assigned with them in the room. "You four stand guard outside the door. Two of you face one way and two face the other way. If anything comes, holler and fire. That will give us time to prepare."

The four men nodded and exited.

Meanwhile, in the room where Seth waited with Master Mal, the pair talked while facing the doorway, ready to strike out their whips at anyone who came in.

"This is the time when all eyes will be on those who are in the top positions, calling the shots. You will find that minus me, you and your sister will be looked to for guidance."

"But we know very little of these universal affairs, Master Mal. We only know what we've witnessed thus far and what we've been told."

"Remember what you've been told by wise men, and use it to govern wisely. If you question something, look into it yourself, or see another mind on it."

"How do you know what to believe then?"

"You will know. Romerians have always been known to feel the truth."

"You know," Seth said, nodding his head, "I understand."

"Good."

A rap came at the door, and Reese stepped inside. "Master Mal, we almost lost Troy, but the Princess saved him."

"I foresaw she would seek to try her first save on Troy. It worked. Good. We should move to a safer location."

"The Princess cannot walk."

"Carry her."

The sudden change in plans caused the slight confusion in the suite, but it was soon under control as one guard carried the Princess over his shoulder and the others guarded them as all followed the lead of Reese. Troy and Kal brought up the rear.

When they came out of the suite, they moved to the right and proceeded down the corridor, checking in with command.

"Command, this is Reese. I have been ordered by Master Mal to move the party from the suite.

"NO!" Jay cried. "We were protecting that level! Go back!"

"I have foreseen that if we stay there we will be caught," Master Mal stated. "Do you question my senses?"

"No, Master Mal. I don't. Alright. How can we help you advance?"

Mal grunted to himself and nodded his head, the boy had learned to listen in his youth.

"Good. Have the men come down to level ten. We will head up the interior ladders to your level. Make sure the Centurions don't get in the ladder wells."

"Very well, Master Mal. You know while the Centurions are attacking they are preparing to fire on us with their ships as well!"

"Don't be distracted with those ships."

"I have to keep them off of us to protect the shields."

"True. Beware of that, but focus, Jay. Your objective is to keep us safe. This ship and those in it save us, can all perish; we cannot."

"Understood," Jay sighed as he looked at Silver, who gave him a nod. "Good news from below. The eastern stronghold is ours."

"That is good news," Mal stated. "Keep up the good work, Jay.'

Mal was pleased. Despite the Centurions attacking, things were working out well on the surface of Shangri-La and out here in orbit. Mal moved down the corridor slowly and cautiously with Reese assisting him. Troy and Kal, in key positions on the team, opened a portal hatch and the group made it through and started up the ladders that led up the interior of the ship's inner framework to each level of the ship. These backways were mostly used by engineers, but in times of war, they were often used to move from one level to another without being seen.

Boots hitting metallic rods of the ladders made clanking noises that reverberated off the walls that surrounded them. Sounds of laser fire blasting on other levels echoed throughout the ship. Reese couldn't tell if they were getting further away or closer to them. Yet he trusted Master Mal's senses as did all of them.

They climbed up several levels until they reached level 1, the last level, and opened the hatch. The group filed out of the hatch and into an empty corridor. Reese quickly ordered his Clavemen around the Senators. By this time, Princess Elaina was standing on her own.

"I think I can walk now."

"Good," Troy replied, wiping sweat from his brow, "Not that you weigh a lot, but climbing several ladders with extra weight is not part of my work out routine."

Cassandra smiled as did Seth, yet Elaina looked offended.

"For a fighter like you, it shouldn't be so bad."

Troy smirked. "Naw," He shook his head. "I was kidding."

Seth coughed, covering his laugh because he knew Troy wasn't kidding. He turned and looked to Reese. "Which way?"

"We head to the control room."

When they entered the control room, Master Jay rose to greet them.

"Thanks be the stars, you all made it!" Jay exclaimed uttering a sigh of relief. "I didn't think Keltor would go to such lengths as to call the Centurions."

Master Mal stepped forward. "It shows how desperate he is to win this battle. However, he knows he will fail. Shatra was his ace in the hole, and as long as she is out of the picture, he no longer has a way to tap into our network."

The ship suddenly rocked violently.

Jay stumbled as did others to the floor. When they recovered, Jay had turned his attention back to the ships outside in orbit.

"Break orbit, come about mark 0219!"

"AYE!"

"Coms, get the other star annihilators on the horn and order them join this battle here!" Jay cried. "There must be a skeleton crew left on those ships"

"Roger."

"Artillery, fire at will at your closest star cruiser!"

"Firing!"

"Launch primary torpedoes!"

"Launching primary torpedoes!"

Chapter Fifty-Four

Rebel Response

The suns of Shangri-La poured light over the jagged peaks of the northern mountain range, casting a bright light to the valley. Gorn stood at the edge of the frozen pond, looking across at the enemy's camp.

"Sir, are we crossing the ice to engage in battle?"

"Notify the men we will cross the pond to fight," Gorn stated without turning his head from the horizon. He took a step on to the ice and noted how solid it was. It didn't take long before the men stood ready and in formation at the edge of the pond, waiting for orders from their leader Gorn.

"We will go quietly and surprise our enemy this morning! Be careful of the ice and tread lightly over it until we get to the other side. We will strike them while they sleep!"

Swiftly but carefully the army moved across the pond and crept closer to its prey. A horn sounded alerting the opposing Rebels of the Clave's advance. In the gradually lightening sky, the forces met on the pond, where light whips, lasers, and swords clashed and blood colored the white snow dark red. The snow-covered ice crunched under their feet until the snow and blood made a slushy mess.

Gorn, using his sword, sliced Rebs as he fought his way forward. He had a flow of a dancer to his steps, leading his troops into battle. They advanced like thieves in the night as daylight peeked from behind the mountain range. The northern mountain range would soon be theirs. There was still yet another force to confront. Gorn called for the communicator.

"Sir, we've taken the valley."

"Yes, this side of the mountain is ours, but we still have the other side."

"But it is good, is it not?"

"Yes, it's good. It shouldn't have been as easy as it was, but I imagine the next fight won't be as easy."

"That's how things usually go. You take the good with the bad."

"Get me Master Markel."

"Aye."

The man stepped to one side and spoke over the communicator. "Gamma Patrol to Alpha, come in."

"Alpha here," Markel responded.

"I've got him, sir.'Gorn stepped close.

"Markel, this is Gorn."

"Good to hear from you. How are things on the northern front?"

"We just took over one side of the northern range. However, we have yet to get the other side. This side was fairly easy, but we expect the other side won't be."

"Be prepared. Those Rebels know our weaknesses. They've been coached."

"Understood. We have the Eastern range."

'Congratulations! Perhaps this war won't last as long as we once thought."

"This is just the beginning, my brother. Zymon and his followers will absolutely not stop."

"I know."

"Proceed to take the other side and then contact me again."

"Roger. Gorn out."

"Alpha out."

Gorn turned to the young man beside him and placed a hand on his shoulder. "This day is not done."

The young man shrugged his shoulders and looked at Gorn. "For things to return to the way they were, it is worth it to continue with the killing, Master."

"I'm glad to hear you say that. Some don't see the need for all the killing and would rather the Emperor continue to rule despite his dictatorial ways that leave some with their needs unmet. The old ways guaranteed everyone had everything they needed….water, gold, silver whatever else. WE must continue fighting for the people."

"Aye, Master."

"Get the men ready, we will climb up and over the ridge tonight." Gorn continued, realizing that saying that they would climb up and over the ridge in a night was one thing, but doing it was yet another. Getting a thousand men safely in position and ready for battle before daylight would be challenging. Despite this reality, Gorn and his men set out to achieve that task. Gorn led the way. Because he worked out daily, he scaled that ridge in record time. Other Clave Warriors and newcomers like Rex, who had stayed active, quickly used the pick axes, and the studded boots to hack their way to the top of the ridge, also. Immediately the ten leaders secured large ropes to trees and lowered them down to make it easier for the remaining ninety in each of the ten groups to scale the ridge. Holding onto the ropes and placing their feet into the tracks honed out by the leaders, even the weakest soldiers made it to the top quicker that it would have taken them otherwise. Before the sun pierced the black canopy over Shangri-La, signaling the start of a new day, Gorn's men ate a hearty meal and rested, before Gorn called them to attention.

"Alright, we will move down the other side of this ridge to the Rebs camp and attack them by surprise!" Gorn announced his plans to the troops. "Form your teams and get ready for descent!"

Moving down the mountain proved easier than the climb up had been. Using the same ropes that they had used before, the troops repelled from the precipice. Just as the last group touched the bottom, enemy Rebs appeared out of nowhere, swords drawn, and attacked, before the Clave could draw their weapons.

The fighting favored the Rebels. Caught by surprise, Clavemen had no time to regroup before engaging in battle and many of the inexperienced volunteers never knew what hit them. The surprise attack had backfired. Gorn, knowing they were in trouble acted quickly. He drew his favorite weapon, his sword, and ordered his troops to follow suit. He knew they could not use lasers or other Clave weapons because of the close proximity of the fighting. They could easily kill their own Warriors.

"Draw your swords and fight for the Clave and restoration of Universal Order!" he yelled.

Swords clanked as they searched for targets on the bodies of their enemies. Red blood, oozing from open gashes of downed fighters on both sides, colored the white snow a crimson canvas of death. Both Rebel and Clave Warriors brandishing their swords which glistened from the morning sun reflecting against them, struggled to avoid tripping over downed bodies that lay on the cold, frozen lake with blood exuding from their fatal wounds, some still gasping for their last breaths.

Gorn, an avid swordsman, tripped over a downed Rebel fighter, who in his last act of loyalty to Keltor before his death, grabbed Gorn's leg, just as he lunged, aiming his sword at the throat of a key Rebel leader who had lost his balance. Luckily the Rebel fell forward as Gorn fell back. The target he had aimed for flew right onto the sword that Gorn had managed to hold extended forward piercing the Rebel's body which landed atop of him. Another Claveman, who was fighting close to Gorn and protecting his back, yelled out to Gorn.

"Master, are you okay?!"

"Yes, I need to get this three hundred pounds off me so I can signal Alpha for back up!"

Gorn managed to free himself from the weight and speak into his communicator. Just as he was about to ask for backup, he heard the voice of the enemy leader shout to his fighters.

"All Rebel fighters! Fall back now!"

Gorn had been so busy fighting that he had no idea that his Clave Warriors had nearly annihilated the entire Rebel force. Immediately the clanging swords stopped as the enemy retreated.

"Gamma to Alpha!" Gorn called.

'Alpha here," Markel replied

"We have taken the other side, but we have lost many men."

"It is good news, but at a costly price. How many were lost?

"About 700."

Whistles came through the line. "Can you hold it with so few?"

"We'll have to," Gorn stated.

"Do your best, but don't engage in another battle."

"Roger. Gamma out."

"Alpha out."

Chapter Fifty-Five

Centurions Attack

The explosion sprayed debris out from the star annihilator in a circular pattern. Cassandra gasped at the sight with blinking eyes. Seth looked at her and smiled.

"Glad we're over here."

"Yeah."

Master Jay, content that the Senators were now safe in the command room, barked out orders for the star ship to continue the battle just outside of the orbit of Shangri-La

"HARD TO PORT!"

"Coming about Master Jay!'

"Concentrate all primary weapons on the closest star cruiser."

"Weapons locked on! Firing!"

Laser fire sprayed out from the starship hitting its target, the closest star cruiser. There was no blast right away because the star cruiser's shielding was high. Instead, the power from the laser blast gave off electro-magnetic sparks that danced over the hull of the ship. It would take several blasts to diminish the shielding, which Master Jay was determined to deliver.

Jay knew that they had to do something to sway the advantage to their side. The Emperor's hand had been played with the Centurions being put into the mix of things. But now, Jay needed to take the lead and make some decisions that would rid them of the threat. This meant that he had to put more Clavemen in harm's way to protect the most important cargo on the ship, the Senators.

"Master Reese and Master Kal, the Senators are safe up here with us. You three go down and deal with those two Centurions."

Nodding, Master Reese, Kal and Troy dashed to the lift and disappeared as the doors shut behind them.

Silver nodded, giving Jay a supportive look of agreement. It had been the right thing to do in this venture. The Clavemen down below decks were only so skilled and probably couldn't take the Centurions. But Master Reese, Troy, and Kal were seasoned Clavemen and knew the martial arts of the Clave well. Jay knew that the threat of the Centurions would be abated quickly with them on the case. It was just a matter of time and fate.

Cassandra sat down in one of the empty chairs of the control room and sighed heavily. "I'll be glad when this is all over with!"

"So will all of us," Silver stated. "But that won't be the end. This is just the beginning of what will be more battles to come."

"Why do you say that?"

"The Emperor will not stop trying to take over the Universe, and there will always be those who oppose the ways of the Order. In the old days, many disagreed on who should govern the universe. Some opposed us, but they were few and unorganized and had evil ways. No one wanted to support them. Then the Emperor organized these groups, causing them to become more powerful. In order to completely take control, the Rebels had to destroy Master Zeger and his entire family. They almost succeeded, but at the last minute, Master Zeger ordered Odan to take you two and go into hiding.

Now we are taking back control, and these battles will continue for some time to cone, I imagine. I doubt they will end unless we rid the universe of the Emperor himself."

"Perhaps that is what we need to do," Cassandra stated,

"That is a tall order," Silver responded.

"How so?"

"No one will be able to get near him."

"He's not that untouchable," Jay butted in.

"He can be killed," Master Mal added. "It just must be the right one to do it."

"Who do we have that can face him?' Silver asked,

"Of all our numbers, there should be one who is capable, Silver" Mal answered.

But that is for another time, not now."

"When?" Silver asked. "When is it time to save the Universe."

"We are not ready!" Mal insisted.

Meanwhile, below decks, Reese, Troy and Kal fought with the Centurions. With three against one Centurion, the odds were in the Clave's favor. It only took three strikes to a Centurion's shielding to render it vulnerable. Therefore if the three of them worked together, they could bring down the Centurion rather quickly. In the confines of the corridors, the Clavemen had difficulty fully extending their arms to deliver effective blows to the target, but they managed to whip without fully extending their arms, a sign of a skilled Clave warrior.

"One more strike and he's shieldless," Kal cried.

The trio moved in unison, taking different angles of attack, preparing to strike their enemy. Then, as a team their laser whips shot out and struck the shielding simultaneously and the power knocked him backwards against the bulkhead, denting it with a loud bang. However, the Centurion was still alive.

Reese rushed to the Centurion before it could recover and plunged his sword into its belly. The Centurion grabbed at the blade but could do nothing but crash to the floor dead with a thud.

"One down and one to go!" Kal exclaimed.

The trio moved on, taking the lift to the level where the last Centurion continued to fight. By the time they got there, the Clave had crashed through two layers of the Centurion's shielding, but it continued its good fight with a rookie Clavemen. Reese, Troy and Kal immediately blasted lasers aimed at the final shield delivering blows that pierced through the last protective shield. The Centurion's inner core immediately short-circuited; it paused momentarily like an old man with memory loss, desperately trying to recall what his mission had been before crumbling to the floor, with electrical sparks and black smoke radiating from the searing heap that had once been a feared assassin. All that remained was a mass of entangled wires and metal without a brain.

Reese tapped his communicator on his wrist. "Master Jay, the threat of the Centurions has been eliminated, Sir."

Master Jay smiled, "Good. Now we can concentrate on those star cruisers. Return to Command Center and escort the Senators back to their lodging.'

"Affirmed."

Chapter Fifty-Six

Clave Ground Battle

R eports were coming in from each command leader that the Clave had taken over the planet of Shangri-La. The Clave had forced the Rebels to retreat from the strongholds at every strategic location. It was only a matter of time before the Clave would be declared the winner of the planet, and the Rebels would resign.

"I think the Emperor will retreat, Markel said to Odan as they evaluated the developments of the past two days.

"It is my hope," Odan replied.

"He's lost!" Markel exclaimed.

"This time," Odan replied.

"It is good. I know he will live to fight another day, but this time we've won! We beat him! This time the Rebels lost, and the Clave will live again!"

"Yes, my brother. We have revitalized the Clave and the Universal Order, but we will still have to fight to keep it going. We cannot just relax and let things go. We must continue to recruit Warriors just as we did in the past, or we risk dying out again. And we must support the Senate!"

"Yes, nothing will be easy," Markel admitted as he gazed through the viewer at the Warriors sitting in different campfires.

"But we have started something that is good here. We have fought for what is right and the people have supported us in this. So we have the advantage now. The Emperor's days are numbered."

Nodding, Markel drank his tea and then sighed, "Yes. It won't be long before someone will seek him out.'

"I foresee that the Clave will be rid of him soon," Odan stated. Just like I got rid of Shatra. Someone will be called to face him."

"Yes. Someone."

Chapter Fifty-Seven

Keltor Learns Assassins' Fate

Emporer Keltor slammed his fist down on the console before him, as he witnessed from a safe distance away his forces scurrying away like timid rats from battle on the northern front. He no longer held any hope that he could maintain control of Shangri-La. The battle for the eastern front had already failed, and hundreds of his loyal soldiers lay dead on the cold battle field, left at the mercy of the victors. He didn't really care about not giving them a decent burial. The reality that he did not have enough troops to engage the enemy again made one thing clear. If he ever needed Shatra, he needed her now. He had put General Zolotan in charge of the operations, and he had failed miserably.

"Damn, Shatra! What the hell were you thinking flying off alone!?" He cursed her for leaving him to fight the Clave without her expertise on how to hit their Achilles heels. Realizing that he had no other choice, he grabbed the communicator and yelled orders to the remaining forces. He knew he had another game plan that was sure to work.

Just after he delivered his orders to his forces, the communications technician received a message from the Centurions cloaked ship.

"Emperor Keltor, an in-coming message from the assassins' ship!"

Keltor smiled. "Post the message on the screen now!" he ordered. He sat back and relaxed knowing that the Centurions had taken care of the Senators making it impossible for the Clave to regain power. As he read the message, his demeanor changed drastically.

"THREE CENTURIANS SENT ON MISSION TO *ARES* ARE
DEAD!"

Keltor bolted from his seat. The sneering grin turned into a frown of
disbelief. "No! This cannot be true!" But the reality of the Centurion's
death sank in. He exploded in a rage, his brow furrowing in disgust,
causing the others in the control room to cower in fear for their lives.
Even the control panel was in jeopardy. The technicians knew that if he
took his anger out by pounding the panel, they would have no way of
communicating.

Finally Keltor regained some composure and turned his attention to
the monitor only to see Clave starships firing on the only remaining star
annihilator, except the ship he was on. His belly knotted and cold sweat
poured from his brow before he cursed Shatra for the final time.

"Damn you, Shatra!" This is all your fault! You knew how much I
depended on you and your knowledge of the Clave! I depended on you!!"
When his tirade simmered down, he did the only thing he could do.

"RETREAT! All ships RETREAT!" Keltor bellowed through his
communication system. "Set course back to Star Point Omega One!
We will take control of the Andromeda Galaxy and the Clave can have
Shangri-La! I am still the Emperor!"

"Aye, aye, Emperor. Coming about!"

The star cruiser zipped into hyperspace speed toward the Stargate,
leaving Shangri-La to the Clave, and the Universal Order Senators,
Masters, and Warriors.

Chapter Fifty-Eight

Jay's Test Results

Master Jay and those on the starship *Ares* witnessed the Rebels' retreat through the ship's viewer screen. Seth and Cassy through their ability to read each other's minds looked at each other in awe of what they knew to be true.

"Look Master Jay! Did the Rebel destroyer ship just disappear from the line of fire?" Seth asked.

"Looks like you are right, Seth!" The enemy ships are no longer registering on the radar screens! Keltor must have called for them to fall back."

The control room immediately exploded. Cheers of victory echoed throughout the control room and into the corridors. The guards Kal, Reese, and Troy poked their heads in the door to see what all the commotion was about. They joined in on the celebration since the Senators no longer faced any immediate danger.

Master Jay gathered himself and contacted the ground patrols to notify them of their triumph.

"Master Jay to Master Markel."'

"Markel here."

"We've won! The Emperor's ship just retreated with all the other star cruisers!"

"Praise the Heavens!" Markel stated. "I'll spread the word down here."

"Master Jay out."

"Master Markel out."

Jay turned to his guests in the control room. "I hope I was able to keep you confidently safe."

"You did a fine job, Master Jay," Cassandra replied and gave him a bear hug. I thank you for protecting us. No one could have done a better job!"

"Yes." Mal added. "Your decision to have Reese, Troy and Kal go down and take care of the Centurions was the strategic point that swayed the battle into our favor."

"I just figured they needed some experience down there."

"Good call," Silver smiled.

Reese, Troy and Kal's faces turned red upon hearing all these compliments. Reese spoke for the guards. "Thank you Masters. We are happy that things worked in our favor."

"What's the situation now?" Reese asked.

"We've won Shangri-La," Jay acknowledged the victory. "The Emperor and his Rebels have retreated. Now I think we should retreat to our quarters and rest."

"It's time to celebrate," Elaina reminded them of the importance of this victory.

Master Mal spoke up and everyone else listened to the words of experience and wisdom. "I'll take them down, Reese. We will all celebrate together when we meet on Shangri-La. Come along, you youngsters! I'm exhausted, and so are you."

In Devin's absence, Silver took Master Mal's arm and escorted him into the corridor and the three Senators followed.

Chapter Fifty-Nine
Revelations, Presentations, and Celebrations

Several days passed before the Senators landed on the surface of Shangri-La in the northern stronghold. They had to remain on the starship longer than they wanted to while the land crews worked to clean up the planet from the harsh signs of battle. Destroying all of the dead bodies, both Clave and Rebel, that lay frozen on the battlefields required special attention or they would be there forever. Markel came up with the quickest solution to this problem.

"This is Master Markel to Justin and Gorn, over!"

Both ground troop commanders responded to the communication at the same time,

"I read you loud and clear, Master Markel!"

When he had the attention of both leaders, Markel spoke into his communicator "I bring you good news! The enemy has retreated and we now have complete control over planet Shangri-La. We now must focus on the tasks at hand in order to prepare the planet for the arrival of the other Masters, Senators, Warriors and volunteers. Divide one thousand men into teams of one hundred each. Order them to split up into teams and take a section of the war zones and use their lasers to destroy each body until nothing remains. Direct all remaining Warriors to devote their efforts to rebuilding and repairing the northern and eastern strongholds and the equipment at both sites, over!"

Justin and Gorn first shouted cheers of relief upon learning that their efforts on the battlefields had not been fought in vain.

Justin acknowledged the orders first. "Yes, Sir! Master Markel. We will get her done!"

"Aye! Aye, Sir! Congratulations for your genius leadership and war plan! I am on it!"

"Over, and out!"

When the planet was finally in decent repair and the war zones cleaned up, Jay landed the *Ares* on the planet safely with the human cargo intact. The ground crew and leaders had gathered for the victory celebration, and to welcome the other Masters, Senators, Warriors, and volunteers to the party.

Master Mal stood before the congregation, hands stretched out wide. "We must continue to fight for what is right in this Universe. Now with Senator Zeger's children in place, we can continue to add more star systems to our ranks. However, we must always be wary of the opposition. Keltor will not stop his efforts to overthrow us. It is the Clave's job and duty to see that the Rebel forces continue to back down!"

Loud cheers rang out on the planet, and Master Mal had to wait for the applause to subside before he continued. "For those who have not had the pleasure of meeting the two new members of our Clave, I will introduce them to you now. Some of you met them before, but you probably don't recognize them. They were mere babies when Keltor launched a surprise attack on the Clave and murdered their parents and siblings so that he could establish his dictatorship throughout the Universe. Thank God our leader Master Zeger had the presence of mind to order Master Odan to take the babies into hiding to save their lives. It is through them that the Clave will rise again and re-establish order so that all beings may have equal freedom and rights.

Now I present to you all grown up, Senator Cassandra and her twin brother Senator Seth Zeger!"

Cassandra and Seth stepped forward amid loud cheers and applause and murmurs of disbelief from the older Clave members, who thought the twins had been murdered with the rest of the Zeger family. As if on cue, Cassandra and Seth raised their hands signaling for quiet. The two were overwhelmed by the unbelievable welcome they were receiving from the Clave.

Tears welled in their eyes as they realized how much their parents had meant to the Clave and how well respected they had been throughout the Universe. Through mental telepathy, they communicated with each other what they felt at this moment. *"Will we be able to earn the same respect as our parents had? Can we really become strong and effective leaders of this powerful group?"*

It was at this moment they missed their parents most though they had never really had the chance to know them at all. After what seemed like hours, the twins raised their hands at the same time to quiet the crowd without speaking to each other aloud.

Cassandra spoke first. "Thank you so much for that outstanding welcome! Seth and I are grateful for all you have done to ensure our safety throughout this entire relocation process. You have earned our trust and admiration in the way you have performed on the ground and in space to retake Shangri-La. My brother and I have been far away and have not seen the horrible ways of the Rebels. But we see it in your eyes and have heard some of your stories. We will stand with you to rebuild the Clave and make it a group to be respected and honored because we will fight for what is right and fair. Once again, young girls and boys will strive to be Clavemen and Clavewomen! Once again the star systems will be united in brotherly love!!"

Again cheers and clapping rang out as Cassandra gestured for Seth to address the group.

"Not long ago I was just a teenager living a carefree life on planet Earth, living with a kind man whom Cassy and I thought to be our grandfather. I had no worries and went about my days doing things that teenagers do on earth: school, chores, girlfriends, shopping, etc. I was happy until one day Master Odan dropped a bombshell on Cassy and me. Hours later, I found myself aboard a transporter heading for a place I knew nothing about. I admit I was angry because I did not understand the necessity for this change in my life. Both Cassy and I have grown up since them. We have met some outstanding and admirable people along the way, and we are both happy to try to fill our incredible parents' shoes. Odan has explained the situation to us and assured us that we have our parents' DNA and that we possess the leadership skills that we have inherited from them which qualifies us for the task. We will do our best to gain your respect in the days ahead. Thank you very much."

The crowd burst into an arousing applause and cheers again. Odan smiled and shed a tear after the twins' speeches. Pride welled in his chest as he had fulfilled the wishes of Master Zeger in not only keeping the twins safe, but also in helping them develop into fine and caring human beings. It was at that moment he knew the twins would succeed.

After several other masters spoke briefly and praised the group for the victory in retaking the planet and honoring those who had fallen along the way, Master Markel praised those men and women of valor who had proven themselves worthy in battle on the ground. Master Jay honored those aboard *Ares* who had risked their lives to protect the Senators from the Centurions. Master Mal, who had been impressed by the young Master's leadership which he had witnessed up close on starship *Ares*, surprised Master Jay with an award for his leadership. When all the speeches and awards ended, loud music blared to signal the beginning of the real celebration.

Happy revelers carved out a section of the celebration site as a dance floor, and almost instantly the area looked like a huge wave of human motion. Some men and women danced together, while solo Clave members and volunteers cavorted, creating styles of their own. Even the Senators joined in the fun. It reminded Cassy of the school dances back on Earth where she loved to show off her moves on the gym floor.

Sensing her thoughts, Markel approached Cassy, extended his hand, and bowed in front of her. "May I have this dance, your Highness?"

Cassandra snapped back to the reality of the moment and instantly allowed herself to be whisked onto the dance floor in the arms of Markel.

"You spoke well tonight, Senator," Markel complimented, leading her to the right.

"Thank you, Master Markel," She replied, smiling. "I didn't quite know what to say."

"You said exactly what needed to be said."

"Thanks."

"You know, you look very beautiful; you remind me of your mother."

"Thank you," Cassy replied blushing as a wide smile spread across her face. She had seen only one picture Odan had shared with them just before they left Earth and had noted the   beauty of the woman he had pointed to and identified as her mother. This was a huge compliment.

A young man strode over to them. "May I cut in?"

"Do you want to dance with this man?' Markel asked.

It was Rex Faraday.

"Why, Markel!" Cassy exclaimed, "It's Captain Rex!"

'Yes, yes. It's good ole Rex. How good of you to come and barge into our little dance here," Markel retorted sarcastically.

"No harm, no foul. But I would like a chance to dance with the lady," Rex insisted, as Markel bowed out of the dance as a fine gentleman should.

Rex then moved in close to Cassandra and wrapped his arms about her waist.

"I've been waiting a long time to get this close to you," Rex whispered in her ear.

"Have you?"

"The moment I set eyes on you I was hooked."

"I bet you say that to all the girls."

"No. I swear this is the first time I've said that to anyone."

"Well, you do know that a Clave warrior cannot have any attachments to anything outside the Clave."

"I know, so I guess the Clave just lost a good man."

"Then you know there is no chance of a relationship."

"Yeah."

"I don't understand then. Why tell me that you find me beautiful."

"Because I do."

"I guess there is no harm there.'

"Nope. I usually say what's on my mind."

Cassandra laughed. "I guess so."

Dancing and revelry continued as the Clave Warriors celebrated victory well into the wee hours of the next morning, fully aware that Keltor had not given up the fight.

The End....